THE FAR FAR BETTER THING

By Auston Habershaw

Saga of the Redeemed
The Oldest Trick
No Good Deed
Dead But Once
The Far Far Better Thing

THE FAR FAR BETTER THING

Saga of the Redeemed: Book IV

AUSTON HABERSHAW

HARPER
VOYAGER
IMPULSE

An Imprint of HarperCollinsPublishers

This is a work of fiction. Names, characters, places, and incidents are products of the author's imagination or are used fictitiously and are not to be construed as real. Any resemblance to actual events, locales, organizations, or persons, living or dead, is entirely coincidental.

THE FAR FAR BETTER THING. Copyright © 2019 by Auston Habershaw. All rights reserved. Printed in the United States of America. No part of this book may be used or reproduced in any manner whatsoever without written permission except in the case of brief quotations embodied in critical articles and reviews. For information, address HarperCollins Publishers, 195 Broadway, New York, NY 10007.

Digital Edition MARCH 2019 ISBN: 978-0-06-267703-7
Print Edition ISBN: 978-0-06-267705-1

Cover design by Patricia Barrow
Cover photographs © taviphoto/iStock/Getty Images (antler); ©Ron-Tech2000/iStock/Getty Images (throne); © TeoLazarev/iStock/Getty Images (smoke)

Harper Voyager, the Harper Voyager logo, and Harper Voyager Impulse are trademarks of HarperCollins Publishers.

HarperCollins is a registered trademark of HarperCollins Publishers in the United States of America and other countries.

FIRST EDITION

19 20 21 22 23   OPM   10 9 8 7 6 5 4 3 2 1

This book is dedicated to
my daughters, Madelyn and Violet:
find the steel inside you, my girls,
and hone it well

There is nothing noble in being superior to your fellow men.
True nobility lies in being superior to your former self.

—ERNEST HEMINGWAY

TABLE OF CONTENTS

PROLOGUE

The Keeper of the Balance, Polimeux II, was a haggard old man with a hook nose and a bleary gaze perpetually fixed on some unknowable, distant horizon. Though he was fairly dripping with gilded amulets and precious stones and clad in thick robes of lush and vibrant purple, he had the look of a beggar mooching coppers down by the docks. This, as Xahlven understood it, was the way with Keepers. Once you achieved the fifth mark in the Chamber of Testing, you lost something of yourself. Some idiots claimed you gained some "higher understanding." Xahlven was pretty sure the only thing that "higher understanding" did was make you lose your mind.

Of course, that never stopped the raggedy old nut from looking down his ridiculous nose at Xahlven. "You are late, young Xahlven."

Xahlven, in point of fact, was *not* late. It just so happened that the other four archmagi had arrived earlier than he had. Still, he put on his best sheepish grin and genuflected to the Keeper on his towering dais at the center of the chamber. "My apologies, Keeper. Time runs differently in the Black College, it seems. I lost track."

The Keeper's displeasure quickly dissipated as his attention drifted to some distant eddy of time and space. Xahlven doubted the old goat had any memory of their brief exchange, and so he took the obsidian throne reserved for the Archmage of the Ether and waited for the opening ceremonies of the meeting to run their course.

The Chamber of Stars stood at the very heart of the Arcanostrum, at the very nexus of three of the world's most powerful ley lines. It was, therefore, a place where the five great energies of existence— Ether, Lumen, Fey, Dweomer, and Astral—were in such vital abundance that they could be seen with the naked eye, pulsating through the walls along veins of precious metal long ago infused into the stones. The four quadrants of the rhomboid room each blazed with the character of their respective energies— Xahlven's part, for instance, was dark and silent, with stagnant puddles forming upon the flagstones and long, unnatural shadows.

Sitting on that ancient throne, he could feel more

power coursing through him than in any other place. It was a good thing, too—his mother's hex was still there, draining away his power at all times, day and night. A week since his duel with her in the Empty Tower, and still he had found no way to remove it. He had often been tempted to try his luck here, with all the power of the Star Chamber at his command, but then his fellow archmagi would doubtlessly notice what he was doing, and he had no intention of showing them weakness.

On the floor of the chamber, between the central dais and the platforms of each archmage, Trevard, Lord Defender of the Balance—the technical archmage of the Astral—walked a circuit of the room, verifying with various auguries that each archmage was indeed who they said they were, and not some shrouded or shape-shifted impostor, simulacrum, or other such ruse. Trevard was a tall, thin man with a severe, humorless face, his forehead creased with frown lines that extended up beneath his mageglass helm. He spent an unusually long time peering at Xahlven, verifying his identity. There was a lot of banging his staff upon the ground and grunting on the Lord Defender's part. Xahlven chose to ignore it.

When he had finished with each of the archmagi, Trevard banged his staff against the floor five times more. "The Great Cabal is complete, all are present. May the Balance prevail!"

The noise broke Polimeux from whatever stupor had transfixed his attention on his hands. "What? Yes . . . yes of course. What of Eretheria, my servants?"

Trevard started speaking almost before the Keeper had finished asking the question. "Necromancy! Necromancy used to field an army of the living dead! This cannot be tolerated!"

The Archmage of the Dweomer, Delkatar—the eldest archmage by far and a conservative relic—smoothed his knee-length beard with one hand. "A lost art, I assumed. Who has found it anew?"

"It has not been taught in the White College for centuries, of that I can assure you." Talian, the Archmage of the Lumen, was looking directly at Xahlven from the opposite side of the chamber, her rose-colored spectacles glinting in the glow of her bright and shiny quadrant. "I am *forced* to assume there has been some kind of malfeasance."

"I can't imagine why you are looking at me that way, Talian," Xahlven said. "I am as disturbed as the rest of you, and necromancy is a *Lumenal* art, remember?"

"Oh, it's just hedge magic, is all." Hugarth, Archmage of the Fey, hooked a knee over the armrest of his brass throne. "Who cares if somebody's animated a few corpses?"

"*I* care!" Trevard said, banging his staff on the floor again. "This so-called 'Gray Lady' is a former Defender who—"

Hugarth laughed. "A former Defender, eh? Well, that sounds as though it's one of those *you* problems, not a *me* problem."

Xahlven did his best not to sneer at Hugarth—even if he was taking the position Xahlven wanted, there was just something so unseemly about an archmage who didn't wear shoes. "Lord Defender," he said softly, "the issue is not whether or not Myreon Alafarr has committed a crime—of that we are all agreed, yes?"

Nods around the hall, except from Hugarth, who merely shrugged. The Keeper seemed not to be paying any attention, which suited Xahlven just fine. He continued. "The issue is how the Balance can be *best preserved.*"

Delkatar banged his staff in approval. "That is sensible. This woman is the instigator of a popular revolt, but the revolt has already *been* instigated, yes? If we remove her now . . . well . . ."

"Chaos," Xahlven confirmed. "We create a martyr—"

"You mean *another* martyr," Talian broke in. She smiled sweetly at Xahlven. "The first one was your *brother.* Or . . . have you forgotten about him already?"

Xahlven barely suppressed a bark of rage. "Yes, yes—of course. *Another* martyr, very well—the *point* is that removing Alafarr won't stop the uprising, it will merely rob it of its moderating influence. The woman wants to create a better, more stable Eretheria. I propose we let her try."

Delkatar nodded while Talian looked pensive.

Hugarth jerked his chin in Xahlven's direction. "And just what are *you* getting out of this, boy?"

Carefully, carefully . . . "A stable Eretheria, Hugarth."

"*If* she wins," Delkatar said.

"*And* if she loses—then the old order will be restored." Xahlven looked around at them all. "Let her continue, because win or lose, the war ends one way or another. Necromancy or no necromancy."

"Necromancy is an *abomination!*" Trevard was livid, his nostrils flaring so wide a sparrow could conceivably get caught in one.

Xahlven couldn't let that one go. "And firepikes aren't? Colossi? Bladecrystals? War fiends? It seems the Lord Defender is perfectly satisfied with all the *other* sorcerous weapons we have permitted to propagate across the West, but when it comes to dead bodies holding spears, *there* the line is crossed?"

"Mind your manners, young man." Delkatar had the temerity to waggle a finger in Xahlven's direction, like he was some misbehaving nephew and not a fellow archmage. "It was *your mother* who brought us to this pass. Don't go blaming Trevard for your own family's misdeeds."

"And do not presume to lecture me about my own family, Delkatar," Xahlven said, keenly aware of how hot his temper was running. These . . . these *idiots*. These self-involved imbeciles! Gods, if there were only poison enough in the world to drown them all in it.

He closed his eyes and took a cleansing breath. Not yet. Not *yet*. His mother took thirty years to have her grand plot come to fruition; he could wait a few more months for his own. *One step at a time, Xahlven.* "Myreon Alafarr must remain in command of the rebel army she is massing in Eretheria. We cannot interfere without making the problem worse."

"If she maintains an army of the living dead—" Trevard began.

"Then we can warn her—threaten her. By all means we can encourage her to stop using proscribed sorcery. I am not suggesting otherwise." *Indeed*, Xahlven thought, *I very much want you to do so, you inflexible old battle-axe.*

Trevard looked up at Xahlven, thinking the suggestion over. "You know the woman. How would she react to such a threat?"

"She will not wish to anger Saldor—her rebellion cannot confront another enemy." This was not precisely a lie. But neither was it entirely true. *Myreon will do exactly what she feels she must, threats or no threats.*

Silence fell over the chamber as everyone mulled this over. Xahlven steepled his fingers beneath his chin. This was the moment he had been scrying for some time—what happened now would alter how his plans would unfold from this moment forward. No doubt his fellow archmagi, too, had scryed this. Manipulating them was the most delicate of arts, stupid though they were. It had taken him only a week as archmage to realize how much he hated them all, but it had taken him almost ten years of constant, painstaking plotting to bring them to this juncture. That they suspected nothing he felt was proof positive of his genius. Now the fools mulled over the time of their own deaths, and it was all Xahlven could do to keep from grinning.

Talian spoke first. "Agreed. As much as I dislike it, Xahlven is correct. Trevard should send her a warning, but we should take no direct action unless she escalates things."

Delkatar agreed as well, and Hugarth shrugged his shoulders and said he couldn't give a damn either way. It fell to Trevard. "I will make preparations to field an army of Defenders at short notice, just in case, but . . . but I am reluctantly forced to agree with the Archmage of the Ether."

Xahlven gave Trevard a shallow bow out of respect. The old battle-mage returned the gesture reflexively and grinned. Xahlven had seen that grin in his scrying pool before—he knew now what happened next, and knew it better than any other person in that hall. With that grin, Trevard had sealed his fate. Xahlven's plot could never be stopped now. Not by Trevard, nor by any other archmage.

For the first time in years, he saw a clear, unbroken path to victory—to an end of the perverse order of the world as fashioned by his mother and a beginning of a new era of his own devising. The board had been cleared of all obstacles—his mother, awaiting her death in Sahand's tallest tower, his brother dead and on the bottom of a lake, and Myreon Alafarr embroiled in a war she could never hope to win. No matter how his mother's hex drained his power, Xahlven couldn't help but smile.

The Keeper of the Balance, Polimeux II—the most powerful mage in the world—wiped a string of drool from his face with a silk handkerchief. "What of Eretheria, my servants?"

"Never fear, Keeper," Xahlven said. "Everything is well in hand."

CHAPTER 1

RUDE AWAKENING

Tyvian awoke with a gasp and then he kept gasping, gulping down air as though he hadn't breathed in days. He was struggling—something was grabbing him, holding him down. He kicked and thrashed and then coarse wool was thrown over his head and it was dark. He tried to scream, but his voice barely seemed to creak.

He fell out of the bed and thumped his face on a dirt floor. He was covered in a wool blanket, which had been pushed up over his head by his struggles. He lay there for a moment, collecting his wits, letting his breathing calm. *I'm alive*, he thought. *The ring brought me back*. He felt it on his right hand—cold, hard, immovable. Hard to imagine so much power packed in so plain an iron band.

The plan worked!

He was lying in a barn. There were no animals present and the big doors were pulled closed. Sunbeams through the windows lit the dust and motes of hay in the air, cutting diagonally across the big, empty room—it was either early morning or evening, then. The place smelled of horse manure and a hundred different kinds of dander. His bed was something makeshift—a couple of sacks stuffed with dirt laid atop a few small crates. A little cook fire was going, the smoke rising up above the hayloft and then out the vent near the barn's roof. Tyvian frowned at it. An open fire in a barn was a bad idea, unless . . .

The door slid open a few inches—enough for a big man with a sword on his back to slip through sideways. He was clad in black mail and had a shaggy mane of black hair striped with gray. When he turned to face Tyvian, he could see that the man had been growing his beard out again. "Well met, Eddereon."

Eddereon smiled, showing his uneven teeth. "Back with us at last, eh? I was beginning to wonder."

"Has it been two weeks?" Tyvian pulled himself atop the makeshift bed. It was now that he noted what he was wearing—a loose shirt, brown and stained, and a pair of green hose patched at the knees and toes. He nearly gagged.

"Those clothes were the best I could find—you'd better plan on keeping them." Eddereon rubbed his beard and squatted next to the fire. "It's been about twelve days since the Battle of Eretheria, which is what they're calling it. How did you know it had been—"

"Your beard," Tyvian said offhandedly as he inspected himself. The wounds were all there, barely scabbed over—each place Xahlven's simulacra had run him through. He felt the tightness of healing skin around each of them. They'd probably scar. "Who won the battle?"

Eddereon stirred a wooden spoon in the little iron cauldron he had suspended over the fire. "Depends on who you ask. The White Army insists it was a great victory for Eretheria, the Dellorans insist that it went exactly as planned, and the Free Houses will insist whatever scoops up the most popular support is the truth."

"The White Army?"

"Myreon," Eddereon said. He pulled out the spoon and licked it. "Hmph . . . I've grown too used to pepper."

Tyvian rubbed his temples, only to discover that he had no hair. Someone had shaved his head. "What . . . what the *hell?*"

Eddereon chuckled. "I know you went to a lot of trouble to fake your death, but not *everyone* believed it. Red hair is likely to stick out."

Tyvian closed his eyes and took a good, long breath. It was the right play. It made sense. But he still felt naked. His goatee, at least, was intact, if a bit ragged. "The Free Houses?"

"The war is shaping up like this: the White Army is putting any noble to the sword who doesn't join the cause and renounce their titles. Turns out this is very popular among the peasantry, who flock to the Gray Lady's banners. House Davram is likely to march on the capital, or is doing so right now—battle is in the wind. Ayventry is under the control of Sahand. That leaves Camis, Vora, and Hadda, all of whom are biding their time to see how Davram fares. Until then, they're the 'Free Houses.'"

"It didn't work, then. My death didn't unify them against Sahand."

Eddereon shrugged. "I have never been very good at politics. It seems to me, though, that if Myreon defeats Davram in the field, the western part of the country will stay at peace—Camis and Vora seem unlikely to get involved, and Hadda will stay neutral until a winner seems clear. That just leaves Sahand."

"Half a war is still a war. And Sahand is better at it than Myreon is."

Eddereon spooned out a brown-black stew of beans and some kind of game meat into a wooden bowl and shoved it in Tyvian's hands. "Begging your pardon, but none of that is your concern any longer, correct? That man—Tyvian Reldamar—he's dead. You're somebody else now."

Tyvian thought about this as he cast about for his

own spoon. "Eddereon, do you by any chance happen to have—"

"New person, remember?" Eddereon held up one hand and wiggled his fingers at Tyvian. "Learn to adapt."

Tyvian cursed and looked down at the stew. It was thick and hot and he realized just how hungry he was. "Dammit all." He pulled out a piece of meat and stuffed it in his mouth. It was tough, but good. Its taste made him remember all those meals Hool had hunted down during their vagabond years. He wondered where she was and if she was well. He wondered if Brana was with her.

"Once you've eaten, you'll need to put on this." Eddereon went into a stall and came back with a pair of boots, a thick gray tunic of wool, a mail shirt and coif, a sword belt with a broadsword, and a black tabard with an elk-skull device, the antlers reaching almost to the collar.

Tyvian looked at it—this had been the plan. "What company are we with?"

Eddereon tapped the device on the tabard. "This is the sign of Rodall's Hunters, also called the Ghouls. They are camped not far away and are waiting for me—a personal favor."

Tyvian poked through the outfit, paying particular attention to the sword. It was competently made, but not the work of a master. It would need a lot of sharpening. "You know them?"

"We know each other by reputation," Eddereon said. "Whereas you were something of a legend in your circle, I was something of a legend in mine. Few sell-swords do not know the name of Eddereon the Black."

Tyvian picked out a bit more stew, resisting the urge to reach for a napkin. "And who am I?"

"Arick Cadronmay of Denthro, hedge knight and my bosom companion, just recovered from his injuries at the Battle of Eretheria."

Tyvian pulled on the boots. They were well worn, but again of decent construction. They fit, too—Eddereon had a good eye for sizes.

Conversation died as Tyvian ate and dressed. He would have liked to bathe, but this being a barn, no tub was present, and he sure as hell wasn't about to scrub down in a feed trough. Sacrifices needed to be made, he supposed. First his hair, then his hygiene.

Why was he doing all this, again? He stopped as he was belting on the broadsword, suddenly alarmed at a gap in his memory. He cast his mind back, trying to confirm all the details. He remembered everything leading up to his coronation with relative clarity, but the night of the ordeal itself . . . well . . . he remembered fire and death and his duel with Xahlven on the rooftop. But how had he gotten there? What else had happened?

He frowned. There was something there. Something on the edge of his memory . . . something Xahlven had told him, right at the end. Something important.

He pushed the thought away. It didn't matter anymore, did it? He was done—free. He'd sacrificed himself for Eretheria, and now the rest of the world and its problems were no longer his own. He wasn't Tyvian the First, he wasn't even Tyvian Reldamar. He was Arick Cadronmay of Denthro, disgraced hedge knight—a common sell-sword and no one of consequence. Tyvian took a deep, cleansing breath.

For the first time in ages—decades, perhaps—Tyvian's life seemed to unfold before him with wild, unrestricted promise.

Eddereon was standing at the barn door. He cleared his throat. "We'd better go. They won't wait much longer."

Tyvian nodded and finished belting on the sword. It seemed too heavy, and it dragged on his hip. He'd never much cared for broadswords—they were balanced more toward the tip than the hilt to give them a heavier stroke, but when compared to his preferred rapier, you lost a measure of control and a few inches of reach. He hoped those few inches and that extra control wouldn't matter much. Given the arc of his life thus far, that didn't seem likely. "Very well. Let's go."

The camp of Rodall's Hunters was a typical sell-sword encampment. It straddled a road on the north side of a stream crossed by a narrow stone bridge. A cheval-de-frise was placed across the bridge on both sides, and it was manned by a half-dozen men clad as Tyvian was and armed with long spears and bows. Beyond this, the tents were arranged in neat rows, and a central pavilion of black and white flew the company colors and had the company standard staked out front—a larger, more detailed version of the device on Tyvian's chest, this including streaks of blood dripping from the antlers and a border stitched with the images of human skulls. Not cheery, but then again, sell-swords traded on their fearsome reputations, and fearsome banners helped keep them in coin.

Eddereon greeted the men on the bridge by name and they let him pass with some slaps on the back and good-natured ribbing about farmer's daughters and so on. They didn't say a word to Tyvian at all.

As they walked through the camp, Tyvian spared a look at the tents. They were small, housing four men apiece, though Tyvian guessed the men would have to be stacked like firewood inside if everyone were to sleep at once. There was precious little magecraft in evidence: the tents were not warded against the elements, the cook fires were stoked with plain wood, and only a few of the men's weapons had the telltale sheen of having been treated with bladecrystal. That meant the company was either low on supplies or perhaps poor. In either case, Tyvian didn't expect much in the way of comfort.

The men were in the process of striking camp.

They knew their duties and they did them, rolling up tents and loading supply wagons in organized teams. Tyvian found himself counting fingers, ears, noses, and eyes—he came up with less than the expected number. Far less, and most of the injuries were not recent. These were veterans, then, not some green company out of Galaspin looking to make some quick coin in the spring campaigns. Tyvian, with his well-fed complexion and a full set of digits, was going to stick out here.

"Cheery bunch," Tyvian grumbled to Eddereon as a man with no teeth and shoulders like a bull glared at him. "You could have found a less . . . conspicuous group, couldn't you?"

"I did the best that I could. The Ghouls will do," Eddereon said and led on, heading toward the central pavilion. Beside the elaborate banner was a pair of guards standing at attention, halberds at their sides.

Tyvian ducked past a pair of men carrying five rolled-up tents between them. "Why are they called the Ghouls?"

"The Siege of Gandor's Gate."

Tyvian tried to remember his history. "That was at the end of the Illini Wars, after Calassa, right? Sahand's men held the castle for two months and started eating their captives . . . but why would *this* company be called the Ghouls if it was the Dellorans who were eating . . ."

Eddereon stopped and gave Tyvian a hard stare over his shoulder.

Tyvian came up short. The realization hit him like a wave—the Dellorans were falling back *north* in front of the White Army. The Ghouls were camped on the *north* side of the river, guarding their southern approaches. Gods. *This is a Delloran Company!*

I'm joining Sahand's service!

When Eddereon saw that Tyvian understood, he nodded and introduced himself to the guards at the front of the pavilion. He was seen inside, but Tyvian was told to remain here. He did as he was told, if only because he was too shocked to think of another thing to do. They were in a Delloran camp! He kept darting his eyes around, expecting at any moment for one of the sundry thugs and murderers surrounding him to notice who he was and sound the alert. Nothing happened, though—the tabard, his shaved head, and the fact that his ordeal probably had adverse effects on his appearance were sufficient to confound anyone who might happen to recognize him, even assuming such a person existed.

But what if such a person did? He might pass casual inspection, but how long until his Saldorian accent gave him away? Did Sahand believe he was dead? Hard to say—it wasn't Sahand he was attempting to fool. What were the odds they would come into Sahand's presence?

What in the hell was Eddereon *thinking*?

A pair of huge wolfhounds emerged from the pavilion, wearing spiked collars. They did not wag their tails or pant or even come close to Tyvian. Instead, they both stared at him with black eyes, stone-still. Tyvian also froze, uncertain what to do. He glanced at the two guards standing there, but neither man said or did anything.

Laughter filtered out of the pavilion and into the morning sun. The man Eddereon was with had a head like a whetstone—gray, with nothing but sharp corners and flat surfaces. He wore plate-and-mail of good quality, and his head was shaved in the manner of knights who still wore a helm on a regular basis. His teeth, evidently worn down with age, had each been capped with platinum crowns. Though half a head shorter than Eddereon, he bore a kind of violent menace that made Tyvian feel he was bigger. He gave the two hounds a low whistle, and the dogs instantly sat at his heels. Their eyes still hadn't left Tyvian.

"Arick Cadronmay of Denthro," Eddereon said, presenting Tyvian, "meet Captain Rodall Gern."

Tyvian knuckled his forehead in salute and bowed for good measure—he was abruptly realizing he had no idea what the etiquette was here. Should he kneel? Would he be kissing rings?

Captain Rodall extended his hand to shake. Tyvian grabbed his forearm and Rodall squeezed his—too hard. "Well met," Rodall said, his voice far higher pitched than Tyvian had expected out of such a face.

"Milord," Tyvian answered.

Rodall hooted a laugh. "You weren't kidding, Ed—high-born and polite. I'm worried I might break him!"

"No danger of that, sir!" Tyvian said, trying to sound more eager than he was.

"Arrogant, too." Rodall shook his head. "On any other day, I'd break your knees and leave a ponce like you behind for the crows. I lost too many men in that shit-eating town full of wigs and women, though, to pass up free help. Can you handle a pike?"

Tyvian nodded. Any moron could handle a pike—what kind of stupid question was that? Still, he couldn't resist a follow up question. "Free, sir?"

Rodall looked at Eddereon. "Thought you told him?"

Eddereon stepped in. "You don't get paid in Rodall's Hunters until you're blooded in your first battle. Gives new recruits an incentive to stick the engagement out rather than run."

Rodall came close to Tyvian and stared down his flat nose. "And once you're blooded, you're *ours*—no deserters in this company, understood? You take off without my leave, and I hunt you down."

Tyvian did his best not to roll his eyes. If he had a copper common every time somebody threatened to hunt him down . . .

"Not impressed, eh?" Rodall yanked out a piece

of Tyvian's beard, making Tyvian wince. He held the hair out to his hounds, which eagerly sniffed it. He then stuffed the little sprig of hair into his belt.

"They know you now, boy," Rodal said, grinning his metal-capped grin. "If you run, well . . ." He reached up to his neck and teased out a leather string that wove through a half dozen mummified human ears. "We'll see how brave you are when I catch you."

Rodall looked at Eddereon, slapped a hand on his shoulder, and nodded. "I need to get back—got a company to run. You're both in tent twenty-five. Would make you sergeant, but the boys would take it wrong, some stranger riding their rumps."

Eddereon saluted. "Of course. Thank you, sir."

Tyvian spoke up, "Hold on—tent twenty-five? I'm . . . errr . . . *we're* to march with the infantry?"

Rodall paused. "We're an infantry company—what the hell else would you do?"

"Well, sir—it seems to me that a man leading a company abroad through enemy territory could use a guide."

"I could cross rougher terrain than this in my sleep," Rodall said. But he turned around and folded his arms—he was listening, at any rate.

Tyvian was getting a death-stare from Eddereon, but he pressed on anyway. "I don't mean the *physical* terrain. I mean the *political* terrain. I know this country—I know its people and its laws. I might be useful to you in the command tent." Deathly silence from Rodall. Then Tyvian remembered to add the word "Sir."

Rodall favored Tyvian with another shiny grin. "Maybe you would at that. Very well, Arick—you will report to my command tent each evening after camp has been set. Understood?"

Tyvian saluted. "Yes sir."

And then Rodall and his giant dogs went back in the pavilion, leaving them alone save the guards. Eddereon put an arm around Tyvian's shoulder and steered him away. "You made a good impression. Well done."

Tyvian hissed at him. "Sahand's service, Eddereon? *Sahand?* Kroth's teeth, man, what were you thinking?"

"Shhh . . . I can explain."

"Explain bloody well quick, you great hairy oaf!"

Eddereon cast a look around—the bustle of the camp was intensifying. There were horns blowing, and men scrambled to load wagons and shoulder their packs. No one was paying them any heed. "Your plan has changed a bit, Tyvian."

Tyvian smacked him in the side of the head. "Call me Arick, you dunce—and who told you to change any plans! The idea was to get out of Eretheria and then we'd lie low. Travelling with the enemy is *not* lying low!"

Eddereon grimaced and sought to explain, but the

big man was having trouble finding the words. "Your mother . . . after the battle . . . she . . . well . . . she was captured by Sahand."

The news hit Tyvian harder than he expected. *She's dead.* He took a step back. A thousand methods of painful, torturous death flashed through his mind, each of them a potential fate for his mother. He wondered which of them it had been, or maybe Sahand hadn't bothered choosing and did them all. He wondered where the body was being displayed. He shook his head. "She . . . when she told me that was the last time we'd speak, I . . . I didn't believe her."

Eddereon took Tyvian by the shoulders. "No, you don't understand. Your mother is *alive*, held captive in Dellor."

Tyvian blinked. "What? Wh . . . why?"

Eddereon seemed not to hear the question. "We have joined the Delloran army because you and I are going to rescue her."

That's insane. Tyvian didn't get a chance to say it, though. The horns were blowing. They were being called into ranks. Rodall's Hunters—the Ghouls of Dellor—were marching north.

And Tyvian was going with them.

CHAPTER 2

IN THE ARMY NOW

Marching, Tyvian quickly discovered, was unpleasant. The Ghouls—nobody in the company called them the Hunters unless the captain was in earshot—were a light infantry outfit evidently famed for their ability to cover ground quickly. The departure from their camp that first morning was considered, leisurely by company standards, even though to Tyvian it had looked as though they were striking tents while people were still sleeping in them.

Somebody shoved a pike in Tyvian's hand—an eighteen-foot-long spear that weighed about eight pounds—and slapped a pack on his back that contained a blanket roll, a quantity of dry rations, a canteen, and some assortment of camping knickknacks Tyvian did not have the time to inspect. Over this pack, that same somebody hung a small target shield and yelled at him until Tyvian was standing in a column with other people with absurdly long spears and large packs.

They were then made to walk. For hours. Eight hours, specifically, with only a brief midday respite to choke down a few iron-hard crackers and a handful of seeds before they were once again bellowed at until they were back in lines, marching again. By midday, Tyvian's legs were screaming with exhaustion. By dusk, they were just numb.

There was very little conversation among the men while marching. Everyone was focused on keeping pace, since the sergeant—the man who had apparently made it his life's mission to scream at Tyvian for any minor infraction—was pacing the edge of the column. He was a toothless badger of a human being with scraggly yellow hair that grew just about everywhere on his head except the top. His name was Drawsher. In another life, Tyvian would have killed him five minutes after meeting him. In this life—this wretched, reduced, quasiexistence he now occupied—he was Tyvian's immediate superior.

"You! Fancy boy! Quit yer lagging!" Drawsher shouted in Tyvian's ear as though Tyvian were deaf. He cracked Tyvian across the backside with a slender rod. A white-hot line of pain bloomed, making Tyvian wince.

"Oy, you think that hurt, Duchess?" Drawsher snarled. "It'll hurt worse'n that if you don't keep pace, damn your lazy arse!"

"I *am* keeping pace," Tyvian grumbled.

"Quiet in the ranks!" Drawsher screamed and hit Tyvian three more times, all across the arse or the back of his legs.

The urge to club the brute over the head with his pike was enormous. Even the ring was ambivalent about it, as it often was in cases of self-defense. But Tyvian clenched his teeth and picked up the pace slightly. Drawsher, evidently satisfied, moved on to find other victims. It turned out there was always *somebody* in the Ghouls who had an arse that needed a few strikes.

Tyvian was not a perfect judge of such things, but when the command came to set camp, he was reasonably certain they'd gone about twenty-five miles in a single day. Tyvian had scarcely been in such a rush in his entire life, and *he'd* been hunted by the Defenders of the Balance across half a continent.

Compared to marching, setting camp was also unpleasant, but in an entirely different way. Drawsher singled Tyvian and a handful of other "bones"—a Ghoul term for raw recruits—to dig a latrine. Tyvian made the argument that the captain had ordered him to his tent each evening after they camped.

Dawsher was unimpressed. "If'n the captain wants to talk to you, then I'm a honey-glazed ham!"

The analogy garnered a hearty laugh from Tyvian's new "companions." This, evidently, was what passed for humor among the Ghouls.

Tyvian was too fatigued to be snarky at that precise moment, but he did devise some choice insults for later deployment while hacking at the rocky Eretherian ground with a glorified garden trowel referred to as an "entrenching tool." It was, evidently, one of those pointless pieces of military paraphernalia that Tyvian had previously given little notice to, but now constituted the majority of his waking thoughts.

It was there, digging a ditch in the dying daylight, that Tyvian formally met his new social circle. Now no longer in ranks and with Sergeant Drawsher nowhere in sight, the Delloran mercenaries began to chatter. The first thing that struck Tyvian about them was their age—he guessed he was at least fifteen years older than all of them. He knew it made sense—it *shouldn't* have surprised him, given he was about their age when he joined up with Carlo diCarlo's pirate crew—but there was something inescapably jarring in realizing he was, in the eyes of the young, an old man.

An additional obstacle to forging any new alliances was that all of these young men were immensely, incurably stupid. They were young men from Dellor, and sometimes Galaspin, who had found marching to Eretheria with the Ghouls a more productive use of their lives than herding cows, breaking rocks, or coaxing plants out of the ground. Unless it had something to do with one of those three activities, they knew exactly nothing about anything.

They disliked Tyvian immediately. His alias, as it turned out, was utterly unnecessary, as Sergeant Drawsher had seen to it that nobody would ever use his name again. He was "Duchess" for now and ever.

"Oy, Duchess!" Hambone, a fat boy of perhaps twenty from Dellor who had been blabbering steadily about his family pig farm, was working his yard-long entrenching tool like it was a murder implement and his victim the earth itself. "Gimme a hand over here!"

Tyvian felt about as motivated to assist Hambone as he would be a urine-soaked street person. "You need to *scoop* the dirt, Hambone. Stop making holes and start actually digging."

Some of the other bones snickered. Hambone threw down his tool. "I done more ditch digging before I was ten than you done your whole fat life!"

Tyvian's tool bounced off a stone. He kicked the stone aside. "And yet you remain terrible at it. Some would call that a miracle."

Hambone came closer. Despite evidently having marched hundreds of miles from Dellor, he somehow had never lost the stench of pigs. "You think you're better than me, Duchess?"

Tyvian looked him in the eye. "Yes. In every field of endeavor, from now until the day you die."

The ring twinged softly, warning Tyvian against

hitting the boy. Tyvian didn't, knowing full well the idiot was going to hit him first.

Or try.

Hambone stood there, fists clenched, fuming. Behind him, some of the other bones egged him on. "Knock him good, Hammy! Piss on his lordship's arse!"

Tyvian waited. "Well, are you going to try and urinate on my arse, or what?"

Hambone swung. Even though monstrously tired from marching, Tyvian ducked the blow easily and ended the fight in as expeditious a method as possible—he hit Hambone in the knee with his entrenching tool. Not hard—just hard enough to make the boy's leg buckle and for it to hurt *really* badly. Hambone fell on his back in the muddy depths of the latrine ditch, howling.

The ring stayed mercifully silent.

The other bones backed away from him, their eyes wide. "Weren't no call for that," one of them muttered.

Tyvian ignored Hambone's groans. "You've joined a company of hired killers called 'The Ghouls,' for Hann's sake! How much bloody fair play did you expect?"

Hambone flopped, trying to stand, but his knee gave way immediately and he fell back in the half-dug latrine. "Help! Oh gods, me leg! Ohhhh!"

This time the ring *did* have an opinion. It gave Tyvian a hard jolt that snapped him out of his staring contest with the other fresh recruits. "Oh . . . very well, dammit."

He slipped an arm under Hambone's armpit and helped him to his feet. Tyvian took a look at his injured knee. It was bulging and swollen—Tyvian guessed he'd maybe knocked the kneecap out of alignment or possibly dislocated the whole joint, though he didn't think he'd swung that hard. Hambone leaned heavily on Tyvian's shoulders—appropriately enough, he seemed to weigh as much as a prize hog. "It hurts! Ohhhh!"

Grimacing, Tyvian walked the idiot to Eddereon, who was examining the blisters growing on one foot outside their tiny tent. He stood as they approached. "What's all this?"

Tears were rolling down Hambone's flat cheeks. "He hit me! Ohhh! Right in the knee!"

Eddereon looked at Tyvian. "Well?"

Tyvian only nodded. "I hit him. Right in the knee."

"You better get him to the medical tent before Drawsher sees."

"Sees what?" Drawsher emerged from behind a pike stand like a troll lumbering out of a hedge. "What happened here?"

Eddereon and Tyvian exchanged quick glances. "An accident, sir. Digging the latrine."

Drawsher looked at the three of them, scratching at his unkempt beard. "Accident, is it? Hey, Hambone—can you walk?"

Hambone shook his head, tears still streaming down his cheeks.

"I can help him to the medical tent, sir," Tyvian offered.

Drawsher laughed in Tyvian's face. "What for? Man can't walk—he's useless. We leave him behind come dawn."

The color drained from Hambone's face. "What? You can't! You can't leave me here!"

Drawsher leaned close to Hambone, as though about to whisper something conspiratorial. Instead, he sucker punched Hambone in the lower abdomen, folding the fat man in half like a bath towel. Nearby, a few other mercenaries laughed.

The ring blazed on Tyvian's hand. "You miserable son of a—"

Drawsher had a dagger out in a flash and pressed it under Tyvian's nose. "Am I going to get lip from you, Duchess? Eh?" He dragged the blade gently along Tyvian's mouth. "If I am, I might as well *take em now*, eh?"

Tyvian kept his eyes on Drawsher's eyes. The play with the knife was scary, sure, but also wildly stupid. Tyvian could have put that knife in Drawsher's own throat in two moves, three tops. His fingers twitched, wanting to. How many two-bit bullies like Drawsher had Tyvian put in the ground? Gods, too many to even bother counting. If there was a reason he was better at digging holes than Hambone, it was because of all the bodies he'd buried over the years.

But I'm not Tyvian anymore, he cautioned himself. *Play the damned part.*

Tyvian let his eyes drop from Drawsher's. "There were wounded riding in a wagon today. I saw them. Why can't Hambone ride, too, sir?"

Drawsher withdrew the knife. He nodded. "Them's blooded men—them's true Ghouls, Duchess. This here bone would be wasted space. Space we need for supplies, for armor—for things what matter."

Tyvian looked down at Hambone, who was still wheezing and moaning on the ground. "What if I carry his load? What if I make up the space that he takes?"

Drawsher cocked his head. "Well now . . . ain't that noble of you, Duchess. Downright gentlemanly." He slapped his knife home in its scabbard. "All right, then—bring him to the healer. But you carry his pack tomorrow, Duchess. And his pike. And *anything else I say.*"

There was mirth in Drawsher's bloodshot eyes. Tyvian nodded—he knew what it meant for him tomorrow. He licked his lips. "As you say, sir."

Drawsher grinned. "Another wrong breath from you, Duchess, and I'll eat your kidneys, understand?"

Tyvian saluted as best he could. Drawsher went back to his rounds.

Eddereon patted Tyvian on the shoulder. "You certainly have a way with people sometimes."

Tyvian didn't answer. He helped Hambone up.

Hambone, pale, managed to say, "What in hell is wrong with you, Duchess? You trying to get dead?"

"Tried, Hambone. Tried and succeeded."

The camp doctor—a hedge wizard and probably non-guild alchemist named Rink—managed to relocate Hambone's kneecap and put the man's leg in a splint. It was the back of a wagon for Hambone for one week. Tyvian, meanwhile, carried double the weight, plus a five-gallon water skin slung over one shoulder.

Despite his inquiries, there was no indication of him being invited to Rodall's command tent. Sergeant Drawsher had Tyvian all to himself.

The first day, Drawsher circled him like a raven. The weight was overwhelming, the pace punishing—the sergeant was expecting a long day of beating the snot out of Tyvian Reldamar. The ring, though, had a few things to say about that. Saving Hambone from abandonment was enough to keep Tyvian upright and marching, the ring's power driving every step. He was still exhausted, still punishing his body in ways he'd never considered possible before, but he kept up. Drawsher barely had an excuse to strike him.

So, in a fit of pique, he assigned Tyvian latrine duty *alone* for three days straight.

Despite being sandwiched in a tiny tent between three men every night—one of whom happened to be Hambone, with his distinct pig odor—Tyvian found himself falling asleep the moment his head hit his blanket roll.

His efforts had two additional side effects. The first and less consequential one was that Hambone had now become his friend. He seemed to think getting his kneecap knocked askew with a small shovel was the best thing that ever happened to him. "Weren't for you," he said one night over the evening's share of mutton stew, "I wouldn't be riding the wagon. Be out there with you lot, marching my legs down to nothing."

"Just say the word," Tyvian said, "and I'll knock you on your arse again. Anytime."

Hambone had found this hilarious.

The second side effect was that Tyvian's time digging the latrine alone allowed him space to think over his predicament in private. While marching, he was too concerned with staying in rank and not dropping his pike (or Hambone's), but in the cool of the evening, alone with his stupid little shovel, Tyvian could take a deep breath and forget, for a moment, that his new name was Duchess and he was the unpaid foot soldier of Banric Sahand's invading army.

Like his sticking up for Hambone, Tyvian's plan to fake his own death had been a selfless act to its core—it had to be, since if it hadn't, he would have died as he plummeted off the roof of the Peregrine Palace into the lake below. As a selfless act, however, it had lacked a certain degree of postmortem planning. He had informed Eddereon to fish him out of the lake and hide him away until he recovered, but had also tasked him with finding a means by which they could leave the country unnoticed. This, he had to admit, Eddereon had done, albeit in the least pleasant way possible.

But now what?

Tyvian had no intention of remaining a member of the Ghouls for one moment longer than necessary. It was only a matter of time before orders from on high would put him (and Eddereon) in an untenable situation vis-à-vis the ring. As it stood, Tyvian knew full well that the mutton they were eating each night wasn't from any kind of elaborate baggage train—the Ghouls were stripping the countryside bare of every chicken, lamb, duck, and cow they could clap their gauntlets on. The villages they marched through locked their doors and shutters as they passed. Sometimes at dawn, Tyvian could see the oily columns of smoke rising to the sky—farms that had been burned by Captain Rodall's foraging teams the night before.

The idea that his mother was still alive and imprisoned in Dellor struck Tyvian as wildly improbable. Sahand was not known for his mercy and, even if his mother were alive, it was only because the torture she was enduring was so elaborate that she had not yet been permitted to expire. Running to Dellor—on foot, incidentally—would accomplish very little except put them in *Dellor*, which by all accounts was one of the least pleasant places in the West. No, Tyvian was not the one to rescue Lyrelle. The woman was on her own.

That fact, though, had yet to penetrate Eddereon's wooly brain. Late at night, while Hambone snored and their other tent-mate, a giant of a man by the name of Mort, evidently wrestled bears in his sleep, Eddereon and Tyvian would sometimes whisper to one another.

"You can't be serious about going to Dellor," Tyvian said one night, throwing Mort's huge hand off his face.

"She's in danger, Tyvian. She's your *mother*," Eddereon said, his eyes barely visible in the slash of moonlight that squeezed between their tent flaps.

"I'm telling you, as her *son*, that Lyrelle Reldamar has never wanted help from anybody, least of all me. If she wound up in Dellor, it's because she knew she would. That means she's either dead already, or well on her way to a triumphant escape. The last thing she needs is your schoolyard heroics."

"Tyvian." Eddereon reached out and grabbed his arm. "Don't you owe her this much?"

"*Owe* her? We're square, believe me." Tyvian yanked his arm free. "Besides, why do you care anyway? What do *you* owe her?"

Eddereon's eyes grew damp. He wiped away a tear with one filthy thumb. "Because, Tyvian—I *love* her."

So there it was. Lyrelle Reldamar had gotten her hooks so deep in Eddereon's idiot heart that he was about to cross a featureless wasteland and assail an impregnable fortress all in the hopes she wasn't skinned, stuffed, and adorning Banric Sahand's trophy case.

It was clear Eddereon could not be relied upon. That meant it would soon be time to ditch him, too.

If he was giving up the hero business, though, what else was there for Tyvian to do? He thought of one of his conversations with Xahlven—the Oracle of the Vale, he had said, knew how to find the Yldd. Find the Yldd and he could remove the ring. He could go back to being himself again—a new beginning, as it were. No more lowly moralistic concerns, no more requisite acts of heroic daring. He looked at the ring in the firelight one night over dinner. It was caked with grime, blackened by the day's efforts. Were it not for it, he would be dead. Of course, were it not for it, he would also never have found himself on that palace roof in the first place. There was so much he owed that trinket and so much it owed *him*, that it had become pointless to pass blame. Besides, he believed his mother when she had told him it was really just a storage unit for and amplifier of his better self. There was no sense arguing that, on some level, all the things he had done at the ring's coaxing were things he thought were right.

But that didn't mean he needed to keep it forever.

Again, that feeling of freedom sought to overwhelm him. If he disappeared one night—if he crept off and got away—there was literally no limit to what he could do. No responsibilities, no debts, not even any enemies! Carlo diCarlo always said he knew how to get to the Vale—hell, if anybody knew something like that, it would be Carlo. All Tyvian needed to do was give the Ghouls the slip, get to Freegate, and then begin the next chapter in his life. The thought of kicking back in Carlo's house, a glass of *cherille* in his hand, while one of Carlo's girls rubbed the kinks from his back and the cramps from his legs . . . gods, it was enough to keep Tyvian going the whole next day with a smile on his face. Not even Drawsher's bawling could crack it.

Tyvian began to develop his plan for escape. The primary obstacle was Rodall's hounds—fooling hounds like that was nearly impossible without sorcerous intervention. At minimum, he was going to need about five gallons of human urine. Fortunately, he knew just where to get it—he had to dig the damned latrine every night. Even with all that piss, though, that would only buy him a half hour or so before they found the trail again. He set his mind to remembering his Eretherian geography—he'd smuggled things through this country so many times, he knew plenty of bolt holes and hideaways. He just needed a safe haven . . .

"Duchess!" Drawsher kicked him in the foot. For the barest second, Tyvian thought that maybe his plan to escape had been found out. But then he noticed Drawsher's expression—that unique kind of bitterness that arises when a bully has to admit they are wrong. "Captain is asking to see you. Hop to it."

Tyvian crawled out of the tent and stood, stretching his aching back. "What's this about?"

Drawsher pointed toward the command tent. "Don't keep the captain waiting, scrub! Move it!"

Tyvian walked toward the captain's tent with an easy gait. "What's the matter, Drawsher—weren't *you* invited?"

"Kroth take you, high-born shit-eating . . ." The sergeant made as though to chase him, fists balled, but something kept him at bay. Probably the fact that if Tyvian showed up to Rodall's tent late and with a black eye, Drawsher would be the one limping for the next week.

Tyvian savored the sergeant's impotence as he went to answer his employer's call. He felt so good at that moment, he even felt the desire to whistle coming on. Then he remembered exactly where he was going and his mood sobered. *After a week of marching and no word, what the hell could Rodall want now?*

Rodall's tent had no guards posted—just two of those enormous dogs curled up and sleeping on the mat before the door. Their heads popped up when Tyvian was five paces away and they watched carefully as he approached. One of them growled—a higher-pitched version of Hool's growl, but nevertheless pretty menacing. Tyvian stopped in his tracks.

Rodall whistled from inside the tent. "Let him in, boys."

Rodall was still wearing his armor—Tyvian was beginning to suspect the man slept in it. His tent featured a folding table with a huge map rolled up and lying across it. Tyvian didn't flatter himself to think that Rodall had hidden his company's exact location and disposition for *his* benefit. The captain was about to receive a visitor, then—a visitor he did not entirely trust.

Rodall looked at him and pointed to a weapons rack in the corner of the tent. "Get a sword and stand behind me. I want the weapon bared and point-down in the ground between your legs—don't say a damned thing, but keep your eyes open and be ready for anything, understand?"

Tyvian saluted. "Yes sir."

As Tyvian was doing as he was asked, Rodall caught him by the elbow and whispered in his ear. "If you breathe a word of anything you're about to hear to *anybody* . . ."

He let himself trail off, leaving the punishment to the imagination. Tyvian didn't have to imagine very hard.

Tyvian got to his "imposing bodyguard" position just in time to hear Rodall's hounds growl at a new visitor. Rodall drew a dagger from a scabbard and slipped it into his boot. Then he slid gently into a chair, the table between him and the door. He whistled his dogs off. "Come in."

A small woman stepped over the dogs and into the tent. She was dressed in a long black cloak, but Tyvian glimpsed a sword at her hip as she took in the tent. She reached up with gloved hands and gently pulled back her hood. Midnight curls, delicate features, blind in one eye . . .

It was Adatha Voth.

Kroth.

Tyvian froze. How many seconds before she recognized him? His heart pounded in his chest. His immediate instinct was to put his borrowed sword through the base of Rodall's skull while he had the chance and then see if he could cut his way out of the tent before Voth put a throwing knife in his spine. Of course, the ring would never permit him to do such a thing—stab a man in the back without cause—so while Tyvian was going through a secondary plan, he noticed something:

Voth had barely looked at him. She had noted his presence and the sword in his hands and the tabard on his chest, but that was it. The beard, the bald head, the poor nutrition and hard marching—Tyvian must not look remotely himself.

He was relieved, and yet . . . after all they'd shared, his pride was just a *touch* hurt.

Rodall eyed her warily, his hand resting on his

knee beneath the table, in easy reach of the dagger in his boot. "Sahand sent you?"

Voth watched Rodall with razor-sharp focus. Tyvian could tell she knew about the knife Rodall had in reach, and Tyvian discerned from some subtle movements that she had just let a small throwing knife drop into the palm of her hand. If Rodall saw this, he gave no sign. "I need to speak with you privately, Captain," she said.

"I might be a stupid old mercenary captain," Rodall said. "But I'm smart enough not to be alone with *you*, assassin."

Voth laughed—that throaty, sexy laugh Tyvian remembered so well from their evenings together in the House of Eddon, in a literally different life. "My dear captain—if I were sent here to kill you, do you really think you would have been told to expect me?"

Told? Told how? Tyvian hadn't spotted any couriers coming or going, nor any messenger djinn. He cast an eye around the room—there, in the corner, was a sending stone. Rodall must be in direct contact with his commanders, which meant he was in contact with Sahand. The risks of his discovery just got even more serious.

Meanwhile, the standoff between Voth and Rodall had not abated. With slow movements, Voth pulled open her cloak to reveal a scroll tube in a concealed pocket. She pulled it out and threw it on the table. "There. This ought to explain things. It seems I'm going to be tagging along with your little band of cannibals for the immediate future."

Rodall opened the scroll case. *Idiot*, Tyvian thought. *If Voth wanted him dead, there would have been a poison needle concealed in the lid.*

The captain glanced at the document, which was sealed with Sahand's personal mark in the wax. He looked over his shoulder. "You—leave us."

Tyvian didn't need to be asked twice. Part of him wanted to stick around and eavesdrop, but Rodall's hounds seemed disinclined toward his company. He decided to play it safe, even though with Voth in the camp he felt *decidedly* less safe.

What was Voth doing here? Could she . . . could she *know* or suspect he was alive? Could Sahand? Was Eddereon in danger? Should he warn him?

The ring throbbed in a dull, monotonous rhythm. *Dammit all.*

He turned back toward his tent. Desertion, it seemed, would have to wait for another day. He slipped back between his three tent-mates, marinating in their manly odors, and tried his best to get comfortable.

For the first time since he'd joined the Ghouls, Tyvian found he couldn't sleep.

CHAPTER 3

EARNING PAY

Tyvian spent the next few days waiting for the other shoe to drop. It never did. Rumors of Voth's arrival were rampant—Rodall's personal whore, some said. Others insisted she was a sorceress. Tyvian refused to offer an opinion. When someone asked what he thought, he'd say he didn't know either way. Voth? Who's that? Never heard of her.

In the meantime, Tyvian was getting a reputation for being the world's best mule. Even Drawsher seemed mutely appreciative of the fact that he'd been carrying Hambone's pack for days without falling behind a step. "That's what yer good for, Duchess," he said once, tapping Tyvian's shoulder with his rod. "Carrying baggage."

Tyvian couldn't help but snort. *If the man only knew . . .*

Hambone got back on his feet just in time for their first battle. Well, a skirmish, more like—Captain Rodall wasn't about to deploy his greenest troops against anything that resembled a dangerous foe. They were mustered into ranks early one morning without explanation and marched to a green outside a small village. There they stood, pikes high—a mute display of force—while Rodall "negotiated" with the village leaders.

Tyvian squinted across the grassy meadow at the motley assembly of peasants with pots on their heads who had dared to oppose them. A few of them had small hunting bows—the kind you used to kill ducks in a pond. The ring throbbed. *If it comes to fighting, this isn't going to be a skirmish. It's going to be murder.*

Captain Rodall, astride his coal-black charger with his hounds at his heels, had advanced twenty paces from the two blocks he'd tasked to this operation— one of pikes, the other of broadswords and shields. He had Drawsher on one side of him and Adatha Voth on the other, both of them also mounted. Despite what he'd heard in the tent, Tyvian had to assume that if Voth were with the Ghouls, she was here to murder someone. Given that Tyvian was not yet dead, he presumed that someone wasn't him.

He very much wanted to sneak out of his tent at night and find where in the camp she was bedded down. He wanted to lurk outside the command tent and eavesdrop on her discussions with Rodall. Of course, he was not alone—the presence of a beautiful woman in the camp was enough to drive half the Ghouls to distraction. Serving as her "escort" in camp had become a coveted position, afforded only those with the longest service records with the company— and "Duchess" didn't rate. Besides, the closer he got, the more likely she'd recognize him, and he had been lucky enough the first time around to dissuade him from trying his luck for a second go.

"Duchess," Hambone nudged him, "what're they saying? We gonna fight?"

Tyvian tore his attention from Voth's black curls. "What?"

"C'mon—do the trick!" Hambone thrust his chin toward the captain's delegation and the three villagers who had come out to meet him.

Mort spat a wad of chewing tobacco into the grass. "What trick?"

Hambone giggled. "Duchess can read lips!"

Mort looked down at Tyvian. Standing nearly taller than Hool, this was a long way down for Mort. Tyvian felt like an ant. "The hell he can!"

"I certainly can, and if you two would shut up, I will." Tyvian adjusted his helm to get the best view. Hambone and Mort fell silent, and he felt the rank behind him leaning in to listen to whatever he was going to say. "I can't see the captain's mouth, so I don't know what he's saying, but I can see the villagers well enough."

Silence for a moment as Tyvian parsed out the words. "Well?" Hambone whispered.

"The fellow's making Rodall an offer. They'll give us a dozen chickens and five pigs in exchange for us marching away."

Mort snorted through his cavernous nostrils. "We're just gonna kill 'em and take 'em anyway."

"But if we just take that much, we can march away and none of us get killed."

Mort spat again. "Them farmers ain't enough to kill me—won't kill nobody in this company. Captain knows it, too. You'll see."

Hambone was grinning. "And then we get paid!"

Tyvian glimpsed nods from the corner of his eye. The Ghouls were excited, especially the bones. If they got to stick their pikes into some peasants today, they'd be eligible for the Ghouls' very generous salary of three silver crowns a week. The ring tightened on Tyvian's finger to the point that it went numb. *And what do you propose I do about it?* Tyvian thought.

He felt a hand on his back—Eddereon, standing right behind him. The big man whispered in Tyvian's ear. "This is going to get ugly. Prepare yourself."

Tyvian nodded, though he had no realistic idea

of what "preparing himself" would look like in this scenario.

The villagers' delegation had finished talking. Tyvian supposed this was the point when Captain Rodall would tell the head villager in which end to stuff his bribe. Before he started speaking, though, Drawsher wheeled his horse and rode back toward the pikes. *Here we go . . .*

Rodall drew his broadsword and cut down the head villager with a savage blow to the temple that took the top of the man's head off. On the backswing, he cut the arm off the lanky boy who was holding the village "standard"—just a plain blue flag on a stick. The third person—an old woman—screamed and fled, clutching her skirts. The captain twitched a finger, and his hounds leapt after her, running her down with ease. Her screams as they tore her apart made the ring blaze to the point that Tyvian's knees felt weak. He leaned on his pike.

Rodall and Voth wheeled their horses and headed back toward the Ghouls. A few arrows struck Rodall's bow wards and bounced off. Voth was laughing.

Tyvian glanced back to see Eddereon clutching his right hand to his chest. Tyvian knew that exact feeling—the ring torturing him. Tyvian felt it too, from a numbing squeeze to a red-hot fire. An iron brand laid across his fingers and blazing up his forearm.

The drums sounded the advance.

Tyvian had little choice but to match pace with

the pike block, but his feet were so heavy he felt like he was wading through mud. Beside him, he heard Hambone say, "Here we go!"

The peasants—about fifty of them—ranged from boys of maybe thirteen to old men two steps from the grave. It was probably the entire male population of the village here. They were armed with hatchets and pitchforks and scythes and other tools of agriculture and husbandry. They had pot lids and barrel tops for shields. He hadn't been seeing things, either—they truly wore iron cooking pots on their heads.

They were screaming with rage.

Some old fellow with an actual rusty sabre—a makeshift sergeant—thrust his blade toward the approaching pike block. Arrows from the back rank of the village militia whistled in low arcs. They mostly missed, but a few managed to plink off the Ghouls' helmets. Tyvian heard one man cry out—probably hit in the leg or arm. The drums doubled their pace, and so did the Ghouls. Tyvian lowered his pike. Over his shoulders, the pikes of the ranks behind him lowered as well. The twenty-five-man block was a solid wall of steel spikes, moving toward the peasants at an even march. The other block—the sword block—was wheeling wide. When the pikes engaged, the swords would sweep down on those villagers seeking to flee. Tyvian could only glance at the other unit between the waving weapon shafts that surrounded him, but he knew what was going on. It was obvious, really. Inevitable.

Half of the peasants charged, throwing themselves at the mercenaries, sledgehammers and wood splitters held high. The other half broke and ran.

It was hard to say who had the worst of it.

The first villager to come within range of Tyvian's pike was a boy—a big barrel-chested lad, a bit like Hambone. He had a pitchfork. The ring atrophied Tyvian's arms—he couldn't do anything. He couldn't stab the boy, but of course he didn't have to. Hambone did, as did the pikeman just behind him and to his left, spitting the farmboy through the chest in two places. In a dying spasm, he threw his pitchfork at the block. It plinked off of Tyvian's mail; it would probably leave a bruise. But then they were marching over the dying boy, their weapons poking holes in the next villager and the next and the next.

Tears streaked Tyvian's cheeks as the fire in his hand burned. It was all he could do to hold the pike, but it hung down at his waist, inert—just a long pole to ward off danger. Five other peasants went down under the foot-long tips of the Ghouls' weapons. Then the order came to drop the pikes and the formation broke up. Swords were drawn. The villagers were routed, and now the slaughter was set to begin.

Hambone whooped, waving his sword in the air, and charged into the fray. Mort was more deliberate, carefully stabbing injured villagers in the spine before advancing.

Tyvian let them go. He supposed he ought to be screaming at himself to get over it—to do something before someone noticed and his cover was blown. He supposed also he ought to have been angry at the idiot peasants who thought threatening a mercenary company with a couple of old men with garden tools was a wise plan. But he remembered, at alternate points in his life, thinking and doing just those kinds of things.

Not now, however. Not today. He could still remember the faces of all those people who had come to his coronation. The ones that had kissed his hands and wept with joy at the very sight of him. The ones that, ultimately, he'd thrown himself off a building to save.

And a fat lot of good that had done.

Somebody smacked him in the back of the head. It was Drawsher—on foot, his eyes wild. "Get your head out your arse, Duchess! Earn your pay!"

Tyvian nodded, his hand still blazing with pain, and dropped his pike. He followed Drawsher as he charged through the village and into a pigsty. The sergeant spitted a young pig with a precise thrust and then passed the corpse to Tyvian. "Hold that! That there's mine, understand? For later."

A woman in a bonnet poked her head out of a doorway and shot an arrow at Drawsher. It stuck in his mail, just below the collarbone, but the bow just wasn't strong enough to pierce deep. Drawsher staggered back a pace, roaring. Then he charged into the house.

Tyvian, still holding the bleeding pig, followed him. He could scarcely think—the pain was so intense. It had never been this bad before. The world was just a tunnel of fire and blood, and at the end was Drawsher's broad back, pieces of his kit jingling as he ran.

They were in the cottage. The woman was screaming, throwing pots and plates and bowls at Drawsher as she sought to keep the butcher's table between her and the sergeant. Drawsher batted the projectiles aside with his shield and leered. "Only gonna make it all the sweeter, duckling! I like the fighters!"

Tyvian dropped the dead pig.

Drawsher glared at him. "Go search the rest of the house, bone!"

Tyvian drew his sword. "No."

Getting through Drawsher's guard took only two moves. Tyvian left his broadsword sticking in the sergeant's eye, its tip pushing through the back of Drawsher's skull and his chain coif and pinning him to a wooden support beam.

The pain torturing him subsided, if momentarily. The woman screamed and fled. *Not even a thank you.* But his next thought was this: *What does she have to krothing thank you for, anyway?*

Numb, Tyvian worked his sword out of Drawsher's

face. He had to put his foot on the man's breastbone to get it out.

Outside there was a flash of fire, and a wave of heat rushed through the open door. Tyvian went outside to see three Ghouls lying on their backs, their bodies smoking. Across the village square, on the roof of what was probably a blacksmith's shop, an old woman was waving around a wand. *A hedge wizard.*

She fired another ball of flame at some more men, but these were a bit more nimble and dove behind a water trough. One of them was Hambone. His face was blistering up from a severe burn. He was screaming.

The hedge wizard powered up her wand again and shot another fireball at a group of the sword block that was trying to advance on the smithy. They scattered.

From the ground floor of the smithy, three men with bows started shooting. With the wizard's wand providing cover, they could take their time and aim well. Two more Ghouls went down.

What the hell do I do now?

"Duchess!" It was Hambone, screaming to him from behind his trough. "Get that bitch on the roof! Get her!"

Tyvian looked down. There was a bow at his feet—the woman's bow.

Tyvian had never shot a bow in his entire life.

A fireball exploded against the trough, causing it

to light on fire. The men hunkered down with Ham-bone, screaming.

The ring sent Tyvian conflicting signals. On the one hand, the Ghouls had already lit half the village aflame and killed dozens of people. On the other, that old woman with the wand was trying to kill his os-tensible friends. His whole right arm tingled with the conflict. He froze up.

In the end, he didn't have to decide. The hedge wizard dropped her wand and clawed at her neck. Behind her, gloved hands twisted a garrote deeper into the old woman's throat.

Of course, it was Adatha Voth.

CHAPTER 4

THE SPOILS

Tyvian spent the remainder of the "battle" in a pain-soaked stupor. The ring inflicted on him every torture, every hurt, and every death the Ghouls perpetrated. He knew he might have picked up a sword and begun a campaign of violence on his own, but to what end? Nothing could save that nameless little village now, least of all him. He might have felt the satisfaction of cutting the throats of a half-dozen rapists and murderers, but that scenario only ended with him running through the fields from Captain Rodall and his dogs, hunting new ears for his necklace.

So he curled himself into a ball somewhere, closed his eyes, and waited for it all to be over. Like a stinking coward. He only wondered, as he listened to the screams of the women and the crying children, how Eddereon was faring in all this. No better, certainly. Or perhaps Eddereon's better self wasn't quite as good as his own.

When it had quieted down some, the horn was sounded for retreat. Tyvian crawled out from beneath the oxcart he'd been hiding under and tried to leave the village without looking at anything. The heat from the burning homes hit him in waves. He had to step over a little boy—perhaps five years old—whose head was bashed open like a melon. One of his tiny, shoeless feet still twitched. The ring burned Tyvian from within while real flames burned him from without. He felt like his bones were grinding together, dry and brittle as sandpaper. He gasped, trying to keep the tears from falling. Somehow, he pressed on.

Back on the meadow where the village's fallen defenders lay, the pain subsided somewhat. Tyvian managed an erect posture; he could look around. On either side of him he saw his tent-mates. Mort had a goat over his broad shoulders, his boots caked in blood. Despite the burns on his face, Hambone was laughing with another man. "Shoulda heard her squeal, mate! Gods, what a ride that was!"

Tyvian threw up.

This caught their attention. "Well, well," Hambone said with a snort, "if it ain't Duchess! Where were you hiding, eh? Missed all the fun!"

Still leaning on his knees, Tyvian spat and struggled to catch his breath. "Yes . . . my . . . my loss . . ."

Hambone laughed at him. "Seems like there's something I do better'n you, after all. Ain't there, Duchess?"

Tyvian couldn't help but choke out a laugh. "Yes . . . seems so."

They were mustered into loose ranks. The lack of Sergeant Drawsher was noticed immediately. Captain Rodall summoned a few of the senior Ghouls—Eddereon included in this—and sent them back to the village to fetch him. Tyvian knew this was bad, but was too wrung out to care. There were few tortures a bunch of Delloran thugs could devise that he had not just experienced tenfold. Having his ears cut off sounded like a refreshing change of pace.

Eddereon and the others came back after a brief search, Drawsher's body draped between them. The men stared. "Kroth's teeth," Hambone said, eyes wide, "who coulda taken Drawsher? He was a beast! An utter beast!"

"Maybe he owed somebody money, eh?" Mort was stroking the goat's head to keep it from bleating. Now that Tyvian could see him from the front, he could tell where the blood all over his boots came from—from his belt hung five headless chickens.

Hambone's eyes shot up. "You think . . . one of *us* did that?"

Mort shrugged, refusing to comment.

Eddereon and the other men carried the body

away. The rest of them were ordered to form into a column and marched back to camp a mile or so distant. The mood, though initially jubilant, had soured notably. The men seemed downtrodden, heads hanging as they carried along their stolen chickens, pigs, and goats, the smoke from the burning village still thick in the air.

Tyvian wanted to scream at them all. *Seriously? You just raped and murdered a bunch of unarmed farmers and you're depressed because the man who beat you with a switch every morning got stabbed through the skull?*

But, as he had the past number of days, he said nothing.

He hated his own silence.

With every step away from the village, the ring's anger eased somewhat, though not entirely. It was there constantly, pushing him toward either justice or vengeance, though at this point Tyvian could not readily tell the difference between the two.

Back at camp, the stolen provisions were confiscated by the company quartermaster and recorded in a massive iron-bound ledger. Each man was searched by a pair of burly sell-swords with hands the size of ham hocks—the process had more in common with a beating than anything else. Men were permitted to keep money and trinkets and such, but food and drink was dropped into labeled barrels. Altogether, the razing of a pastoral Eretherian village was extremely organized.

When it came to be Tyvian's turn, the men turned

up nothing. The quartermaster, who had gold-rimmed spectacles clipped to a long, booze-rotted nose, actually looked up from his ledger. "Nothing?"

Tyvian shrugged. "Nothing I wanted."

Everyone looked at him like he'd just pulled off his own head and tried to bowl with it. The quartermaster blinked, his eyes magnified by his spectacles. "You know that these provisions are important for the company's survival, yes?"

"I'm very sorry for not doing my part," Tyvian droned. "Um . . . sir."

The magnified eyes of the quartermaster narrowed. "What is your name?"

"Duchess."

"Your *real* name?"

"Ty . . . ahhh . . . blast it . . . Arick of . . . somewhere."

If the fact that Tyvian didn't remember his own name raised any suspicions, the quartermaster gave no sign—Tyvian imagined people joined mercenary companies under false names all the time anyway. The man scribbled a note and waved him off. Tyvian went back to his tent and waited for his comeuppance to arrive.

It came at sundown. Tyvian's whole block was mustered. Captain Rodall was there, hands resting on the pommel of his broadsword, which was currently stuck point-first in the ground. Beside him was Voth, who was sitting on a large rock and cleaning under her fingernails with a stiletto.

Eddereon had evidently been given a field promotion to sergeant—the benefits of being a legendary mercenary, Tyvian supposed. After Eddereon had inspected his unit and noted that all men were present, saving those few wounded in the action that day, he took his place at Rodall's right hand. The captain nodded at his new sergeant and then flashed a silvery smile at the men. "Sergeant Drawsher was killed by a broadsword to the eye. One thrust, quick and hard—right through the back of his skull." Drawsher nodded, scanning them, one by one. "No Eretherian pig's boy or grandpa did this. It was one of our own."

Tyvian felt the tension in the unit ramp up. He could tell that men were holding their breath, that others were tensing for what was to come next. He didn't do anything, though. With Voth sitting there, looking at the men, anything to distinguish himself from the crowd might be a death sentence in more ways than one.

Rodall was still talking. "We can't stay here long. We march tonight, so we're going to settle this quick. The man who killed Drawsher can step forward now, and we'll have it done with quick and painless. If he doesn't, well . . ." Rodall's silver grin sparkled in the fading sunlight. "I just kill two of you at random and call it even. If the rest of you find out who done it later and take things into your own hands, can't say I'd mind that, either."

Silence. Tyvian clenched his teeth. Had anyone seen him? Would someone turn him in?

Rodall walked down the line, sword over one shoulder. "Can't say as I blame a man who'd put steel through Drawsher. He was a certain kind of son of a bitch, for sure. He was a cheap death, too—no children, no wife. No death pay for me to spend, eh?"

Tyvian held his breath as Voth's gaze passed over him and paused, just for a moment, before moving on. The ring was beginning to throw fits again, squeezing and burning and pinching. It wasn't about to let two others die for his deed. *Dammit, dammit, dammit!*

Rodall stopped two-thirds through the line and pointed his blade at one of the younger bones— Tyvian didn't remember his name, just the size of his ears and his creaky voice. "You. Step forward."

The boy fell to his knees. "Oh, please, Captain sir, I didn't do it! I swear, I—"

Rodall thrust his sword down through the boy's open mouth and into his chest cavity. Blood fountained up and the lad's arms and legs twitched for a moment, then he was still. Rodall put his foot in the boy's chest and pulled the sword free. The body tumbled backward, his legs pinned beneath him. The men nearby stepped back.

The ring made Tyvian wince so hard he actually cried out. He closed his eyes, trying to swallow the pain somehow. There was no escape.

Rodall stepped in front of him. "Something you want to confess, Duchess?"

Tyvian clenched his teeth. "N . . . no."

Rodall snickered. "Step forward, then."

"Begging your pardon, sir!" Hambone broke in, his voice quavering. "But . . . but Duchess didn't kill nobody, sir! He . . . he couldn't have—he spent the whole battle curled up like a baby! Like . . . like a little girl, sir!"

Tyvian looked at the stocky Delloran pig farmer with openmouthed shock. "Hambone, shut the hell up!"

Rodall turned toward Hambone. "Would you like to take his place, bone?"

Hambone was pale. "W-With respect . . . s-sir . . . I ain't no bone no more. Blooded today, see?"

Rodall laughed and looked back at Eddereon. "You were right, Ed! These boys have spunk, don't they? Ha!" He looked back at Hambone and the smile dropped from his face. "Step forward and on your knees, *bone*."

Hambone gulped. "I . . . I . . ."

Rodall pointed to the grass. "Knees!"

Hambone looked at Tyvian, his eyes wide, mouth hanging open—he looked like a man about to drown. He stepped forward on wooden legs. He slowly sank to his knees.

Dammit all! Tyvian stepped between Hambone and Rodall. "It's me! I did it. I killed Drawsher!"

Hambone looked poleaxed. "Wh . . . what? You did no such thing! Duchess, don't be stupid!"

"Hambone, you insufferable dunce, between the two of us, the stupid one is *always you!*"

Rodall laughed, his platinum-capped teeth flashing. He motioned Hambone up with the tip of his sword. "Back in ranks!" He pointed to a spot on the grass a bit in front of the line of men—somewhere they all could see. "Kneel over there, Duchess. And be a man about it this time."

Eddereon stepped forward, "Sir, if I might—"

"Shut it, Ed," Rodall snarled. "This little priss cost me two men now. I'm going to get back my money's worth."

Tyvian walked forward. The ring, for the first time in hours, fell silent. He wondered to himself if its resurrection powers extended to decapitations. He decided he just wasn't that lucky. He got to the spot indicated and knelt. Voth was looking right at him, her good eye squinting, her head cocked.

What the hell. Tyvian winked at her.

Rodall's armored boots clanked up behind him. "You know I lied about the painless thing, right?"

Tyvian spoke over his shoulder. "My mother always told me not to trust a Ghoul."

Rodall kicked him hard in the kidneys. Tyvian gasped and fell on his face. The tip of Rodall's sword, still slick with the blood of its last kill, pressed between Tyvian's thighs and slid, slowly, toward the crease of his buttocks. Tyvian clenched—this . . . this was going to hurt. A lot.

"Rodall!" Voth shouted. "I pick him."

The captain's sword paused. "What?"

"I have my pick of men—I pick *him*. Don't damage him."

Rodall's sword didn't waver. "This is a discipline issue, Adatha! I settle it *my* way!"

Voth hopped down off her rock and walked right up to the captain. "And when I report back to the prince and tell him you weren't entirely cooperative with me, how do you suppose he will react?" She pointed at Tyvian. "Do you think he might have to settle a 'discipline issue' of his own?"

"Are you *threatening* me? In front of my own men?"

Voth chuckled. "Don't bother, Rodall—I'm not a girl who gives an arse about your problems. I'm a representative of your damned employer, and you *do what I say.*"

Tyvian lay on his face in the grass for another few moments, the feeling of a broadsword between his thighs. Then, finally, it was withdrawn. "Take him, then, but keep him out of my sight, understand? I'd hate there to be an *accident.*"

Voth grinned up at the armored sell-sword captain and faked a curtsey. "Accidents can happen to quite a lot of people, Rodall. *Especially* when I'm around."

Tyvian rolled over and got a look at Rodall's face. It was positively feral with anger—Tyvian had seen raccoons trapped in barrels who'd looked happier. He roared at the block of soldiers, "Dismissed!" Then, spitting on Tyvian's chest, he stormed away.

Tyvian staggered to his feet. Voth was there, helping him up. Her lips were close to his ear: "Well, well, well—aren't *you* full of surprises, *Tyvian*."

Voth's tent was a palace compared to the canvas doghouse Tyvian had slept in for the last two weeks. It was lit by a brass feylamp dangling from a chain. Thick Kalsaari rugs carpeted the ground; a circular bed with silk sheets occupied much of the available space. No sooner had they entered than Voth threw Tyvian on it and pounced on him.

Tyvian had been expecting to be murdered or, if not that, at least yelled at. Instead, he found Voth kissing him with the kind of reckless passion usually reserved by starving men for bread. She had her arms locked around his neck, her legs straddling his waist, and her lips so firmly sealed around his own that Tyvian couldn't have escaped if he wanted to.

As it happened, he rapidly discovered that he *didn't* want to. He let her midnight curls surround his face, soft and smelling of fresh leather, and put one hand on her back, pulling her close. She moaned appreciatively and kissed him hard. With that encouragement, Tyvian threw caution to the wind and put his other hand firmly on her arse.

Voth broke the kiss. "Take off your clothes."

"Isn't there . . . well . . . shouldn't we talk about—"

"No." Voth pulled open her vest and shirt with a savage tug. She was wearing nothing underneath. "Strip. Now."

Tyvian did as he was told. He did not regret it.

Outside the tent, in the camp around them, Tyvian heard a lot of commotion—they were breaking camp, getting ready to move. In Voth's arms, however, the world outside seemed distant, unimportant. It was like another life—some kind of nightmare he'd woken up from.

When they had finished their lovemaking—if that was the proper word for something that left that many scratches on his back—Voth rose from the bed and got dressed immediately. She wasn't a cuddler, apparently. He also noted that the singular piece of clothing she *was* still wearing—and had been during the entire amorous episode—was a slender stiletto sheath strapped to her calf. He couldn't help but smile at her.

She tossed his hose at him. "Get dressed. We've got to get packed up or they'll leave us behind."

Tyvian motioned to the bed. "Are we going to talk about what the hell just happened here?"

Voth smiled at him. "It was good, Reldamar—is that what you need? I've never enjoyed a dirtier man. There—get up." She began throwing things into a large chest.

Tyvian got up, pulled on his hose, and started

hunting around for his shirt. "Not that—though compliments are always appreciated. I mean . . . well . . . do I even need to ask?"

Voth rolled her good eye. "Fine, fine—I was paid to kill you. That didn't mean I didn't find you attractive. Now that you are dead and my former employer is dead, there is absolutely nothing stopping me from having my way with you, and I intend to do so whenever I feel like it. Is that satisfactory?"

Velia Hesswyn is dead? Tyvian pushed the surprise away in favor of more pressing concerns. "What's to stop you from turning me in to Sahand?"

"Absolutely nothing, and I'm so glad you understand our relationship at this point." Voth banged the lid of the trunk closed. "You're mine, Tyvian Reldamar. I have you by the balls in several different ways, and not all of them unpleasant for you."

There's always a catch. "All right, so besides my occasional *romantic* attentions, what exactly do you need me for?" Tyvian pulled on his shirt.

Voth was belting on a Galaspin sword—a kind of shorter, heavier rapier or narrower broadsword. "That is need-to-know information, and you do not yet need to know." She waved him outside. "Now get out and get ready to carry my things."

CHAPTER 5

BETWEEN THE LIVING
AND THE DEAD

The mudlark, filthy and toothless, pulled the canvas off the dead bodies like an artist unveiling his life's work. He bowed low and gestured to the stinking, rotten corpses with fingerless gloves. "For inspection, Your Highness . . ."

Artus wrinkled his nose at the smell, but didn't retch—he'd seen enough rotting flesh in the past week to get past that particular affliction. Michelle had prepared him an enchanted handkerchief that would protect him from the stench—he had it in his sleeve now—but he refused to use it. Everybody might think him a prince, but he'd be damned if he behaved like one. Bad enough he was receiving guests in the ruins of the Peregrine Palace with a pair of undead bodyguards—the White Guard—flanking him.

Artus crouched in front of the closest body. Like all the others, it had been dragged from the bottom of Lake Elren, where it had probably been rotting since the Battle of Eretheria City two weeks prior. It was hard to tell what this man had looked like in life; scavengers from the lake bed, probably freshwater crabs and various fish, had eaten away much of the man's face. The pallid flesh was caked in black mud from head to toe. The clothing had been of fine quality, but now it was practically impossible to tell the color or precise style. Artus looked anyway, seeking identifiable characteristics—none.

The mudlark twiddled his fingers in anticipation. "You can see, Your Highness, this one's the right size, the proper height. Hair seems like it was red, yes?"

Artus grabbed the corpse's right arm and looked closely at the worm-eaten fingers. They were bare. "Not this one."

The mudlark hid his disappointment well. "It was but a guess, Your Highness, of course, of course. But *this* one," he motioned toward the second body, "this one was found with quite a lot of valuable magecraft on his person."

Artus shifted his attention to the other body, which was, if anything, in worse condition than the first. This one appeared to have caught on fire before plunging into the lake, given the state of the skull. "Do you *have* any of that magecraft?"

The mudlark smiled his toothless smile and bowed. "I'm afraid I weren't the first to the body, Your Highness. Other . . . what's the word—other *entrepreneurs* got there first."

In other words, the body had already been rifled over and anything valuable pawned. There was a whole industry of secondhand luxury sales that had sprung up almost overnight in Eretheria. A fellow who walked down North Street in Westercity could buy the heirlooms of at least twenty different noble lines off a cart for short money and pawn them again in Saldor or Ihyn for five times what was paid. Artus had seen survivors of the palace massacre—the lucky ones—clutching their signet rings and going through the boxes of discarded golden earrings and jeweled brooches, hoping to find signs of their loved ones' fates.

He had wandered there himself in the days following the battle, walking up and down the rows of little pawnshops, trying to pick out something that had belonged to Tyvian in a window somewhere. It was impossible—he had no idea what Tyvian had been wearing that night, and so he had no idea what might be there. Tyvian's collection of jewelry was comprehensive, after all. The only thing Artus *knew* Tyvian was wearing that night was not the kind of thing that would show up in a pawn shop window.

So he had to resort to more *direct* means.

"Do you know what was taken?" he asked the mudlark, trying to look the man in the eyes.

The mudlark bowed rather than meet his gaze. "Some wards enchanted in some brooches, I think, and three rings, all silver. He might've also had a blade, or maybe just a scabbard—I didn't get a good look, more's the pity."

Artus picked up the right hand of the corpse. There, nestled on the ring finger, was a plain iron band. His breath caught. *No.*

The mudlark smiled. "Your Highness sees it, eh? I knew it! I knew it! I told my brother and he didn't believe me—looking for something on the right hand, I tells him, and maybe a ring. And there it is!"

Artus thrust at finger at man. "Watch it with the big smiles, friend. This was . . . might have been . . ." He couldn't quite finish the sentence for the tears that sought to choke him.

The color drained from the mudlark's already pale face. He bowed deeply. "Oh! My apologies, Your Highness! I was forgetting myself! Of course, of course!"

The stink of rot nearly made Artus gag again. Clenching his teeth, he grabbed the ring and worried it off the corpse's finger. A fair amount of dead flesh came with it. *Damned thing still doesn't wanna come off.*

The ring was lighter than Artus had expected. He brushed away the filth and death until he could see it clearly. He produced Michelle's enchanted handkerchief and rubbed it clean.

The mudlark was still bowing. "I will not trouble Your Highness in his time of grief. If all's in order, I'll just collect my reward and—"

"Wait!" Artus held up a hand. The mudlark froze as the two White Guards silently stepped forward, their ivory *volto* masks peaceful as always.

Artus held the ring up to a shaft of sunlight pouring in from a hole in the distant palace roof. There, etched on the exterior of the ring in his hands, was the inscription A.V.B. WITH LOVE. Artus threw it on the floor. "That isn't the right ring."

The mudlark did not rise from his bow, but he did shuffle backward. The White Guards matched him, pace for pace. "Please, Your Highness—a mistake, is all. A misunderstanding!"

Artus found himself shouting. "You tried to trick me! You wanted to dupe me into thinking this was the king's body!"

The White Guards loomed over the mudlark, their long spears gleaming, their white robes perfectly still. The toothless, filthy man trembled beneath their non-gaze. "No! I swear! Please, Your Highness! Mercy!"

Artus's heart pounded in his chest. He knew he had only to give the order and the undead constructs would kill this man instantly, without hesitation. There would be no repercussions, either—he was the Young Prince, beloved by the people, fresh back from his first victory in battle. He *wanted* to do it, too—this disgusting scavenger, looting dead bodies to sell their things to weeping widows and haggard old knights. The last two weeks had been nothing but death and blood and grief, and there were always men like this—grinning, soulless husks—making a few coppers off it. It made him more ill than the stench of any dozen corpses.

The mudlark had his face pressed to the floor, his whole body trembling. Artus took a deep breath. "Get out of here."

The mudlark cocked his head. "Wh . . . what? Truly?"

Artus turned away and waved him toward the door. "Just go. Don't come back."

The mudlark stood slowly, eyeing the stone-still White Guards still flanking him, and gave Artus a cautious salute. "You're a good man, Your Highness. A good man, blessed by Hann."

"Vanish already."

The mudlark left at a dead run. When he was gone, the two White Guards silently retook their places behind each of Artus's shoulders. He looked at them both, not for the first time wondering who or what they had been in life. Myreon had spread the word that they were Eretherian peasant levies killed in the spring campaigns of years past and buried in mass graves outside the city. Artus wasn't so sure. Though you couldn't see what they looked like, thanks to the masks and the white robes, Artus was pretty sure some of them were too short and too

small to have ever been men-at-arms. He had, however, resisted the urge to unmask any of them. In the
end, he just didn't want to know.

"Artus? Are you in here?" Artus turned to see Michelle entering through a servants' entrance at the far
end of the hall, her gown of bright green flowing like
a cloud behind her slender silhouette.

"Over here!" He waved. And then she was there,
draping her thin arms around his neck and planting
a soft kiss on his cheek. The feeling of her lips made
his spine tingle.

"You were missed at the celebration! Everyone's
asking for you." She looked down at the two bodies
lying on the floor. Her face fell. "Oh Artus, why do
you do this to yourself?"

Artus leaned his forehead against hers. "Do what?"

"The mudlarks. You dragging every person with
a pulse in here to ask them about red-haired men.
You're torturing yourself."

Artus placed a hand on his chest, feeling Tyvian's
letter in the pocket where it always rested. "He's alive,
Michelle. I know he's alive."

Michelle sighed and gave him another kiss, this
one on the temple. "I know, my love. But if he is, then
he wished to appear dead, and from what you've told
me of him, he probably did it for a good reason."

Artus frowned. "No. He was just . . . just running
away again." The words hurt to say, like a knot in his
chest he couldn't remove. They always were followed

by an unspoken phrase, one that echoed in Artus's mind as loud as thunder: *Except this time he didn't take me with him.*

Michelle seemed to sense his tension. Her delicate hands played with his hair. She pulled him close. "You've got to stop this, Artus. People are beginning to talk. They say you're mad with grief."

"Well, maybe I am." Artus pulled away from her. He found himself staring in a full-length mirror hanging on the wall. He was almost six feet tall now, with broad shoulders that supported a cape of royal blue linen clasped with gold at his throat. A shirt of enchanted mail, a mageglass broadsword, riding boots of fine Eddonish leather. Sandy blond hair that fell in ringlets just below his ears, a close-short goatee that was filling in nicely for once. Artus had trouble reconciling the man in the mirror with the street urchin who had once been in his place. The one who'd stuck with Tyvian Reldamar through a hundred adventures, only now to be alone.

Gods, he thought, *even Brana . . .*

Michelle came next to him, and wrapped her arms around his waist, and put her head on his shoulder. He felt some of the tension bleed out of him—Michelle always had that power, it seemed. She was so thin, Artus felt as though he could break her with one hand, and yet she'd become a kind of anchor for him. Without Hool and without Tyvian, Artus felt adrift for the first time in years. Even Brana would have offered a companion in disorientation. But instead of a gnoll-brother to wrestle with, now he had responsibilities, *expectations*—he was the Young Prince of Eretheria. Without Michelle there to hold him, he thought he might have gone mad.

Michelle gave him a squeeze. "You have duties to attend to, my prince."

Artus's stomach fell at the sound of those words—*my prince*. "Right. Sure—of course."

"You'll be a great leader, Artus. I know it. You just have to believe in yourself."

Artus didn't answer—he had no idea what was appropriate to say and didn't want to argue. It never felt right, arguing with Michelle, so he just let the young noblewoman hang on his arm as they walked out of the hall.

Outside, on the muddy ground of Peregrine Palace's once beautiful gardens, a great celebration was underway. Casks of beer, stacked in a pyramid, were tapped one after another to serve endless rows of peasant men in bleached white tabards—the soldiers of Myreon's new army. These men were the guests of honor, and a whirling carnival of musicians and dancers and games of chance had been erected to celebrate their victory. *His* victory.

Someone in the crowd recognized him. Beer tankards were raised and a thunderous cry of *HUZZAH, THE PRINCE* echoed off the scorched walls of the palace. They also saluted Michelle, who waved happily to the half-drunken, gleeful mob. Artus found himself searching their faces for his friends, all dead or gone. *Brana would have loved a party like this.*

"Go on," Michelle whispered into his ear. "Wave to your people."

They aren't my people. But Artus waved anyway. He smiled. He let himself be led across the gardens to the opposite wing of the palace. They might have arrived there without ever going outside, but Artus guessed Michelle wanted to be seen with him. She was staking her claim, as it were.

It was presumed by the world at large, if silently, that he and Michelle were to be married. They had not discussed this expectation themselves, though—there was something . . . delicate between them, Artus knew. Like dew on a spiderweb, he feared poking at it too much might ruin something forever. He could not tell how much of their relationship was based on . . . well . . . on him being a prince. Which he wasn't, no matter what Michelle said. But, at the same time, he was in no rush to dissuade her from thinking he was.

Artus had a hard time verbalizing such feelings. This little slip of a highborn girl, with her sharp features and her soft voice, seemed able to drive him mad with a gesture. He had not ever been in love—he hadn't ever thought he'd be that lucky—and now that he might be, he found himself full of doubts. Did she feel the same way? Was she using him? What if he wasn't *really* in love? What if he was stringing her along, only to ruin her later? The thought of making her cry was agony. The thought of his promise on that hellish night in the palace—that he would never let her go—haunted him. Who was he to take such an oath?

But, for all of that, when Michelle held him, when she laughed at his jokes, when her eyes shone with admiration of him—as they often did—he felt a warm glow deep inside, powering him forward. His heart rose into his throat at the thought of her smile or the feeling of her lips against his, and he knew that he would be a prince if he had to, if that meant he would have her. He suspected, though he didn't know, that this *was* love.

But he had no one to ask.

The prisoner—the leader of the now-defunct Army of Davram—was located in the least damaged wing of the palace. It was in this wing that most of the administrative "staff" for Myreon's burgeoning White Army was based, and so he and Michelle had to pass by rows of burly guild types—blacksmiths, carpenters, stonemasons, and the like—who had come to comprise most of Myreon's officer corps, in order to reach their rooms. They also cheered as Artus passed and doffed their hats to Michelle, smiling their gaptoothed and gold-capped smiles. Michelle elbowed him and told him to wave, so he waved.

These men were like a different species when compared to the kind of people who used to loiter about the Peregrine Palace. They were loud and poorly dressed, they laughed too long and smoked pipes indoors, but they had the unique distinction of being respected community leaders *without* being of noble birth. Loyalty to guild—a network of masters and journeymen and apprentices that stretched across the whole of Eretheria—was the foundation upon which Myreon was building her revolution.

But not a one of them was a professional soldier.

"Don't look so worried," Michelle whispered as they rounded a corner to reach their rooms.

Artus scratched his head. "*Shouldn't* we be worried?"

"Yes, of course," Michelle said as she opened the door. "But there's no reason to let *them* know that!"

Artus thought this over as he walked to a door flanked by two more of Myreon's eerie White Guard.

He took a deep breath. "Are you sure about this? You want it to be me?"

Michelle kissed his hand. "The Gray Lady insisted, and I agree with her. You are the only person here he will respect."

"He tried to kill me!"

"You're a prince, Artus—act like one." She stepped away from the door and waved him on. "You'll do fine!"

Artus straightened his cape and nodded to the guards. They stepped forward and threw open the doors. There, on the other side, in a bedroom watched over by two other White Guards, was Valen Hesswyn.

He was still muddy from the battle in the shallows

of the Fanning River the day before. He had a bandage over his head and his tunic was stained with blood. He had the expression of a man drained of all his vigor— like an invalid, resigned to death. He looked at Artus with dull eyes. "You. They would send you, wouldn't they?"

"I'm a prince. Nobody sends me anywhere," Artus lied. "How are you feeling?"

"Go to hell."

"Oh, so not that badly, then? Great—we were worried you'd caught quite a beating."

"We?"

"Myreon, Michelle, and I," Artus said. "You're lucky the White Guard were there to break it up— those peasant levies of yours were really planning to give you a stomping."

Valen sputtered. "What? White Guard?"

Artus jerked a thumb at the guards on either side of the door. "I'd say you should thank them, but I don't think they'd care much. C'mon—get up. Myreon wants to see you."

A flare of resistance lit behind Valen's eyes. Artus could see him weighing the risks of attacking him, of making a break for it. Artus tensed and moved his weight to the balls of his feet. He didn't want Valen to wind up killed by the White Guard, and if Valen made a move . . .

The moment passed. Valen seemed to come to his senses. "How's your stomach?"

The place where Valen had stabbed him—only barely healed—twinged slightly. Artus laughed despite himself. "Oh, is that you taunting me? Adorable. Come on, jackass—the Gray Lady hasn't got time for this."

He turned and walked away.

Valen had little choice but to follow. The White Guards fell into step on either side of him, matching his pace perfectly.

The palace was largely in ruins. Several grand galleries had collapsed, scorch marks peppered the walls, and rubble and bodies were still being cleared away by teams of commoners. In places, the sun shone through holes in the vaulted roofs. Though Artus had grown used to this over the past weeks, to Valen they were a revelation. The young knight stared, open-mouthed, at the wreckage.

"I take it I'm to be ransomed, then?" Valen asked as they descended a half-crumbled marble staircase.

"Nope," Artus said absently as a beefy stonemason bowed to him and insisted on kissing his hand. Artus's skin crawled as it happened, but he let it happen anyway. He was supposed to be royalty, so here he was, being royal. When the man rose, he gave Valen an ugly look before returning to his repair work.

Valen gaped at them both. "What do you mean, 'nope'? Look at the damage done here! You *must* need money! My grandmother will pay!"

Artus winced. He had been hoping he wasn't going to be the person who had to say this. "Valen, your grandmother is dead. She didn't survive the battle at Fanning Ford."

Valen froze. "What? You . . . you didn't give her quarter?"

"She refused to surrender to our field commander, so he killed her."

The White Guards pulled open the grand doors to the Congress of Peers. Valen suddenly looked sick. He sank to one knee. "Why . . . why would she . . . why . . ."

Artus looked down at him, remembering at once that Valen was only a few years older than he was and that he had just learned that his grandmother—the most important person in his life—had been killed. No matter how much of a witch old Velia Hesswyn had been, that still had to hurt. He spoke softly, so that no one nearby could hear. "The field commander was a carpenter, Valen. Your mother refused to surrender to a carpenter. She tried to blast him with a wand, and so he had to kill her." Artus offered Valen a hand. "Which is where you come in."

Valen glared at the hand for a moment, but again some kind of internal battle was waged and, in the end, the civilized part of Valen won. He took the hand and allowed himself to be pulled to his feet. There was now something different about Valen—Artus could see it. His eyes were clearer now, his jaw set. *It's because he knows he's the Count now. That's all it took for him to be ready to accept that responsibility. Saints, what I wouldn't give to feel that certain of anything.*

The destruction inside the Congress was almost absolute. The benches were wrecked and burned, the floor was scorched and stained with blood, and part of the great domed ceiling had collapsed. At the far end of the great room, the Falcon Throne rested in pieces, scattered all across the dais. *Sahand's message to us all*, Artus thought.

A space had been cleared beneath the center of the dome. There stood Myreon, her blond hair ragged from lack of care. She wore gray robes that made her look like a beggar, but she was surrounded by people listening to her every word. At her side stood a short, broad man with a bald head and thick beard—Gammond Barth, the carpenter who had put an end to Velia Hesswyn. He had a war-hammer— the implement of the countess's demise—slung over his back. When he saw Artus and Valen come in, he nudged Myreon and pointed.

"Ah, Valen Hesswyn," she said, her voice clear. "So glad to see you're feeling better."

"Necromancer!" Valen shouted. "The Defenders will make you pay for this!"

Myreon didn't react to the threat. "I'm very busy and I don't have time to quarrel, so I will make this brief: House Davram is finished. Your army, such as it was, has either joined me or is lying dead on the banks of the Fanning River. Your knights and noble vassals are crushed and are currently resting in the dungeons of the Young Prince here. Your attempt to put down my revolution and restore the old order in Eretheria is over. In short, you have no bargaining position. Do you accept this?"

Valen stared at her, speechless.

Artus watched him for any sign of that reckless anger from earlier. "It's true, Valen. Don't say something stupid."

Valen looked at Artus. Artus did his best impression of a princely posture. Whatever he did, it had an effect on Valen. He swallowed hard and looked back at Myreon. "What . . . what is to become of me? My people? My family?"

"If I were to listen to the advice of some advisors," Myreon said, "I should execute you and all your bloodline as traitors to their own people. But I am not so bloodthirsty as all that." Over her shoulder, Barth scowled at Valen. *He* had been calling for Valen's head on a plate since his capture.

Myreon pressed on, "Instead, I want you to renounce the Hesswyns' claim to the County of Davram *in perpetuity*. You are no longer rulers there—Eretheria is changing, and there is no more room for petty tyrants fighting private wars every spring. Instead, you and your vassals will swear yourself to Prince Artus's service—you will become officers in his White Army, the army of Eretheria, of which I am general."

Valen looked as though he had just been stabbed. An expression of complete shock bled into one of absolute horror. Artus tried to put himself in Valen's shoes, but couldn't. Yes, he was being asked to give up his birthright and the birthrights of all his House, but so what? For all the years Artus had spent among the rich, he could never get used to how entitled they felt. Especially toward stuff they never earned.

Myreon watched Valen closely. Perhaps she saw some of his horror, perhaps she understood, but whatever the reason, her tone softened and she placed a hand gently on his shoulder. "Sahand is still abroad in Eretheria, Valen. He controls Ayventry—all of us are in danger. There is a future for you and your family, just not the same one as before. Join me—we could use your help, your advice. I am painfully short on people with real military training. We need you."

She reached into her robes and produced a piece of parchment—a declaration renouncing his claims that Artus knew she'd spent the better part of the night before drafting, stacks of Eretherian law books next to her desk. "We're winning this war, Valen. You can get on the winning side now, or rest with the losing side in the dungeons. What will it be?"

Valen looked down at the parchment. Everyone was staring at him—Artus knew if he signed that paper, it would be a terrible blow struck to every count and viscount and earl and petty lordling in Eretheria and beyond. It would be a nobleman not renouncing just his claims, but the claims of all his relations. The end of a way of life that stretched back centuries.

The truth was, they *needed* him to sign—Valen had more military experience than any of them, even at his age. He also could command the loyalty of a few dozen knights currently in the dungeons. Armored cavalry like that would be crucial in the war ahead.

But they were his enemies—had been his enemies as recently as yesterday. Artus couldn't see how this could go any way besides Valen ripping up that parchment and spitting on it.

To his complete surprise, Valen spoke to Artus next. "Do you vouch for this?"

"Wh . . . what?"

"Do you, Prince of Eretheria, vouch for everything she says? A future for me and my family? My personal safety and that of my vassals?"

"You have my word, Valen. And I've always been straight with you, haven't I?"

Valen reached a decision. He looked Myreon in the eye. "Get me a quill."

She smiled. "Get me a quill, *ma'am.*"

CHAPTER 6

CRIMES OF WAR

The outskirts of Eretheria City had become one enormous armed camp. The levied soldiers of every peer, lord, and knight in Eretheria seemed to be pouring in from the countryside, their lords' pikes on their shoulders, and pitching tents or laying out blanket rolls on the nearest unoccupied patch of grass. Tabards of every color wandered the streets, all of them singing the praises of the Young Prince, the Gray Lady, or Good King Tyvian. Or all three at once.

Since the defeat of House Davram at Fanning Ford, Myreon's recruiting problems had been solved. Funding was also secure—Hool's vast wealth, left to Tyvian when she departed and then passed on to

Artus—was more than sufficient to arm and fund the revolution, at least in the short term. What remained was a far more difficult problem—logistics.

The first step involved organizing the volunteer soldiers into companies. As they were already familiar with the House system, that was where Myreon had started—men who arrived to volunteer in the army were directed to camp down with volunteers who once served the same House as they had. These five companies soon had to be divided into ten companies—there were *that* many of them. Myreon still had a couple of accountants counting heads, but she estimated she was leading an army of nearly three thousand men.

This first step led very quickly to a new problem—infighting. As it turned out, the Hadda boys weren't too fond of the Davrams, the Vora and the Camis groups fought like cats, and just about nobody liked the Ayventry bunch. That was to say nothing about the stragglers and wild hillmen and other ragtag bands that were scattered about, all of them lured to Artus's banner on the promise of an end to the campaign system and an overthrow of the five Houses that had pushed them out of society for so long.

Myreon's solution to this problem was similarly simple to the company organization: an enormous quantity of lye. All soldiers in her army were ordered to bleach their tabards white. Any house emblems were also to be thrown away. They were to be *one* army, she insisted. The White Army—the army that would save Eretheria. She didn't want men walking down the street and thinking they were "Hadda" men or "Vora" men—they were Eretherians.

The White Army had been laundering their clothing for two days now. The bleaching process was imperfect—even enchanted lye couldn't get *all* the color out of a green tabard, for instance. The visual effect was that the White Army was less actually white and more just plain drab. Observing her men from horseback as they floundered around a public fountain, the water frothing with soap, Myreon was starting to wonder at the wisdom of it all—just that morning her accountants had informed her of just how much she was spending on washing clothes and it was a breathtaking figure—but orders were orders, and if this whole army thing was going to work, she couldn't second-guess herself. She had to be strong, resolute. Artus might be the crowd-pleaser, but Myreon was the backbone. And the brains.

And pretty much everything else, to be honest.

"I've seen rebellions before, but never like this one." Myreon's breath caught at the voice—Argus Androlli. He was also on horseback, his staff in one hand. Somehow he'd managed to ride up next to her without any of her White Guard noticing. But of course, he was a mage. He could manage that.

Myreon resolved not to be flustered. "At least they'll be clean. In body, in spirit, in cause."

"Men are never clean. You were a Defender long enough to know *that*, Myreon."

Myreon smiled at him. "That's the past. I'm the future."

"We need to talk." Androlli looked at the volunteer soldiers surrounding them. A couple of men had picked up axes and spears and were giving the Mage Defender ugly looks. "Is there somewhere private we can go?"

Myreon held up a hand and the men with weapons paused. "You're not thinking of *arresting* me, are you, Argus?"

Androlli gave her a tight smile. "As you can see—I am alone. I'm not suicidal, Myreon. And I'm not about to burn a hundred peasants with wood-axes to ash to bring you in. I came to talk. I'm actually doing you a favor."

"Oh, yes—you're *famous* for your favors, Argus," Myreon said. "This way. We'll talk in my field tent."

Myreon motioned for some of the men to move aside, and move they did, though they didn't look happy about it. She and Argus rode side by side past rows of burned out houses and looted shops until they were out of the city entirely. Myreon's tent—a tall, gleaming white pavilion—was easy to spot among a sea of patched and yellowing canvas that comprised the ten companies of the White Army. As they rode there, volunteer soldiers hailed her as she passed, but no one challenged them. Other than a few chickens and careless children running around, they proceeded unhindered.

"You're mad, you know," Androlli said when they had at last dismounted. "This army—it's a joke, Myreon. You're going to get chewed apart."

"Argus, you know even less about armies than I do." Myreon snapped her fingers and the White Guards on either side of her tent's entrance pulled back the flaps. "Come in, before somebody out there tries to lynch you."

Androlli followed her inside, but not before giving the White Guard a long, disgusted look. The tent's interior was comfortable, if rustic, with a thick Rhondian carpet covering the muddy ground and a few portable folding chairs of hardwood and canvas. A large round table—also collapsible—occupied the center of the room. It was piled high with various correspondence and ledgers full of figures. Myreon waved her hand over them and laid a brief gibberish curse on it all—she didn't need Androlli reading her letters or reporting her supply figures back to Saldor.

This done, she sat down and summoned a White Guard to bring her a glass of water. "Well, what was it you wanted to discuss?"

Androlli nodded toward the white-clad, masked creature standing serenely behind her. "Do you really need to ask?"

Myreon was prepared for this, of course. That

didn't mean it was going to be pleasant. "I didn't create it, Argus. I'm merely controlling it."

"Hardly a nuance a Saldorian judge will appreciate," Androlli said, still standing.

"As I implied back at the fountain—you can't exactly arrest me, Argus. I'm in the middle of an armed camp—an armed camp full of men who think *the Defenders* killed their king and threw him off the top of a cathedral. You so much as poke one firepike out of Eretheria Tower, and the White Army will burn it to the ground."

"I already said I wasn't here to arrest you, Myreon. Necromancy is a crime, but it turns out it's not a severe enough crime to necessitate an international incident. Besides, it is the opinion of Lord Defender Trevard that it is better *you* lead the White Army than anyone else at the moment. Sahand is still a threat and still must be defeated. Until such time, it is the official decision of the Arcanostrum to remain neutral toward your little revolution."

"Then why are you here? Why are you wasting my time?"

"I came to warn you, Myreon," Androlli said. "There are limits to Saldor's patience."

"Meaning?"

"Meaning you cannot employ battlefield-scale sorcery and still expect Saldor to remain neutral. You can't deploy *those*," he pointed to the White Guard, "in a battlefield role and expect us not to intervene.

Battlefield necromancy has been forbidden for over a thousand years, Myreon. There's a *reason* for that."

Myreon chuckled. "The reason is that Saldor doesn't like anybody *else* using sorcery to win wars. That's it."

Androlli shook his head. "You sound like a radical, Myreon."

Myreon stood up. "I'm a mage leading an army of peasants in a revolution—you're damned *right* I'm a radical! And I won't have my victory dictated to by the likes of *you!*"

Androlli's face was red. "No more Fanning Fords, understand? No more undead legions engaging in battlefield roles! The Lord Defender nearly broke a rib, he yelled so much—he wanted you petrified for a full century over that. Some of the masters calmed him down a bit and many of the archmagi took your side, but the threat still stands. If you deploy sorcery like that again, Trevard will muster the Grand Army of Saldor and burn your foolish revolution to ash. Do I make myself clear?"

Myreon felt her heart thumping in her chest. "Yes, Argus. Perfectly clear."

Androlli took a deep breath. "Good."

"Get out."

Androlli snorted. "What, no escort out of the camp?"

Myreon tilted her head slightly and a pair of White Guards came to flank him. "There—happy now?"

Androlli's nostrils flared at the two animated corpses. "You can dress them up in white all you like, Myreon. You're still keeping company with the stolen corpses of the dead."

Myreon glared at him—a gesture that was sufficient to have the two White Guards practically frog-march Androlli out of her presence. She waited until she heard him mount up and ride off, the White Guards still escorting him. Then she let out a long, slow breath.

He was right. Fanning Ford had been a step too far, perhaps. It was one she had been forced to take—she never would have won the battle without them—but she had no excuse anymore. The living soldiers of her army now vastly outnumbered the dead ones, and it was for the best that way. Even with their white garb and masks, the constructs made the volunteers uneasy. The story about them being the bodies of former conscripted soldiers come back to help Eretheria win its freedom had helped a lot, but the sight of the White Guard in battle was too unnerving for the living to be fully comfortable. If she wasn't careful, they would sap morale, and if Fanning Ford had taught her anything, it was that morale was key. An army that was frightened was an inefficient army, and an army that ran away was no army at all.

She didn't have much time to think about it, though, before her role as general took over the rest of her day. She had Valen Hesswyn and his cavalry to attend to, she had company commanders to interview and appoint, she had supplies to requisition from . . . well, from somewhere, and a thousand other duties that kept her on her feet until the sun was well below the horizon.

Over dinner, the guild accountants delivered their report. "At this rate of expense, assuming the army grows no larger, you will run through the Royal Treasury in two months."

Myreon nearly choked on her wine. "That *can't* be true. How can that be true?"

The accountant was a young man in a starched ruff that extended past his shoulders, making it look as though his pointy head was being served on a white platter. His hands fiddled at his sides—he was evidently uncomfortable talking to a sorceress. "Please, Magus—the calculations are good. Food is . . . very scarce. And so it's become *unnaturally* expensive. In fact, *everything* is becoming more expensive for you . . . errr . . . *us*. Everyone knows you are—and pardon me for saying so—*desperate* for supplies, and quick. There's no competition."

Myreon tightened her fist. "I'm being cheated, you mean."

The accountant looked at his apprentices—two girls who seemed to have frozen in a permanent state of midcurtsey. They didn't meet his eye. He tugged at his collar. "The numbers are good, Magus. I'd swear by them."

"Then what do you recommend we do?"

The accountant stiffened. "I am not a military advisor, Magus. I couldn't possibly—"

"It wasn't a military question. It's a financial planning question." Myreon gave him a hard look. "Answer it."

"Well . . . if I were you, General Alafarr, I'd see about winning this war very quickly."

Myreon dismissed them with a growl. But the words stuck.

After dinner, she went down into the sewers. One last time.

The necromancer, whoever he had been, was long gone from his bloodstained haunts. Myreon assumed he had been killed in the battle for the palace. In any event, he had never reappeared. His grisly workshop and subterranean ritual space was hers now. Hers if it were anybody's.

The ritual had been running smoothly since it had been invoked. The great veta inscribed by the old blind necromancer still glowed with power, lighting the subterranean cavern as bright as midday—there was enough Lumenal energy to keep it running for months, perhaps years. Its power sustained the life force of all five hundred of the White Guard, and additions and small edits made by Myreon since then had expanded it so that, if need be, she could raise five hundred more. If she wanted, she could build even more on her already considerable power.

Yet Androlli was right; the White Guard were an abomination. They could and probably would serve to prevent her from achieving her goals. Necromancy, by its very nature, was wrong. This ritual had served its purpose. It was time for it to end.

It would be a relatively simple matter to disrupt the ritual. The bigger the ritual, the more delicate it was—a concentrated arc of Etheric energy and the whole thing would implode, just like Sahand's master Fey ritual in Daer Trondor had been undone by a snowball. Myreon was confident she could protect herself from the ensuing blast of Lumenal energy—she had dark thoughts aplenty to power an Etheric shield around herself.

Such dark thoughts, however, were what gave her pause. The accountants were *also* right—she needed to win this war. The challenges ahead of her were harrowing, indeed. Sahand's army had withdrawn from the city, yes, but it was still abroad in the countryside. Tales trickled into the camp daily—Delloran soldiers slaughtering villages, putting inns to the torch, stealing crops and livestock. Those people needed protection. It was why the White Army had come into existence in the first place.

To protect the people, Myreon needed to defeat Sahand. Sahand was a soldier with a lifetime of military experience. He had been conquering nations since before Myreon was born. His soldiers were well trained, blooded, and experienced. By all reasonable measures, Myreon and her White Army were doomed to failure.

Why, then, should she pass up any advantage? Why disrupt this ritual? So that she wouldn't anger Trevard? She was no Mage Defender anymore—who cared what that stiff old man thought?

If Sahand were in her place, would *he* dispel the ritual? Would *he* give up his one edge against his opponent?

Of course not.

Androlli had warned her not to use the White Guard in a battlefield role. Fine—there were probably numerous other uses for them. Uses she couldn't rely on others to fulfill.

Myreon subtly adjusted her stance before the ritual. She wasn't going to dispel it at all—no. Instead, she set about enchanting a linking stone, which would let her bring the power of the ritual with her, wherever she went.

When the White Army marched—and soon it certainly would have to—the ritual was coming along. And so, too, would come the White Guard.

CHAPTER 7

IN THE SHADOW OF SAHAND

The Citadel of Dellor was among the most ancient fortresses in the known world. Built to defend against foes unknown in ages long forgotten by some warlock king whose name was now lost to history, it was a vast, sprawling military structure—a five-pointed star of thick stone walls and flat defensive turrets squatting at the edge of the Great Whiteflood River.

There was no earthly reason to have a fortress this big in a land as remote as Dellor—it could have easily housed an army of well over ten thousand men, fully provisioned and not even forced to share cots in the seemingly endless barracks. However, there was also no feasible way to knock it down and many reasons it could be useful to a man like Banric Sahand.

Chief among these reasons was how impressive it was—the endless corridors filled with artfully concealed murder-holes and arrow slits, the cleverly disguised booby traps, and the many secret doors and passages belied a level of engineering ingenuity lost to the modern age. With every tour of the vast castle, Sahand was able to convey a very important message to just about anyone:

I am unassailable and thus invincible—remember this.

At that moment, the person being given this impression was a fleshy-cheeked young man—no, a *boy*—who, as it happened, was the sitting Count of Ayventry. He was a distant cousin to the late Count Andluss and the rest of Andluss's also-dead family. His trembling parents had presented him to Sahand two days before, and Sahand had taken an immediate liking to the puffy young dunce. He was stupid enough to have no idea he was being used and greedy enough to go along with whatever Sahand said, so long as it worked to his advantage. His name was Fawnse.

Sahand put an arm around the young count and guided him into the last stop on their tour—an underground, artificial harbor concealed within the fifth point of the Citadel's star. This point jutted into the river and, behind a huge stone gate, was an artificial waterfront big enough to accommodate ten huge barges, currently under construction.

Fawnse's eyes nearly popped out of his skull in surprise. "Wow! You have *ships*, too?"

Sahand smiled. "Those are just transport barges, Your Grace—without any good roads, the best way to explore the lands of Dellor is by river. The same goes for my troops. With these barges, I'll be able to keep my people safe from bandits and trolls and such."

Fawnse tipped his head upward, trying to encompass the whole of the vast vaulted ceiling in one glance and nearly falling over from the effort. "It's amazing!"

"So you see that I am a good friend to have, yes? Aren't you glad you came to visit?"

Fawnse nodded. "Oh, very much so! And to think my mother was so worried—she thought you were going to kill me!"

Sahand laughed. "I only kill my enemies, Fawnse— and you are no enemy of mine, are you?"

"No sir!" The boy answered, his eyes falling back to the barges and the swarm of workers hammering nails and sawing logs to aid in their construction. The vast chamber echoed with the sound of wood being bent to human use.

Sahand still had his arm around Fawnse. He gave the boy a hearty squeeze. "Fawnse, how are you liking being count?"

Fawnse smiled. "Fine, my lord. Just fine. My bed is huge!"

"So you wouldn't mind remaining count, then? For, say, a long time?"

"No, my lord!" Fawnse grinned. "It's been the greatest honor of my life!"

"And what are your thoughts on the so-called White Army—the upstart rebels who mean to usurp you?"

Fawnse snickered. "I have eight thousand levies and five hundred heavy cavalry that will *show* them what I think of them!"

Sahand nodded—the boy was overestimating his cavalry by at least a hundred fifty, but by no more than that. Add that to his own companies of light cavalry—two hundred strong—and the twelve companies of Delloran regulars and mercenaries he had in Eretheria, and that gave them an army of about four thousand men, give or take, plus those eight thousand worthless levies. Fawnse no doubt assumed he would be making his stand outside Ayventry, just as many other counts had over the years—wait until the enemy shows up, muster your armies on the broad fields surrounding the city, and have a very civilized pitched battle on some sunny summer afternoon.

This, of course, struck Sahand as a very stupid thing to do.

"Fawnse, I'm glad to hear you are a fighting man at heart. That is why I've made a strategic decision." He guided the boy out of the harbor and into a great hall where a vast round table had been set up and, upon it, an enormous map of Eretheria. Little wooden soldiers (for footmen) and horses (for cavalry) were scattered about the map—Sahand's troops were black, spread out like a net across the Eastern Basin and the Great South Plains, while Ayventry's were red, concentrated in the county at the very northern tip of the mountains and the basin. The forces of that resilient old hag, Ousienne of Hadda, were a smattering of yellow along Lake Country, which extended from the northern tip of the Tarralles to form the northern border of the Great South Plains. There, represented by a small cluster of white, still down by the coast near Eretheria City, was the White Army—the rebels who had made Eretheria an unsackable prize and forced Sahand's retreat north.

"My men are retreating north, as were my orders." Sahand gestured to his forces. "As they go, they are under orders to burn, loot, and pillage."

Fawnse frowned. "That isn't allowed, I thought."

"Ah, Fawnse—it is time I gave you an important lesson in statecraft: *everything* is allowed if no one can stop you." Sahand didn't wait to see if the boy understood or not. He pointed to the map, and specifically the two roads that ran north from Eretheria—the Freegate Road and the Congress Road. "When the Young Prince and his Gray Lady advance from Eretheria, they shall either travel up the Congress Road, which means they are headed for Lake Country, or the Freegate Road, which will take them directly to us. Either way they go, they will find no fodder on the land and only miserable, starving peasants in their way. This will force the Young Prince to slow down, to forage more widely, and to deal with the suffering of his own people."

Fawnse nodded slowly, squinting at the table. "What do my men do?"

Sahand pointed at the picture of a tower perched at the northern spur of the Tarralle Mountains, astride the Freegate Road. "Unless the White Army secures an alliance from Lake Country—which they will not—the only way to pass the Tarralles is under the ramparts of the castle of Tor Erdun."

Fawnse brightened. "The Earl of Tor Erdun is my uncle!"

Sahand nodded while the boy beamed at him. "So now you see what I want you to do with your men: take them—all of them—to Tor Erdun. Make certain your uncle is well supplied and stocked with fresh troops and take command of the garrison yourself. In a matter of weeks, a starving army of rebellious peasants and poor hedge knights will have to lay siege to it, and then my forces, which will have retreated into the mountains," Sahand moved a few black pieces into the Tarralles with a long stick, "will cut them off from behind. The rebellion will be crushed and you, Your Grace, will be the savior of Eretheria."

Fawnse clapped his hands and cheered. "A wonderful plan! I'll go and tell my captains right away!"

Sahand grinned. "Yes, do. My anygate remains open, linked to your castle. Come back and visit anytime, Fawnse!"

Fawnse bowed and left at a run. When he had gone, Sahand nodded to one of his lieutenants, who took care to bar the doors behind him and clear the hall of anyone but Sahand's inner circle. "Inform my companies to fall back toward Ayventry. I want the city fully garrisoned by my own armies once Count Fawnse's troops have gone."

His men leapt into action, pulling out sending stones and seeking to make contact with Sahand's far-flung forces. As they worked, Sahand folded his arms behind his back and strolled onto the balcony that overlooked his secret harbor. There, the large, square barges were halfway complete. They would be able to ferry over a thousand men across the Whiteflood in a single trip—an invasion force.

One of his captains was beside him at the rail. "Sire, won't the boy tell people about these barges? Won't he reveal your plans?"

Sahand arched an eyebrow at the man—he was young, newly promoted. Perhaps a little overbold in speaking with his prince. Still, Sahand was in a jovial mood. "I do not show my plans to fools, Captain."

The captain puzzled this over for a moment, chewing his moustache. "A clever ruse, sire."

Sahand seriously doubted the fellow had any idea what he was talking about. He laughed. "That includes you, too, Captain." Sahand slapped him on the back. "Now, bring me Arkald the Strange. We need to discuss my prisoner."

Arkald the Strange, personal necromancer to Prince Banric Sahand, could not sleep. No matter how many fur blankets he piled upon his bed, no matter how well he stoked the iron stove in his small chamber, no matter what potions he concocted to ease his way into slumber, he lay shivering and awake each and every night, his eyes wide open. Staring upward. Knowing that, on the floor just above him, a nightmare walked. And waited. And plotted.

No amount of pleading was able to dissuade the Mad Prince from using the top floor of Arkald's tower for a prison. Never mind that it was Arkald's preferred ritual space. Never mind that it was incoherently dangerous to keep the prisoner alive. He had thrown himself on his face before Sahand, tugging at the hem of his fur cape. "Please, Your Highness! Kill her! Just kill her, I beg of you! For all of our sakes!"

Sahand had only grinned at him. Always fearsome, Sahand's smiles held something extra special these days—one cheek had been torn away in battle, and now one could see his teeth all the way back to his molars on one side. When he smiled, he seemed part crocodile. "No, Arkald. One does not destroy so useful a vessel of knowledge as this. Certainly not out of fear. She is to be your captive and you her jailor."

"No!" Arkald had gasped.

Still that horrible, half-human smile. "Yes, Arkald. I trust your terror of her is sufficient to make you a very *efficient* and *thorough* guardian of our permanent guest. And of course, I don't need to tell you what happens if she dies in your care, do I?"

What could Arkald say? He touched his forehead to the stone floor of Sahand's throne room and swore it would be done.

The ritual space at the top of Arkald's tower had been Astrally warded. Arkald had spent days etching the runes on the outside of the tower, using a rickety wooden scaffold that hung from the tower's roof and suspended him hundreds of feet in the air. When they were complete, the runes rebuffed all the energies except the Astral—the fifth energy, the medium through which the other four moved. Any sorcery based in the four—Ether, Lumen, Fey, or Dweomer—would be impossible.

As for the Astral, Sahand had assured Arkald that the prisoner was sufficiently mutilated to make any significant spellcraft impossible. Arkald, of course, did not believe this for a moment, and so every day he made a point of siphoning as much of the Astral as he could into a ritual of his own—a spell to unwrite and then rewrite books by locally reversing and then advancing the flow of time. Such a spell was enormously taxing—so much so that Arkald's own work and study had to fall by the wayside—but it was essential. His survival depended on it. If that woman were able to cast even a single spell . . .

And so, Arkald the Strange did not sleep. His appetite left him. He feared what wine or beer might do to his wits, and so he refused these, as well. Within a week, he appeared every bit as skeletal as any of his creations ever had.

Once a day, Arkald mustered all of his modest courage and made the ascent up the claustrophobic spiral staircase to what he had come to call "the cell," carrying a light wooden tray with bread, cheese, and a pitcher of water. He took care to carry no weapon and left all his charms and rods and wards behind. They would do him no good in any case.

The cell itself was fourteen feet across. There was nothing in the room save a stool, a clay chamber pot, and a pile of dirty straw. The trap door to the roof had been nailed shut, and the only window had been fixed with inch-thick iron bars. Through this poured the morning sunshine, bathing the sparse chamber in a cheery orange glow.

There, huddled within a threadbare robe and sitting upon the stool in the full light of day, was Lyrelle Reldamar—the most terrifying woman in the world.

She had been roughly used in her journey to Dellor. Her thumbs were missing and one eye was still swollen shut. Her face was an array of yellowing bruises, and her hair—once the color of spun gold—was torn and matted and dirty. Each night up here, with no fire to warm her, must have been hellishly cold; Arkald could see it in how her shoulders shivered at the slightest breeze.

And yet, each morning she smiled at him. "Good morning, Arkald. How are you today?"

Arkald placed the wooden tray on the floor, staying well out of arm's reach. He circled her, his back to the wall.

Lyrelle watched him, her keen eyes tracking him like a cat tracks a mouse. "I must apologize again for imposing upon you. I know how important your work must be to you."

Arkald frowned and picked up the chamber pot, carrying it to the window. He said nothing, even though he wanted to yell at her. No, more than that—he wanted to rush downstairs, get a knife, and stab this woman through the heart. Then she would be dead and gone and out of his life forever. Gods, the League might even forgive him for the death of Renia Elons and then he could escape this tower and Sahand and go far, far away. Somewhere quiet. Somewhere no one would bother him again.

"Your silence betrays you, Arkald," Lyrelle said as he dumped the contents of the pot out the window. Thanks to the bars it was, as ever, a messy job. A splash of cold urine dripped over the sill and trickled to the floor.

Arkald stepped back and inspected his robe and shoes, making sure nothing had spattered on him. "Be quiet!" he snapped, but his voice didn't come out quite as the bark he'd wanted it to. It was more of a bleat, a pathetic honking sound.

"Why, Arkald, if I cannot speak with you, with whom can I?"

Arkald wrung his hands. "No one. You can remain silent. Say nothing!"

Lyrelle frowned. "That seems needlessly unpleasant for both of us." When Arkald stiffened, she went on, "Clearly this is an ordeal for you as well as me. Surely a bit of civilized conversation would not be out of order."

Arkald began to circle back toward the door. "Hurry up and eat or I will leave and you will go hungry."

Lyrelle drew her head up. Her glamours were gone and she had not sipped *cherille* in some time, but even still—even with the wrinkles beginning to grow at the corners of her eyes and the white beginning to streak through her hair—there was something regal about her. She made Arkald feel as a donkey in the presence of a parade horse. "If you take my food, I would starve."

"What is that to me?"

"I am an old woman, Arkald—two decades your senior, I should think—and my health in this frigid prison is not the best. Were I to take ill as a result of malnourishment, I could die."

Arkald frowned. "I have healing poultices. Illbane powder."

"None of which will function in this room." Lyrelle raised an eyebrow. "Do you mean to suggest you would remove me from this tower, even for an instant? Even to save my life?"

Arkald said nothing, but his scowl probably said enough.

"I thought not. So, as you are unwilling to starve me and as *I* am unwilling to eat without some manner of conversation, I suggest you remain and chat a while as I enjoy this feast you have brought me."

"It's a trick. You're trying to trick me."

Lyrelle smiled. "Oh, Arkald—of *course* it's a trick. But I've played it, see? I have forced you to talk with me while I eat. Not so very sinister, is it?"

Arkald looked at the tray, the pitcher. "I could just leave and come back later!"

"And leave me with a clay pitcher with which to brain you as you come through the door? Now, now, Arkald—that seems risky, don't you think?"

Dammit, the woman had a point. He shuffled his weight from foot to foot. "What would we talk about?"

"Assuming the doings of your master are not up for discussion, nor are suggestions for how to escape this efficient little trap you've set, I'm afraid I don't have much to discuss. The rumor mill up here is rather . . . sparse." She scooped up the bread with one four-fingered hand. "Why don't you tell me about yourself?"

"No."

Lyrelle took an awkward bite. "No? Very well, why don't you tell me what it's like to work for Banric Sahand."

Arkald shook his head. "That's a bad idea."

Lyrelle chuckled. "Oh, Arkald—worried I might tattle on you to your prince? Please. That old brute would never believe a word I said. Come now, Unburden yourself. You and I could spend the day telling each other all the various things we hate about Banric Sahand, and nobody—least of all Sahand himself—would ever be the wiser. When else will you have an opportunity like that?"

Arkald opened his mouth and then . . . stopped. This was it—this was how it started. This was how she was going to get inside his head. "You are going to stay here until you die. If you want to spend the day without water, that's up to you. I won't be made into your tool."

He marched over, quite close to her, and picked up the pitcher and the tray, throwing the cheese onto the ground.

Lyrelle fell to her knees, clutching at his robes with her mutilated hands. The regal woman from moments before was gone—a wild, miserable desperation filled her face. "Oh, please, no! No, Arkald! Leave me the water, please! I'm sorry!"

Arkald pulled himself free as though he were being bitten and fled the room, slamming and barring the door behind him. From inside, he heard his prisoner begin to sob.

He knew that kind of cry. He had cried that way himself many times since being brought here. They were tears of despair. They hurt him to hear, but he tarried by the door anyway to listen. Perhaps it was an act—a trick.

Lyrelle Reldamar wept for almost an hour. She screamed. She cursed Sahand and her son, Xahlven. She beat weakly on the door. Then, eventually, Arkald heard her lie in the straw and slowly cry herself to sleep.

Then, on wobbly legs, Arkald descended to his own room—his own cell—and sat before the book he had forced time to unwrite and rewrite endlessly. His hands trembling, he began the ritual again.

"Necromancer!" A voice bellowed from the stairs below—a guard. "The prince wishes to see you!"

A bolt of fear struck through Arkald's throat. It took him a moment to find his voice again. "Yes. I'm . . . I'm coming."

The guard waited for him. Like most of Sahand's men, he was a meaty block of a human being in a mail shirt. Standing next to him, Arkald felt like a little boy about to be spanked by his father. The guard said almost nothing—only grunted and poked him in the back with the butt of his spear when he wanted Arkald to walk faster.

The Citadel of Dellor was too huge to heat effectively, and so it was a long, cold journey down the stairs of Arkald's tower and through the long galleries and cavernous halls to Sahand's private chambers. The doors were tall and studded with iron, their latches fashioned in the shape of a wyvern's claws. There were two guards posted on either side of them, as usual, as mail-clad and humorless as the guard who'd fetched him. Arkald's escort prodded the necromancer forward. "The necromancer, as ordered."

The two soldiers opened the doors and motioned for Arkald to go in. Holding his breath, Arkald forced himself to pass over the threshold into Sahand's inner sanctum. The doors boomed closed behind him.

He was alone.

Or, more accurately, he was alone with Banric Sahand.

Sahand's private parlor was decorated with the faded banners of the many mercenary companies and petty lords he had crushed on the fields of battle over the years. They hung from the high rafters and along the walls, all of them varying degrees of tattered and bloodstained, many charred, and some so faded that their devices were barely recognizable. At the other end of the room was a high-backed chair of dark wood, carved into the image of a wyvern rising in flight—an echo of the great chair of steel that stood in the Mad Prince's formal throne room. This one looked rather more comfortable, which had the perverse effect of making it somehow more sinister—Sahand preferred to *relax* in a chair that looked like a monster and surrounded by the tattered remnants of his enemies.

A hunk of bloody meat and a goblet of what was probably oggra rested on a table before Sahand's chair. Sahand was using a wicked-looking dagger to slice off chunks of the red meat and spear them to be popped into his mouth. There was no chair for Arkald. Indeed, there was no other furniture at all apart from a huge manticore-skin rug that stretched from the doors to the foot of Sahand's table.

Arkald stood perfectly still, as though trying not to wake the manticore rug.

It was a full minute before Sahand looked at him. When he did, he pointed the knife at him and waved it to indicate the necromancer should come closer. Arkald went halfway across the rug and stopped. "You called for me, sire?"

Sahand chewed his meat with gusto, his ruined cheek giving Arkald a perfect view of the process. Red juice squirted across the table. "You don't bow, Arkald. Why is that?"

Arkald instantly fell to his knees and abased himself. "I'm sorry, sire. I . . . I forgot . . . please . . ."

Sahand laughed, the bloody remnants of his meal leaking from the holes in his face and staining his close-cropped beard. "Stand up, stand up—if I cared so much about protocol from you, I'd have killed you long ago. It's enough to see you shiver when you're in my presence."

His heart pounding, Arkald staggered back to his feet. "As you say, sire."

Sahand dabbed at his face with a bloodstained handkerchief and took a careful sip of oggra. "Tell me about Lyrelle."

Arkald's breath caught. He couldn't *know* what she said to him, could he? This . . . this was just chance, yes? He licked his lips. "She . . . she suffers greatly, sire."

Sahand sawed off another chunk of meat. "Good—I'm glad of it. And her health?"

"She . . . she appears sickly, sire. She may catch ill, given the cold."

Sahand paused. "Is that a note of concern I hear, Arkald?"

"No! No sire!"

Sahand frowned at him. "So you're saying you don't care if she dies?"

A bolt of terror shot through him again. A trap—it was a trap! "I . . . I mean, yes, of course I *care* but . . . but . . . but only because *you* commanded me to keep her alive and . . . and . . . so therefore I care, but not *really.*"

Sahand laughed at him. "You are to provide her no comforts, understood? Not so much as a new blanket. If I learn you have been coddling her, I'll take *your* thumbs as well."

Arkald remembered to bow this time. "Yes, sire."

Sahand returned to eating for a moment, leaving Arkald standing there. Arkald's stomach rumbled. It occurred to him that he hadn't eaten all day. Even before Lyrelle Reldamar had played havoc with his appetite, food was difficult to come by for Arkald—Sahand did not pay him. He was not in Sahand's employ in any economic sense—he was Sahand's permanent guest. He had to barter for food from the kitchens, and few people there had much interest in feeding a necromancer. He'd lived on crusts of bread, pork gristle, and thin soup for years now. Sometimes he managed a little beer or wine, but only if he stole it.

It occurred to Arkald that Sahand was eating in front of him on purpose. Every hunk of meat the Mad Prince swallowed was just another reminder of Arkald's absolute inferiority—of his servile wretchedness. He could do nothing but watch, his empty stomach groaning.

"What does she say?" Sahand asked at last.

"Sire?"

Sahand was looking at Arkald intently. "About me, about anything—what does she say?"

Arkald shivered—a draft from somewhere, or so he told himself. Here was the moment he could tell Sahand about Lyrelle's attempt to turn him. Perhaps . . . perhaps Arkald's show of loyalty would be rewarded somehow. Sahand *did* reward him from time to time. Perhaps he could ask for some payment or new clothing or even an assistant or something.

"Well, Arkald?"

Arkald realized that he had not said anything yet. He opened his mouth. "She . . ." he trailed off.

"Yes?"

"She weeps, sire. She curses your name and her sons." Arkald took a deep breath. "She despairs."

Sahand glared at him for a moment. Arkald tensed, awaiting the violent backlash for the lie. What bones would the Mad Prince break this time?

But Sahand only smiled. "Good. Very good." The Mad Prince waved him away. "You may go, Arkald. Give me regular reports."

Arkald bowed and took his leave, uncertain of what he said in response—probably "yes sire." He was out in the halls and alone a minute later. He ducked into a sawtooth alcove—some ancient defensive measure—and tried to slow his heart from racing. He'd lied. He'd lied to Banric Sahand.

And he'd gotten away with it!

Arkald wept.

But this time with relief.

CHAPTER 8

DARK TIMES

Myreon stood amid the ruins of the little village, flanked by her White Guard. At her feet was the body of a little boy, his head smashed. She could scarcely look at him. There was nowhere better to look.

Barth's scouts had spotted the smoke at dawn as the White Army moved north. True to her plan, she had insisted the army keep moving—the scouting party would catch up later. Myreon had also insisted on inspecting the ruins in person. "If I'm fighting a war," she had said to the old carpenter, "I should at least know what it costs." As she looked at the body of the little boy, facedown in the mud, she now had her answer.

But there was no going back now. There was no going back the moment she signed the necromancer's contract in the sewers. This path—this war—was going to be her legacy, her life's work. The cost in blood had to be worth it. She would *make it* worth it.

Barth, wearing a dented breastplate intended for a smaller man and a feathered cap intended for a larger one, came out of one of the more intact houses and went to Myreon's side. His face was still, but his eyes were full of barely constrained rage. "There were some survivors. Found 'em in a root cellar—women and children." He shook his head and took a few deep breaths. He wiped at his eyes.

"Who did it?" Myreon was surprised at how calm her voice was. Her years of sorcerous training, she supposed—one's emotions needed to be under control, or else the Fey leaked into all of one's incantations.

Barth spat. "The Ghouls. On Sahand's personal orders, I shouldn't wonder."

"How many dead?"

"About a hundred or so. Half of them unarmed." Barth's voice cracked. "Just farmers! Gods, Magus! How much more of this have we got to stand, eh? This is the fifth village hit, and that's just what we've heard of! Hann's mercy . . ." He shook his head and snuffled. "These aren't men we're fighting. Not men."

Myreon laid a hand on his shoulder. She tried to think of something inspiring to say, but there was nothing. She just left her hand there, and the old carpenter let it stay as his hulking shoulders shook with silent tears for a moment. Finally, he wiped beneath his eyes and took a long breath. "When . . . when this all started, Magus. When I fought with you in Eretheria, you promised a better world. This isn't better."

Myreon took her hand away. "I know, Barth. I'm sorry."

A peasant soldier, tall and lanky, ran up. After a wary eye at the silent White Guard, he pressed a knuckle to his temple in salute. "General, we've collected the dead . . . except . . ." His eyes strayed to the dead child.

Myreon stepped back. "Yes, of course. When they are together, leave them. The White Guard will bury the bodies."

The peasant soldier gently lifted the dead little boy and walked away. The man's face was pale, his eyes sunken.

Barth grunted. "It ain't natural, having the dead bury the dead. There should be a priest. There should be friends and family. Wine to ease the passage."

Sahand is counting on us slowing down, on us burying our dead. He uses our decency as a weapon against us. Myreon didn't say this, though. She changed the subject. "Which way did the Ghouls go?"

Barth shrugged. "Seems like they cut across country, though I can't say why. Those bastards set a hell of a pace—we can't match it, especially not off the roads."

"So they get away," Myreon said.

"So they get away. Again." Barth said, his voice tight.

It had been the way ever since they set march—Sahand's army, working in small bands and in supernatural coordination, scattered across the countryside, burning and pillaging but never engaging in battle. It was a bizarre, perverse strategy. No one on her command staff had ever seen the like of it before. But of course, none of them were really soldiers. Even Valen Hesswyn barely qualified.

Sahand, on the other hand . . .

"You're dismissed, Barth," Myreon said. "Catch up to the army. I'll be back by sundown."

Barth nodded and left, pulling himself awkwardly into the saddle of a sturdy pony and trotting away. The men in the scouting party went with him, their heads bowed, their bleached tabards stained with blood and ash.

Soon there was only Myreon and the White Guard. She had brought fifteen of them, and with a tap of her staff, those fifteen silently moved to just beyond the village, where the dead had been laid out in the afternoon sun. Myreon passed the women and the children, doing her best to separate the horror of their deaths from the fact of their bodies. That was how she had to think of them now—merely inert objects, decaying matter. She willed the White Guard to begin digging the grave—one great trench into which all these people would be rolled and then covered.

Then Myreon came to the men. These she examined more closely, walking down the line and trying to judge age and height and the extent of their injuries. She found twenty of them who were more or less intact and who were of approximately the right frame and size. She had the White Guard separate out these and arrange them in a wide circle, foot to toe.

The first of the two spells she intended to cast was a desiccation spell that would eliminate the fluids in the corpses, effectively mummifying them. This was difficult work, as the sun was strong and the Ether weak in the area, but she had done this several times now and was getting rather good at it. The process took two hours.

Then came the easy part. Myreon removed the linking stone from her belt purse—a small crystal orb that glittered with the sunny power of the Lumen. With a few words and a little coaxing of the ample Lumenal energy in the grassy field, the dead men of the destroyed village rose as one. They were met by a White Guard who held out a box of tunics and volto masks. At her urging, the newly risen dead dressed in their new garb—white shrouded, masked, and ready to serve.

"I'm sorry," she said to the dead, despite herself. "I'm so sorry to do this to you. You deserved better."

The animated corpses, of course, had nothing to say. They fell into a column behind her, marching with eerie precision. Her steps heavy, she turned away from the village and began the long journey to meet with the White Army. Behind her, the only things that moved in the ruined village were the bodies of dead men burying dead women and children.

Though she was surrounded, she was also alone. She realized she was often alone now. People's eyes did not shine for the Gray Lady as they once had. No one embraced her, or asked for her blessing, or beseeched Hann on her behalf. Necromancers did not receive such welcomes, even if their efforts were for the good. Even Artus . . . well . . . they had never been close, she and Artus. And Tyvian's death and what had happened in the palace had only alienated him further from her. Now he had Michelle and the adoration of the peasantry to occupy most of his time anyway.

No, Myreon was alone. Alone to bear the terrible burdens this "war" was laying on her shoulders. She had no one to confide in, no one to weep with. She had to be seen as stronger than everyone. Her arts and Artus's gleaming reputation were what made the White Army function, and no crack could be shown in that facade. And so she wept in moments like this—when she was alone but for the abominations she herself had helped create, and where no one would ever see.

Barth was right—this *was* worse. The initial euphoria of their early victories was long gone, wiped away by the march north. The spring campaigns might have ended, but this war was a darker thing than they had ever been. No Eretherian lord ever burned the fields of his enemies. No Eretherian knight sacked villages or permitted his men to rape women or murder children. It was undreamed of. Even when Perwynnon rode against Sahand the first time, their battles had observed the conventions of the Common Law. But now, all bets were off along the Great South Plains. Sahand had no compunction about running a war that made people suffer on purpose, and it was just this lack of decency that was going to let him win.

Their only chance was to get to Tor Erdun, and soon—to take the pass before Sahand could fortify it. So she drove her army onward, refusing to let Valen pursue this or that mercenary company as they tried to coax the White Army into a pointless chase in the Eretherian hinterland. But every village they found like this slowed them down, and every order she gave forbidding action sapped morale. They were low on supplies already, and morale was perhaps even lower.

Her army needed a victory—needed it so badly she felt as though the fate of all of Eretheria, or decency *itself* hung in the balance. And she would do anything—*anything*—to secure that victory.

She marched into the gathering dusk with her undead soldiers all around her.

She would make it worth it. She would make it all worth it.

Artus put his hand at the level of his cheekbone. "He would be about this tall, with red hair. If you heard him speak, he'd sound like a lord, but with a foul tongue. He'd probably be wearing a sword—a rapier."

The three peasants kneeling on the floor of Artus's tent exchanged glances. They were a father and his two sons who'd been on a harrowing journey—first fleeing from the Peregrine Palace, then dodging Sahand's men in the fields, and finally finding their way to the White Army. They were haggard with travel, but had insisted on being brought to see the Young Prince. Artus had barely waited for them to kiss his ring before he started asking questions.

The father cleared his throat. "If I had news of that kind, Your Highness, I would tell you for sure. But . . . no, sire. We've seen no such man."

Artus nodded. He'd known the answer as soon as he saw their faces. He knew that they knew what he was asking, too. He bade them rise. "I'm sorry for everything you've been through, really I am." He reached for his purse.

The father bowed. "Begging your pardon, sire, but we'll not take a copper from you."

Artus blinked. "But you must need it. Please."

All three shook their heads. The father had tears in his eyes. "You don't understand, my prince. It's not you who owes us. No sire. It's . . ." He sniffled. "It's us who owes you."

Artus took the man's hand and shook it. He put a hand on his shoulder. "If you need anything, let me know. And thank you."

All three of them teared up then. They all knelt again before leaving, muttering blessings and invoking Hann's name on his behalf. When they at last retreated through the flap of the tent, Artus fell back into his chair. He rubbed his face—he felt like he'd just run a mile. "Gods and saints . . ."

Michelle came from behind a curtain in the tent that walled off her bedchamber. She pressed a goblet into Artus's hand. "You know money isn't going to solve their problems, Artus."

"What else can I do? What else can I offer them?" He gestured to his fine clothes and the sumptuous tent that surrounded them. "How can I be living like *this* and they think it's an insult to take my coin?"

"You're *prince*, Artus—you *deserve* all this." Michelle sat in a chair next to him. "You need to start acting as your station commands."

Artus scowled. "The hell I do! I'm not a lordling! I'm not like Valen . . ."

Michelle pursed her lips—a sign that she was angry. "Valen isn't like you, no. Valen *wishes* he were like you. You're a natural leader, Artus. You have the bearing of royalty. You need to stop acting like a peasant."

Artus knew he should have left it at that—he knew he could walk away and just let the statement hang, but he couldn't. He thought of his mother, his sisters—all so far away, across the mountains, living in a four-room farmhouse. "I *am* a peasant, Michelle. It's in my blood! I'm no more a king than those three are!"

Michelle paled. "Don't *say* that, Artus! I know you grew up in common surroundings, but you *mustn't* lower yourself like that!"

Artus took a sip of wine. "And why not? What's so bad about being common?"

"Because people don't die for *common* men!" Michelle snapped. "Because you are leading an *army* that believes in you! Do you know how much of this army's cohesion relies on their opinion of you? Do you think *Myreon* commands their loyalty? No—it's you, Artus. Only you."

Artus froze, staring at her. Gods, she was *right*, wasn't she? Everybody was counting on him to be . . . to be what? He was a farmboy and a cutpurse and a pretty decent tail and a more than decent brawler, but a prince? It was absurd. *Tyvian, what the hell did you get me into?*

Michelle took his hand and squeezed it. "You are doing fine, Artus. You're doing just fine."

"I don't belong here, Michelle. I'm not cut out for this."

She grinned and kissed him on the nose. "Then it's a good thing I'm here to tell you what to do."

The tent flaps opened and Valen ducked inside. He looked out of breath. "Artus . . . Your Highness, I mean."

Artus stood up. Valen's face was grim. "What? What is it?"

Valen motioned for Artus to follow. "You'd better come see this."

Valen filled Artus in on the vague story of how Barth's scouting parties had caught the Delloran—the accounts Valen had received varied widely—but what was certain was this: he had been a member of the Ghouls and he had almost certainly been left behind. He had a nasty arrow wound in his thigh that had become infected despite being bandaged. Evidently, the Ghouls felt the cost of amputating a leg and feeding the crippled man indefinitely was too high, and they'd dumped him.

Much of this, though, Artus had to piece together later. He *should* have heard it firsthand, but instead of bringing the man to him for questioning, the soldiers of the White Army had kept him for themselves.

The Delloran, stripped naked, was in the middle of a ring of jeering White Army volunteers. He was delirious with infection, his nose was broken and eyes nearly swollen shut from the beating he'd received. On three sides of him, their teeth bared and growling, were three hunting dogs. Somehow, they were the least feral element of the scene.

The Delloran swatted at the dogs as they darted in and out, testing him. He couldn't stand and was therefore rolling around on his back, his whole body trembling. The peasants roared for blood. One of the dogs rushed in and caught a hold of the Delloran's hand in its jaws and began to worry it back and forth. The Delloran screamed, blood pouring down his arm, his other hand beating ineffectually on the dog's head. Another dog got a piece of his good leg—by the thigh—and began to drag the Delloran along in the mud with short, sharp tugs. The man's screams were mingled with barely coherent pleas, then names Artus couldn't recognize, and appeals to Hann's mercy.

Artus had seen enough. "Hey! Stop! Stop it!"

No one heard him. Nobody paid the least attention. They were chanting for blood, their eyes fixed on the grisly scene, shouting themselves raw. Artus wished he had a horse, but it was too late to have one fetched—the prisoner would be dead before then.

Fine—the old-fashioned way it is. Artus pushed aside a man at the back. When he tried to slap Artus back, Artus caught his arm, twisted it, punched him just beneath the nose hard enough to knock out teeth. The man dropped like an empty sack. The next two men Artus pushed apart with each hand on a shoulder. They went to curse him, but then noticed who he was and recoiled. A third man—this one close to the action—jabbed his elbow back at Artus's face. Artus ducked it, kicked him in the back of the knees and grabbed him by the hair.

By this point, word had spread—the Young Prince was here and he wasn't happy. A hush fell over the crowd. They fell to one knee almost as one. The only sound left was the snarling of the dogs—the Delloran had passed out.

Artus dragged the peasant he had by the hair into the ring and threw him facedown in the dirt. Then he drew his sword and, with three quick strokes, killed the dogs. "Whose dogs were these?"

Silence.

"I asked you all a *question!*" Artus searched the bowed heads for some sign of the guilty party, but there was nothing. He couldn't even see their faces.

Artus kicked the man at his feet. "You—explain yourself!"

"Begging your pardon, Your Highness, but . . . but . . ."

Artus whacked his arse with the flat of his sword. "Out with it!"

"He's a Delloran, sir!" The man squealed, "He's only a Delloran!"

"He's a man!" Artus yelled. "And you were going to feed him to the dogs? A human being?"

Again that still, sullen silence. Artus didn't need them to speak—he knew what they were thinking. *But they've done the same to us. To our children. To our wives.*

He looked down at the naked Delloran. He still lived, but only barely. He nodded toward the White Guard, who had been waiting patiently at the crowd's edge for orders. "Take him to the healers. I want him to be able to talk to us, and soon."

The white-robed undead stepped forward quietly and picked up the Delloran between the two of them with no sign of strain. The crowd of peasant militia parted for them as though their state was contagious. Artus glared at them. "I want you all to think about this: What makes you better than the Dellorans, anyway?" Artus held up his bloodied sword. "As of this moment, it's one thing less than before. Take care you don't become the thing you hate." He wiped the blade of his sword on a peasant's back, leaving a streak of blood, and sheathed it. "Where is Gammond Barth? Have him sent to my command tent straight-away!"

Valen gave Artus a cruel grin. "With pleasure, sire."

Artus stepped over the bodies of the dogs and left, not looking back. Behind him, the silence remained.

Later, in the command tent, Valen brought in Barth as though he were a bouncer escorting a man out of a bar. When Artus related what had happened, Barth shrugged. "You might think I can tell these men what to do, Your Highness, but I don't. Not all the way. The men said they was going to take him to you. I believed them."

Artus wasn't buying it. "The hell you did, Barth!

You know better than anybody how angry the men are—you *knew* this would happen!"

Valen nodded, his arms crossed. "I want names, Barth. Those men are to be hanged."

Barth sneered at Valen. "And what, then the White Army starts decorating the trees with Eretherian bodies? Just how much rope do you think we have, rich boy?"

Valen took a step toward Barth, his hand falling to his sword. "These men violated the conventions of war!"

Barth stepped right up to the young knight, nose to nose. "Kroth's teeth, you naive ponce! There *are* no bloody conventions of war—Sahand keeps proving that, day in and day out! The more you cling to your toy soldier ideals, the worse this is going to get."

"Toy soldier ideals? My men are the only real soldiers in this entire army! Unless they learn some discipline, *your* peasant mob is going to be the death of us all!"

Artus stepped between them and pried them apart. "Stop it, both of you! We're only a few days out from Tor Erdun—we can't afford to lose either of you in some stupid brawl!"

Valen retreated to a chair and sat down, pouring himself a cup of water from a clay pitcher. He put his elbows on his knees and leaned forward. In the flickering lamplight, he looked haggard—much older than his eighteen years would imply. "We need to do *something*."

Barth also found a chair, but on the opposite side of the tent. He was squinting at the map in the dim light. "The closer we get to Tor Erdun, the more we're bumping into Sahand's forces. I keep getting reports—unconfirmed, mind, but I believe them. We're close. If we send out a probing force, we might just be able to engage someone or something."

"That isn't the general's plan," Artus pointed out.

Barth spat. "Hang the Gray Lady, and pardon me for saying so. She's bloodless as a witch. Her plan's all well and good for beating Sahand, I suppose, but it won't do nothing for all those poor souls what he's burned out of house and home!"

Valen nodded slowly. "You know I hate to admit this carpenter is right about anything, Artus—*sire*—but he's right about this. You are prince. This is *your* army, not hers."

Artus looked between the two of them—Valen was right, they hardly ever agreed. Here it was, then—the thing Michelle had been saying. *His* army. He was prince. At his word, they would all do whatever he said. Right now, they wanted permission to go tearing off after some splinter of Sahand's army—on a bloody gnome hunt—and where would that get them? Maybe some satisfaction, but beyond that? Nothing. It was what Myreon said Sahand wanted them to do.

Barth had his hands balled into fists. "Only give the word, sire! We'll bring the bastards to justice!"

"I don't think so . . ."

Valen grabbed Artus by the upper arm and shook him, as though trying to wake him up. "Take *command*, sire! Stop doing whatever that sorceress tells you to!"

What would Tyvian do? Artus wondered. It was a question he asked himself daily, but he never seemed to come up with a reasonable answer. Long-term plans were always Tyvian's forte. *Pretending* he was Tyvian didn't give Artus any magical powers in that regard. Still, he could think of one piece of advice Tyvian would probably have given him, if he were there.

Listen to the former Mage Defender, not the carpenter or the teenaged knight, you bloody dunce!

Artus couldn't help but laugh.

"I don't see what's funny," Barth said.

Artus controlled his expression. "No. We carry on as ordered. Myreon is right."

Barth's face darkened but he, too, got his expression under control. He bowed. "As my prince commands." He stomped out of the tent.

Valen watched the carpenter go. "You better hope she knows what she's doing. This army can't afford to lose a battle."

"Well, we'd better not let that happen, then."

CHAPTER 9

ON-THE-JOB TRAINING

The next few days saw the Ghouls take up a steady march overland, cutting across roads and farmland and woods without much care to the terrain. Captain Rodall set an ambitious pace for such uneven territory—anybody following them would have a hell of a time keeping up. As it was, they were only limited by the speed their supply wagons could make, and these were enhanced with wheels enchanted to make the progress relatively smooth. Tyvian wondered how many people would ever have guessed that the most expensive and useful tactical weapon available to the Ghouls was a bunch of wagon wheels.

Tyvian had a lot more time to think about things,

now that his role in the company had completely changed. He had gone from raw mercenary recruit to the indentured servant of Sahand's personal assassin overnight. He was not altogether certain it was a step up. For those first few days, Tyvian's duties were mostly sexual in nature. The rest of the time, however, Voth had him follow her around like some kind of lapdog, carrying her sword, her cape, her hat, or whatever else she didn't feel like burdening herself with. She trotted him around the camp like a trained pony. The looks he got from the men were a mixture of envy and pity—a grown man being bossed about by a slip of a woman? The Ghouls spat when they said his name . . . which was still Duchess.

Part of him—an old part, a deep part—wanted to challenge some of these hulking brutes to a duel or two, just to show them who was boss. Voth, though, had reminded him of just how thinly he was being tolerated by the captain. If he gave the Ghouls any excuse to run him through, he was good as dead. Rodall would have his head, and there wasn't a damned thing he could do about it.

So Tyvian held his tongue and endured the slights and kept his head down. And in the evenings, he had Voth all to himself. He told himself this was adequate compensation. And it almost was.

On the fourth day since the massacre at the village, the company came to a halt and set camp by the bend of a little stream that was flowing north. If

Tyvian's geography was as good as he'd hoped, they were close to the southern edge of Lake Country and the County of Hadda. Hadda was technically neutral in the conflict between the White Army and Sahand, but they wouldn't welcome Delloran boots on Hadda soil at all. At night, Tyvian could see the lights of a castle no more than two or three miles distant—the Ghouls' own campfires had to be visible to the castle, as well. Captain Rodall was announcing his presence, whereas before they had been moving so as to make it difficult for others to follow. This was a part of some larger game, but Tyvian couldn't guess at what. It was like trying to predict a *couronne* strategy by the location of a single piece.

That night, Tyvian tried to hold Voth in his arms, at least for a few moments. She twisted away, giving him a lopsided grin. "Now, now, Duchess—you don't want to give me the wrong idea, do you?"

"I assure you, I was merely offering to keep you warm a bit longer. A tiny little thing like yourself must freeze in these cool evenings."

Voth laughed and got dressed in a flowing silk robe of glossy black and embroidered with thread-of-gold. "My blood runs hotter than you think, Reldamar."

Tyvian lay back on the bed and thought of Myreon. He found himself thinking a lot about Myreon lately, particularly in this bed at times like this. Myreon would have stayed in his arms all night, holding him close. He would play with her strands of golden hair, feeling her breath push softly against his neck. He grimaced at the memory. He tried to think back, tried to pinpoint exactly where it had gone so wrong for the two of them. He couldn't think of one thing, but rather hundreds of little mistakes, of small little splinters that eventually killed whatever romance they had. Most of them were his fault, he was sure. *Gods, what a dunce I am.*

Voth snapped her fingers at him. "Hey, I don't like you like that."

"Like what?"

"Thinking. Your thinking tends to have fatal consequences."

"It isn't as though I'm given much else to do."

"Is that a complaint I detect? Surely not from the man whose life I saved from a grisly end." Voth examined her dead white eye in a mirror, poking at it softly. She did this a lot. "Besides, I've got good news for you: your slate of duties is about to increase."

"And how's that?"

"You and I and Eddereon the Black and two others of the sergeant's recommendation are about to part company with the Ghouls and go on a little side-mission."

Tyvian sat up. "Who are the other two? What are we doing?"

"The men I think you know—two morons known as Hambone and Mort. The mission is, of course, still need-to-know."

"So what has this to do with me?"

Voth picked up a small vial of some kind of oil and poured a drop into her dead eye. "These men need to be brought up to speed with what we're going to be doing. I'm leaving the small unit tactics and such to Eddereon, but you I need to take over some of the more delicate aspects of their training."

Tyvian cocked his head. "Such as?"

"These men need to be able to pass for Eretherian knights."

Tyvian nodded. Those two words—*Eretherian knights*—were enough for him to put a number of pieces into place and establish context for a number of different things, not the least of which was why they were here, a scant few miles from Hadda's borders. He now knew what they were about to do—it should have been obvious, really, given Voth's talents. They were about to kidnap and murder someone, and Tyvian had a pretty short list of who that might possibly be.

All of them were friends.

The next day, those selected by Voth as members of her "team" were left with minimal supplies, two horses, and Voth's own tent. The rest of the Ghouls moved on, heading southwest. Witnessing it from the outside for the first time, he was surprised at how quickly the whole company was able to pick up and move. They were gone from sight before the sun had fully risen. Voth's little party was alone.

Mort, Hambone, and Tyvian were compelled to stand at attention while Eddereon went through any personal belongings the three of them had and presented them to Voth. Mort had a lock of hair from some mysterious brunette, some obviously shaved gambling dice, and an assortment of partially mummified chicken feet. Hambone had a smooth white rock, a compact Book of Hann with a flower pressed between the pages, and some brass knuckles. Tyvian had nothing whatsoever.

Voth eyed the pathetic little pile of mementos with a sardonic grin. She was standing on a large rock, her hands on her hips, as though she were about to give a stirring speech. She wasn't. "Easy duty's over, boys. It's time for some real work."

Mort shifted his lantern jaw back and forth. It made a cracking sound. "What we doing?"

Eddereon smacked him in the ribs with a swagger stick. "If she wants to hear you talk, she'll ask you a question!"

Mort remained at attention, but Tyvian could feel the huge man tense up beside him. "Easy, Mort," Tyvian whispered.

Voth kept talking. "Prince Banric has a mission for us. The details of that mission are none of your business. The purpose of that mission is none of your business. The only things that are your business are two facts: first, you do what I say, and second, if you don't do what I say, I'm allowed to kill you. We clear?"

Tyvian and his two companions nodded.

"Good." Voth hopped off the rock and headed toward her tent. "Each of you is going to come in here, one at a time, and we're going to get you out of those clothes." Tyvian half expected her to give him a wink at that last part, but she didn't. For the rest of the day, Voth was very businesslike.

Though Tyvian wasn't given the details, he had been involved in operations like this often enough that he could make a pretty good guess. The cover story would be this: Hambone and Mort would be masquerading as hedge knights who deserted the service of House Hadda in order to sign with the White Army. Tyvian and Eddereon would impersonate their squires, while Voth would be in the role of runaway farmgirl or similar—probably recently escaped from the ravages of Delloran soldiers. Desperate for experienced blades, the White Army would welcome them with open arms.

Then, once in the army, it was only a matter of finding a way to get close enough to whoever the target was to grab them, kill them, and vanish in the dead of night. Tyvian appreciated the tactical simplicity of the plan—armies on the march were confusing affairs, and everyone lived in tents. Slitting a throat in the night was very much within the bounds of plausibility.

All of it, though, relied upon Hambone and Mort making convincing hedge knights. Given that hedge knights tended to be filthy and poorly educated, Hambone and Mort had a head start in their preparations. The rest, though, was up to Tyvian.

During the day, Voth went out scouting and Eddereon ran the three of them through drills. These were mostly exercises in stealth and silent coordination. Tyvian had done things like this many times, and he found it fairly easy. Mort and Hambone were less able. They got an earful of Eddereon's gruff bark: "Hambone, why can't you have ankles like Duchess? Sounds like you're walking with a bone loose!"

Then, in the evenings, while Voth and Eddereon discussed tactics in her tent, Tyvian coached the two Dellorans in basic etiquette. On this particular evening, the challenge was eating with flatware.

Tyvian sat with a wooden tray across his knees on which were displayed a wedge of cheese and some strawberry preserves. The fork was an awkward wooden thing—gods knew where Voth had even found it—but Tyvian was able to spear a slice of cheese precisely, dip it in some of the preserves, and maneuver it into his mouth as smoothly as a pilot berthing a ship in his home port. "There, see? Easy."

Hambone was throttling his own fork like a broadsword. "Why can't we just use our hands? Don't rich folk use their hands?" He looked down at his own little platter of cheese and preserves, his forehead furrowed.

Mort had his fork held backward—as though intending to use it to murder someone in bed—and stabbed a piece of cheese with violent force. The tray shook and some of the preserves flew off and hit Hambone in the cheek. Tyvian winced. "Mort, it's cheese, not your mortal foe. More gently."

"I don't do things gently, Duchess," Mort growled. He bit the cheese off the end of his fork, teeth bare.

"If you don't do this gently, you'll likely wind up dead."

"Bah, what do you know?"

The expression on Hambone's face reminded him suddenly of Artus—particularly sullen Artus, when he was about fourteen and felt the world was devoted to his personal misery. He could see Artus scowling at him from across a campfire, rolling his eyes at his lesson. He remembered the boy's laughter; his bright, open face. The memory hurt somehow—so sharply that, for a moment, he looked at the ring. But no, that wasn't it. He only missed him. He only wished he could have spoken with him one more time.

"What's the matter with you, eh?" Mort was eating the cheese with his fingers now. The fork was nowhere to be seen.

"Mort, did you eat the fork, or are you just stupid?"

The big man rolled to his feet. "You want to say that again?"

Hambone stood up, too, and placed himself

between Tyvian and giant mercenary. "Hey, big man—take it easy. He's just following orders, right? It's what we're all doing, eh?"

"I don't like it when folks call me stupid," Mort said, more to Tyvian than to Hambone.

Tyvian remained seated. "Then perhaps you shouldn't do so many stupid things." He slowly tightened his grip on the fork. It might not be all that useful in hard cheese, but if Mort got too close, the big oaf was going to lose an eye.

Hambone patted Mort gently on his chest. "C'mon, Mort—the sergeant'll have your ears."

"Sergeant, my arse! His name's Ed, and he used to fart in our own tent."

Hambone laughed nervously. "You want to tussle with that old fighter? You heard the stories about him, right? Eddereon the Black . . ."

Mort, still glaring at Tyvian, backed off. "I'm going for a walk. Sleep with one eye open, Duchess—you hear?" He rolled his shoulders and backed away into the falling dusk.

Tyvian watched him go, shaking his head. "You know, Hambone—one of these days I'm afraid I'm going to have to stab that man."

Hambone turned around and forced a grin. Tyvian could tell the color had drained from his face a little—he was frightened. "Just like you done old Drawsher, eh?" He laughed, but it was too high-pitched to be genuine.

Gods, Tyvian thought, *he's afraid of me!*

Quiet fell between them. The crackle of the campfire complimented a soft chorus of crickets by the riverside. Somewhere, out there in the dark, they could hear Mort blundering around. At length, Tyvian cleared his throat. "Why'd you stand up for me?"

Hambone blinked and rubbed smoke from his eyes. "What?"

"The captain was going to kill you. Why step up for me? You could have held your tongue like everyone else. Why?"

Hambone got a stick and prodded at the fire. "Well, you and me are friends, ain't we?"

"I broke your knee with a shovel, Hambone."

Hambone shrugged. "I deserved it, right? Expect you'd done the same to ol' Mort, eh?"

Tyvian smiled. "You're learning, at least."

"See, what I don't get is this: How's a man who knows his way in a fight as well as you do—a man who can best a professional sell-sword like Drawsher—go all weak-kneed in battle? Hann's boots, Duchess—you was weeping like a girl. That part I ain't made up!"

Tyvian thought back to the village. It made him shudder. "You call that a battle, do you?"

"C'mon—you know what I mean."

Tyvian looked into the fire, trying to burn away the sounds of the screams, the smell of blood. "Here's what I don't understand, Ham. How's a fellow who stands up for his friends, who forgives them, who protects them from harm—how's he do what you did back in that village?"

"Do what?"

Tyvian scowled. "Don't make me say it. You know what you did."

"Oh." Hambone frowned. "*That*." He paused, searching for the words, then shrugged. "Weren't everybody else doing it?"

"That's no kind of answer."

Hambone's expression darkened. The silence dragged out again. "I don't want to talk about this no more."

"Sure. Maybe you should just *think* about it, instead."

Voth came into the circle of firelight. She was dressed plainly—a woolen cloak, a peasant's dress, stained and dirty. A bloody bandage was bound across her dead eye. "Up." She pointed at Hambone. "Get into costume. Do you remember your heraldry?"

Hambone's jaw dropped open. He looked like he had been shot. "I . . . uhhhh . . ."

Voth rolled her good eye. "Kroth's teeth. Duchess, you stick close by this oaf and make sure he makes the right grunts at the right times or we'll all end up dead. Training time is over."

Tyvian stood up. "How close is the White Army?"

Voth's head snapped around, and she glared at him. After a moment, she laughed. "How much of the plan do you know already?" When Tyvian shrugged, she laughed again. "Just don't get any stupid ideas. I'll be watching you. Closely."

Tyvian made a courtly bow. This only made Voth laugh harder. "Gods, I *do* like you, Duchess. It will probably be the death of me, won't it?"

Tyvian smiled. "One can dream."

Eddereon had the horses saddled and Voth's tent packed up. Due to some Astral enchantments on it, it was unusually collapsible—small enough to be slung across the back of a saddle with little trouble. Mort and Hambone were each in mail, but of a higher quality than the stuff the Ghouls had issued. Where they had found a suit large enough to accommodate Mort's massive shoulders, Tyvian could only guess. None of his guesses seemed plausible.

The illusion of Mort and Hambone as Lake Country hedge knights on hard times was completed primarily by Eddereon and Tyvian, each of whom dressed in a tabard with the heraldic markings of their supposed masters. A good eye for heraldry would identify the two sell-swords as errant lances from somewhere in the Forest of Barrents, related very indirectly to the Earl of Barrentry on his mother's side, and from a largely disgraced corner of that line. Tyvian guessed the family names they were using as aliases hadn't been seen or heard of in the capital for at least two decades.

They set off south while it was still dark and rode until dawn. How they knew their way in the dark was a secret possessed by Eddereon alone, since he was in the lead. By the time the sun was up, Tyvian could see spirit engine tracks, cutting through the farmland like a black ribbon. That would put the Freegate Road to the west. How far indicated how far north they had come. If Tyvian had a slightly better eye for distances, he'd be able to pinpoint their exact location in Eretheria. As it was, he was reduced to the same kind of vague dead reckoning that had kept him alive before Hool had entered his life and travelling through the wilderness got a thousand times easier.

A wave of nostalgia threatened to overtake him yet again, and Tyvian stuffed it down before it could crest. What, was he supposed to live his life in regret now? Constantly moping for the old days? Tyvian felt that, more than anything else, was a sign of a man getting too old. *Hang the past. Focus on what's ahead. A new life. A new you.*

Thinking of Hool, though, did raise a concern. He walked ahead with Eddereon for a bit, scouting the land alongside the old Northron. "We may have a problem if we enter the camp. Hool—she could sniff me out."

Eddereon shook his head. "She's not with the White Army."

"How can you be so sure?"

"There is a trail of dead Dellorans stretching from here to beyond Ayventry that suggests your friend the gnoll has other plans. I overheard Captain Rodall discussing the reports on several occasions."

Despite himself, Tyvian smiled. "She's on a rampage. Avenging me."

Eddereon looked grave. "No. Not you." He turned and waved to Voth and the two "knights."

Tyvian's smile sank away. *Not me. Then who?*

Oh Gods—Brana . . .

For the rest of the morning, Tyvian's stomach felt tied in knots. Had he eaten anything, he might have thrown up.

They found the White Army shortly before midday. A troop of ragtag men in hunting greens came upon them from a copse of trees. When it became clear they weren't Dellorans and were travelling with a wounded peasant girl, they cheerfully informed them where the army could be found without any further questioning. "So much for security," Tyvian grumbled when they were out of earshot.

"Cheer up, Duchess," Voth said, "at least we didn't have to kill them."

Tyvian was holding Hambone's fraudulent banner aloft. He looked up at the "knight" to see he was pale and sweating. "I don't know about this," Hambone said.

"Shut the hell up," Mort growled. "You want to get us killed?"

"Both of you shut up!" Eddereon snapped. "Follow Duchess's lead."

The White Army was huge—twenty times or more larger than the Ghouls, judging from the number of tents. It was also twenty times more disorganized. Tyvian's brief stint in the Delloran army had shown him the militant precision Sahand expected of his bannermen and sell-swords—the army moved like a single organism or machine, oiled and seamless. The White Army seemed to be some kind of mass migration of angry men with spears. Tents were arrayed haphazardly, and other than a few masked men in white walking around who seemed to know what they were about, the rest of the army seemed uncertain whether they were meant to pack up camp, dig in, or practice marching.

"They need more sergeants," Eddereon said.

"The only thing they don't need more of is people," Tyvian countered, noting one group of men limping along without any shoes, their feet bloody and raw.

They had gone a good ways into the camp before they were stopped by a fellow in a dented breastplate and carrying a mace. He directed them to the quartermaster's tent, where they could "sign on."

The quartermaster was an older man, but built like a barn. He squatted on a stool and was hacking away in a ledger with a quill. Tyvian could tell from here that he was a man unaccustomed to writing.

When he saw them, he picked a pair of spectacles off his nose and folded them up. "More? Gods, it's turning into a busy day."

Tyvian bowed. "Sir, may I present Sir Hubert Macrole and his esteemed cousin, Sir Jorris Dalvert, both of the Forest of Barrents."

The quartermaster wiped ink off his fingers by rubbing them on his sleeve and extended a hand to shake. "Gammond Barth. I'm a carpenter, but you'd best get used to shaking my hand anyway." He grinned.

Tyvian shook—the old man had a grip like a vise. Tyvian looked up at the two Dellorans and gave them a hard stare. Mort was the first to react. "We've come to kill Dellorans."

"Then you're in good company. We'll be happy to give you the chance, just as soon as we find some." Barth laughed. No one else did.

It was now Hambone's line. "Oh! Uhhh . . . we . . . we've got some smarts!"

"*Intelligence . . .*" Tyvian coughed.

Hambone's cheeks reddened. "Right—intelligence. About Tor Erdun!"

Barth stopped laughing and looked serious. "Truly, son? You're not telling tall tales, are you? We had our fill of those, understand? We'll throw you out if you're lying, horses and armor or no."

Voth made a good show of looking shy as she

came forward and curtsied. Just watching her performance made Tyvian's ring clamp down. "Please, sir—I'm the one what told them. I'm from Tor Erdun. The Dellorans killed my father. He . . . he was a miller . . ." Tears welled in her good eye. Her body shook. The effect was perfectly realized. Though he knew it was a lie, even Tyvian felt moved.

Barth put his arm around her. "Oh, you poor thing. Come on, come on—let's get you something to eat and you can tell me all about it."

"You want us to stay?" Mort asked, though it was somewhat unclear who he was asking—Barth or Voth.

Barth shook his head. "She's in good hands, lads—you've done well. Get yourself settled and come back in a bit. I want to hear her story first and then yours later. All right?"

Mort and Hambone exchanged glances. "Yeah . . . uhhh . . . okay." Hambone shrugged. He scooted in his saddle, as though willing the horse to back up but not being really sure how to do that.

Tyvian grabbed the bridle before anything untoward could occur. "We'll leave her in your capable care. Our thanks."

Voth and Barth disappeared inside the tent. If Voth's target was the White Army's quartermaster, that man was as good as dead. He had a sense it wasn't, though. Looking around at the chaos of the White Army's camp, it was pretty clear that the quartermaster was *not* Myreon's primary military asset. It only remained to be seen who was.

"That went well!" Hambone observed, smiling.

Mort was more pensive. "Ain't over yet, Ham."

Tyvian grimaced at the failure to use Hambone's alias. "Come on—let's find somewhere to pitch this tent."

CHAPTER 10

THE JAWS OF VENGEANCE

The Delloran patrol had not died quickly. Though Hool had come upon them unawares, they were good fighters and tough, for humans. But there were only eight of them, and two of them had been sleeping.

And none of them could see in the dark.

At dawn, Sir Damon Pirenne—now just "Damon"—joined her in the ruins of the little camp where it stood beneath a dead tree on the slopes of a windswept hill somewhere around the place where Eretheria ended and Galaspin began. As usual, he was nervous around the bodies. Especially the ones Hool had impaled on tree branches. He rubbed his bald head while looking at them, his face grave. "Was that strictly necessary?"

Hool looked at the Delloran, upside down with a tree branch sticking through his stomach. "It was the easiest way. Would you rather he had stabbed me?"

Damon sat down on a log—the same log where the Dellorans had been sitting the night before, when she had killed them. He kicked at the ashes of the campfire. "I'd rather we *avoided* these patrols, instead of hunting them down."

Hool shrugged and went back to going through the Dellorans' packs for anything useful. She threw a packet of dried rations at Damon. "Keep these. Just in case."

Damon mutely stuffed the rations inside his own pack. He looked pale and tired and sad for some reason—he had looked that way for almost a month now. Though the top of his head was still hairless, his beard had become long and scraggly, and his nice shiny clothes were now mudstained and tattered. Hool considered asking him if he wanted to go home, but every time she asked that question, he only got grumpier. He also only answered it one way: *I made an oath and I will see it kept.*

Hool upended another sack. More pointless garbage—bladecrystals, knives, socks, a bag of teeth, a few copper coins. She could not figure out why humans marched around with so much junk.

Damon was still looking at the bodies. "I'm worried about you, Hool."

Hool snorted. "Why? I'm not hurt."

Damon's warm brown eyes fixed on her face. "Yes, you are."

Hool found herself unable to meet his gaze. She put her ears back and dumped out another sack. She heard a weird *twang* and looked down—a musical instrument of some kind. It had a long neck and a bulbous body and was strung with some kind of animal tendons or something. She kicked it. "What a stupid, big thing to—"

Damon was on his feet. "Don't break it. Please."

Hool had her foot raised, ready to crush it. She paused. "Why?"

"I want it. I used to play."

"So?"

"Hool, I'm not very useful to you. I could at least try to be entertaining."

Hool set her foot down. "I am seeking revenge. It isn't supposed to be entertaining."

Damon came over, gingerly stepping over a headless body, and picked up the lute or guitar or whatever it was. He cradled it in his hands gently, as though it were a baby. "This is actually a very nice piece."

"They probably stole it from some farmers they killed," Hool pointed out.

But Damon ignored her. He plucked a few strings, making the instrument squeak. "Needs tuning."

"You can do that later. We have to get going. These ones will be noticed missing soon." Hool gestured vaguely to the carnage around her. "Are you ready?"

Damon slung the instrument over one shoulder and took a steadying breath. "Lead on, milady."

So they headed off.

By Hool's standards, they had to travel slowly thanks to Damon being a human. They travelled light, though, and still faster than any other humans on foot. Hool was constantly alert for the sound of hoofbeats, but they were far enough off the main roads and trails that people on horseback were uncommon. Other than a string of dead patrols and slaughtered couriers, they left no signs behind them. Damon had proven adept at hiding his tracks and, despite his age, was strong and healthy. The journey was going well so far—Hool had no reason to think it could go better.

Still, she often thought about leaving Damon behind. He was right—he wasn't very helpful. He could fight, but not as well as Hool. He could travel, but not as fast. He could keep watch, but not as ably. By all measurable accounts, Damon was a liability.

Besides, this was not his fight. He didn't understand. He didn't understand that killing those patrols was not only *right* but also *important*. It was not just Sahand she hunted, not just his blood she wished to see spilled. She wanted all of Dellor to tremble at the sound of her howl. She wanted to stain the ground red with the blood of every black-hearted murderer in Sahand's service. Every fiber of her being demanded this of her.

With every bearded sell-sword she strangled, every scarred soldier's throat she tore out, the sound of her Brana whimpering before his death grew just a little duller. She felt that his spirit, watching her from the stars at night, rested all the easier in knowing that his killers were receiving justice. This was something Damon did not understand. He could not. He had no children, no family. He was just a stupid man who said he loved her. If she left him behind, both she and he would be better off.

But she didn't.

Their long day of travel brought them north out of the foothills of the Tarralles. According to Damon's map, that put them somewhere in the County of Ayventry, on the border with Galaspin. It was a wide, flat place, full of farmland and small country cottages. In the distance was the occasional village, the lights of their houses glowing warmly in the night. Hool could tell that Damon wanted to go toward those lights, to be out of the wilderness and among his own kind. But he never said so, following Hool on her cross-country journey until well past sundown.

At night, Hool permitted no fire. Damon hugged his tattered cape around his shoulders, rubbing his hands together. The moon was bright—almost full— and the lands around them glowed silver beneath its gaze. Far away, a farmhouse poured thin smoke into the air. At this distance, Hool could smell the manure of the horses and the scent of fresh hay. Crickets chirped in the tall grass. She took a deep breath, trying to savor the peace. But the anger would not let her.

She thought of that last night with Brana, sleeping under a starry sky like this. Her heart fell and she balled herself up. She didn't want to see it anymore. She didn't want to remember. She just wanted the hole inside her filled.

Damon began to tinker with his lute, his ear bent over the strings as he softly plucked one after the other and turned the pegs at one end. The sound drowned out the crickets. It made Hool's hair stand up on end. "Stop that," she growled, her face still hidden.

"Just a moment, just a moment," Damon said. He gave a peg a final twist. "There."

Hool opened one eye and peered from beneath one paw. "There *what?*"

Damon cleared his throat and placing four fingers on the neck of the instrument, strummed a chord. It was deep and resonant and seemed to hang in the air. Then, Damon began to sing.

> *The pride of Man is broken now,*
> *His kingdoms burned to ash.*
> *And there can be no greater grief*
> *Than that of Tal Torash.*

Torash was brave, Torash was strong.
He smote his foes, knew right from wrong.
But when death came for his fair queen,
There was no comfort left for him.

"Stop it," Hool snapped, sitting up. "Stop that right now."

Damon set the lute down. "Was it that bad? I'm a bit rusty, I'm afraid."

"No," Hool said, more suddenly than she intended. "It was not bad. I don't like that song."

Damon picked the lute back up. "A different one?"

"How many songs do you know?"

"As a young man, it was my habit to impress ladies with my musical talents in hopes to win myself an advantageous marriage." Damon shrugged.

Hool frowned. "That didn't work, did it?"

Damon laughed. "No. But I did learn a great, great many songs."

Hool considered this. "Play another one. But not a sad one. Play one about victory."

Damon strummed the strings idly, traversing through a series of chords. "Is that where you think we're headed toward? A victory?"

Hool laid her ears back against her skull. "You're changing the subject."

"I was just asking a question."

"Play something happier. Do it."

Damon bowed his head. "I never deny the request

of a lady." He began to strum again, this time faster, in a steady rhythm.

> They call me Captain Piper, lads,
> the bravest man you've ever seen
> Who's got a thousand ships at call
> To fly my banner green.

> And when my foes consider, lads,
> the strength o' my battling arm,
> They throw their weapons to the ground,
> Rather than come to harm.

> Captain Piper, master mage,
> Captain Piper, holy sage,
> Captain Piper, lover true,
> Captain Piper, here for you!

Hool snorted. "That's a stupid song."

Damon stopped playing and chuckled. "Yes, I suppose it is. Never failed to get the ladies' eyes rolling."

Silence fell. In a few moments, the crickets were back and chirping. Damon was looking at Hool, his steady brown eyes glittering in the moonlight. Hool turned away from him. "You don't need to worry about me."

"Hool, you are the only person in this entire world I worry about."

"Well stop it!" she said.

"You are taking too many risks, Hool. You need to slow down. One of these days, your insane little raids are going to get you killed."

"You can't tell me what to do," Hool growled. "I'm in charge, remember?"

"You can't honestly think you can kill every Delloran between here and the Citadel, can you? And even if you do, what will that accomplish?"

Hool looked back at him, her teeth bared. "Revenge! Revenge is what it will accomplish, you stupid man! This is a mission of *revenge*! Why can't you understand that?"

Damon put up his hands. "Nobody is arguing that Sahand doesn't deserve it, Hool! But there is no reason you need to destroy yourself—"

Hool pounced on him, knocking him onto his back. She growled in his face. *"You do not understand! You don't have to understand! I am in charge and you obey! Got it?"*

Damon, his eyes wide, nodded slowly. "As you wish."

Hool climbed off him, suddenly ashamed. She said nothing else—she only backed away and curled up for the night. In time, Damon picked up the lute again and strummed it softly. It was to this music, not the crickets, that she finally fell asleep.

She dreamed of her pups. And fire.

CHAPTER 11

TOR ERDUN

Altogether, it took the White Army nearly two weeks to march up the Freegate Road from the Great South Plains to the northernmost spur of the Tarralle Mountains. There, the road wound its way around and over gradually steeper hills until, at last, it camped on the slopes beneath Mount Erdun and the Citadel that bore its name.

Tor Erdun commanded a wide and low pass through the mountains and had been a trading post for many years. Even with the advent of the spirit engine, Tor Erdun and the Freegate Road remained popular, not just with the poor compelled to use it, but also with the wealthy guilders and nobles in this region of Eretheria who could avoid a side trip to Hadburg in Lake Country and just cut through the mountains. Accordingly, the Earldom of Tor Erdun was a very valuable fief, and the Citadel there was no stranger to siege.

The castle itself was large and well provisioned, guarded by sheer cliffs on three sides and on the fourth by a fortified gatehouse and a tall curtain wall. The wall itself was enchanted—this Myreon could easily tell with a few simple auguries—making it impervious to conventional siege weapons. The Citadel consisted of three towers: one was very tall, where the castellan could survey all approaches to the castle for many miles. The other two were comparatively squat and flat and broad, their crenelated tops acting as platforms for war machines designed to shoot down enemy flyers like griffons and to rain death on any army marching up the winding road to the pass.

At the base of the cliffs, sheltering within the protective range of the Citadel's weapons, the town of Erdun rested, peaceful and unwalled. From where the White Army was encamped, the town was perhaps two miles distant. On the fields surrounding it was camped another army—the Army of Ayventry, its tower-and-rose pennants snapping in the cool mountain breeze. Myreon lowered the viewing glass. "That is a *lot* of cavalry."

Artus took the glass and looked. He could make out a number of banners, but most of them blended together. "There's got to be about three hundred of them."

Valen, in full plate and on horseback, shifted nervously in the saddle. "Most of the peerage of Ayventry, I'd guess. And us with only fifty horse. I hope you have a plan, Magus."

They were standing at the edge of their own camp, a cordon of White Guard surrounding them. All of the senior staff were here. She looked at Barth, who was dressed in his dented breastplate and leaning on his massive war-hammer. "Where are the Dellorans?"

Barth spat in the grass. "My scouts haven't spotted a blessed thing. If they're nearby, they haven't mustered in force as yet. My advice would be to strike quickly before they can."

"A frontal assault uphill across open ground at that army and against that castle would be suicide," Valen countered. He looked at Barth. "You said some miller's girl knew of a secret way inside? Can she be trusted?"

Barth bristled. "I know a woman's tears when I see them, boy. She's honest." Then, to Myreon, "General, if we can get a force of men—young Valen's knights, perhaps—into the Citadel, we can probably take it. As the lordling says, most of their men are in the field."

"That would be a very *costly* victory, Barth, and this isn't the last battle we'll have to fight," Myreon said. "Let's call for a parley first."

"What? And after what they've done? They're

traitors! To the crown, to the land, to the people—
we're not here to make deals, general!"

"Come off it, Barth!" Artus said. "They outnumber
us three to one, at least. How much blood do we want
on our hands?"

"You talk about the blood on our hands, sire, but
you forget about the blood on *theirs*." Barth pointed
up the slope to the enemy camp. "Children, hanging
from trees. Villages slaughtered."

"Those were Dellorans," Artus countered.

"Just so, my prince. And with Ayventry backing
them up with every step. Traitors all, I say!"

Valen maneuvered his horse a bit closer to Barth.
"You're out of line, Barth. Watch your tone."

Artus held up a hand to Valen. "Calm down." He
looked at Barth. "I understand there are at least two
companies of our own army made up of Ayventrymen. Perhaps I oughta have them turned over to you,
then? So you can strip them naked and feed them to
dogs?"

Barth's face turned red, but he said nothing.

Myreon looked at the three men. "Are we done
now? Anyone else have some piece of masculine anatomy they want to swing around?"

Nobody answered. Artus, at least, had the sense
of shame to look at his feet. Myreon waved to the
closest courier. "Arrange a parley. Flag of truce, no
weapons."

The man—the *boy*—nodded and took up a pole

with a white flag. Then he was off like a jackrabbit, running across the fields on his errand.

Myreon tapped her fingers on the linking stone at her belt. "Now we see what they say."

The courier did not return for several hours. Myreon hadn't enough military experience to know if this was usual or not, but judging from the dark expressions of both Barth and Valen, she guessed it wasn't a good sign. She left orders to begin mustering the companies by type of arms—archers, halberdiers, pikemen, and swordsmen. Thanks to the esoteric nature of many of their armaments, these were to be loose designations.

The White Guard were dispersed among the ranks as they usually were. If she closed her eyes and touched the Linking Stone, she could see through them, hear through them. She got a feel for the mood of her army this way—she could overhear heated conversations, could see the tension among the men as they sharpened axes and tended to frayed laces and makeshift shields. They were eager for battle, but were they ready? How could the White Guard best help? She'd been keeping the undead in reserve, using them as her eyes and ears and, if needed, her voice— she could speak through any or all of them at any time. But a good communication system wouldn't solve everything.

In her tent, Myreon pored over maps of the Citadel that, Valen assured her, were up to date. The miller's daughter had described a small door at the base of the cliff that eventually granted one access to the castle, but it was both too narrow to use as a point of serious entry and also on the far side of the village, meaning any who did attempt it could be easily exposed before they got there. Inserting a small team and hoping for the best seemed the only way, as there was no other option to get inside the castle without enchanted siege equipment, and her army had very little of that.

By the estimates of both Valen and Barth, the army camped outside the town was a full five thousand strong. Even with the extra volunteers the White Army had picked up along the march north, she had only about three thousand men to draw on, and a lot of those were poorly armed—and even worse-trained—irregulars. They were a mob more than an army. And the enemy had the high ground, to boot.

That left the White Guard.

Androlli's warning against deploying them in "a battlefield role" still hung with her. The last thing they needed was another enemy, least of all coming from Saldor, with all its sorcerous might. But the White Guard were also the only tactical edge she could think of—the temptation to send them to breach the secret door in the dead of night and murder everyone inside the castle was perversely large. But word of such an act would spread and spread quickly. No doubt the augurs of the Defenders of the Balance were scrying this battle and had been for weeks. If she used them in so blatant a fashion, they would be lost—and so would the White Army.

But Tor Erdun was only the first obstacle. Beyond it lay the city of Ayventry itself and Sahand's army—a smaller force, perhaps, but a more dangerous one. She couldn't let her own army break here, at its first engagement, and leave Eretheria defenseless in the face of Sahand's vicious mercenaries.

The voices of so many people seemed to crowd her thoughts as she considered the terrible options at her disposal. She thought of Tyvian's warnings about civil war, about Lyrelle's admonition against this kind of violence. She thought of poor little Bree, hugging her, *believing* she could save everyone. But she couldn't. No matter what she did in the next few days, a great many people were going to die. Good people. People who didn't deserve this.

The cause had to be worth it. If this was the price she had to pay, then the goal had to be a lofty one. Freedom for the people of Eretheria, an end to their needless suffering. Equality before the law. All that and more.

"General!" An old man in bleached-white livery saluted from outside her tent. Myreon emerged, squinting in the noonday sun. "The courier has returned, Magus," he said.

Myreon caught the look in the man's eye. "What happened?"

The courier had been flogged perhaps twenty times. The boy had arrived back at camp strapped over a mule, his bare back a ruin of blood-red ribbons of flesh. Though barely conscious, he was still able to deliver a letter. Myreon read it with her hands trembling with rage.

> *Your Highness,*
>
> *I cannot help but think you are insulting me by sending this peasant as courier. I do not take kindly to such insults, and so I have expressed my displeasure upon your boy's back. My doctors inform me that he will not die. I am merciful, as you see.*
>
> *I am prepared to parley with you this afternoon. Bring your witch and your walking dead—I do not fear you. You stand on my lands by birthright, and the Tower and Rose stands strong. I will hear your demands and then you will hear mine.*
>
> *Yours in kinship,*
>
> > *Fawnse Kadrian,*
> > *Count of Ayventry*

"Well?" Artus asked, looking over her shoulder.

Myreon folded the letter up. "He's young and arrogant. His tone of address was insulting to your lineage. But he still wants to meet."

Barth shook his head. "You'd still meet with him

after he did *that*? You could practically see the boy's ribs!"

"It was a stupid show of strength," Myreon said, cutting off what was sure to develop into another rant. "I think Fawnse's situation is worse than we imagine. He wants to look strong to hide his weakness, but it's his weakness that compels him to meet."

Artus nodded. "So what do we do?"

Myreon laid a bow ward on Artus with a touch of her hand and did the same for herself. "We go and see where the weakness lies."

The parley was prepared in under an hour. Myreon sat astride her dappled gray mare before a rank of her best armed soldiers—deserters from the Davram levies, mostly—with Artus on one side and Sir Valen on the other. They were unarmed, as requested, though Myreon—as a sorceress—could not realistically be described as such.

Across from them, so far as to be only specks, the corresponding delegation from the Ayventry side trotted toward them. Just like Myreon's party, they were flying the white flag of truce.

Artus examined them through the viewing glass. "I don't see any signs of treachery."

"One of them could be a sorcerer," Valen grumbled.

"Then it's a good thing I'm here." Myreon gave him a sharp look.

Valen grinned and shrugged. "Yes. I suppose that's a good point."

"Smooth, Valen. Real smooth." Artus chuckled. The two of them smiled at each other, sharing the laugh.

Myreon sighed and urged her horse forward. She would never understand Artus's ability to forgive and befriend people who once wanted him dead or in chains. And she even counted herself among that number.

The two parties met at approximately the middle of the vast hillside that separated the two armies. There wasn't much to distinguish it—a muddy spot in the middle of an empty pasture. Myreon figured all of the town's goats and sheep were probably locked up in pens and barns, safe from the hungry eyes of the White Army. And hungry they would be, too, if this battle didn't end quickly. Barth insisted they were less than two days away from running out of food, and, thanks to Sahand's scorched earth strategy, their supply lines stretched all the way back to Davram and Eretheria. Bandit raids were already becoming a problem.

Fawnse Kadrian, the Count of Ayventry, was only a boy—younger even than Artus was when Myreon had first met him. He was wearing ornate, enchanted plate mail but he didn't have the shoulders for it—his

head looked too small between the gleaming paul-
drons, like a boy trying on his father's armor. He had
a piggish little face and dark eyes that darted back
and forth between his retainers and Myreon. When
he spoke, his voice cracked. "No sorcerers! You could
enchant us!"

Myreon spread her hands to show all her fingers.
"Then we would be in violation of the truce, which
would result in an immediate battle, yes? We are
trying to avoid that."

"I know who you are." Fawnse pointed at her.
"You're the Gray Lady. You murdered my cousin in
cold blood."

Myreon glared at the boy. "Count Andluss was
killed by a drifter who knew a simple trick and a
series of bodyguards too stupid to anticipate it."

"Insult!" Fawnse's eyebrows leapt up. He pawed
for the hilt of a sword that wasn't there. "Did you hear
that?" he asked one of his lieutenants. "Did you hear
what she said?"

Artus cleared his throat. "Maybe we should begin
by introducing ourselves. I'm Artus of Eddon, Prince
of Eretheria."

Fawnse seemed to see Artus for the first time. His
expression changed immediately from one of outright
hostility to one of furtive caution. He eyed Artus like
a duelist gauging an opponent's style. "You will forgive me for saying so, but you are very informal for a
prince. Tell me, have you sat on the throne yet?"

Myreon scowled—she wasn't sure which she despised more: this boy's attempt at political intrigue, or the fact that he was so bad at disguising it. "The issue of legitimacy is not in question here. What *is* in question is whether we are going to lay siege to your castle or not."

Fawnse laughed. "You can't siege Tor Erdun! I have it garrisoned with two thousand men! You can go no further, General."

Valen looked at Myreon out of the corner of his eye. Myreon knew what he was thinking. Two thousand men? In *that* tiny castle? Where were they sleeping, the chicken coops?

Artus tried a different tactic. "We aren't your enemies, Your Grace. We are merely the enemies of Dellor and of Sahand. If you let us pass, no harm will befall a single vassal of yours, nor will we take anything without paying for it." He nodded to Valen, who produced a tightly packed purse and threw it to one of Fawnse's men. The man grunted as it hit him—it was heavy. "There's a lot more where that came from," Artus said.

The man undid the strings on the purse and poured out a handful of gold marks. The man's eyes nearly popped out of his head. He held out the handful of gold to Fawnse. The young count slapped it away. "Bribes now? Who do you think you are dealing with? How many times do you think you can insult me before my cavalry rout you from the field?"

Artus forced a smile. "Your Grace, if you could just—".

"You will listen to my demands!" Fawnse held his hand out and one of his retainers put a scroll in it. He unfurled it and began to read. "'Your rebellion is unlawful, your prince is illegitimate. You will surrender your leaders to me and the commoners shall be permitted to depart in peace. Those of noble birth will be ransomed back to their Houses. Those commoners who incited revolt'"—Fawnse sneered at Myreon—"'shall be beheaded for treason.'"

Myreon looked the boy over. His fingers gripped the parchment too tightly. His cheeks were a little sallow—indeed, Fawnse looked positively jaundiced. His two men looked no better—deep bags beneath their eyes from lack of sleep. An unhealthy pallor to them, too. She did her best to put on a winning smile. "Those are relatively poor terms you offer, Your Grace."

Fawnse furled the scroll. "I am willing to hear your counter-proposal."

Artus fiddled with his reins, causing his horse to dance a bit. "Well—"

Myreon cut him off. "We reject your proposal, Fawnse. Tomorrow we have a battle."

The Count of Ayventry's mouth fell open. "Wh... what? *What?*"

Myreon began to turn her horse around. "If you wish to offer your unconditional surrender before then, you know where to find us. Tell your servants they'll be well treated, too. Unlike you, I don't whip couriers."

Artus was staring at her. "But . . . Myreon . . . we haven't—"

"Let's go, Your Highness." Myreon flicked the reins and off she went. She didn't look to see if they were following her—they would, she knew. For the first time in what seemed like forever, she felt light in the saddle.

Because she knew exactly how to win this battle.

CHAPTER 12

UPHILL BATTLE

That night, on Myreon's orders, every man in camp had a cup of beer in his hand—the last few casks were tapped and drained, much to the joy of the army. The fires were stoked high, too, burning through more of their fuel than was strictly wise. It wouldn't last the night, but then Myreon didn't need it to. The camp echoed with good cheer and the sounds of voices raised in bawdy song. The noise echoed off the cliffs and up out of the valley—Myreon had no doubt it could be heard for miles.

In the midst of the merrymaking, Myreon worked some necromancy. It was easy enough to do—the song, the bright fires, the happy mood—made the

Lumen rest thick in the camp. The Lumen—the energy of life, of growth—was also the energy of undeath. This was a paradox to the untrained, who expected the living dead to crave the dark and draw power from the Ether—the energy of death. Of course, these people failed to understand what necromancy actually was: the giving of life.

By her sorcerous command, the White Guard slipped out of the camp, utterly silent as always, and crept up the slope separating the White Army from Fawnse's forces. Most of them she tasked to some basic manual labor in the fields—they dug with shovels and spades without rest and without complaint for some hours. A select group of others, though, infiltrated the camp of the enemy, disguised with some simple glamours and basic shrouds to make them difficult to recognize as undead in the dark. Their unnatural quiet and the distraction poised by the White Army made it easy for the constructs to slip past the sentries. Also there were fewer sentries than there probably should have been. This confirmed her suspicions.

Peering through the eyes of her undead servants, Myreon got a good look at the enemy camp. It was as she expected—as the meeting with Fawnse implied and the lack of sentries indicated. The army of Ayventry was starving, on the very edge of disaster. Everywhere the White Guard looked, they found famished soldiers in worse condition than her own, eating chipmunks and gnawing on roots. As peasant levies of House Ayventry, they were modestly equipped—good boots being the primary piece of kit that caught her attention—but they were angry. They squatted by their sputtering fires and spat curses. Not all the curses were directed at her, either.

At the center of the camp were the pavilions of the knights. They were not substantially better off in terms of food. They complained to one another. They fought over trifles. From what she heard through the ears of the White Guard, they had been stationed here for three weeks. They had eaten through their supplies in ten days. They had stripped the town clean of its meat and grain in another seven. It had been four days now without proper food. The situation in the castle, they said, was worse.

And of course it was—an army of eight thousand camped in one place for nearly a month? And in the mountains, too? What was Sahand *thinking*? The soldiers outnumbered the townspeople by seven or eight to one! This was a small trading post, meant to accommodate a trade caravan of hundreds, not an army of thousands. Even with supplies working their way down the Freegate Road from Ayventry, it was a hundred miles away. And from the way Fawnse's man had stared at that gold, it was clear they didn't have the money to pay for much in the way of supplies, anyway. Sahand had set this army up to fail. It made Myreon's skin crawl to consider why, but that didn't matter at the moment. What mattered was winning the day.

At her willed command, a dozen different White Guards stepped into the firelight in a dozen different gatherings throughout the Ayventry camp. They spoke with her voice:

"The Gray Lady bids you good evening, gentlemen. As a champion of all Eretheria, she invites you and your friends to join her in her camp this evening. There is food and song and good cheer, and no one will do you harm. At daybreak, any who remain here will fight and die for Count Fawnse. Any who join the Young Prince may take their ease tomorrow, and watch the battle from a safe distance."

Then they each cast down a pouch of silver crowns and departed, leaving the shocked Ayventry men to wrestle with their own allegiance—and each other, trying to get the coins.

Some of the men attacked her messengers—plunging knives into their bodies or hurling stones at them. The White Guard, of course, were unconcerned with such assaults. They retreated in good order, and the men who attacked them were too frightened to follow.

But many *others* followed. In the light of a half moon, the red tabards of thousands of Ayventry men stumbled down the slope in the dark toward the light and life of the White Army. There, at the foot of the hill, Barth and his best men were there to welcome them.

This will eat through all our supplies, Barth had warned when Myreon explained her plan to him.

Better lost food than lost lives, Myreon had responded.

The Ayventry deserters were given a full share of stew and bread, clean water and, if they had descended early, a taste of beer. Myreon had seen to it that they were welcomed like brothers, invited to join the White Army men around the fire. No weapons, no threats, no trouble.

It worked. There were a few fights, true, and a few Ayventry men trudged back up the hill before dawn, but most of them stayed. There were so many of them, it was like a new, third army had grown up overnight—twenty-five-hundred men slept in borrowed tents and lounged around enemy campfires when the sun rose.

In the morning light, the White Army stood in ranks, ready to advance on the field of battle. Now, instead of being outnumbered by more than two to one, Myreon's forces had the clear numerical advantage. This had another effect on the empty-bellied legions of Count Fawnse: footmen began to quit the field. Through the viewing glass, Myreon saw dozens of men throw down their spears and tear off their tabards, to the anguish of the knights put in charge of them. Unrest and ill-discipline spread through the Ayventry ranks like an evil wind.

Valen shook his head as he witnessed this. "I can't believe it. Just like at Fanning Ford. It's the same damned thing all over again."

Myreon gave him a cool glance. "The master is always alarmed to discover his slave has desires beyond his own."

Valen scowled, but had the good sense to bow his head. Artus, in the saddle beside him, put a hand on the young knight's shoulder. "You saved a lot of men's lives that day, Valen. You spared your county a lot of pain. You should be proud of yourself."

Valen nodded. He looked at Myreon. "You can think what you like about my grandmother, but she wasn't an evil woman. She wanted the best for her family and for her county—most of the peerage is the same. They just—*we* just lost perspective."

Myreon pointed to the long rank of enemy knights moving up to try to flank the White Army. "Their loss of perspective is about to attempt to ride us down as we advance."

She nodded to Barth, who was on foot alongside a long rank of archers. At her signal, Barth raised a baton. "Archers! Ready!"

A few hundred peasants nocked arrows and drew to the corners of their eyes, sighting the colorful plumes and bright pennants of the encroaching Ayventry heavy cavalry. Barth's voice boomed across the battlefield. "LOOSE!"

The arrows flew in a gentle arc, hitting the forward knights in the enemy formation. There was comparatively little effect—the armor of the knights was thick and the bows they had in numbers weren't formidable Galaspin longbows or even crossbows, but rather simple hunting weapons. At this range, they lacked the power to punch through plate, to say nothing of whatever bow wards or sorcerous guards the knights had active. A few knights went down or fell off their horses, but not enough to make much of a dent in their numbers. It was all right—they weren't supposed to. Myreon just wanted them goaded into action—she wanted the knights to be eager for blood. To get their adrenaline racing.

A few more volleys rained down on the knights as they closed, the thunder of hooves now clearly audible even over the din of the White Army. The archers were recalled and the footmen called forward, spears and glaives and hook-ended bills held out and braced against the earth—ready to receive a charge.

At just under a hundred yards distant, that charge began. A clear trumpet note sounded, the knights' lances lowered, and their horses leapt forward. The slope was steep enough that the knights couldn't lean in—they had to balance their weight atop their mounts, so as not to fall—but the momentum of the attack was undeniable. Even though she knew what was about to happen, Myreon couldn't help but tighten her grip on the reins and cast a few powerful guards on herself and her mount. The call of the trumpet, the flash of the lance tips—many enchanted to explode on impact—the heart-stopping rumble of the hooves; the sight of stray arrows pinging off invisible walls of force surrounding the knights. Myreon's instincts called out for her to run. Instead, she shouted, "Steady! Steady men of Eretheria!"

Barth did her one better. "HOLD, YOU BAS-TARDS!"

The White Army, with full bellies and dreams of victory, held fast.

The charge never reached the lines.

The first knight to hit one of the deadfall traps was a standard bearer. The horse pitched forward as its front legs vanished into a shallow trench concealed by grass-covered cloth. As it screamed, the man flew from the saddle and landed, face-first, in the dirt and kept rolling. Another horse fell. And another. And another. One horse would fall and take out another few nearby. Knights tried to pull their mounts up, tried to keep their mounts from trampling their friends who fell in front of them—it was too late, though. The trenches the White Guard had dug through the night were working.

When the remains of the cavalry hit the pike line, it was not with the force of a wall of steel a hundred men wide, but instead a few isolated knights slamming into the White Army's ranks and being pulled from the saddle in the ensuing melee. In a matter of moments, the might of Ayventry lay strewn across the battlefield, injured and dazed and dead. The shrieks of man and beast echoed through the air.

It wasn't over.

Myreon raised her staff. "Now!"

Barth picked up his war-hammer and hefted it over his head. "FORWARD!"

With a triumphant cry, the White Army headed up the hill. On foot, disorganized, hurt, and wildly outnumbered, the dismounted knights didn't stand a chance. Most surrendered at once, but some fought— Myreon didn't take the time to observe how it all went. Barth knew his job and she left him to do it.

She, Valen, Artus, and the remaining cavalry began their own advance toward the ragged Ayventry lines at the top of the hill. With the destruction of their heavy cavalry in front of their eyes, they seemed hesitant to give up the high ground and join the fray. Arrows began to fall among Myreon's troops, not in waves but piecemeal; the bow wards she had woven for the front ranks of knights were sufficient to bat them aside. When they were within a few hundred yards, she began to throw some missiles of her own—balls of fire and lightning, designed more to terrify than to kill. It was enough. When the knights of the White Army hit Ayventry's flank, the men there were disordered and uncertain. The shock of their enchanted lances into the ranks was the last thing the Ayventrymen's nerves could take. They broke and ran, getting tangled with the blocks of infantry to their right who were trying to organize a push back against the advance from the White Army center. Sheer panic and confusion ensued.

The world got smaller for Myreon. She was in battle now, her Defender training coming back to the fore. She smote to the left and right with her staff, drawing on the sunny weather to blind the enemy with sunblasts. She lost track of exactly who was beside her—at one moment Valen, at another Artus.

And then she wasn't beside anyone—she took a sharp blow to the back from a polearm. The guard she had woven earlier took most of the impact, but the force of the blow knocked her off balance. For one frightening moment, she felt the world tumble—light and dark, light and dark. The breath was knocked out of her. She had been unhorsed. Her horse, panicked with the battle, had kept running. She stood up.

Ayventry soldiers seemed everywhere, but most of them had the fight already sapped out of them. She worked her sorcery and advanced. They saw her, blazing with power, and fled. And for a moment she was able to pause and survey her surroundings.

The White Army was churning its way uphill, engaged with blocks of Ayventry pikes in several directions, but with superior numbers and morale winning the day. Fawnse's army—now almost com-

pletely comprised of peasant levies and footmen—
was falling back toward the town and beneath the
protective range of Tor Erdun's siege engines.

Looking around, she spotted Sir Valen riding, his
sword drawn and bloody, the banner of the White
Army in his off hand. "Valen!"

He spotted her and pulled up his horse. He snapped
his visor back, revealing a face wild with the madness
of battle. "General! They're retreating—not quite a
rout, but close enough!"

"Harry them! Chase them right back into the
town—spread the word. We don't let up until that
town is ours! Then get inside that door and dig out
Fawnse!"

Valen smiled and slapped his visor back down.
"Yes ma'am!"

Myreon headed the other direction—toward the
blocks of White Army footmen headed her way.

Artus kept riding, arrows plinking off his bow wards,
his enchanted shield gleaming in the sunlight. Valen
was back on his right again, banner held high. To his
left was one of the hedge knights from Hadda—a
giant fellow swinging around a huge mace with
less-than-expert skill. Behind was the other Hadda
knight, who was mostly holding on to his horse for
dear life, his head down. Somewhere along the line
they'd lost the rest of their escort—to the left and

right they heard the crash of steel against steel and the screams of the injured and dying.

Ahead of them, men in red tabards fled in disorganized mobs, their weapons discarded. Sometimes a brave soul would step forth with a halberd or spear and Artus or his companions would ride him down with barely a break in their horses' stride.

Then they were in the camp. Artus threw a handful of sparkstones as they passed, lighting tents aflame. Valen swung his sword in graceful arcs, striking off heads. The big fellow did something similar with his mace, crushing skulls. He could feel the mood of the men he faced *break* somehow. For the first time in his life, he witnessed the change from an orderly retreat into a true rout. No one was fighting back now. No one was even looking behind them as they ran. When they had ridden straight through the enemy camp to the side closest to the town, Artus held up his hand and called a halt.

His horse was hot beneath him, its nostrils flared, and he could smell the pungent sweat wafting up from beneath its barding. He'd just pushed the animal at a near gallop uphill for the gods knew how long. It was probably best he give the creature a moment to collect itself. He looked around.

It turned out they were not alone—a dozen or so of Artus's knights were blazing their way through the camp, too. They were now situated to the rear of the main Ayventry force, which was also retreating from the determined advance of the White Army. He supposed he might have ordered everyone to turn around and charge their rear, but he was skeptical that a dozen knights charging an army of thousands was going to make much difference. Besides, that wasn't the plan. Valen waved the banner, calling the other knights to him.

Ahead was Erdun town. At another time in another lifetime, the place might have been picturesque—a quaint mountain town with steeply shingled roofs and colorful flowerboxes in every window. Today, though, the town was boarded up and its streets were muddy and packed with panicky Ayventry levies trying to force their way into houses or hide in stables. Above the town, at least two hundred feet up, loomed Tor Erdun itself. Artus could see activity on the battlements—the glint of steel as men rushed from crenel to crenel.

"We're in range of their siege engines, aren't we?" Artus asked Valen.

Valen put back his visor and looked up. "I should say so, sire. But I rather doubt they'll be tossing trebuchet stones into their own army's camp."

At that moment, a boulder the size of a large barrel arced over the ramparts and tumbled toward them. Artus froze with terror as he watched it pass just over them and land with a heavy *boom* in the camp just behind them. Then the projectile exploded, throwing carts and tents and equipment and men twenty feet into the air. A piece of rock struck Artus squarely on the back and knocked him out of the saddle. The big man's horse went down when its back leg was taken out, and Valen barely managed to keep his seat as his mount reared in terror.

Artus rolled onto his back and sat up. He had to shout over the ringing in his ears. "You were saying?"

Valen pointed up. "Look out!"

Two more enchanted boulders struck the earth nearby. One hit near a trio of Artus's knights, blowing them into bloody pieces in the blink of an eye. The other struck a barn on the outskirts of the town, reducing it to a cloud of wooden splinters accelerating in all directions. Artus held his enchanted shield up to take most of the blow. Valen cried out—a one-foot spike of wood was wedged between his pauldron and his breastplate; blood spilled down his armor.

The big hedge knight was on his feet. "They're reloading. To the village! Quick!"

Artus helped Valen out of the saddle and they ran toward the town. Some of his knights, still mounted, rode with them, their eyes fixed on the battlements above.

"They won't bombard the town," Valen said through clenched teeth. "They wouldn't dare."

No one challenged them as they rushed past the boarded-up houses. Any enemy soldiers they saw fell on their faces at the sight of Artus's gleaming shield or Valen's bloody sword, begging for mercy.

The trebuchets released again. Everyone in the

streets of Erdun froze, tracking the trajectory of the deadly boulders.

Valen was wrong once again.

The first boulder hit in the middle of a street, blowing the front walls of two houses inward and setting them ablaze. The second crashed through the inn with a direct hit, obliterating half the massive building with a deafening explosion. The third landed in an empty pigsty and left a crater of mud deep enough to make a swimming hole.

"Saints," Artus swore. "What in blazes does that little prick Fawnse think he's doing?"

The town erupted into pure panic. The fleeing soldiers in the streets scattered like mice. Townspeople shot out of cellars and charged from locked doors to come to the aid of their neighbors. Women were screaming in one of the burning houses.

Artus's knights formed a defensive perimeter around him, swords drawn, but no one attacked them. Artus was at a loss over what to do—what *could* he do?

The trebuchets loosed again. Three more houses were crushed. Dozens were killed, all of them either townsfolk or Fawnse's own levies. Artus could scarcely understand the sheer inhumanity of it.

But he didn't need to understand. He needed to act. "Valen, get the townspeople out of here."

Valen had lost his helmet somehow. "Sire?"

"Get them back to our own lines if you have to! See to it!"

Valen flinched as a trebuchet stone exploded on the other side of town. "You have to come with me, sire—we have to get you to safety!"

Artus gestured to the madness around him—burning houses, fear-mad soldiers, boulders raining from the sky. "We're in the middle of a battlefield, Valen—where the hell would 'safety' be, anyway? Go—do your duty!"

Valen nodded and was off, shouting at the closest few men—knights of Davram who had surrendered at Fanning Ford, mostly—and headed off, kicking in doors and trying to pull people out of burning houses.

That left the two Hadda knights, whatever their names were. The big one was staring dumbly at the devastation around them while the broad one was crouched into a ball, holding on to his helm as though it were a hat in the wind. Artus yelled at them both. "We've got to stop Fawnse!"

The big one said nothing. The other one squeaked, "We're . . . we're gonna die!"

Artus put out his hand. "You'll only die if you stay here. But come with me, and I'll make us all heroes."

The man looked at Artus's hand. "Are you crazy?"

Artus forced himself to smile and shook his head. "This won't even be the craziest thing I've done *this year*. C'mon, boys—we've got a castle to take."

The man pointed up the cliff face toward the castle. "But there's two thousand men in that castle!"

"And I promise to leave some for you—come on!"

The man reached up and took his hand. Artus hauled him to his feet just as another trebuchet stone blew up a stable nearby. Instinctively, Artus pushed the man behind him and held up his shield, warding off the shrapnel that would have torn the two Hadda knights to ribbons. When he turned back around, they were both blinking at him, stunned.

Well, they'll either follow me, or they won't. Artus took off running toward the cliff face, still with one eye upward.

The two knights followed.

They didn't have to fight their way to Tor Erdun's bolt-hole door. All they had to do was dodge the destruction raining on the village and avoid the screaming people running for their lives. Always keeping an eye on the battlements above, Artus decided the trebuchets on the second siege turret were now throwing boulders at the armies themselves. Given the deployment of his own soldiers, Fawnse had to be dropping explosive ordnance on his own men as often as the enemy, but the boy-count seemed not to care. He had to be stopped, and the bolt-hole was the only way.

The door was small—Artus would have to duck to go through it—and well-concealed behind a bush. Had it not been for the miller's daughter's knowledge of the castle, they would never have known where to look. The door was perfectly round and iron-banded, with no doorknob of any kind on this side—a door to escape from, not enter through.

Behind them both, another explosion rocked the town. It made Artus flinch. "Dammit! How are we going to get in?"

The big knight hefted his huge mace. "Stand back." He slammed the weapon against the door with all his weight. The wood cracked down the middle. Then the other knight was there, a battle-axe in both hands, hacking at the breach. In under a minute, the door was broken open.

The big one was almost the first through, but Artus grabbed him by the shoulder. "Royalty first."

The giant man refused to budge. "That's not the plan . . . umm . . . sire."

Plan? What plan? Artus didn't have time to argue— he just sighed and shoved the enchanted shield into the big fellow's hands. "Lead with this, at least."

In they went. The tunnel beyond was small—almost claustrophobic—and lit with illumite in tiny sconces every twenty paces or so. Artus couldn't imagine trying to escape a castle this way—fleeing in the dead of night, terrified by what was happening behind you, stumbling and crawling down through the dark. Of course, now that he was thinking about it, stumbling and crawling *up* through the winding tunnel toward a castle full of people who wanted to kill him sounded little better. He had originally thought this was a clever trick on their part, but now he was realizing that it wasn't so much a "plan" as a brash course of action.

Story of his life, he guessed.

The giant knight was ahead of him, shield held up in case of ambush. Behind Artus was the other one. It occurred to him suddenly that he knew almost nothing about either man—nothing about their allegiances, their provenance. He couldn't even tell if they were really knights—he certainly had never seen knights ride as terribly as they had. What if he was wrong about them? It wouldn't take much for the man behind him to draw a knife and plunge it into a chink in his armor as they climbed. The hair on the back of his neck stood on end.

After what seemed like forever, the big fellow grunted as he ran into something. "Hold on—it's a door. I think we're there!"

"Hurry!" Artus whispered.

The knight fumbled in the dark. "Found the handle. Here we go."

There was a ray of light and a breath of fresh air. Artus followed the lead knight into a storeroom, probably in the foundations of the castle. It was bare—picked clean. Myreon had been right; the defenders were starving. A woman poked her head into the room, eyes wide with fear. A servant, probably—she must have heard the door open.

The knight behind him drew a knife but Artus caught his arm. Artus smiled at her instead. "It's all right—we mean you no harm!"

The woman—no, the *girl*—cocked her head when she looked at Artus. "Are you . . . the prince?"

The big knight pushed past her and peered into the hall beyond. "Nobody coming."

The girl's eyes widened. "You *are!*" She fell to her knees, caught Artus's hand, and began kissing his knuckles. "Thank Hann! Thank all the gods!"

The two knights exchanged glances. The big one grunted at the other one. "Well, Ham?"

The smaller one—the one named "Ham"—shook his head. "I dunno, Mort. It don't seem right."

Mort's hands tightened around the shaft of his mace. He held "Ham's" gaze for a good long moment, and then relaxed, nodding.

Artus cocked an eyebrow at them, but before he could ask what it was about, the maid was tugging on his arm. "His Grace has gone batty, sire! You've got to stop him!"

"That's the basic idea, ma'am. Now, where can I find the little louse?"

The girl blushed deeply, which for just a moment obscured the thinness of her face and the bags under her eyes. "I know the best way. Follow me." She slipped past Mort with a curtsey and led them up the stairs.

Artus caught his eye as he passed. "What was that about, just now?"

Mort's wide face was impassive. "Nothing. Just a bet we had."

Artus frowned at the lie. "Did you win?"

The big man shook his head. "Nope."

Nope? That settled it—these men were no knights. But if they wanted to kill him, he guessed they would have just done so. For all he knew, that was what the "bet" was about, but he didn't have time to suss out every plot in the world right now. First things first.

The girl led them through the crowded castle via the corners and back hallways known only to the servants of a great house. The soldiers they saw were too exhausted to put up much of a fight or too unwilling to die for Fawnse—they pretended they didn't see the three armored men creeping through the castle or surrendered before Mort could smash them into paste with his mace.

Then they were at the base of a long staircase. The girl pointed upward. "He's up there, at the top of the tall tower. Go quickly, please."

Artus kissed her hand. "I am in your debt."

She blushed again and curtsied and then they were running up the stairs, weapons drawn. They heard Fawnse screaming before they were halfway up. "They aren't stopping! Why aren't they stopping! Why aren't they fighting them? Traitors! Cowards!"

When they were at the open trap door, Artus nodded to Ham and Mort. "Quickly now, but leave the count alive."

They nodded in return and then charged into the room. Fawnse had three men with him—the two that had been his retainers at the parley and an older man tied to a chair. Artus didn't take the time to make sense of the situation—he swung his sword at the back of one of the men's knees, cutting through the mail there with the bladecrystal-enchanted edge. Just behind him, Mort's mace took the other man in the hip, the force of the blow propelling him through the window of the observation tower and into the empty air beyond. Ham tackled Fawnse in short order, before the boy could draw a wand.

"No!" the boy-count shrieked. "NO! Unhand me! Treachery! Treachery!"

Artus finished off his man with a sword thrust under the armpit and drew his broadsword out, crimson with blood. He put the tip of the blade at Fawnse's nose. "Surrender."

"Never! You're no prince! You were supposed to be my prisoner! I was promised!" Fawnse's fleshy cheeks were purple with rage. They were also wet with tears—he'd been crying. *But over what?* Artus wondered.

"If you don't surrender, I'm going to kill you, prince or not." Artus raised his arm as though about to thrust.

The man in the chair spoke up. "Kill him! Run him through, my liege! If you have any sense of justice, see him to hell!"

Artus looked over at the man. He had a white beard and clear blue eyes. His face was marred by a massive purple bruise. "Who are you?"

"The Earl of Tor Erdun and the rightful castellan

of this fortress. Fawnse is my nephew, though I hereby renounce any relation, Hann help me!"

Outside, another trebuchet stone exploded below. Artus didn't have time to figure this all out. "Surrender, Fawnse! Surrender or the trebuchets toss you next!"

Fawnse's rabid angry expression melted into simple tears. His body shook with sobs. "It's . . . it's not fair . . . it's not fair . . . I was . . . I was supposed to win! Me! *I was promised!*"

Artus put up his sword. Ham and Mort threw the Count of Ayventry on the ground, where the boy curled himself into a ball and continued to weep. Everyone stared at the sight.

Finally, Artus shook his head. "Somebody stop those damned trebuchets, strike the colors, and open the bloody gates. This battle is over."

CHAPTER 13

BACKUP PLAN

Tyvian's role in the Battle of Tor Erdun had been intentionally minimal. Without a horse of his own, he couldn't ride with the knights and was left behind. This was just as well—Tyvian had very limited experience riding a horse *toward* danger, and Artus would have spotted him anyway. As for joining the infantry, that had been avoided most easily by hiding in Voth's tent as the call to muster went up. Predictably enough, the White Army lacked sufficient sergeants or similar persons to go kick shirkers out of their bedrolls. Given the soldiers' collective hatred of Dellor and Ayventry, however, such men were hardly needed. The vast majority of men had turned out in good spirits.

Left alone in the camp, Tyvian had slept in late with Voth, for once, at his side. They only woke up to the deep boom of enchanted trebuchet stones detonating in Erdun town. He pulled on a shirt and some hose and went out to look.

Eddereon was standing outside the tent, his hand shading his eyes as he looked up at the castle far, far above. His face was grim. "They're bombarding the town. It's burning."

Tyvian followed his gaze to see the black plumes of smoke billowing from the base of the cliff, visible over the chaotic debris of the battle that was still raging at its foot. He felt the ring twinge. "Do you feel it, too?"

Eddereon rubbed his ring hand. "Yes. Nothing to be done, though. We should have joined the battle."

"Artus would see you. He'd know you anywhere." Tyvian squinted into the rising sun. "It's up to him and Myreon to stop it."

The two of them watched, side by side, their rings jabbing them every time an explosion echoed over the battlefield. Tyvian found himself holding his breath. *Come on, boy*, he thought, *do something. Stop them.*

He felt another twinge, coming not from the ring, but deep in his spine. He wanted to rush out there and fight. To take up a sword next to Artus and help Myreon win her battle and bring a better day to Eretheria. He balled his fists and clenched his teeth. *No. You've done enough.*

But the fact of it didn't help. He felt impotent. Useless. Forgotten. He sat now on the sidelines and watched others claim glory. It did not feel good, but Tyvian knew from hard experience that charging off to right wrongs didn't feel any better. They usually felt worse.

When the trebuchets did, at last, stop and the Ayventry banner was struck from the spire of Tor Erdun, a loud cheer erupted from the massed ranks of the White Army. Tyvian joined them, clapping his hands. He looked over to see Eddereon smiling as well, but not at the castle—at him. "What?"

Eddereon stuck out his hand to shake. "I never officially welcomed you back."

Frowning, Tyvian shook it. "To what?"

Eddereon's big hand squeezed his tight. "To the human race."

Tyvian pulled his hand back. "Let's not get overly dramatic. We should have been out there, you and me. We should have helped them."

"You did help them, Tyvian. Without you, none of this would be happening. This victory was something you sacrificed your old life for. Don't forget that."

In the aftermath of the battle, orders came down that the camp was to be struck and the army to move through the pass the following dawn. The remainder of the afternoon was spent looting the battlefield by those who still had the energy to do so after a hard day's fight. Tyvian and Voth joined the mobs of scavengers tearing good boots off the feet of dead Ayventrymen. They were not there to loot, though, but to reconnoiter.

The gossip running downhill was that Prince Artus had taken the castle nearly single-handedly, with only two of his most trusted knights at his side. Voth had a dark expression when they heard this from a skinny fellow in a bloodstained tabard with a large collection of shoes hanging around his neck by the laces. Tyvian heard her mutter, "Those two fools better be dead."

Tyvian pretended he didn't hear. *Hambone and Mort just screwed up, eh? What a bloody surprise.* He suppressed a grin as they kept walking up the slope toward the village.

Though the White Army had won, losses were severe, primarily because Count Fawnse's fit of pique took the form of exploding boulders. It was impossible to get a firm count of the dead, but Tyvian estimated the casualties would run well over a thousand either dead or too injured to be any more use in any further battles. The knights of the White Army, such as they were, barely existed at this point—the word was that less than ten men lived, assuming you counted Hambone and Mort, which Tyvian felt was perhaps overgenerous. What remained to be seen was whether Young Prince Artus could convince any of the Ayventry peers to join them. As the White Army was preparing to invade Ayventry territory,

Tyvian felt that was a slim hope—nobody was going to convince peers to invade their own lands and besiege their own castles. Not even the "Young Prince."

Prisoners would be a serious problem, then. Tyvian spotted a row of men in padded tunics—men stripped of their armor, in other words—walking, hands on their heads, in a row down the hill. Captured knights—at least a hundred of them. There were also more red tabards on newly shoeless levies than could be reasonably counted. Destroying the army of Ayventry was going to prove more costly than fighting it, he'd guess.

Then there was the carnage of Erdun town. The only structure left standing was the hardy Hannite church at the center, its stone walls protected by ancient wards imbued by priests several centuries dead. The church had sheltered a significant number of townspeople, but not a majority. Those who had opted to hide out in their own cellars or homes to protect from looting had died as the rocks fell. Again, counting the dead was beyond him—Tyvian merely stared at the ruins of a once prosperous town, unable to verbalize his horror. He had travelled through here many times in his life. He had always enjoyed the grand fireplace in the common room of the Passage, and the taste of the mulled cider the innkeeper kept by the barrel behind the bar. Now only the fireplace remained—a lone cairn of stone in the midst of charred wooden beams and rubble.

It was a disaster. No, it was an *atrocity*. He couldn't

believe what he was seeing. Eddereon's words came echoing back to him: *Without you, none of this would be happening.*

He felt sick.

Voth, if she felt the same way, gave no indication. She surveyed the damage with apparent disinterest. "Let's get to the castle."

Tyvian followed her, his body numb. If Voth had elected to stab him dead, right there on the battle-field, he didn't think he'd care.

A crowd had formed in the small courtyard of the castle. It was packed with an even mix of White Army soldiers, Ayventry prisoners, and townspeople who had survived the bombardment. All of them were howling for blood, which was perhaps predictable. What was peculiar was that they were all demanding the same person's blood—the Count of Ayventry.

Ducking just inside the portico, Tyvian and Voth hid toward the back of the crowd, hoods pulled up to conceal their faces. Standing on a balcony over-looking the courtyard were Artus, Myreon, Barth, and a bearded old man Tyvian recognized as the old Earl of Tor Erdun. The young count was nowhere to be seen.

Artus was trying to calm everyone down by waving his arms. It was having a limited effect. "Please! Let us speak, will ya?"

"He's a murderer!" a woman in the crowd shrieked. "Death to him! Death to them all!"

Roars of approval from the crowd. Tyvian wondered what the woman defined as "them."

Myreon raised her staff and tapped it down, which caused a heart-stopping boom to echo through the courtyard. Everyone fell silent. "There is little doubt that Count Fawnse has committed a grave crime. He is currently in our custody and, when the time is right, he will stand trial for his deeds."

This was unpopular, even among the people standing on the balcony. Barth's expression was so grim, Tyvian would not have been surprised to see lighting shoot out of his beard at any moment.

"No trial!" shouted a man in a white tabard. "Death now! Bring us a headsman!"

The crowd cheered.

Artus looked frustrated. "Look, we can't just go chopping off heads! Isn't that what this whole war is about to begin with—injustice? Fawnse is just a kid! He deserves a trial."

"Why?" screamed a man with a bloody face. "So you can let him go? So you can ransom him back to Sahand?"

Artus tried to say, *of course not*, but the sentiment was drowned out by a sea of jeers. Tyvian looked at the crowd—he saw rage and fear in a lethal mix of faces.

Myreon once again restored order with a booming blow of her staff. "People of Eretheria, we hear your concerns. I understand your anger—we all share it. His Highness is right, though. We must not become a mob—we must remain a people."

Voth grunted. "Fat chance of that," she muttered. Tyvian noted that she was watching the faces on the balcony with keen interest. From his angle, though, he couldn't tell whose face she was lingering on.

"For now," Myreon continued, "we must win the war first and punish its criminals later. We must take Ayventry and scatter Sahand's armies once more—then, and only then, can we discuss the fate of Count Fawnse."

"Booooo!" the crowd howled.

Artus cut in, "Remember who *put* Fawnse here! Remember who started this war! It's Sahand—always Sahand! Fawnse is just his tool, and a stupid tool to boot! Let's stay focused, okay?"

More boos. Voth turned away from the crowd and grabbed Tyvian by the arm. "I've seen enough. Let's go."

They left, arm in arm, like actual lovers. Walking down the winding road that led to the town ruins and then the battlefield and the camp beyond, Tyvian had a lot of time to think. Sahand *had* placed Fawnse here, and with a force far too large for the land or their provisions to support. Sahand had also ordered his mercenary companies to delay and distract the White Army, therefore slowing them down. He had to have known how this battle would go. He *had* to have known he was starving his own allies into some kind of horrific debacle.

Sahand was brutal and, at times, terribly obtuse about some things, but he had always been a keen military mind. Assuming, therefore, that putting an immature and inexperienced commander in charge of a large, underprovisioned force was not a *mistake* but, in reality, a *ploy*, what then was the ploy?

Well, for one thing, he had inflicted heavy casualties on the White Army *and* saddled them with enormous numbers of prisoners. He'd also angered them, goading them to come for him. Ayventry, as everyone knew, was not suited to resisting a siege, so what was the point of drawing the White Army to attack him at Ayventry?

Unless it was all a trap.

But what kind of trap? And for whom? And what could Tyvian actually do about it?

Voth squeezed his arm. "Stay with me now, lover. You make me nervous when you think that hard."

Tyvian nodded. He forced himself to smile at the pretty assassin. "Yeah. Me too."

When Mort and Hambone didn't return from the castle, Tyvian assumed that they had either betrayed Voth or been compromised. According to Voth, however, neither was precisely true—they'd just "lost their nerve." The mission, it seemed, was still going. They needed to keep a low profile, though, just in case the two Delloran soldiers *had* given them away.

Searching for any particular person in a disorganized camp of thousands of people would have been a difficult job for trained professionals, and that was assuming the person you were searching for was an amateur and unaware of their risk. In the White Army, they had no professional manhunters among them and, furthermore, Voth was a consummate mimic. A roll in the dirt, some white powder in her hair, and a couple minor glamours, and she looked just like a middle-aged washerwoman with a blind eye. She didn't even have to switch tents—she just sat out front with a washboard and a bucket and scrubbed Tyvian's hose and it was as though the farm girl had never existed. As it turned out, though, nobody ever did come looking. Ham and Mort, it seemed, hadn't turned them in. At least not yet. Voth kept up the act, just in case.

Tyvian was hiding in plain sight, too. It was astonishing how well it worked sometimes. Here he was—the crowned king of Eretheria—and not a single one of his subjects recognized him in the least. There had to be scores of people he actually *met* on the night of his coronation, and still nothing. Tyvian didn't know how to feel about that. Part of him wanted to laugh at the absurdity of it all—here was a war being fought over his death, and not a damned one of them could pick him out of a crowd.

Voth stopped washing. "You can finish this. I'm not your servant."

Tyvian waggled a finger at her. "Appearances are everything, Adatha—don't get cocky."

Voth rolled her good eye. "That nephew of yours is full of surprises, isn't he?"

"He isn't my nephew. We are of no particular relation." Tyvian frowned.

"Good," Voth said, walking past him and into the tent.

Tyvian followed. Inside, the tent was dark, lit only by the faint glow of campfires bleeding through the thick fabric. "He's why we're staying, isn't he? He's your target?"

"Too many questions, Reldamar." Voth snaked her arms around Tyvian's waist and pulled him close to her. She kissed him on the throat, then the chin, then the lips.

Tyvian pushed her away. "If you're planning to kill Artus, then I'm a liability. That means you're going to kill me next, yes?"

Voth sighed. "You always manage to ruin things." She sat on the bed, hugging herself.

Tyvian had seen this before. "The same exact trick as last time? You sulk, I come to comfort you, and then I find myself poisoned?"

Voth said nothing. Her silhouette, just barely visible in the darkness, showed her to be facing away from him. But her shoulders weren't shaking with sobs. There was no sniffling. Nothing like last time. Though perhaps that was part of the trap.

"I meant those things I said, you know," Voth said at last. Her voice was barely a whisper.

Tyvian kept his distance, hand close to his knife. "What things?"

"In your house. Just before I poisoned you," she said. "I meant those things."

"You mean about feeling kinship with me? About you hoping I actually . . . wanted you?"

Voth said nothing for a moment. "Once I'd met you, once I'd figured out who you were . . . I didn't really *want* to kill you, you know. Not really."

"So, what, you poisoned me out of a sense of professional pride?"

Voth turned her head. Her teeth caught just enough light to glow white in the dark. She was grinning. "Of course. It was a contract from the Countess of Davram—I wasn't about to renege. You understand, don't you?"

Tyvian silently slid his knife out of its sheath and concealed it behind his back. Then he gingerly sat on the bed beside Voth. "Yes, I understand. I think."

"I lost my eye to my father's knife," Voth said. "The world is a hard place and a woman has to be hard right back. That's how I am."

"Then you'll have to kill me."

Voth arms were still crossed in front of her chest, hands on her shoulders. She didn't move. Tyvian, so close to her, remained coiled, ready to strike. What weapons did Voth have about her person? A poison needle concealed in her clothing? A hidden blade?

"I still don't want to kill you, Tyvian," Voth said. She bowed her head. "I knew it when that animal Rodall had you on the ground. I was . . . I was *happy* you were alive. I hadn't even realized I was sad before that, but when you looked at me and gave me that wink . . ."

In spite of himself, Tyvian grinned and nudged her with an elbow. "Don't take it too hard. I have that effect on a lot of women."

Voth laughed. "I have never been so stupid as I am with you, Tyvian Reldamar." She leaned her head against his shoulder. "If I tell you I'm planning to kill the Young Prince, will you stab me with that knife behind your back? I can't kill you, but can you kill me?"

The ring, of course, shuddered with warning. Tyvian, though, didn't need it. He presented the blade to Voth, hilt first. "My murdering days are over, Voth. I'd just as soon not kill anyone anymore." He grinned. "Especially not you."

Voth took the knife out of his hand and threw it, point-first, into the ground. She then wrapped her arms around his neck and kissed him. Tyvian pulled her onto his lap.

The petite assassin hugged Tyvian close, pressing her cheek against his. She whispered in his ear, the softness of her voice making his hair stand on end. "I have some good news for you, Tyvian."

Tyvian was fumbling with the laces in the back of Voth's shirt. "Which is?"

"We aren't going to kill your friend the prince." She slapped his hands away and untied the laces herself. "Sahand wants him alive."

"Oh. Lucky him." Tyvian buried his face in the nape of Voth's neck. The ring twinged, concerned for Artus, but Tyvian ignored it. He had more pressing matters to attend to.

CHAPTER 14

A MEETING OF ESTEEMED COLLEAGUES

The problems the White Army faced became evident even before they moved through the pass. Myreon bent over travel-worn campaign maps and argued with Barth and Valen and Artus and even Lady Michelle while their soldiers hiked up the winding trail that led up through the mountains and then down again. The whole process, Barth guessed, would take them two days. In three, they'd be mustered on the other side and ready to march on Ayventry—a straight shot down the Freegate Road over relatively flat ground.

The initial euphoria over their victory had worn off quickly in the command tent. First there were the arguments over who should garrison Tor Erdun—Valen wanted one of his surviving knights, Barth wanted one of his guilder friends. Then there were the arguments about what to do with the prisoners—kill them, let them go, or keep them hostage, there was no answer that satisfied everyone. Necessity and basic decency told Myreon that they should just be set loose, but she also knew what that meant—hundreds of people preceding their army into Ayventry, telling everyone they saw about the White Army, its size, disposition, and weaknesses.

And Sahand was out there, waiting. Myreon knew it. Ayventry was a trap.

"When we come down out of these mountains," Myreon said at last, weary from argument, "we are going to be weakened by casualties, short good officers we cannot spare, and preciously low on food. Meanwhile, Sahand's men are rested, disciplined, aware of our disposition and movements, and sitting on a mountain of supplies stolen from every village and hamlet from here back to Eretheria City, not to mention the support of Ayventry itself, who we have now terrified right into Sahand's arms."

A heavy quiet drew out.

"So"—Myreon slumped into a chair—"they have all the advantages here. We have none. Suggestions?"

Silence drew out. Valen was wearing his arm in a sling, the shrapnel wound in his arm still healing. Artus was singed all over to the point where he looked like he had fallen asleep in an oven. Barth's face was a storm cloud of anger and frustration, and his big, knobby hands were busy strangling the life out of his own war-hammer. They were all on edge, and there was still at least one more battle to go.

Michelle looked around at each of them, her slender frame like a reed among the tree trunk men. She curtsied, looking at Myreon and blushing.

Myreon put her chin in her hand. "Yes, Michelle?"

"I realize this probably sounds obvious to you all, but . . ." Michelle paused.

Myreon snapped her fingers. "Out with it, girl!"

"Couldn't we just use some kind of, you know, *magic*?"

Silence. All eyes turned to Myreon where she sat, head in hand. She closed her eyes. *There it is.* "You're aware that Saldor has laws against that kind of magic, yes?"

Michelle nodded, still blushing. "But the last time somebody defeated Sahand, *they* used that kind of magic."

"That was different. That was Saldor *itself* using battlefield-scale magic. I'm pushing things with the White Guard as it is. The Defenders have been *very* specific about the consequences should I go any further than I've already gone."

"Begging your pardon, Magus, but . . . so *what?*"

Artus was beaming at her. "My lady has a point, Myreon. We can't lose now. Too much is riding on it."

"You don't know what you are all asking."

"Indeed we do not, Magus," Valen said. "But . . . as we have no other options . . ."

"There *must be* other options."

Barth eyed the White Guard, standing stone-still in the shadowed recesses of the room. "I'm no great lover of sorcery, Magus, but you've already raised the dead to fight with us. How much worse could it get?"

Myreon pressed her lips together, but held her tongue. That was the statement of an uneducated man. Looking around, she realized she was surrounded by the uneducated—Valen was the closest one got, and his knowledge probably didn't extend much beyond Eretherian history and heraldry. But she knew. Lyrelle Reldamar, when she pushed the late Keeper Astrian X to sanction greater use of sorcery on the battlefield, had changed the whole world. She had made it more dangerous. No more than a century ago, magecraft was rare and the common people had little knowledge of it. This, of course, was a tool used by the wealthy to cement their control over the poor—an injustice—but indulging in the kind of sorcerous warfare her advisors were suggesting . . . that was something else. That led to very dark places. Androlli—and the Defenders—were right.

Artus put a hand on her shoulder. "Myreon, we trust you. *I* trust you. You've led the people to victory three times now—I know you won't let us down."

Myreon looked up at him. Where in all the hells

had this *man* come from? This handsome, tall, strong man with a gleam in his eye and a voice warm as sunshine? Wasn't this Artus—that boy that always hung around Tyvian Reldamar? And yet here she was, getting swept up in that same magic that seemed to afflict everybody in this army when he spoke to them. *How in the names of all the gods does he do that?*

Myreon knew, of anybody there, *Artus* would understand. She put her hand over his and looked him in the eye. "It means going to the League, Artus. Do you really want me to involve them?"

Artus shrugged. "It's either that or we all get slaughtered by Sahand. Barth's right—how much worse can it get? It can't hurt to ask, can it?"

Myreon nodded and dismissed everyone to their duties. Then she put her face in her hands. Oh, it could hurt to ask, all right.

But she was going to have to ask anyway.

Being a secretive organization, the League was obsessed with security. Most communication was done via the untraceable correspondence of the network of enchanted letterboxes—one of which was left in Myreon's possession after the disappearance of the old blind necromancer. The magecraft was sufficiently sophisticated that she had only a basic sense of how they worked—they operated on the same principle as an anygate, except much smaller and easier to use. Correspondence, however, had its limits. Everyone dealt in pseudonyms, for one thing, and it was difficult to know who one was corresponding with. As Banric Sahand was evidently a member of the League (or at least *was*), Myreon had no way of knowing whether her letters were being read by the enemy. She had to presume they were or at least could be, which meant her requests for aid had to be very carefully worded.

It wouldn't be the first time, though, for this was how she had acquired the formula to create the linking stone. She had written certain members of the League she "knew," courtesy of her letterbox's previous owner, whom his "esteemed colleagues" referred to as "Requiem," and asked certain oblique questions regarding how to best continue Requiem's work in the field. If Sahand had intercepted that one, it was no giant secret what she was doing with a linking stone and, if Sahand hadn't, it would take some doing for somebody to figure out what exactly her intent was. Or so she hoped, at least.

If she wanted to acquire more help than the occasional spell formula, however—if she wanted large-scale military support, for instance—correspondence simply wasn't secure enough. Any number of League members might forward her letters to any number of others (though they would have to be copies, as no letter could be sent through the letterbox twice), and it did not stretch the imagination to see Banric Sahand, sitting in some forbidding chair, reading her requests with a grin.

So Myreon decided to write the Chairman to request an in-person meeting.

The League had three officers who loosely managed the complex web of independent and rogue sorcerers comprising the organization. The Secretary was in charge of informational security—policing the letterbox network, specifically, and supposedly also spying on members who were out of line. The Treasurer maintained the League's physical assets, which evidently included a number of hidden laboratories, safe houses, and various stashes of money. Last, the Chairman was the steward of the Black Hall—the semi-real pocket world where League meetings took place—and was also in charge of disciplining erratic members or assigning members to assist in various group efforts. As both the Treasurer and the Secretary ultimately reported to the Chairman, he was the de facto ruler of the League, if indeed something that decentralized could be ruled.

Surprisingly, he quickly agreed to Myreon's request for a meeting. So it was that Myreon found herself in the Black Hall for the first time.

The structure of the place was fascinating—a thirteen-sided hall, terraced, descending to a black pool, still as death, known as the Well of Secrets. Tyvian had told her about it once (and its limitations in actually detecting the truth) in a long and winding story he had found knee-slappingly hilarious. Now that she was actually here in the flesh, Myreon felt cold and terrified.

Via convention, she was wearing a shroud to disguise her face. She made herself look like a stern old woman—a governess type—with a tall silver wig that spilled down to her midback. She took care to lean on her staff a bit, just to complete the illusion. This proved a fortunate precaution, as she was not, evidently, the Chairman's only meeting for the day.

At the top of the terraced hall, she could see the Chairman—who appeared to be Rhondian man with sun-baked skin and lesions all over his face—in conference with a completely unshrouded Banric Sahand. The Mad Prince looked up as she entered and, for a moment, Myreon wondered if perhaps somebody had adopted a shroud of Sahand as some kind of joke, but Sahand's recently ruined face and hard eyes would be subtle details for anyone but someone close to the prince to miss. When he spoke, any doubts Myreon still had were dispelled. She would know his voice anywhere. "Very well then—I see you have another meeting. I will depart. Send me the names when you have them."

Then the Mad Prince turned and left, heading out the opposite side of the Hall. Myreon shivered.

The Chairman looked up at her. Even at this distance, she could see that his eyes were icy blue and piercing—an odd match for his Rhondian face. "Welcome to the Black Hall, my esteemed colleague."

Myreon didn't know what the etiquette was here, or even if there *was* an etiquette, so she opted for a polite nod. "I'm pleased to be here."

The Well of Secrets flickered with the lie, but the Chairman only smiled. "Everyone is unsettled during their first visit. Please, come closer." He waved Myreon down the terraces until she stood across the well from him. Despite herself, Myreon found herself squinting at his face. There was something familiar about him, but she couldn't put her finger on what. "Was that Banric Sahand?"

The Chairman sighed. "Though I would ordinarily decline to comment on the identity of any one of our members, the Prince of Dellor makes a point of scoffing at our security procedures."

Myreon couldn't help but ask, "What did he want?"

"If he were to ask me the same question of you, would you like me to answer?"

Myreon pursed her lips and nodded. "Fair enough."

"Now, what can I do for you?" The Chairman asked.

Myreon grimaced. "First I need to know to what extent I can trust you."

"You can trust me to the extent that you can trust anyone, I suppose."

"That's dodging the question." Myreon pointed at the Well of Secrets. "Don't think I don't know how this thing works. Answer me."

The Chairman smiled. "Good. Good—that's a good instinct. I like it. Very well, I will rephrase my answer: you can trust me to help you as long as our goals coincide. How does that suit you?"

Myreon looked at the well—nothing—but still not enough. "And your goals are?"

The Chairman cocked his head for a moment, considering something. Finally, he sighed. "The destruction of the Arcanostrum and the political structures that support it."

No glimmers from the black water. It was the truth, if a frightening one. "That's . . . ambitious."

"No less ambitious than your own quest to upend all of Eretherian society, I would say." He waved away Myreon's look of surprise. "Now, now—don't be alarmed. You can't expect to lead the first army of undead soldiers in over sixteen hundred years and maintain anonymity for long. Everyone in the League knows of the Gray Lady. You are quite popular. In many ways, your current quest is in keeping with the ancient purpose of this League. You and it are both devoted to the idea that people are best at liberty to pursue what they will, without a tyrant choking them at every turn."

Myreon narrowed her eyes—an evasion. "And what are you devoted to?"

"I have already told you. Come now, surely you didn't come here just to pump me for information. Have I adequately satisfied you that I am an ally, or do you wish to depart?"

"Do you give your word that you will not share information about me or my plans with Sahand?"

"I have no intention of doing so, no."

The waters were still and dark—not a lie. Myreon took an easy breath. "I need battlefield-grade sorcery. Something to give the White Army an edge against Sahand." She explained the strategic dilemma she was facing, all the while trying not to give away too much. Well or no well, she didn't trust this man.

There was something about him, even behind his shroud, that she found too dreadfully familiar. Was he someone she had arrested at one point? She tried to remember the voices and mannerisms of all the rogue wizards she'd caught during her career as a Defender and their sentences. The list of persons who had already served their term of years in Saldor's penitentiary gardens was short, and none of them fit. They were dabblers and mischief makers, not arch-sorcerers in control of international conspiracies.

When she had finished, the Chairman rubbed his chin. "Hmmmm . . . I may have something for you—something that could settle a battle quite quickly and very much put Sahand's armies on their back foot."

"What is it?"

"I should stress that it is extraordinarily dangerous." The Chairman looked her in the eye. "It should not be used lightly, if at all. Its effects are likely very . . . thorough."

Myreon held his gaze. *Something about those eyes . . . so familiar.*

The Chairman looked away, gazing deeply into the Well of Secrets. "Tell me, have you ever heard of the Seeking Dark?"

An involuntary chill travelled up Myreon's spine. "The Bane of Vorn the Terrible. The superweapon that ended the Third Mage War and saw the end of the last Warlock Kings. Gods—you *have* that?"

"No, we do not," the Chairman replied, "but the League knows where it is—a small part of it, at any rate—and I know how you can get that part."

Myreon felt cold. The Seeking Dark had, according to legend, killed an entire kingdom's worth of people in a single night. How was not clear—every sorcerous text Myreon had ever read or heard of had refused to even speculate. It was held up as the perfect example of why the Arcanostrum existed and what the Defenders existed to stop—sorcery of such terrible potency that it was unstoppable, uncontrollable, and cataclysmically fatal. She could scarcely believe that the Chairman was offering it to her—and yet the Well had remained dark. He was telling the truth.

Her voice was breathless. "And . . . in exchange?"

"You will give it to the League when you are done." He didn't say "for study." He didn't say "for safekeeping," either. *He intends to use it.*

"Perhaps it would be best if I didn't," she said, backing away from the well.

The Chairman shrugged. "You may, of course, continue your pursuit of justice in your own way. The historians agree on one thing, however: a quick war is always preferable to a long one."

Myreon's mind leapt to the dead little boy in the village, facedown in the dirt. To Barth's tears. To Erdun town, burned to ashes. *How many more towns will it be? And what of Ayventry—a whole city!* She forced herself to stand tall. "Where is it?"

"At the ancestral estate of the Reldamars— Glamourvine." The Chairman smiled.

It was the smile that did it. The smile and those eyes—she'd seen that look before, or a version of it, on Tyvian's face a thousand times. But this wasn't Tyvian.

Xahlven Reldamar was Chairman of the Sorcerous League.

And he wanted her to break into his own house.

Myreon's whole body erupted in goose bumps, but she kept her voice steady. "When do we leave?"

The Chairman—Xahlven—motioned to one of the thirteen doors to the Black Hall. "Right now."

CHAPTER 15

FRONTAL ASSAULT

The Great Whiteflood—the longest river in the world, stretching from Dellor in the north to Eddon in the far southwest—was still and flat and the color of slate on a cloudy day. It looked cold and vast and forbidding. Hool paused on its banks, feeling a shiver travel up her spine. "We have to get across."

Damon sat down next to her, his feet dangling over the embankment. He was panting. It occurred to Hool that she had been running for the past several minutes, and that Damon had actually managed to keep up for a short way. He was getting in better shape.

He looked worse, though. He wore a cloak of

beaver pelts now, with a deep hood; his good boots were worn and patched, and all vestiges of the clean, perfumed knight she had known in Eretheria had been scrubbed away by the harsh expanse of the Wild Territories they had just crossed in two weeks of hard travel. "Might we . . ." He struggled to catch his breath. "Might we pause for a moment to put together a feasible plan?"

Hool put her ears back—he was just saying this because he was tired. "No. We go on."

There, across the three-mile expanse of the Whiteflood, rested the city of Dellor and its infamous Citadel. It was the biggest single structure Hool had ever seen—almost like a city in itself. No, not a city. It was too *solid*—almost like some giant made of stone had laid itself down to sleep and then frozen there. The walls and the turrets presented themselves at angled intervals, like the teeth of a sleeping beast. Its high towers flew Sahand's banners. Somewhere— somewhere within there—the object of her hatred rested, thinking himself safe. She was going to show him how wrong he was.

Damon had moderately recovered from their run. He rolled over onto his stomach and turned himself so he could survey the huge fortress and the small city appended to its outer walls. "How do you propose we get across? I can't swim that. I daresay you can't either."

Hool snorted. "We just need a boat, stupid."

Damon made a show of searching his clothing. "I seem to be fresh out of boats, Hool."

"Well what is *your* smart plan, then?"

"If we go downriver to Dunnmayre, we can take the ferry over. This is what I said before."

"Dunnmayre is a town. They will recognize me. It won't work. Besides, that will take two days at least. I want Sahand dead tonight." Hool searched up and down the banks of the river for any sign of habitation. There was precious little. The land on which they stood was not farmable and was barely suitable for livestock—a cold, gray-green tundra stretched out in every direction, fading into the jagged mountains of the Dragonspine in the east and the green-black fir trees of the Great Forest to the west. To the north, the Whiteflood.

Hool growled, "There must be *something*."

Damon shook his head. "Very well. Let's have a look."

Into the dusk, Hool prowled the banks of the river, keeping herself hidden behind the scraggly trees and thorn-covered bushes that cropped up along the shore. Damon followed along at a distance, strumming his lute as he went. He was the lure—or at least such was Hool's plan. Boaters on the river would see him and, hearing his music, draw closer. Then, when they were close enough, Hool would pounce and steal the boat.

There *were* boats on the river, too—a great many,

traveling to and fro, their flat decks piled with lumber and casks and crates—but they all stuck to the northern bank of the river, most of them pulling up alongside the great triangular arm of the Citadel that thrust into the river itself. It seemed no boats came their way because there simply wasn't anything on the south bank to draw them, music or no.

No boats came. No people. Not even any animals.

Hool growled to herself all that night. If this was what Dellor was like, she hated it. It was ugly and cold and empty and cruel. It was a place where nothing grew except brambles and scruff grass. She hated the idea that she would have to spend yet *another* day here, where the air smelled only of snow and pine and cold mud.

Yet they had no choice, which rankled Hool even more.

The next day they doubled back over the same ground, Damon walking ahead, Hool stalking behind. Still nothing. Dellor refused to grant them any stroke of luck. Hool wanted to howl.

Damon, though, he had only smiles for her, and his stupid jokes, and his pretty songs. She did not know how he could sing in a place like this.

The second night on the banks, they lay side by side between two big boulders, hiding themselves from everything around. The stars—bright and innumerable as they had been on the Taqar—were visible only in a jagged strip of unobscured sky. It was cold, but Damon strummed his lute and quietly sang a song about summer and the flowers a man picked for his wife.

Hool waited for it to be over before saying anything. "Why are you not upset?"

Damon raised a bushy eyebrow. "I beg your pardon?"

"We have been wandering this awful place for days, but you are not mad or grouchy or whining. Why not?"

Damon laughed. "Would you like me to complain more often?"

"No," Hool said. "But I don't understand. You complained in Ayventry and Galaspin and the Wild Territory, and those were all a lot nicer than this."

Damon thought about this, then said, "They were. I think that was why I complained."

"Explain!"

Damon searched for the words for a few moments, idly testing out some chords on his lute. They sounded awful. "All my life I was taught to struggle to be wealthy. My mother, my sisters, and I were poor, our father having fought on the wrong side of Perwynnon's war and paying for it by losing his life and his lands. As the only son, I had to work my way back up the ladder, as it were. If my sisters were to find good husbands, I had to distinguish myself on the field of honor. If my mother fell ill, I needed to win a tournament to pay the doctor. So I did—I fought and I worked and I struggled and I got my family a small house in the city and I saw my sisters married off to kindly gentlemen and I saw my mother buried with honor."

"I am waiting for this to make sense," Hool growled.

Damon laughed. "I was miserable. I felt like a . . . like this wretched thing. A nobody. Gods, I *was* a nobody. A passably good duelist, but landless and fairly poor and without prospects, and the lack made me miserable. When I entered your service, I saw everything that I ever worked for wiped away—my good name, my titles, my ties with family—"

"You didn't have to do that! I told you that!"

Damon held up one hand. "Please, let me finish." When Hool settled down, he continued. "The complaining I did before was a . . . a residue of my old life. I could only see what I was losing. Now . . . now that I've lost everything, I can finally see what I have."

Hool's ears perked up. "What could you *possibly* have? A lute? A sword?"

"I have a beautiful sky. I have peace in my heart." Damon smiled at her. "And I have you."

"Me?"

"You never believed me when I told you that I loved you. But I do. Not as a man loves a woman, perhaps—that is never to be—but I still love you more than I ever loved any woman, Hool of the Taqar. I am simply blessed to share in your adventures, wherever they lead."

Hool stared at him. "That . . . that is the stupidest thing anybody has ever said to me."

Damon shrugged. "I never claimed to be very smart."

Hool turned away from him. "Let's go to sleep. I don't want to talk about this anymore."

"As you wish."

Hool tried to let herself doze off, but it didn't take. Instead, she found herself counting the breaths of the strange man pressed against her, feeling the beat of his heart, and puzzling over his words.

It took a long time before she found sleep.

At dawn, they came upon a boat.

It was a small craft—perhaps fifteen feet long and narrow and pointed at one end, like a giant woman's slipper. There were two men aboard, each with fishing poles. Hool did not wait for them to notice her from her rocky hiding spot—she pounced upon the boat, intending to hurl the men into the water.

Instead, she immediately capsized the boat.

Hool fell into the water and instantly panicked. The wet was so cold it stole her breath and so dark it obscured her vision. Her nostrils filled with its watery stink. She thrust down with her feet—she could *stand!* Relief flooded her limbs.

The men were shouting. They swam to shore and were running away. Roaring, Hool charged out of the water after them.

The closest one—an old man—had a paddle that he swung like a club. Hool caught it and tore it away from him before slapping him to the ground with the back of one hand.

"Papa!" screamed the other one—a boy. He had out a small knife and he pointed it at Hool. "Arghhh!" he yelled, slashing through the air. "Back! Back, beast!"

Hool picked up a rock and threw it, hitting the boy in the shoulder hard enough to break a bone. He yelped and fell to the ground, dropping the knife. Hool sprinted over and kicked the knife away. Grabbing the boy by the scalp, she lifted him off the ground.

"Hool!" Damon shouted, scrabbling out of their hiding place. "Stop! Stop, by all the gods!"

The boy squirmed in her grasp and Hool slammed him on the ground. "Why?"

Damon crouched by the man. "They're *not* your enemies, Hool! They're just fishermen, for Hann's sake!"

Hool looked down at the boy, who was wheezing with pain at her feet. "These are Sahand's people. These are Dellorans!"

Damon shook his head. "Are they wearing tabards? Mail? These aren't the ones who killed your Brana or your Api, Hool! They're just as much the victims of Sahand as you are!"

Hool frowned down at the two fishermen. She stepped over their prone bodies. "Fine. Just get in the boat."

Damon let out a long breath. "As you wish."

They rowed out into the river. Well, Damon did, anyway. Hool sat toward the bow, the Fist of Veroth across her knees, focusing on keeping her center of balance in the middle of the wobbly, thin boat. She scarcely could look around at first. "I think this boat is broken!" she called.

"It's not broken. Just hold still!" Damon dipped his oars into the water and pulled. The boat shot forward and at good speed. With every sweep of his oars, the Citadel grew closer. And closer.

And bigger.

The walls—weather-scarred and ancient—seemed taller than the clouds. Looking at them made Hool feel very small indeed. Her heart raced. This was her goal. This was where she was supposed to be.

"How do you propose to get in?" Damon asked.

"Keep rowing," Hool said, her eyes fixed on the towering battlements. "Don't distract me."

There were riverboats ahead—large, flat-bottomed barges. These were the kind they'd been watching from the opposite shore the last two days, piled high with all manner of supplies. Hool pointed at them. "Follow those."

The men aboard the boats used sails or oars or long poles to push themselves toward that outer spur of the Citadel's huge walls. As they got closer, Hool could make out the base of the wall—it stood open! It didn't close off the river, it let the river in!

Her ears perked up. "See?" She twisted to look at Damon. "There! We can get in there!"

Damon looked pale. "Hool, there will be guards."

She waved the Fist of Veroth. "I will kill them. Go!"

Damon obeyed.

Ahead of them, one by one, the barges full of supplies vanished into the belly of the Citadel. What seemed like a small crack at the base of the wall yawned in front of them—a fifteen-foot-tall opening that stretched for fifty yards from the shore. Sniffing the air, Hool could smell the forges and coal fires beyond, and the scent of sorcery beneath that. She heard the jingle of mail and the creak of leather and the clomp of boots on stone—Delloran soldiers.

Her enemies.

They were almost in . . .

Until a chain sprang up on front of them, wet and rusty from the river. In the gloom of the entrance, a rough voice called out. "Halt! Who goes there?"

Hool gripped the Fist of Veroth with both hands, the raw power of her rage funneling into it at once. She stood, for once confident in her balance aboard the little boat. She roared into the dark gloom. "I am Lady Hool of the Taqar! Your master, Banric Sahand, murdered my pups! Now I come to take his hide as my own and wear it as a warning to others! Stand aside or die!"

The Fist of Veroth flared with fiery brilliance, lighting the gloomy opening beyond. Hool could see two squat stone battlements rising out of the water, each packed with soldiers armed with crossbows. She showed them her fangs and howled.

"Hool!" Damon yelled from behind her. "Get down!"

Hool didn't listen. He was just a frightened little man. This was her moment—she would not be a rabbit.

Today she was the lion.

The crossbows clacked even as Hool made her first swing. Four bolts caught her in the chest, arm, stomach, and leg. Her body crumpled, but she still had the energy to strike the water with the enchanted mace. A huge wave exploded upward where it hit, coupled with a thunderclap that made the air itself shake.

Hool willed herself to her feet again. She willed herself to pounce into that darkness, to swing her mace again and again.

But her legs would not obey. She coughed, and felt blood spill down her chin and from her nostrils. The boat was spinning, bobbing like a cork. She felt Damon's hand clutch around her wrist. Then there was his face, yelling, but he sounded so distant. "Hool!" he said. "Hold on! Just hold on!"

He went back to the oars.

Hool tried to rise one last time, but the bolts were deep inside her and, next to her, she could feel the Fist of Veroth grow cold and dark.

Whimpering, she closed her eyes.

She had failed.

CHAPTER 16

MIND GAMES

Lyrelle Reldamar did not stoop to scratching little marks into the walls to count the days. She knew how many days she had been here. She knew how many hours. If she could not remember something as trivial as that, what point was there to going on?

Indeed, that was the question she entertained most often of late. She was maimed, old, and completely extraneous now—whatever chance she had to manipulate events was past. All her plots were finished that night in Eretheria, just as she had suspected. She just hadn't expected to live. She wondered daily why she continued to bother.

Out her window gave her a view of the Whiteflood

and beyond it the stark countryside of Dellor. Nothing but rocky, windswept hills and scraggly yellow grass. The smell of snow was always in the air, and the wind was like knives when it blew.

Sooner or later, she would take ill. There was no doubt. The hard cheese and stale crackers, the flat, tepid water—in his caution to contain her, Sahand courted her death. In the beginning she had thought to escape—there were ways, especially given that her jailor was a grandiose coward. In any event, she had stopped trying very hard to turn him—why bother escaping? All she did from time to time was weep and do her best to look pathetic when the poor little wretch came to feed her. Neither of these things were much of a challenge.

She ran her index finger along the scabbed-over lump of flesh to which her left thumb had once been attached. Perhaps this was what she deserved. After all those decades making the world dance, surely a quick death was too much to ask in return. Fate wished to see her suffer, and so she suffered. There was no need to get indignant.

She heard a rattling of keys in the lock—Arkald coming to deliver breakfast. She pulled herself out of a slouch and faced the door, waiting. When he came in, he would notice how thin she was becoming, thanks to the light of the sun pouring through her gauze-thin robe. She let her face droop, but not too much—she wanted to look tired, but also look like she was trying to hide it. It was a pointless game, she knew, but she had very little else to do. Playing head games with Arkald was literally all she had left to entertain her.

The door popped open only a few inches—just enough for Arkald to poke his bony, hairless head in. The expression on his face told her immediately that this was not an ordinary visit. His eyes, fairly alight with terror, looked her up and down—confirming her existence—and then popped out again.

Lyrelle took a deep, calming breath. Not a visit from Arkald, then. She adjusted her posture once more, this time seeking to banish any indication of discomfort or fatigue. She flattened her skirt against her legs and brushed her hair away from her face.

She sat prepared to face Banric Sahand.

The door was pushed open all the way, hard enough so it banged against the wall. Just like Sahand—never a gentle touch where a blow might do. The Mad Prince swaggered into the cell with a criminal leer—one would think he intended to seduce her, absurd as that was. He was wearing his fur cloak and a long dagger at his belt, but no sword—a nod to her as a dangerous adversary, she supposed, though the idea that she might thumblessly wrestle a blade away from the old campaigner was completely ludicrous. When he spoke, he grinned widely, his teeth glinting through the ragged hole in his cheek. "Lyrelle."

Lyrelle nodded politely. "Good morning, Banric. How go the wars?"

Whatever she had said she struck a nerve. Sahand's gloating expression melted away, replaced by cold fury. He strode across the cell and slapped Lyrelle with the back of a gloved hand. Lyrelle felt as though she had been struck by a horse. She fell on the ground, the room spinning.

Sahand was yelling at her. "You *knew*! I'll be damned if I know how, but you *knew*!"

Lyrelle took her time rising while she digested this information. *Interesting.* She spat blood onto the floor. "I'm quite sure I don't know what you're talking about."

Sahand yanked her off the ground by the collar of her robe and slammed her against the wall, pinning her a foot off the ground with his meaty hand around her throat. The impact knocked the breath out of her lungs, leaving her wheezing. "Who do you think you're dealing with, eh?" He thrust a thick finger under her nose. "I *know* you, Lyrelle. I've known you for forty years. I know how your mind works."

Lyrelle forced a thin little smile. "If that were true," she choked out, "I would have been in this tower long before now."

Sahand snapped his fingers behind him. "Arkald! Come!"

The bony necromancer poked his head through

the door as though expecting it to be lopped off. "Yes, sire?"

Sahand twirled a finger, indicating the walls of the little cell. "Inspect every inch of this chamber—I want to see where the flaw is in your prison."

Arkald bowed deeply. "I assure you, Your Highness, there *is* no flaw. I was most careful."

Sahand whipped his head around to glare at the necromancer. "Do. It."

As Arkald scurried away, Lyrelle kept herself composed, despite the pain in her face and the pressure on her throat and jaw. Blood leaked into her mouth from a split lip. "You have such a way with people, Banric."

Spittle sprayed out from Sahand's ruined cheek. "I *know* you have been advising them somehow. It's the only way they could have evaded that little trap— the *only way*—and I want to know why. What do you hope to gain? Rescue? Ha! They're a thousand miles away! So what is it, witch? What is your foul little scheme this time?"

Lyrelle smiled at him. She sifted through all the possible things that could have come to pass since her capture—which could it be? The use of "they" indicated a group, and the reference to a trap implied that Sahand was reluctant to face "them" directly. There really was only one logical surmise. "You can't defeat them, Sahand—they are people defending their homes and their children. No number of mercenaries can stop their anger."

Sahand dropped her to the ground. When she landed on all fours, he kicked her in the ribs so hard she gasped with pain and rolled onto her back. He planted a knee in her shoulder and drew his dagger, placing it at Lyrelle's throat. She focused all her will on keeping her gaze steady, unblinking. This only made the Mad Prince angrier. She felt the blade begin to bite. "Give me one good reason not to kill you now!"

"Easy enough, Banric: because you haven't killed me *yet*. Because you *need* me for something, or suspect you do. And until you are sure I am no help to you whatsoever, you are going to keep me alive." Lyrelle watched his face carefully. Sahand's eyebrows rose and told her everything she needed to know—she was *right*. "Just like the old days, isn't it, Ban?"

The Mad Prince withdrew his blade. Then, without warning, he struck her in the face with a closed fist. The blow made her whole head rattle; spots danced in her vision. Lyrelle groaned with pain and clutched her face.

But Sahand wasn't finished.

Straddling her, he struck her again. And again. And again. Each strike crushing bones in her face, knocking teeth loose. Her world shuddered with pain and blood. Between each strike, he growled at her. "You! Are! Not! My! Equal!"

She lost consciousness, but came to again before the beating had ended. Now he was kicking her—

in the stomach, in the ribs. Hard enough, again, to break bones. Lyrelle could not move—she felt as though she were filled with shattered glass. Sahand stood over her, his eyes wild as a rabid dog. "I *told you*! I told you it would end this way for you! Didn't I? Did you think Banric Sahand was not as good as his word, bitch?" He swung his arms wide, as though gesturing to some grand vista. "Look what I have become! Look what I have built! Look where I am! And look at where *you* are."

Lyrelle could see through one eye. Her voice was there, but weak. She whispered the words, but Sahand didn't hear. He had to lean down to hear her.

"Ban . . ." she breathed, "we are in the same place."

He stood up, as though bitten. His mouth was agape. He tried to say something, but failed. Instead, he only smiled—a forced, rakish grin that had once won him the hearts of many ladies in a time very long ago, but was now hopelessly ruined by the ravaged mess of his face and the permanent furrows of anger that creased his brow.

Eventually, he collected himself. "If I suspect you of aiding my enemies again, I shall spill more of you on the floor than a little blood." He pointed a finger at her good eye. "Remember the pain, witch."

Lyrelle said nothing, lying limp. He left, slamming the door and locking it behind him. Only after he had gone did she permit herself to smile. *He leaned down to hear what I said. He needed to know.*

Perhaps there *was* some reason to live, after all.

She let herself drift to sleep.

When she awoke, she was lying on a cot. Still her cell, but in a cot, not on the ground. A blanket lay over her. Sitting on her stool, wiping her face with a warm, damp rag, was Arkald the Strange.

"Arkald . . ." She smiled at him.

He flinched. "Oh . . . oh gods . . . oh gods . . ."

"What is it?" she asked, her voice so weak she could barely hear it herself.

Arkald blinked. Lyrelle thought she saw a sparkle of tears. "What did you say to him? What did you *say* to make him . . . do *this*?"

"Why Arkald, I didn't know you cared."

The necromancer shook his head. "Don't joke. You are badly hurt—*badly* hurt. You . . . you could die. If there is internal bleeding, if one of your bones is too badly broken . . ."

"You speak like a doctor."

Arkald shrugged. "All necromancers are doctors. Well . . . pretty much all. How do you think we get into it?" He shook his head as he wrung out the rag, dripping pink water into a bucket at his feet. "They think we *love* death—nonsense. We hate it. We're the only ones who try to . . . try to *undo* what it's done. That's what you damned magi never understand. Never."

There were a lot of things Lyrelle might have said to this—that perhaps focusing one's efforts on those already dead rather than those currently alive was a waste of time. That necromancy's attempt to "reverse" death merely parodied it and always had. That she'd known a great many necromancers who were hardly doctors. But that wasn't the play here. That wasn't the angle. "Tell me about it, Arkald. I know . . . I know so little of necromancy."

"First tell me what you said."

Lyrelle smiled, making Arkald flinch again. *Gods—what did he do to my face?* "I reminded him of the man he once was. Proud men hate that."

Arkald gently touched the inside of her wrist, reading her pulse. "And who was he?"

Lyrelle thought back—gods, it had to be over forty years now. Her, not yet married, just earned her staff. And Sahand—the big, barrel-chested Northron with the big voice and the big laugh and the big dreams. Always a lady on his arm. Always a tale of daring to share and a cup of good drink and a slap on the back. And that smile, so long gone. The memory ached—oh gods, how it ached.

Lyrelle sighed. "He was nobody special." Then, she paused. "Except to me."

CHAPTER 17

CHILDREN OF A SCHEMER

Glamourvine on a spring evening had a certain scent—of fresh flowers and rich soil, of evening mist clinging to vines. The scent threatened to throw Myreon back in time—she was a teenager, struggling with the weight of her training. She could always come here for comfort, for safety. The thought of Lyrelle Reldamar not being here—of the house standing empty—made her want to cry.

The Chairman—Xahlven—had not accompanied her. He had merely shown her the way to open the doorway from the Black Hall to Glamourvine's grounds. "What about the wards on the property?" she had asked. "How did you get through those?"

Xahlven, his shroud never slipping, gestured toward the yawning black portal. "It has taken the combined effort of many of our best magi to pierce the Archmagus Lyrelle's defenses. It took weeks to get this far, and is only possible because she is not at home. The other defenses we believe you will be able to pierce, but you must go quickly."

So she had. But now, as she walked across the lush lawn toward the front door of that grand old manse, she felt like a thief. No, like an ink-thrall come in the night to rob her own kin of their money just to get what she needed.

The sorcerous defenses of Glamourvine were subtle—Myreon could detect nothing on the doors or windows. No alarm was raised, no fearsome golem or other construct came forth to challenge her. After some hesitation, she put her hand on the doorknob.

Nothing happened.

She turned it and went in; the door wasn't even locked. *Like she was expecting me.*

When she was an initiate in the Arcanostrum, it always seemed as if Lyrelle was expecting her. She would get away from her classes and skip morning exercises and flee here, quite sure the great archmage would be appalled at her arriving unannounced. But the door was always open, the tea was always hot, and a bed was made up. Once Myreon had come while Lyrelle was out, but found a note instead: *I left some books out for you in the library. Please enjoy them and I shall return soon.*

The books left out had changed her life. They had been histories of Saldor, and they had driven her to become a Defender and pledge herself to the Gray Tower when she achieved her first mark. *She knew all along,* Myreon thought as she wandered through darkened halls. *She has always known me better than myself.*

Myreon couldn't fool herself into thinking this moment was any different. Lyrelle must have expected this, too. Myreon just couldn't decide if that was a good thing or a bad thing.

The halls were familiar to her. Myreon couldn't help lingering in certain rooms as she passed, remembering conversations and arguments with Tyvian's mother over this and that. It was strange—for all the years she came here, she never once crossed paths with Tyvian or Xahlven. Tyvian, of course, had run off by that time—living as a pirate with the infamous Carlo diCarlo, it was said—but Xahlven was a master mage in the Black College. Somehow, though, they'd never met. It occurred to Myreon that she had felt more like Lyrelle's daughter than anything else. This house, with all its understated opulence, felt like her home.

And yet it never was that for Tyvian. So strange.

Xahlven had told Myreon where to find what she was looking for. In the Treasure Hall, where the ancient heirlooms of the Reldamars were kept,

Myreon passed by relics and artifacts on pedestals and racks—a crown, a sword, the skull of some fearsome beast, a stand where once might have rested the Fist of Veroth. Myreon counted the artifacts until she arrived at the number thirteen.

She was standing before a small ebony jewelry box on a stone pedestal. Its lid was carved into a leering, demonic mouth, ringed with fangs. It looked so much like what she had expected to find, Myreon almost reached out to touch it by reflex. She stopped herself, though. *Touch it*, Xahlven had warned, *and your death will be extremely swift.*

Myreon conjured a light into the tip of her staff and held it before the pedestal, casting a sharp shadow on the wall behind. Securing her staff in place with a simple telekinetic binding, Myreon slipped around the deadly pedestal and moved to inspect the shadow instead. With a trembling hand, she reached forward toward the *shadow* of the jewelry box . . .

Her hand alighted on something solid, though wholly invisible and undetectable by any means Myreon possessed. Even still, once she had found it, it was a simple matter of feeling for its edges and picking it up. When her hands emerged from the shadow cast by her staff, she was holding a cube of black, battered iron—some kind of heavy chest or coffer. It was sealed closed as though by intense heat—something had welded the edges of the lid into the rest of it. It was cold to the touch—so cold it burned her hands. Myreon could sense its incredible, terrible age. She wanted very much to get away from it. To put it down and run and never look back.

Which meant this was *definitely* what she was looking for.

"You do not need to use it, Myreon."

Myreon yelped in surprise and dropped the blackened chest. Lyrelle was standing right there, dressed in green velvet. But no, it couldn't be Lyrelle—velvet wasn't in season. Even *Myreon* knew that. It had to be a simulacrum. Myreon forced herself to stop trembling. "I'm doing what I need to do."

Lyrelle—or the simulacrum of her—pointed at the chest. "*That* is a thing best left unopened. Spidrahk's Coffer contains no solutions to any problem you wish to solve, my dear. All it contains is death."

"Death is a kind of solution."

"No," Lyrelle said, smiling, "death is merely representative of a transferal of responsibility. The problems that led to the desire to cause death—my death, for instance—are not solved by my absence, merely deferred and postponed. It is an attractive proposition to suggest that death settles all conflict, but in point of fact it merely transforms or otherwise changes the nature of that conflict."

Lyrelle didn't feel like arguing with a shade, so she let Lyrelle's simulacrum declare what it wanted. She never took Lyrelle Reldamar for a pacifist, though. One thing in the exchange stood out, of course: "You aren't dead, you know."

The simulacrum's manicured eyebrows arched upward. "Am I not? How very unexpected. Xahlven ought to have been more thorough."

"You are a prisoner of Sahand," Myreon said. "You mean you didn't predict this?"

"I am an imperfect and impermanent copy of Lyrelle Reldamar, my dear—I am not privy to all of her machinations. I can tell you emphatically, however, that I expected myself to be deceased by this point." The simulacrum sighed. "Given that I'm in Sahand's custody, I suppose we can write that off as a kind of rounding error. I doubt my death is too far in the future."

Myreon closed her eyes. The thought of such a painful death burned, even if her opinions of Lyrelle had shifted of late. "What was your purpose here?"

The false Lyrelle smiled. "To make of you one last entreaty. And to say good-bye."

Myreon picked up Spidrahk's Coffer. "You don't want me to use the ancient superweapon—noted. This is the good-bye part, I suppose."

Lyrelle took Myreon's hand. "You always do the right thing, Myreon. I always believed that. I always have trusted that about you. So did Tyvian."

Myreon felt tears welling in the corners of her eyes. She wiped them away—a ridiculous ploy, playing upon her emotions like that. Utterly predictable for a Reldamar. "Is that all?"

"I'm sorry for everything I put you through. I was not some heartless spider. I loved you like a daughter. That was never an act, never a ploy. You are a good girl, Myreon, and I'm very proud of you."

Myreon drew back from the illusion. "I'm going now."

Lyrelle's simulacrum bowed. "Good-bye, my dear. Good-bye forever." Her image, so perfect, so serene, seemed to fade away into mist and then was gone.

Myreon hefted the black iron coffer and left without looking back. It was hard to see her way out—she was blinded by tears.

Xahlven watched in his scrying pool as Myreon departed Glamourvine. She had the coffer—good. As usual, the woman was incredibly predictable. No wonder his mother had made her into such a tool; no wonder his brother had enjoyed having her around. She was almost like a trained animal in a maze, doing whatever you wished so long as the proper reward was dangled. With a wave of his hand, he dismissed the vision.

The offices of the Archmage of the Ether were a literal labyrinth of folding nonspaces and deep shadows. They were, themselves, hidden within the broader maze of the Black College itself. Those who achieved their First Mark in the Chamber of Testing and wished to apprentice to a mage of the Black

College had to first learn how to enter it. In some cases, it took people years to figure out. It had taken Xahlven three days. He had been fifteen.

Now he held the secrets to not only the Black College and the Archmage's Labyrinth, but to the Arcanostrum as a whole. He knew as much—no, *more*—than even Lyrelle had gleaned in her tenure here. He knew as much as the Keeper of the Balance himself except, unlike the Keeper, he retained most of his sanity.

He stood and stretched, his black robe billowing behind him from a sharp draft—someone was coming. Though he was reasonably certain of who—or rather *what*—it was, he brushed his fingers over a few of his rings, activating a variety of defensive wards. The demon, when it appeared, was little more than a dark silhouette with a pair of pale yellow eyes. He knew it delighted in causing terror, so he took care to show no outward sign of unease, though being in the same room with the entity was hardly calming.

"I see you, wizard." Its voice seemed to emerge from several different corners of the room at once, a hoarse whisper dripping with malice.

"I trust you have eaten well?"

"The woman in the tower has given me some sustenance, yes, but her guardian is much more succulent. His terror is deep and broad."

Xahlven nodded. This demon enjoyed bragging

about its conquests—a further attempt to unnerve others—so he suspected it was telling the truth. Or a close facsimile thereof. "The astral wards still hold?"

"Most unfortunately. The woman is beyond my reach . . . my touch. Her dreams . . . how they would be to feed upon . . ." The demon burbled to itself for a moment. The eyes vanished and reappeared in various shadowy corners of the room.

"Tell me what she has said to her captor," Xahlven said, holding up a shadowy vial of Black Cloud, "and I will give you this."

Xahlven felt an invisible caress as the demon smelled the vial of concentrated Etheric ink. It made his hair stand on end. "Very fragrant, but what is it to me?"

"Slip this in the food of any child—the merest drop—and they will have nightmares to feed you well for a year."

The demon giggled, the laughs coming at Xahlven from all sides and with all different voices. "And if I use it all at once, I shall feast indeed!"

The corner of Xahlven's mouth tightened. "Yes. That too."

"We are in agreement," the demon announced. "Give it to me."

Xahlven held tightly to the vial. "Report first."

The eyes vanished for a moment and then returned, this time at Xahlven's eye level. "The woman has said little. She merely bleats pleasantries to her guardian, who only grows more afraid. She taunted another just today—a man who plants fear in all who see him. He beat her for her insolence. Beyond this, she has said nothing of consequence."

Xahlven pulled the vial inside his cloak. "You are certain?"

"I tell you she has said nothing! Nothing! Give me my prize! Give it!" The demon's eyes grew larger, as if it were getting closer. Despite himself, Xahlven shuddered.

Xahlven extended his hand. "Very well—take it." The vial vanished into the dark. "There is more, of course. In exchange for more information."

The laughter echoed again, from all directions. "As you wish." And then it was gone.

Somewhat spent, Xahlven sank into a chair of bone and ran a hand through his golden hair. With one hand, he attempted to conjure demonfire—it worked, a pyre of green flame sprouting from his palm—but he couldn't sustain it. He could feel his control slipping almost immediately—embarrassing, really, as this was something he learned to do over twenty years ago. He let it flicker out of existence and cursed his mother for the ten-thousandth time.

He cursed her for living. He cursed her for the wheedling little hex she had placed on him. He cursed her, now, for not giving any clue for how to remove it. Having the damned thing leeching off him was like trying to dance in iron manacles. Were it not for his mother's hex, he could have taken Spidrahk's Coffer himself. Were it not for his mother's hex, his plans would be nearing completion, instead of having to founder about as Myreon Alafarr blundered her way through an unwinnable war.

He had been forced to utilize more and more demons as surrogates, that last one the most dangerous of the lot. It was, of course, a matter of time before it betrayed him, but he needed it. He needed it to keep watch over his mother, to make sure she didn't escape, and to possibly give him some clue as to how to remove the hex. The worst of it was just how damned petty it all was. Lyrelle was doomed, his plan was going to work—all the hex did was slow things down, make them arduous. It was the last, petulant act of a woman too spoiled to recognize her own failure.

Xahlven sighed and poured himself some wine, taking care to purify it of any poison before drinking.

"Well," he muttered to himself just before taking a sip, "at least that fool Tyvian is dead."

Tyvian couldn't help but wander among the tents of the White Army. Here were *thousands* of people dedicated to avenging him. The army Myreon built in the fires of Eretheria. The army convinced it would bring Sahand to justice.

And it was an utter shambles.

Ever since Tor Erdun, the best way Tyvian could think to describe it was a kind of rolling, riotous festival. Music echoed over the cheap canvas tents—tin whistles, old-fashioned lutes and newer Rhondian guitars, the occasional flute. There were, bizarrely, a lot of street performers—jugglers, fire-eaters, contortionists. There were priests, preachers, and monks. Prostitutes, too—with special tents set up on the outskirts of the camp. There was that skinny fellow he'd seen after the last battle, but this time with a wagonload of shoes, selling them for a copper a pair. And he wasn't the only such entrepeneur, either.

All this—this strange, festive atmosphere—was alongside grim-looking men, filthy and many shoeless, clutching a bill or pitchfork or honing an old wood axe on a whetstone. Boys and gray-bearded men with leather caps and makeshift barrel-top shields muttered the latest gossip over crusts of stale bread. These were the soldiers—the reason the army existed at all—and they didn't look all that soldierly, despite having won all their battles thus far. Tyvian, in his false livery and mail, drew baleful looks from most of them.

Here and there the White Guard stood in isolated numbers of two or three—stone-still, the eye sockets of their masks sightless and black. A little reminder of Myreon's power, perhaps, or maybe they served some other purpose. In any case, Tyvian avoided them. This was easy, as everybody else did too.

The taking of the Citadel of Tor Erdun was all anyone was talking about. The Young Prince had single-handedly defeated twenty knights in the castle while *simultaneously* rescuing the goodwives and grandchildren of Erdun town and everybody in between, batting away trebuchet stones with his enchanted shield as though he were playing tennis. Everyone swore that they knew somebody who had seen all this, though no one in the part of the camp Tyvian explored had actually been there themselves. It was, Tyvian was assured, Hann's own truth. It was proof that the Young Prince was the true heir, they said. Only the pure of heart, guided by Hann's grace, could perform such feats. Somehow, Tyvian had managed not to laugh at them.

"Was the prince injured?" Tyvian asked.

The two men—wearing bleached and threadbare Davram livery and leaning on halberds—both spat tobacco juice into the grass. "Naw," said one, "he had that enchanted shield of his."

The other shook his head. "I heard he didn't. I heard he walked straight through the fires in Erdun to save some widow and now he's all burned."

The first grunted. "Shame if he had to ruin that pretty face. Think the Lady Michelle would still have him if he were all burned up?"

The second grinned, showing a big gap in his

teeth. "If she don't, I know a tent where she could find some finer looking gentlemen, eh?"

Tyvian shared the laugh and begged his pardon to get away from them, only to run almost headlong into a cordon of White Guard. He froze in place.

They were leading a procession that included Myreon on a gray horse, her head hung low, her hands clutching some object on the saddle in front of her. No fanfare to announce her, no shouts of encouragement from her soldiers—the chatter of the camp died, the music stopped, and everyone parted for her, their eyes downcast.

Tyvian did the same, fading back a bit into the crowds in hopes of going unnoticed. The White Guard looked neither left nor right, but moved with an unnatural precision—each of their steps in perfect synchronization, though they were merely walking and not marching. They seemed not like people, but rather like automatons in an Eddonish clockwork. He supposed, in a certain grisly sense, that was what they were now—tools. Extensions of their mistress's will.

Myreon passed by. She looked spent and lost in thought, her golden hair in disarray around her shoulders. Her eyes were ringed by dark bags and remained fixed on some distant thing—some knowledge or goal that she bore alone. He felt an impulse to step forward and call to her, to see if he could help her or listen to her troubles. Indeed, the ring flashed with heat, prodding him to do just that.

But he clenched his fists and held fast. *No*, he told himself, *I won't be king again. I won't do that to these people. I won't do that to myself.* So he only watched Myreon pass, knowing she was struggling with something, suffering under some burden. He grimaced at the ring burning him. *Let her bear it—she made this army, she wanted this war. Let her wage it.*

A heavy hand fell on his shoulder and Tyvian spun, hand on his knife.

But it was only Eddereon. "You and I must speak."

Tyvian looked around. No one was paying much attention—everybody was too busy chattering over what that iron box was in the general's lap. It occurred to Tyvian that this was the first time he and Eddereon would be able to have a candid conversation for weeks. "You're goddamned right we need to speak!"

Eddereon pulled him behind a wagon full of battered pots and pans. "We have a problem."

Tyvian shoved him. It felt good to shove the sergeant. "Stop saying things I already know! You know what she was planning? Artus was the target all along!"

Eddereon grimaced. "Mort and Hambone were supposed to bag him in the castle and then Fawnse was going to demand a surrender, but they didn't have the guts, I guess. If they had, I'm guessing it would be Fawnse's army walking to Ayventry, only to find Sahand's taken over . . ."

"Eddereon"—Tyvian pointed at his filthy, bearded visage—"is this the face of a man who wants to discuss military strategy with you? Now, what are we doing now? Voth never shares anything with me—she's too suspicious."

"She's already reported back to . . ." Eddereon looked around and then lowered his voice. ". . . Her *employer.* I was sent to find you—something new is in the works."

Tyvian frowned. *So Voth has a sending stone too . . . interesting.* "And?"

"We are to remain embedded with the White Army."

Tyvian shook his head. "Really? She won't get another try at Artus—not now."

Eddereon nodded. "Worse than that, the longer we're stuck here, the slimmer the chance of getting to Dellor to help your mother."

The comment brought Tyvian up short. He looked at Eddereon. "What? Are . . . are you *still* on that particular fantasy? Gods, man—let it go. Nobody can save my mother. Not even my *mother.*"

A troop of women came by, crowding the pot-seller's wagon. They seemed angry over something—a dispute over the provenance of the man's wares, it seemed. Eddereon put an arm around Tyvian and they walked away. The big Northron whispered in Tyvian's ear, "Just because it is unlikely to succeed, doesn't mean we shouldn't *try!*"

Tyvian rolled his eyes. "This entire bloody army is an argument against that particular maxim. I don't know what Sahand has planned, but after seeing the Ghouls, I'm quite certain his forces are going to chew these people apart."

"Also true." He flexed his ring hand. "I'm just not equipped for this life anymore. Gods, I've been in agony ever since that village—"

"You and me both." They waited for a column of footmen practicing their marching to pass and continued on their way. "So we can't stay here, but if we give Voth the slip, we can't continue north without having to pass through occupied territory while marked as deserters. Is that about the shape of it?"

Eddereon nodded. "She'll report you immediately. Sahand would spare no expense to hunt you down."

Tyvian shook his head, eyeing a drunk man sleeping between two tents. "But if I'm caught *here*, the whole premise this army is founded on evaporates—I faked my death and thus tricked them into this foolhardy revolution. Sahand is even *more* likely to win. Hell of a pickle you've gotten me into, Eddereon. The hell of it is that we can't even strangle Voth in the middle of the night and solve our problems—thanks to *these*." Tyvian waggled his ring at him.

Eddereon shrugged and stepped over the drunk. "This is why I came to you. You're a smuggler. Smuggle us. We've got to escape, and before the next battle. I have a bad feeling about what's about to happen."

He thought of the look on Myreon's face. "Me too, and I had a feeling we were going to need to come up with an exit plan. I've been thinking on it for a few days."

Eddereon grinned. "So you've already got a plan?"

"I do," he said. "But you're not going to like it."

CHAPTER 18

A NIGHT OF KNIVES

The city of Ayventry—a pleasant trading capital of colorful roofs, ivy-colored walls, and beautiful stonework—looked bigger than Myreon remembered, but perhaps that was because it was flying Sahand's colors from every turret and spire in the city. All the black and silver, all the devices of a dozen different mercenary companies—each more sinister than the last—somehow transformed the city into something malevolent, like a beast sitting astride the Freegate Road.

It was hard to count the black tabards atop the city's low walls, but Myreon tried anyway. They looked endless—and well equipped and well disciplined and . . . gods. *What have I done? Where have I led us?*

Barth lowered the viewing glass. "I think it's clear where all the food went in this country. Never seen a better fed bunch in all my days."

"Should we ask for a parley?" Artus asked, shuffling in his saddle.

"Why?" Myreon grumbled. "So Sahand can shoot us when we get within range?"

"He'll be making a deal while sitting on all the goods," Barth said. "Never the best idea to do that, especially with a fellow they call 'the Mad Prince.'"

Valen rode up and handed Myreon a report of his inspection. "We're in another impossible position here, General. We have ladders and some rams—we can probably get over that old wall—but we'll never take the city. We can't breach the castle even assuming we get to it, not with all of Sahand's strength inside the walls."

"And we won't be turning them against Sahand, either." Barth spat on the ground. "Those bastards are collaborators—every one of them. Damned Ayventrymen. Stab you in the back for a copper, and no mistake."

Myreon again found all eyes on her, and on Spidrahk's Coffer strapped to her saddle. "No."

Barth threw up his hands. "What's the point of having the damned thing if you won't use it? Why'd you bother getting it in the first place? We might have been here two days earlier if you hadn't gone off to who knows where!"

"Mind your tone, Barth," Artus said, glaring down from the saddle at the old carpenter.

Barth knuckled his forehead. Myreon could tell his heart wasn't behind it, though. Barth had been troubled ever since Tor Erdun. He had raged at Artus and her more than once over their decision to spare Fawnse and to release their prisoners. She was beginning to wonder if the war was becoming too much for him. No one, though, had the same connections with the common people that formed the White Army's rank and file. From simply a political point of view, relieving Barth of his duties would be a mistake. *That sounds like something Tyvian would have said,* she thought, frowning. She wasn't sure if that was a good thing or a bad thing.

The old carpenter also had a point. The battered, ancient box seemed to glower at her from her lap, cold and heavy. She knew very little about how it worked, but she had puzzled out the basics: if she used sorcery or force to pry open that box, it would be released. Once released, scores of people would die for miles around. She couldn't be certain it would be just her enemies, either. The legends only spoke of it being used to decimate a whole kingdom in a single night. It said nothing of whether the bearer of the Dark survived its use.

Xahlven, though, had said that this was only a

piece of the whole. It might not be so destructive as the original, or perhaps it could be more easily controlled. The simplest solution was to send the White Guard bearing the box, have them sneak into the city in the dead of night, and then pry the box open. It sounded so easy it was actually frightening.

But how many innocent people would die? How could she be certain it killed Sahand's men and not the citizens of Ayventry? Collaborators or not, she was here to *save* Eretheria, not destroy its second largest city and everyone in it.

She shook her head. "We can win without that kind of sorcery. We showed that at Tor Erdun—there's no reason we can't do it here, too." Myreon watched Valen, Artus, and Barth. All three of them looked dubious.

Artus, though, was putting on a brave face. "All right then, General—what's the plan?"

"Once it gets dark, Barth, I want you to muster the infantry. Then we will make a frontal assault on my say-so, but not before."

"More of your tricks with the walking dead?"

Myreon gave him a hard look. "You wanted me to use sorcery, and this is the sorcery I choose to use." *And if Saldor comes down on us, perhaps at least I will have spared the world another atrocity like Erdun town.* "It is time our fallen brothers and sisters had their revenge, don't you think?"

"It ain't natural and you know it." Barth spat again.

"War never is," Myreon countered. "You all know your duties—attend to them."

In order for Tyvian and Eddereon's plan to neutralize Voth and escape to work, they needed Voth to make the first move—they needed to nab her just before she took action against Artus. Voth, however, was biding her time as they came down out of the mountains. Therefore, Tyvian, Voth, and Eddereon spent a lot of time together on the road.

All of them knew the game they were playing even though all of them pretended they didn't. Voth had quickly identified Eddereon and Tyvian's alliance, and of course she had—the big Northron was about as subtle as a war horse. Tyvian, for his part, took note of all the times Voth was out of sight and tracked her movements as best he could—that last was damnably difficult, too, as the petite woman seemed able to vanish in a blink of an eye. Tyvian's solution for minimizing this was to be with her as often as possible, preferably in the midst of some amorous embrace.

It was a strange thing, their relationship. Stranger even than his affair with Myreon. While that had been characterized by constant bickering, there was a certain trust between them—Tyvian always knew that, no matter what, Myreon was a good and decent person and could be relied upon to do the good and decent thing. With Voth, there was no arguing, no accusations, no anger. She was easy to be with—she had a sharp wit Tyvian loved, and smiles came easily to her lips. They never fought. But there were secrets between them—deep, dark secrets that went far beyond their current game of cat and mouse. He felt like he knew Voth, but he did not. When her body was pressed against his, it was all too easy to forget this. He got the sense that Voth felt the same way.

Since her confession to him after Tor Erdun, they had spent every night in each other's arms. Voth was always hesitant at first, lying tense and restless beside him, but gradually she relaxed and nestled against Tyvian's sculpted torso, her hair flowing beneath his chin and filling his nostrils with its scent. He would lie awake as she slept, breathing her in.

Sometimes, late into the night, he would wake up to find her crying. He never stirred; he never asked what was wrong, as he would have done for Myreon. He only lay there and kept his breathing steady and let her press against him, her tears dropping gently on his chest. He knew it was not his place to ask.

One morning, he went outside the tent to find Mort and Hambone there, squatting around the fire with Eddereon. Ham offered Tyvian a sheepish grin. "Hey, Duchess."

Tyvian decided to pretend nothing was potentially amiss by squatting beside them. His posture, however, kept his boot knife in easy reach. "We thought you'd run off."

"We're in the Young Prince's retinue," Mort said. "He keeps us close."

"And busy," Hambone added.

I bet he does. There was, in that moment, a little surge of pride in Tyvian's chest. Artus didn't trust these two. Artus was having them watched. Which meant, of course, *he* was being watched right now, too. Hopefully not by anybody he knew in his old life.

"We need to speak to—" Mort began, but Tyvian cut him off.

"Yes, of course—you need those tunics laundered. Just a moment." He got up and went into the tent.

Voth was there at the seam of the door, listening. "Those idiots," she said. "They've got a tail."

"I'm betting the tail is *also* an idiot," Tyvian said. "And we can probably use this to your . . . or, well, *our* advantage."

The two fake knights were invited inside the tent, and the four of them had a hushed discussion while Tyvian found Hambone and Mort fresh clothing. It was decided they would remain close to Artus and behave like total angels. "Then, when his guard is down . . ." Voth was assuming they all knew what she meant.

In the case of Mort and Hambone, Tyvian didn't think that was a guarantee. But he had no intention of doing Voth's plotting for her *entirely*. After all, he was only helping this much because he was trying to get *her* guard down.

So things went for the next few days—Mort and Hambone returned for regular reports in the guise of getting various things from their tent or giving Tyvian various orders.

As the sun set on that first day camped outside of Ayventry, the army was restless. The infantry had been called to ranks—according to Voth's dimwitted spies, they were going to storm the walls in the night. The rest of the camp—the gaggle of entertainers, merchants, prostitutes, servants, pages, and even the few remaining knights—sat around their campfires and strained their ears for some sign of what was to come next. The White Guard had departed all at once, slinking into the darkness for some task as yet unknown. It seemed like the world was holding its breath.

Tyvian thought Myreon's plan was obvious enough. The White Guard would serve as some kind of diversion or perhaps be used to burn the gatehouse or kill sentries. As Sahand moved to react to this probing attack, Myreon would command her army of angry Eretherians to assault in earnest. As plans went, it was reasonably clever. But if Myreon thought that Sahand wasn't expecting something like this, she was woefully underestimating him.

Again, there was that urge to talk to her. To help her, somehow. He had seen her again that afternoon, coming back from observing the city. She looked so tired—gaunt, even. She was giving too much of herself to this army, to these people. Gods knew how much strain maintaining the control of the White Guard must put her under. He wanted to find her and tell her none of this was worth it. These people—this rabble of Eretherian patriots—didn't love her and never would. That distinction they reserved for the Young Prince.

Of course, Tyvian *had* told Myreon all that. It hadn't made any difference. Myreon wanted to bring justice to the land. It didn't matter that she was the only one.

He thought again about his choice to fake his death. He had done it to avert a civil war, and it had worked after a fashion. But even this war—the battles fought and the battles yet to come—was a lot of blood spilled. He tried to think of a way he might have stopped it, too, but he couldn't think of anything. Had he remained and become king, the civil war would have been assured and Sahand would have won out in the end. That would have been worse.

Or so he told himself.

Around Tyvian's campfire sat their little band of spies. Hambone and Mort and Eddereon in their mail, Tyvian in his faux livery and mail shirt, and Voth in her washer-woman disguise. They passed around a little strip of salted pork—the only one they had—each gnawing off a small piece before sending it along. It did nothing to fill the echoing hunger in Tyvian's belly.

Voth glanced up at the moon, as though checking something. The hair on the back of Tyvian's neck stood on end. *Tonight is the night.* He looked over at

Eddereon, whose black eyes were there to meet his. The former mercenary nodded almost imperceptibly. He had seen it, too.

Voth grinned at Hambone and Mort. "Can I trust you gentlemen?"

Hambone was gnawing on the pork. His eyebrows shot up and he answered with his mouth full. "Whatcha mean?"

"It isn't typical for men in your situation to swear fealty to one master and still remain loyal to another, is it?" she said. Tyvian couldn't see Voth's hands—they were beneath her apron. She must have just slipped them there. There was a tightening in his gut. He wanted to warn them, but knew that opening his mouth would be a death sentence for them, anyway.

He wondered, briefly, when he had started to care so much.

The two Dellorans exchanged glances. They understood what was being asked.

Mort, always the more cunning of the duo, rubbed his fat orange beard. "The Young Prince is a fine enough boy, miss, but he's no Sahand."

Hambone considered this statement and, at length, nodded. "Yeah. Yeah, he's right."

Voth smiled. "Good. Because a certain other prince has promised us all a grand sum if we complete our mission to his satisfaction. And I'm afraid you won't be able to do so if you lose your damned nerve again."

Mort's face was grim. "What do we have to do?"

"Just stand ready to do whatever I tell you to," Voth said.

From somewhere in the distance, a man cried out in pain. There was a clash of steel from elsewhere. Some shouts of alarm.

Voth stood up. "That's our cue. Follow me."

Tyvian and Eddereon locked eyes once again. "Ready?" the big Northron asked.

"As I'll ever be," Tyvian said.

They followed Voth deeper into the camp, just as the alarm bell started to ring.

Artus was in his tent having his armor strapped on by one of Valen's lesser cousins—a boy of about twelve with a weak chin and tangled mop of brown hair who trembled each time Artus looked at him. It was a weird feeling, being feared. He had so little experience with it, he had no idea how to act—should he comfort him? Scare him more? Say nothing?

Even though it was late, Michelle was up, hands clenched in her lap as she sat on the edge of the bed. "There's no reason you should go to battle. You *know* this!"

"If I don't go, everyone will wonder why I'm not there," Artus countered. "I'll be fine—it'll be dark and I've got a magic shield."

"That *glows in the dark!*"

"Oh, right—good point." He lifted his arms so the boy—his page, Artus supposed, though such a thing hadn't been formalized yet—could slip his mail shirt over his head and arms.

Which was when the screaming started.

At first, Artus wasn't sure what to make of it. The page stopped in his duties, his head popping up like a deer in a meadow. Artus grabbed his sword off its stand, but didn't draw it. "Did you hear that?" he asked Michelle.

Michelle stood up. "Are we . . . being attacked?"

"No, that's impossible," Artus said. "We're watching the gates."

Another scream. A clash of steel.

Michelle put a hand to her mouth. "*All* of the gates? Even in the dark?"

The alarm bell began to ring.

Artus drew his sword and moved to leave, but Michelle caught his arm. "No! Don't—they're after you!"

Artus blinked. "What? How do you know?"

"Calassa, Artus! Remember the Battle of Calassa—Sahand's biggest defeat!"

Artus stared at her. Michelle had just said the *only* thing he remembered about the Battle of Calassa.

"Finn Cadogan, the famous mercenary captain, led a band of his Iron Men into Sahand's camp the night before the battle and assassinated Sahand's officers. *Sahand's doing the same thing!*" Michelle looked around the tent. "We've got to hide you somewhere!"

Outside, some men in armor rushed past. Artus thought he heard Valen's voice.

"Don't be ridiculous." Artus turned to talk to his page, but the boy was gone already. "Great. Michelle, can you lace on my breastplate?"

"Are you crazy?" Michelle yelled as she dumped the contents of an armoire on the ground. "The assassins might be here any second!"

Artus frowned at the clothing all over the ground. "Ummm . . . that's kinda the reason I feel like my breastplate might be, you know, *important to have on*."

The sounds of fighting were becoming louder and more widespread. *Gods*, Artus thought, *how many men are out there?*

Michelle pointed into the empty armoire. "Get in! I'll tell them you went to find Myreon."

"What, am I supposed to hide in a bloody box while they kill you?" Artus shook his head. "*You* hide in there! But only after you lace on my damned breastplate!"

"Sire!" The Hadda knight who called himself Mort ducked inside the tent. "Glad I've found you!" Behind him was the one called Hambone, who looked troubled.

"What's the situation?" Artus asked.

"This." Mort hit Artus in the jaw so hard he knocked him clean off his feet. The world spun. Michelle screamed.

He managed to roll onto all-fours. Mort loomed

over him, a tidal wave of muscle. Artus got his feet under him and leapt upward, taking the big man in the chin with the top of his skull. Mort groaned and staggered backward. Artus, though, was already moving. Three hard uppercuts into Mort's stomach and then a left hook to the jaw and the man went down. He was still dizzy from the cheap shot, though, so when he looked around, the tent seemed tilted to one side. "I . . . I really shoulda seen that coming . . ." he muttered, spitting blood.

Hambone was in front of Michelle, his arms spread. "Easy now!" he was saying. "Easy, easy!"

Michelle screamed and threw a folding chair at the chunky man. *"Artus! Help!"*

Artus kicked out Hambone's knee and, as the man fell over, Artus went behind and locked his head in a sleeper hold. He heard Hambone gag.

But Mort was back up, this time with an iron candelabra. He hit Artus between the shoulders, which hurt like hell. He threw his weight to one side, causing Hambone to spin around and catch the second blow in the face. Blood spurted across the tent canvas and Hambone choked, spitting teeth.

Artus was under Hambone now, the choke hold still in place, but it was an unenviable position. Michelle was still screaming. "Run!" he yelled. "Get help!"

Mort threw the candelabra down and caught Michelle as she tried to run. She punched and kicked and bit, but Mort was in mail and Michelle's twig-like arms had all the force of a kitten's paws.

And it wasn't just Mort and Hambone anymore.

A sword—his sword—pressed against his cheek. "Let him go, Artus. Sahand wants you alive, but he said nothing about wanting you pretty."

Artus looked up. There, sighting down the length of his own broadsword, was a beautiful girl with one eye and a wicked grin on her face. He recognized her instantly: Adatha Voth. The woman who tried to kill Tyvian Reldamar.

Artus released Hambone, who rolled off him, coughing and sputtering. Artus kept his hands up, where Voth could see them.

"Michelle," he called, keeping his eyes fixed on Voth. "Are you okay?"

"She's tryin' to bite me fingers, if that answers you," Mort growled.

Voth backed away and motioned with the tip of her blade. "Up. Slowly now, or Mort sees how breakable your skinny little harlot is."

Two more men entered the room. He heard a voice—also familiar, though he couldn't quite place it—say, "The way is clear, but not for long."

Artus didn't take his eyes off Voth, nor did she take her *eye* off him. He watched for a slip, a distraction—nothing. He could see now how dangerous she was. He could see how she might have gotten the drop on even Tyvian. "You'll never get out of this camp alive. There isn't a man here who wouldn't die for me."

Voth smiled. "I believe that is the idea, yes." She jerked her chin in the direction of the armoire. "In the box with you, boy."

Artus shook his head. "No. You'll have to kill me first."

"Wrong." Voth spoke to the two newcomers. "Put him in. The girl too, Mort."

The two men grabbed Artus by the arms and muscled him toward the armoire. He wanted to shout, wanted to struggle, but then he saw Michelle, her delicate throat in the meaty paws of that oaf, Mort, and he held his tongue.

They pushed him into the armoire and Michelle followed quickly after. Then, for the first time, he caught a glimpse of the two men who had put him there. His eyes widened, but before he could find the words to say, the doors were slammed shut and locked.

Artus gaped into the darkness, Michelle trembling beside him.

The two men had been none other than Eddereon and Tyvian-goddamned-Reldamar.

CHAPTER 19

OVER THE TOP

"General!" The boy—a page, Myreon thought—
came to attention beside her stirrup. "It's a sneak
attack! The Ghouls of Dellor are burning the camp!"

Myreon tore her attention from the doings of the
White Guard for long enough to look down at the
page. "Is Sir Valen handling it?"

"Trying, sir—umm—ma'am! He needs reinforcements!"

Myreon cursed. She didn't have time for this, especially not now. "Talk to Barth! I'm busy!"

"But General!"

Myreon shooed him away with her foot. "Go!"

She focused again on the linking stone in her hand.

It glowed with a clean, white light—here, on the Freegate Road, they were astride a ley line that travelled from Eretheria through to Freegate, making the link between the subterranean ritual and her distant army bright and clear. Through it, she could sense the doings of her undead minions and could relay commands through the summoned djinn that acted as invisible sergeants, wielding the White Guard as a perfectly synchronized military force.

They were on top of the wall now in three different places, their bodies riddled with arrows but otherwise operating at peak efficiency. As she had predicted, the psychological aspect of fighting the living dead was overcoming their rather substantial weaknesses in actual combat. Sahand's troops on the wall were in a panic, retreating and locking themselves inside the square, fat turrets of the old wall and calling for reinforcements.

The White Guard were not especially strong and did not possess the specialized weapons to breach a turret door. They also hadn't really managed to kill or wound a great many of Sahand's men, comparatively. That was not their task, however. When Myreon could see that the walls were clear and the defenders distracted, she willed her minions into the second phase of her plan.

Dozens of undead soldiers reached under their robes to produce coils of rope, which they then looped around a sturdy crenel or sconce or similar and threw the rest over the wall. Even if Sahand's men had a sudden fit of courage and broke out of the turrets and gatehouses, they'd be hard pressed to cut all the ropes before the real soldiers—the living soldiers—got there.

Myreon let herself return to the world around her. "Now! Advance! Sound the advance—double time! Quickly!"

The drums began. Myreon herself rode down the back of the line, shouting at her men to hurry. "Bring your ladders! Men of Eretheria, your moment is now!"

Uneasy over the sneak attack to their rear, the White Army was slow to move—armies, at the best of times, were ponderous things, and in the dark and confused with an enemy to the rear was not the best of times. Yet move they did, urged on by the bellows of Gammond Barth and his lieutenants—all of them guilders of good reputation and fearsome character. Gradually, as it became clear that the walls were comparatively undefended, the men began to run faster and faster across the grassy field between them and the old walls.

Myreon followed the army forward, even while she desperately wished to know what was happening behind her. *No*, she told herself, *that's what Sahand wants—that was his plan all along.* She put a Lumenal enchantment on her eyes to let her see better in the dark. It showed her the great mass of the White Army scrambling up ropes and ladders even as the arrows of the Dellorans in the turrets rained down on them. There was no stopping them now—the walls were as good as breached. She heard the *thok* of axes biting into wood—they were attempting to breach the nearest gatehouse. Good, all to plan.

Rubbing the linking stone, she commanded the White Guard down off the walls and into the streets of the city itself. They took up defensive positions on key streets, their spears angled outward to receive a charge. They were engaged in combat almost immediately by Delloran infantry. The White Guard would lose—no doubt about that—but it would take time for the Dellorans to hack them apart to the point where they would be unable to fight.

She feyleapt from her horse to the top of the walls and, waving her men aside, blew the door to one of the turrets with the Shattering. As the first man charged in, Myreon laid a blade ward on him, and just in time for a sword aimed at his throat to be turned aside. On her other hand, a gatehouse door had been wrenched open and a bloody battle was joined. Sahand's men were better trained and better armed, but they were outnumbered and unnerved.

In a brief moment of respite, Myreon looked back at the camp. It was burning, orange fire licking upward from dozens of tents. In the blazing light she could see the silhouettes of men fighting—a desperate, brutal kind of combat fought in disorganized pockets.

It's all right, she told herself, *the soldiers are with me—if Sahand burns the camp, we are still an army. By morning, we'll have a city instead.*

And that was when the White Guard, as one, ceased to function.

Only Myreon felt it, but the sudden change to the ley was so forceful she felt kicked in the gut. She staggered against a wall. "Wh . . . what?" She lifted up the linking stone—it had gone dark. Someone had interfered with the ritual back in Eretheria. Gods knew what the kickback from the miscast must have been, but it didn't matter. The White Guard were now nothing but dead bodies. The reinforcements—Sahand's troops—were all on their way now. From the top of the wall, she scanned the mayhem around her, the press of bodies in bleached tabards, until she found a man with a horn. "You! Blow the advance! We need to get off this wall and into the streets, *now!*"

The man put the horn to his lips and started to blow, only to get an arrow through his hand. He howled, the instrument knocked clear over the wall. Myreon grimaced and worked a basic illusion—that of a horn, sounding the advance. It was hastily done and didn't sound especially realistic, but it was loud and she didn't think anybody was going to be discussing sound quality in the midst of a melee.

It worked. The gates of the one gatehouse they'd claimed were thrown open and hundreds of White Army footmen swarmed through, halberds held low.

They met the Dellorans in the marketplace beyond, and the clash of steel and the screams of the wounded grew louder still.

Myreon threw a ball of fire at the nearest block of Delloran pikes and then, reinforcing her wards, leapt down to the streets below. The battle had begun now in earnest.

It was going to be a long night.

Voth led Tyvian, Eddereon, and the two Delloran pseudo-knights out of the camp and away from the battle. Mort and Hambone had the armoire between them, running at a steady pace despite the weight. Tyvian and Eddereon, swords drawn, menaced away anybody who came close. It worked—very few wanted to challenge a squad of men carrying furniture when there were a lot of other men running around with torches trying to burn down tents. They were outside the camp in a matter of minutes.

"Oy!" Hambone called out. "This here is heavy! Let's have a rest, eh?"

Voth pointed to Tyvian and Eddereon. "You two—switch off with them! Hurry up! The rendezvous point is less than a mile off."

Tyvian found himself carrying the back end of the armoire. It was devilishly heavy, made more so by the fact that Artus was inside throwing his weight around in awkward ways. It was like carrying a trunk with a wildcat inside. *Good lad*, he thought to himself, *keep it up*.

The ring was like a hot dollop of lead on his finger, dragging his arms down and punishing him with every step. Eddereon must have felt the same way, as he kept releasing the armoire with his ring hand to shake it around. They were at the rear of the party, now—Voth, Mort, and Hambone were scouting ahead, Voth lighting the way with a small feylamp. It was all the two of them could do to keep up.

"Eddereon," Tyvian panted. "Do you . . . have the materials?"

Eddereon glanced over his shoulder. He also sounded winded. "Yes."

"Don't hesitate! When it's time, just go for it. I'll back you up."

"This won't work, Tyvian," Eddereon said, adjusting his grip on the armoire. "She isn't right for this."

Tyvian's shoulders and arms burned with fatigue. "None of us were. Just do it!"

Behind a small tool shed built beside a rusty old pump, there was a wagon with a two-horse team already hitched. Voth leapt into the seat. "Throw it in the back—come on!"

Eddereon and Tyvian, with the last of their strength, hoisted the armoire into the bed of the wagon and hopped up next to it. Voth was already ordering the horses forward. Tyvian rested against the side of the wagon and looked back for the first time. The camp burned with dozens of individual fires. "Kroth's teeth—the whole thing is going up. All this over Artus?"

Eddereon's face looked bloody in the flickering red glow of the night. "No—all this for a symbol."

Tyvian pursed his lips. Of course, of course—Artus was not a boy, he was a *prince.* Though they were concurrent states, they were not equivalent. Sahand wanted a prince captured, and if that meant a whole camp needed to burn, then so be it. It was just too easy to forget the world saw Artus differently than he did.

"He saw us," Eddereon whispered. "He recognized me."

"Me too. Which is why we can't screw this up."

Eddereon frowned—wanting to argue further perhaps—but there was no time. He nodded. "I'll be ready."

The wagon rattled down a rutted old road that circled the city walls. The battle left them behind—they passed one gate, two. At the third gate, Voth swung the wagon toward the city. They were now on the northwest side. The gate in front of them was small and looked unmanned. When they came close, Voth threw back her hood and called up to the gatehouse. "I am Adatha Voth. Open in the name of Banric Sahand!"

They didn't have to wait long. The gates swung open on counterweights and they rode through—no one challenged them. Once the gates boomed closed behind them, Voth began to relax a bit. She smiled back at her team. "We are all going to be rich beyond our wildest dreams, gentlemen."

All four sets of eyes turned toward her did not reflect the mirth she had expected. "Gods, don't tell me the lot of you were *taken* by the whole Young Prince myth, were you?"

Hambone looked at his hands. "He were a good sort."

Mort prodded his swollen jaw. "Hell of a left, I'll give the boy that."

Voth pulled up her sleeve, revealing a leather bracer in which were sheathed four throwing knives. "Nobody give me any reason to use these." She pointed at Tyvian. "Especially *you*."

Mort whistled low. "Lover's quarrel, Duchess?"

"Something like that," Tyvian said. He kept his eyes on the streets, on the windows of the houses they passed. Not a light in any of them, and everything boarded up as though for a storm. The city wasn't abandoned, though—people were hiding, probably huddled in their root cellars or under beds, waiting for the battle to end.

Tyvian looked at Hambone. "I've got to know—why'd you choose Sahand over him?" He kicked the side of the armoire, which still thumped occasionally from the efforts of its prisoners.

"Whatcha mean?" Hambone asked.

"The Young Prince here saved your life—you said so yourself. He treated you with respect, he counted you among his friends. Why betray a man like that for a man like Banric Sahand?"

Hambone laughed. "That don't even make sense."

"What doesn't?"

"You can't understand 'cause you're not from Dellor," Mort said. "If you're from Dellor, you understand."

Eddereon was trying to catch his eye—Tyvian knew Eddereon wanted to spring their trap, and now, but he couldn't. Not until he got his answer. "Try to *make* me understand, Mort."

In the distance, a church bell began to ring. It was echoed by another, and then another. Eddereon sniffed the air—it smelled faintly of smoke. "The White Army has breached the walls. If we're headed to the castle, we'd better hurry."

Voth chuckled. "We're in no danger, trust me."

Tyvian turned his attention back to the Dellorans. "Well?"

Mort prodded at his bruised jaw. "In Dellor, we've got nothing—*nothing*. There's barely any food, no big cities, no roads worth using—nothing like this down here." The big man shrugged. "Tell you a story: when my da was a boy, he watched my uncle and his parents starve to death one winter, only he didn't know it was happening. They just kept passing the food down, ya know? Kept the youngest alive. Fur trappers found him come spring. He thought his family had just been sleeping. For a week."

Hambone nodded. "That happened to my cousin. Happens often enough, if you catch a bad break. My sister was taken by folk like that—they lost their claim in the mine and went to banditry."

Tyvian's mouth had gone dry. "What happened to her?"

Hambone shook his head. "Never found out. Figure they ate her or something. Some folk do that."

"*Did* that," Mort corrected him. "Not since Sahand. He put a stop to it."

"My father joined Sahand's army when it went south," Hambone added. "He didn't come back, but Sahand paid my mother his weight in silver for not bringing him home."

"You southlanders think about Sahand, and you think of an invader," Mort said, "but we see him as a provider. Everything I got—everything my family's got, everything anybody I ever knew got—they got from the hand of the Prince of Dellor." Mort pointed at the armoire. "The boy prince can keep his *respect*. Me? I'll take food for my family and my weight in silver to my wife. No one else can give me that."

"By pillaging other countries?" Tyvian asked.

"Look around," Mort countered. "You shits got enough."

Tyvian *did* look around—at the quaint little

houses and the cheery tavern signs, the flowers in the window boxes and the glitter of the occasional iron street lamp, the pretty statues and the plazas full of big trees. Mort was right. They did have enough. More than, in fact.

Tyvian reflected that the last time he had been here was when he first met Artus. The boy had been a filthy street urchin then, a foot shorter and skinny as a colt. Tyvian had picked him off the street for his profile, considering it inherently aristocratic. Now the boy was a prince, and Tyvian was about to dump him right back in the place he'd found him. The irony left a bad taste in his mouth.

Almor Castle—the seat of the counts of Ayventry—seemed to spring out of nowhere, popping into view as they rounded a corner as though they'd turned the page in a storybook. The castle was comparatively new, having been rebuilt after the end of the last war. It had a contemporary style—soaring windows and dagger-sharp spires, flying buttresses and a gold-leafed central dome. Tyvian didn't need to be a mage to know that, while the place looked fragile, it had enough wards and defensive abjurations placed upon it that it could likely withstand any conventional siege.

Unlike the rest of the city, Almor was positively bustling with activity. Delloran mercenaries were marshaling in the plaza before the gates and marching off to repulse invaders, and the battlements were full of Sahand's command staff, eyeing the battle on the other side of the town through Kalsaari spyglasses and dispatching couriers here and there. Somewhere in there was an anygate that led directly to Sahand himself—Tyvian would bet his life on it—and that was where they were about to go.

He and Eddereon were running out of time.

They couldn't spring their trap in the field, and not in the gates, and they certainly couldn't spring it in a plaza full of Delloran soldiers. They had to do it now. Tyvian nodded to Eddereon.

Eddereon reached over the side of the moving wagon, grabbed the rim of the wheel, and broke it with a quick, ring-enhanced wrench of his hand. The wagon lurched to a halt, causing Mort and Hambone to tumble over into the front of the wagon bed and almost sending Voth flying onto the backs of the horses.

"Kroth's teeth!" she snarled and hopped down to the street to inspect the damage. "Krothing cut-rate wheels!"

Tyvian pointed up the street toward the brightly lit plaza full of Dellorans. "It's a short walk. We can carry it the rest of the way, right?"

Voth looked at him, one eyebrow raised. "Is that you . . . *volunteering* for physical labor?"

Despite himself, Tyvian grinned. "I've got to hand it to you—you're sharp."

Then Eddereon threw the armoire on top of her

with one quick heave. The petite Voth was pinned to the ground as completely as if a horse had sat on her.

Hambone looked poleaxed. "Wh . . . what are you doing?"

Tyvian drew a dagger and placed it at Hambone's throat. "I don't want to kill you, so don't make me."

Mort was quicker on the draw—he charged Tyvian, spearing him against the side of the wagon and knocking Tyvian's head against the top of the wheel. Lights flashed in his eyes along with the pain.

Eddereon was on the big man in an instant, grabbing him by his sword belt and heaving him across the street like a bale of hay. By that time, Hambone had his sword drawn. Voth was gasping from under the armoire. *"Help! Help! Treachery!"*

Eddereon charged after Mort, his sword out. Tyvian faced Hambone, drawing his sword more from ingrained muscle memory than intent. The world still seemed to wobble a bit from his knock on the head.

Hambone slashed at Tyvian's face, which Tyvian parried without needing to think about it. "Ham, put up your sword—you don't need to do this."

"You put up *your* sword!" the Delloran countered. "You've gone mad!"

There was a clash of steel behind Tyvian, and Hambone's attention was momentarily diverted toward Mort and Eddereon's fight. Tyvian took the opportunity to knock the sword from Hambone's hand with the flat of his blade. Then he put the tip at Hambone's throat. "Yield!"

Hambone blinked at him. "What's 'yield'?"

Then Mort, flying backward from some blow of Eddereon's, slammed into Tyvian's side. Again, Tyvian found himself smashed against the wheel of the damned wagon.

Hambone turned and fled toward the castle, waving his arms. "Danger! Help! Traitors!"

"Kroth." Tyvian dropped a second dagger into his hand and cocked it back to throw—Hambone's broad back made an easy target, and he was silhouetted perfectly by the light of the castle.

But he didn't throw.

Mort was dead weight—whether unconscious or fatally injured, Tyvian couldn't tell. Blood poured from his mouth. "Tyvian!" Eddereon shouted. "The armoire!"

"Right!" Tyvian hacked the lock off the doors and threw them open. "Artus!"

Artus didn't answer—he was unconscious. So was Michelle. He checked their pulses—still alive. "We should have knocked in some damned air-holes."

"*Reldamar!*" Voth shrieked, one arm batting against the side of the armoire. "I knew it! I should have known! You're dead, understand? Dead! I'll find you, wherever you run!"

"Adatha, darling, whatever makes you think I'm

leaving you behind?" Then, ignoring the ring's protests, he kicked her in the face hard enough to knock her out.

"Stop!" It was a small column of Delloran mercenaries, headed their way. Hambone was in the lead.

Eddereon picked up Artus, and Tyvian moved the armoire aside to throw Voth over one shoulder. That left Michelle. With one arm, Tyvian reached down and scooped her up—with the ring pulsing its power through his muscles, she seemed to weigh next to nothing.

Which was good, because now they had to run for it. They heard barking.

Of course the Dellorans had dogs with them. Big, mean-looking ones.

Laden with their human cargo, Eddereon and Tyvian sprinted down an alley into the street beyond. The dogs were hot on their tail, though, covering the distance between them at blistering speed. One set of jaws clamped down on Michelle's dress, which fluttered behind Tyvian like a cape. He yanked it free with a tearing sound and kicked out at the closest dog, but it leapt back. And its four friends were right behind it.

"This way!" Eddereon called. He'd bashed in the door to a thaumaturge's shop. Tyvian darted up the stairs and through, dogs literally nipping at his heels. Eddereon slammed the door on them the moment they were in.

The clambered around in the dark for a second before they found the stairs and headed up. Voth's head knocked vials off of shelves, and Michelle's torn dress pulled over chairs and small tables. Some combination of distillations mixed and started a fire behind them. At the moment, Tyvian considered this an advantage—it would cover their escape.

The dogs' human handlers arrived. They were through the door immediately, armed with axes and maces and other weapons of indiscriminate violence. It didn't take them more than a moment to hear Eddereon and Tyvian knocking around on the stairs and they were after them, fire or no fire.

Eddereon led the way up to the attic and then to a narrow window. He passed Artus out onto the roof and put out his hands. "Voth!"

Tyvian handed her over and Eddereon transferred her outside, too. Then he went. "Come on!"

But the Dellorans were there. The first one went to chop Tyvian in half like a slender tree. He leapt back, but in the process, dropped Michelle. She hit the floor with a thump and stirred. "Wha . . . Artus?"

Two more Dellorans in the room. Tyvian hadn't space beneath the eaves to draw his sword, and the one with the axe was between him and Michelle. The soldier took another swing and Tyvian ducked back again, this time taking him halfway out the window. "Michelle!"

Eddereon grabbed him by the back of the shirt and hoisted him onto the roof. "Let's go!"

"No!" Tyvian scrambled to go back inside, but found himself eye to eye with a Delloran with a dagger in his teeth. He grabbed the hilt of the dagger and pulled, slashing through the man's cheeks, but there were more where that came from—there was no getting in. And the building was on fire.

Eddereon had Artus and Voth each under and arm. "We've got to go! They'll get her out—she's too valuable alive!"

Then he ran along the spine of the roof and leapt to the next house over.

Eddereon was right—they needed to go. Voth could wake up any second, and the plan was not yet secure. Michelle being held prisoner was better than all of them dying in a house fire. Tyvian, his ring squeezing his hand numb, followed Eddereon across the rooftops.

It was time to look for a forge.

The iron ring did not create itself, after all.

CHAPTER 20

THE SACK OF AYVENTRY

The battle raged through the night and into the next day. At some point the battle lines became blurred—no longer were blocks of pikemen and halberdiers maneuvering down streets and holding plazas and marketplaces, but now bands of four or five soldiers from either side were ambushing one another in alleys or shooting arrows down from rooftops. Desperate combat in close quarters, knife against cudgel in the dark. By dawn, the gutters were choked with more blood than the city's sewer demons could eat.

It also became clear to Myreon that she had lost control of her forces. With no camp to return to, the White Army fought with a vicious desperation. While in the field, the disciplined ranks of the Delloran forces were vastly superior, in the cramped lanes of Ayventry, the battle was far more even. In a way it was a repeat of the Battle of Eretheria, but this time the two sides were equally equipped. Sahand's men died in nearly equal proportion to Myreon's own. Bodies clogged the streets so that carts could not get by. Houses burned, and the screams of those trapped inside echoed in Myreon's head.

All of it—the whole battle—had transformed into something different than all the battles before. The orderly pretense of warfare had been stripped away, as had the gleaming moral righteousness of the war's cause. Myreon was witnessing something vicious and barbaric. It was a bonfire that she could not extinguish or even temper—she could only watch as it burned.

She had hoped the Dellorans would surrender. They didn't, however, even as her forces encircled them and drove them back toward Almor Castle. She had hoped the people of Ayventry would rise up with the White Army to throw off their occupiers, but this also didn't happen. They screamed and fought and cursed them. Houses were found booby-trapped. Men were murdered in the dark. To the people, *Myreon* was the invader—the wretched necromancer, come to claim their bones. She was the murderess who had thrown their young Count in a dungeon and now came to destroy their only protector—Banric Sahand.

Then, by dawn, the word had spread that the Young Prince and Lady Michelle were captured—kidnapped in the night by the Ghouls of Dellor, who had murdered good men in their tents in the dark and then vanished into the countryside. By that point they had effectively corralled the remaining Dellorans in the city inside the castle, more or less. The city was virtually theirs. Myreon had hoped a simple parley could win the day.

But the men of Eretheria hadn't marched this far and hadn't bled this much to let Ayventry steal their prince and laugh at them behind their enchanted walls. Myreon was sitting in the common room of a tavern appropriated for her use when she received a bloodied and weary Valen Hesswyn, his helm clutched under one arm, his lips trembling. "The sixth company have begun burning the Garden Row."

Myreon looked up from a hastily drawn map of the city. "What? On whose orders?"

"No one is taking orders anymore, General. I just broke up some looters sacking the library. There's a lynch mob hanging any man they find not in a white tabard. It's chaos out there, and it's getting worse."

"Well? Don't just stand there—*do* something!"

Valen seemed to collect himself. He stood up straight. "I'm going home."

Myreon was already in the middle of doing something else, so it took her a moment to hear what he'd said. "What?"

"I'm going home, Magus." Valen put his helmet on.

Myreon rose, her staff in her hand. "You swore an *oath!*"

"I swore an oath to the White Army!" Valen barked back, his voice cracking. "I swore an oath to the Young Prince! And they're both gone now, General. You wanted me to protect Eretheria? How can I do that when they're killing each other? Is there some spell you can use to make this"—Valen gestured out the window, which showed burning houses and carnage littering the streets—"make this go away? Because I can't."

Myreon blinked. Valen Hesswyn, the de facto Count of Davram, was weeping. *Gods,* she thought, watching his shoulders sag, *he's barely nineteen. Just a boy.*

Valen wiped beneath his eyes and flicked the tears away. "My men are dead. My house is ruined. What . . . what *more* can you ask of me?"

Myreon had a lump in her throat so hard it hurt. "Go."

Valen blinked. "What?"

"Go home. You're right." She looked him in the eye and shook his hand. "There's nothing more you can do. I release you from your oath."

The tears welled again beneath Valen's bloodshot

eyes. "These people . . . these *beasts* don't deserve you, General. They never did."

Myreon waved him away. "Just go."

Valen drew his sword and saluted her, then presented it to her, hilt first. She accepted it, and he went.

She took a moment to collect her thoughts, and then went outside herself. A cordon of weary men in white were blocking off the street, just out of easy bowshot from the castle. Barth was sitting on a barrel, tending to a deep cut along his scalp. "Barth!"

He grinned, holding up a helmet with a deep gash. "Look at that, eh? Battle-axe, right to me temple. Helm saved my life. Fine workmanship, that. Could kiss the bloody smith."

"Barth, get your men in line!" Myreon yelled.

Barth glanced at the rank of pikemen nearby. "They are in line. What are you talking about?"

Myreon gestured around. "Where's the rest of them? Where's the rest of the damned army?"

Barth looked up at her and, in his eyes, she could see that he understood her question. He understood it the first time. He licked his dry, cracked lips. "They're doing what armies do when they capture enemy cities."

Myreon gaped at him. "There was to be no pillaging! No looting! It's the Common Law!"

"This isn't that kind of war, Magus—you said so yourself." Barth stood up and cracked his knuckles. "These here bastards have murdered our wives, burned our villages, and stolen our crops, and here we are, at last, in their city. What did you expect?"

"That was Sahand, not *Ayventry!* These people are *Eretherians*, like you!"

Barth shrugged. "A fine sentiment, Magus, but I'm old enough to remember the *last* time Ayventry-men did this. Except then we had Perwynnon to talk sense into us." Barth grunted a laugh. "Gods, could that man give a speech, too. Talked us right out of killing the lot of these two-faced Ayventry shits and salting their bloody ground. Made us feel like the better men for it, too—made us think we'd done right. But now, look where we are again—betrayed by the same shits."

Myreon pulled herself to her full height, which was a few inches taller than Barth. "You are to recall your men and get them in ranks—that's an *order!*"

"Kroth take your bloody orders, General," Barth spat. "This stinking city needs to pay for all it's done to me and mine, and that is a long bill, let me tell you."

Myreon flinched at the venom in the old man's tone. She softened her voice, trying to find the stalwart old ally she'd leaned on since that first bloody night in Eretheria. "What about the cause, Gammond? What about justice for your people and a new beginning? Don't throw that all away."

"You ever notice, Magus, that you and your Young Prince were the only two folks ever talked about that 'justice' idea? Not a man you spoke to ever said he wanted things to be just, and if he did, he didn't mean it. You, you're an idealist—I admire that, I do—but when you live a life long as I have on this end of the shit-shovel, you understand that some things you just ain't gonna get. Justice? Too expensive for men like me. But revenge? That there's cheap and readily available."

Myreon stepped back from him, scarcely able to understand what he was saying—she just refused to accept it. "Remember what Artus said when they were going to lynch that Delloran prisoner? Barth, this makes us just as bad as they are!"

Barth's eyes blazed in anger. "The hell it does! *I* didn't kill my daughter in the street because she was in the tax-man's way. *I* didn't send my son off to a rich man's war for nothing, only to have him die with an arrow in his throat. *I'm* not the wicked man here, Magus. I'm the avenger." Barth rubbed his cut head, his anger subsiding. He sank back to sitting on the barrel. "If you knew what you were about, you would be, too."

Myreon drew back from him, horrified. "I'll stop them. You'll see. I won't let this happen."

"You're too late, girl. Your prince is gone and now we men of Eretheria are free to do as we please, with no high-handed shit on a pretty horse to tell us what we need."

Myreon leveled her staff at him, its end burning with Fey energy. "Traitor!"

Barth stared Myreon in the eye. "You go on, General. Kill me right here. Won't make a spot of difference now. Today, Ayventry dies, Sahand gets his arse kicked, and tomorrow my people *go home*. They don't need me anymore and they don't need you, either. The war's over."

Myreon shook with anger, but she didn't release the spell. Instead, she backed away from him. Barth laughed. "Like I said, girl—you're too late by half."

Myreon fled into the streets.

Tyvian and Eddereon worked until dawn. The hardest part was forging the ring—neither of them were smiths, though Eddereon had done this before.

Once before.

After a night of fumbling in the dark while a battle raged outside and heating the fires and melting the iron and pouring it into the mold that Eddereon had fashioned, the last part—the most crucial part—was actually the easiest. It was also the most terrifying.

Voth was tied up, her sending stone taken, and then she was stripped of all her many, many daggers and garrotes and poison needles. She thrashed and she screamed into her gag, but there was nothing she could do but watch as Tyvian held the still-hot ring in his right hand—his ring hand—and see it glow with sun-bright light, so intense that the interior of the forge was lit as bright as day.

Tyvian felt as though his hand, then his arm, then his whole body was glowing along with the new ring. He was empowering it somehow, though this was magecraft far, far beyond his experience. It was primal, primordial, even—a sorcery bereft of the complex incantations and centuries of practice and refinement that modern magecraft relied upon. To a simpler soul, it would look as though the power of the god were flowing through Tyvian and into the simple ring in his hand.

He seized Voth's wrist. She struggled, but he held her still. "It's all right, Adatha. I'm not going to hurt you." He saw the terror in her eyes and added, "I am sorry about this."

He forced the ring onto the fourth finger of her right hand. It was too large and, for a moment, Tyvian thought that he had screwed it all up somehow. But then it collapsed in size, all at once, and with the barest gust of air and a soft pop, sealed itself onto her hand.

Voth was screaming, her eyes wild. But then, when there was no pain, she stopped.

Eddereon was on the other side of the room, sitting beside Artus, who was now sleeping comfortably. In the pale light of predawn, Tyvian could not see his face. "You can cut her loose now. I hope you're right about this. I don't think she's right for the ring."

"I'm sorry, Eddereon, but I didn't exactly have the chance to interview her mother at length over her positive qualities," Tyvian said. He loosened the knots in Voth's bindings and stepped back.

It took the assassin alarmingly little time to wriggle out of her bonds. The moment she was free, she cart-wheeled across the room to where a hatchet had been left on a workbench and raised to throw it at Tyvian.

The ring stopped her. Just as it had him, a life-time ago.

Tyvian smiled. *I was right.*

"What . . . what did you *do* to me?" Voth clutched her wrist, looking at her hand like it were some kind of alien appendage.

"Adatha, let me explain—"

Before Tyvian could finish, she flew across the room, hands outstretched, ready to throttle him. Again, the ring stopped her cold. She struggled with it, just as he had, forcing one foot in front of the other as the ring tortured her into submission. "No . . . no . . . noooo . . ." she growled.

Tyvian took a steadying breath. "This would go a lot more easily for you if you just sat down and lis-tened for a moment."

Voth crumpled onto the floor. She was crying, "What . . . what did you do? What did you *do*?"

Tyvian held up his own right hand. "You aren't alone, Voth. What is happening to you now happened to me, once." He pointed at Eddereon. "That is the man who did it to me, too. He has one of his own. Welcome to the club, as it were."

Voth was on all fours, trying to collect her breath. "Why can't I kill you, you son of a bitch?"

"The iron ring seeks to . . . to *focus* your better impulses and excise your worst ones. You can't kill me because to kill me would be wrong."

"Says who?" Voth asked with a breathless laugh.

"Says you, actually. The ring gains its power from you. It contains the best parts of your soul." Tyvian licked his lips. He really couldn't believe he was doing this—it was surreal. He had, at some point, *become* bloody Eddereon. Gods, what a strange life.

Voth sat up and grabbed the ring with one hand, trying to pull it off. She screamed at it. "Get this thing off me! Get it off!"

"I know how you feel, believe me." Tyvian shook his head. "But it's permanent, I'm afraid. The good news is you become much harder to kill."

"And you become a better person," Eddereon added.

"Yes, that too," Tyvian said. "Though I've found the 'being hard to kill' part more beneficial, to be honest."

Voth glared at him, pure murder in her eyes. "Why? Why me? Why not just *kill* me and get it over with?"

"If we'd let you go, you would have revealed me to Sahand. And I couldn't bring myself to kill you."

"Killing you was my vote," Eddereon said, checking on Artus. "But Tyvian's a better person than me."

Voth pushed herself away from the two of them

until her back was to a corner. She hugged her knees to her chest. She was still trembling. "So what happens now? Do we go about the countryside, righting wrongs or some nonsense?"

Eddereon shook his head. "If only it were as easy as all that."

Tyvian looked at him and then back at Voth. "Truth be told, we really hadn't planned much further than this."

Artus stirred, causing both Eddereon and Tyvian to leap up. "Artus?" Tyvian asked. "Artus, can you hear me?"

The boy's eyes fluttered open. "Mi . . . Michelle? Where?"

"Calm down," Tyvian said, taking up his hand. "You're safe for the time being."

Artus sat bolt upright. "Michelle! Where is she?"

Tyvian held up his hands, trying to calm him. "Don't go running off after your lady love, Artus. You need to focus. You need to take a deep breath and get your bearings."

Artus's eyes locked on Tyvian. "You! You're *alive*!"

Tyvian nodded. "Yes. I—"

Artus punched him in the nose. "You lousy son of a bitch! What is the goddamned idea, leaving me like that? Do you know what that was like? Do you know how that made me feel?"

Tyvian tried to formulate an answer, but his face hurt too much. "Artus . . . really . . ."

Artus grabbed Tyvian by his tabard and shook him. "Everybody thinks you're *dead*! They think I'm crazy! Gods, they think I'm a *prince*?"

Tyvian smiled at him. "Well, you do have that nice jawline."

Artus's anger melted from his face. He laughed. And cried. And still laughed. Then he pulled Tyvian into a tight hug. "Oh, gods, Tyvian! I've missed you. I've missed you so *much*."

Tyvian found himself returning the hug. His eyes blurred with tears. "Me too, boy. Me too."

Eddereon slapped Tyvian on the back. "Tyvian— Voth!"

Tyvian released Artus to see that Voth was gone. But where? Not the door—he and Eddereon were sitting by that. Up, then! He charged to the ladder that led to the low roof of the smithy and climbed it as fast as he could. What if he *had* been wrong about Voth? What if she went to Sahand and told him he was alive anyway?

He got to the roof, expecting to see Voth skipping away down a street. Instead, he found her standing, stone-still, by the fat chimney. She was staring at something.

Tyvian looked, too.

The city was burning. Not too far away, a group of thin, desperate-looking men in bleached tabards were dragging people out of their houses and beating them in the middle of the road. Not far beyond that, a man hung by the neck from a streetlamp. He was still kicking.

"Gods," Tyvian said, the ring blazing to life on his hand.

Voth's mouth hung open. "We've got to get out of this city. Now."

Tyvian took her by the hand.

She did not pull away.

CHAPTER 21

MYREON THE DESTROYER

Myreon emerged from the boardinghouse with the ashes of twenty men covering her hands. Twenty of her own men. Men who had cast off their humanity and become beasts. She screamed.

Two hours had passed since she learned of her army's descent into madness. Two hours of her running up and down the streets, screaming commands at looters and lynch mobs. The first groups she met had the decency to look ashamed—to hang their heads and leave their beaten victims on the street. But she was only one woman, mage or not. When she left, the men came back.

She talked to some of them. Interrogated them in alleys at the point of her glowing staff. She asked them why. The responses varied, but all had a central theme: *These people were hoarding food, these people were harboring the enemy, these people betrayed us . . .*

These people . . .

There was no getting around those two words. The good men of the White Army—the revolutionaries Myreon had led across the country to rid it of evil and injustice—had in them the same malice she was trying to stamp out. Appeals to the cause fell on deaf ears and empty stomachs, and all they cared about was that Ayventry had more than they did, and that they got it by helping Sahand. And now the city would be made to pay.

Then there was the boardinghouse. The housemaster had opened his doors to widows and orphaned girls—women with no one to guard them and nowhere to go. He had barred his doors and boarded his windows and kept them all quiet in the dark, waiting for the chaos outside to end. And then someone had found them.

The housemaster put up a fight and killed a man. He died shortly thereafter, and the blood of their comrade gave the hungry, desperate men of the White Army every excuse they needed. Word spread—a house full of Ayventry whores, ready for the taking. That was how Myreon had come upon it. Three floors of rape, of screaming women, of weeping girls beaten bloody by weapons intended for Delloran mercenaries. Weapons paid for by Myreon's own gold.

It was all Myreon could take. The Fey filled her like a volcanic eruption, and she cleansed the house of every man in a white tabard, burning them to the bone, one by one. There was nothing they could do to stop her—she was inevitable as death.

This battle had ceased to be a battle. This was no longer war. Myreon began to doubt whether she had ever actually known what war truly was. She wondered if any of these people had known. Horror and pain and senseless violence and pointless suffering and the blood of children. *If only I'd known this would happen.*

Myreon leaned against a wall in an alley and sank to the ground, head in her hands, weeping. *Tyvian told me. He told me and I didn't listen. This was what he wanted to stop. This is what he died to prevent.*

And it had happened anyway. She'd been a fool to think she could change the world from what it was. She'd been a fool to think the world was made up of good people. She, of all people, should have known better.

They were right. Oh gods, Lyrelle and Tyvian and Xahlven—they've been right this whole time!

This world—this *horror*—belonged to men like Sahand: brutal, cruel, heartless men who amassed power and doled out favor and punishment, who were loved and feared in equal measure; men who stole and murdered and raped their own follow-ers and were thanked for the privilege. They were butchers, leading their followers to the slaughter-house, laughing the whole way.

I won't be part of it. I won't let this continue.

She reached into her satchel—there, hard and heavy, its edges cold to the touch, was the iron box. The Seeking Dark of the Warlock King Spidrahk—another terrible weapon from another monster of history.

If there could not be justice, then there was ven-geance. If there could not even be vengeance, then perhaps there could be punishment. Judgement.

They had all earned it, in the end—her people, their people, Sahand's people. Nothing Myreon was about to do was unwarranted.

Myreon stood up, Spidrahk's Coffer in her hand. She looked at it, wondering how best to break it open and whether she ought to do so standing back or holding it in her hand. She decided she did not care. Not anymore. If she died, she only hoped her death would mark the end of this atrocity.

"In the name of Polimeux II and all the Keepers before him, I claim thy power, Ancient Ones. May it work my will." And, with that, Myreon disintegrated the box with a sharp pass of her other hand. It crum-bled to dust easily, leaving only a single globule of shadow in her palm.

The shadow began to grow, flowing out of her

hand and pooling on the ground like thick, viscous smoke. It surrounded her, swirling faster and faster until she could feel it driving the Lumen from the ley of the city and flooding it with the Ether. The day grew dark, the shadows lengthened. The sun was occluded by unnatural darkness.

Some looters in the street, dragging a sack of flour, stopped to stare at her. Myreon glared and felt a deep hatred well up—not from her, but from the swirling shadow around her feet. It shot out at them and ink-black tentacles seized them before she knew what was happening. Where the tendrils touched, the men's skin grew gray and their hair sloughed off. Then their clothing and armor. Then their flesh.

In moments, nothing but bleached bones remained. And the Seeking Dark grew larger, feeding on its first victims' fear and pain. It flowed from Myreon in all directions now, catching up anyone in its path and consuming them in the barest flicker of an eye. With every death, it grew, splitting off new branches of deadly Etheric energy.

It sought to flow through the broken windows of a house, but Myreon planted her staff and steeled her will. *No,* she thought, *only the soldiers. Only the killers. Only the thieves and the rapists and the monsters.*

But the Seeking Dark did not heed her. Instead, to her horror, it filled the house to the roof, black shadows spilling from the chimney. The screams from inside were brief, high-pitched.

There had been children in there.

Myreon screamed. "NO! NO! OBEY ME!"

But the swirling shadows merely grew larger, more powerful, swifter. Her screams fed them like a spring feeds a river. But Myreon kept screaming anyway, kept battering her will against the Seeking Dark, achieving nothing. She fell to her knees, her body quaking with horror.

And the city around her died.

Eddereon, Tyvian, Artus, and Voth fled along the rooftops whenever they could. The streets were too dangerous. Roving mobs of half-starved soldiers with maces and hatchets were hacking and bashing their way into locked homes to loot or kill or burn what they found there. It was all Tyvian could do to blot out the screams for mercy, the cries of pain. The ring was ablaze, hotter than the fires around them.

Eddereon and Voth felt it too. Like himself, Eddereon had his right hand clutched in a fist and pressed to his chest, his face pale. Voth, though, was not so numb to the ring's compulsions. She groaned in anguish, her eyes rolling back in her head. "Damn you . . . damn you . . . make it . . . make it stop . . . gods, please . . . please . . ."

Tyvian wound up carrying her across his shoulders, focusing on the next leap across the next narrow alley, on placing foot after foot on the steeply angled roofs. The act of helping her allayed the ring's rage somewhat, but not enough. The world had become a tunnel of horror.

"Where's Michelle?" Artus was yelling. It occurred to Tyvian that he had been yelling this for some time, except he had been too distracted to hear him. Now Artus had him by the arm. "Where is she? I won't leave without her!"

Beneath them, a man was being beaten with clubs as he used his body to shelter his wife. Tyvian had to clench his teeth against the incredible pain. "This . . . this is not the time . . ."

Artus's grip tightened. "Tell me, dammit! I *need* to know!"

Voth, delirious, was gnawing at her ring finger. "Somebody . . . somebody do something. Gods . . . oh merciful Hann . . ."

Tyvian adjusted his grip on Voth. "We have to get out of here, Artus—I can't argue right now!"

Eddereon leapt into the alley below, sword drawn. The first attacker he split in half, his sword passing from the collarbone all the way to the hip. He left the blade in place and kicked the body into the others, blood fountaining in all directions. The woman screamed.

Artus kept his eyes locked on Tyvian. "Tell. Me."

Eddereon killed the next man with his bare hands, locking his arms around his head and twisting until something snapped. The other two men struck him with their clubs, but the old mercenary did not falter.

He caught one club by the business end, ripped it from the owner's hands, and then broke it over the side of that man's skull. The fourth one ran away.

Tyvian felt the briefest surge of relief as the woman was saved. "She's in Sahand's custody. There was nothing I could do."

"Well, what's the plan for getting her back?"

Eddereon was climbing back up to the rooftops. Tyvian pointed toward the city walls, only a block or two distant. "Step one: get the hell out of this city."

"Well, that's a start, at least." Artus's face was grim. He knelt to help Eddereon up.

Then the sky went dark. For a moment all of Ayventry went quiet as the grave. Tyvian turned to look out across the city. "What is happening?"

Above the rooftops on the other side of town, a swirling, amorphous *darkness* appeared—like a hand of infinite fingers, black and semi-substantial. It dove into the streets, quick as a gale. And then the screams could be heard.

The ring went icy cold and the pain stopped immediately. It was so abrupt that it made Tyvian gasp. He looked at Eddereon—his eyes were wide. He had felt it too.

Voth gasped for air. "What . . . what's that?"

A torrent of pure darkness flooded the street below, sucking up anybody it found there. From their shrieks, Tyvian doubted whatever was happening to them was good. "Run! Run run run!"

Voth dropped off his shoulder and led the way, vaulting the next alley with acrobatic grace. They all followed. The darkness below began to fill the alleys, too—like a river of shadow, it swelled higher and higher. It would not be long before it was able to reach the roofs and then . . . then Tyvian greatly hoped they were somewhere else.

They sprinted for all they were worth, leaping alley after alley, clambering across rooftop after rooftop. Artus stumbled once, but Tyvian was there to scoop him up. A black tendril lashed out from the roiling dark below and caught the end of Tyvian's scabbard—he didn't even pause to see what happened to it. Or to wonder why, suddenly, he could feel the breeze on his back instead of the weight of his mail shirt. "Go! Go!"

The wall was a bit shorter than the spine of the roof of the closest house, but it was a longer jump. Voth hit it at a sprint and leapt clear across the gap, landing with a crash atop the battlements. Eddereon was next, smashing chest-first into the catwalk and barely scrambling up. Then Artus, who did much as Eddereon did but was helped up by both Voth and the old mercenary.

Tyvian jumped next. He felt the grave chill of *something*—something black and horrible—sliding across his ribs and legs, trying to pull him back. He lost momentum midleap—he wasn't going to make it. He reached up for the wall . . .

Voth caught his hand. Tyvian slammed against

the wall, nearly pulling Voth over, but then Artus was there and Eddereon and he was dragged up just as the shadow behind him claimed his boots.

Then it was over the wall. Luckily, some future looter had left a ladder right there for them to climb down. Then they didn't stop running until they were atop a low hill almost a mile outside of Ayventry, with nothing around but untended farmland. They bent over their knees, panting. Voth threw up. Artus fell on his back, staring up at the sky.

It was daylight again.

Tyvian turned and looked back at the city. The shadow was gone, but so was any sign of life. The fires still burned, but the screams, the cries, the howls of rage had ceased. Even at this distance, it was clear what had happened—some gross act of sorcery had killed every person within the walls.

Eddereon sat down. "What in the name of all the gods was that?"

"I don't think the gods had anything to do with it," Tyvian said.

He looked down at himself for the first time. His mail was gone—rusted clean off his body. His sword, too. Where the thing had touched him was dead skin, peeling off. It was as though he had been burned, but with no pain. His hands began to shake. Scary stories of his mother's, told to a boy disinclined to remain in his room after bedtime, came bubbling up from the depths of his memory. *No, it can't be.*

Artus looked at Tyvian. "Do you think . . . do you think Michelle was there?"

"Sahand was going to move the two of you to Dellor immediately after capture," Voth said, wiping her lips on her sleeve. "I'd bet anything she's still alive."

Artus gave Voth a cautious nod. "Thanks."

"You think being held *alive* by Banric Sahand is an improvement over being dead?"

Artus flinched and looked back at the city.

Eddereon put a hand on Tyvian's shoulder. "Are you hurt?"

Tyvian couldn't stop staring at the devastation of Ayventry. Even though they had ceased, the death screams of the city still echoed in his ears. He felt ill. "The ring. *The ring* made this happen."

"What?" Eddereon blinked at him.

Tyvian wiped his eyes—there were tears. "Gods know how many thousands of people just died—and gods know how many thousands more are about to die—because of *this*!" He held up his ring hand.

"You're upset," Eddereon said. "You aren't thinking clearly."

Tyvian pushed him. "No, I am! I very much *am*! What has brought us to this pass but my good bloody intentions! Huh? What made me become king? What made me fake my death, eh? The desire to fix the world—to make it a better place, to help my friends, to protect strangers. That's what let

Xahlven use me to cause the Saldorian Crash! That's what got the whole world into this mess—my god-damned *conscience!*"

"Calm down," Eddereon said.

"No! You said as much yourself, at Tor Erdun." Tyvian pointed back to the smoking ruins of the once-beautiful city. "Is this better, Eddereon? Tell me truly, is the world better off for this having happened? Because if I'd *left* goddamned Myreon as a goddamned statue in goddamned Saldor, *this city would still be alive!*"

Eddereon opened his mouth to speak, but Tyvian cut him off. "Don't say it. It's all bullshit! The whole Krothing thing—every bit of it. I was right the entire time. The world is a terrible place and nobody's good intentions are going to fix it. No one's."

"What about heroes?" Eddereon said, his voice soft.

Tyvian looked away. "No such animal."

"This is all very fascinating," Voth said. "But what happens now, my captors?"

Tyvian said nothing. He sank to the ground, head in his hands. What did it matter what they did now? Who cared?

Artus stood up. "We go north."

Tyvian snorted. "Sure. Why not? Starving in the wilderness sounds lovely."

Artus glared down at him. "If Sahand has Michelle, I'm going to get her. And you're coming with me."

"And if I don't?"

Artus extended his hand. "That's not how this works. C'mon—don't make me drag you."

"This will all end poorly, Artus," Tyvian said, looking at his soot-stained hands. "You should know by now that there are no happy endings."

Artus pulled Tyvian to his feet. "I think it's like this: if you haven't reached the happy ending, you're not at the end yet. We need to keep going."

Tyvian did his best not to scoff at the truism. Even after all this, the boy still had a lot to learn. Nevertheless, Tyvian found himself hoping that somehow Artus would never learn it.

CHAPTER 22

BEAST AT BAY

Dunnmayre was little more than an outpost—a clutch of rough-hewn log cabins behind a stockade fence, pressed up against the three-mile-wide expanse of the Great Whiteflood as though it were planning to board its own ferry. The lumber mill—the largest building by far—collected logs floated here from nearby lumber camps and cut them into planks and then shipped them on wagons along the rutted, muddy road north to Dellor-town and the Citadel. The sound of the saw chewing through wood and the smell of sawdust permeated the air. Hool drew herself deeper under her blankets, trying to ward off the smell. She badly wanted to sneeze.

If she did sneeze, however, she would also be forced to cry out in pain, and then their cover would be blown and she and Damon would probably die. Instead, she did her best to curl in a ball beneath the blanket, the crossbow bolts tearing at her insides, and tried very hard not to rock the little boat while Damon pulled it up on the riverbank.

Hool heard the jingle of mail and the scent of honed steel a minute or two before Damon noticed the guard. "Hey!" The guard had a gravelly voice, used to yelling. Hool thought he also sounded sick. "State your business!"

"Good morrow, sir," Damon said. Hool could imagine the goofy smile he was giving the man. "I am in need of assistance."

The guard stomped over to the side of the boat and tapped it with the butt of a spear. "What's in here? You can't trade furs without paying the tax, you know. And if these is poached . . ."

Damon laughed. "They aren't furs! That's my dog."

Hool felt her hackles rise at the notion, but kept the growl to herself. It was easy enough with the pain—any exertion would be enough to make her pass out, and she knew it. Besides, as much as she hated it, this was the best plan Damon and she could come up with.

The guard prodded Hool with the butt of the spear, making her whine. "Sweet merciful Hann, what a monster! He must be fifteen stone!"

"A bard needs a big dog if he's to survive way up here." Damon forced a chuckle, but he sounded nervous. "That brings me to my business—is there a veterinarian in town? See, some hunters mistook my dog here for a bear—understandable, really—but now he's shot and I'm in *desperate* need—"

The guard grunted. "Gods and garters, man—say no more! There's a man in town what can help you, I reckon. And he could do with a bard, too, more's the fact. He runs the inn over yonder—the Dragon."

"The one in the big tree?" Damon asked.

"The same. It'll be a copper to leave your boat here and a copper to bring in your dog."

Hool heard the jingle of a coin purse and Damon asking, "How much to rent a wheelbarrow?"

Once inside Dunnmayre's stockade, the smell of sawdust grew even stronger. Hool, cramped and nearly fainting with pain and lost blood, couldn't *help* but sneeze. The pain from the convulsion was such that she howled at nearly full volume and practically passed out.

Damon, red-faced and struggling to push the wheelbarrow, hissed through the blanket still covering Hool. "Will you please keep it down? Half the village just looked at us."

Hool only growled. "Then stop hitting all the bumps!"

Damon puffed as he piloted them around a corner. "The road is nothing *but* bumps."

The Dragon was huge—Hool could see up into its boughs as they rolled beneath them. The tree had to be ancient—Hool had never seen a tree so large before—but from the smell it was strong as well as old, healthy with river water and clean winter air. The inn built into its boughs also seemed old, as the tree had grown up around its walls, knotted branches wrapping it up in a lover's embrace. From the sound and smell of things, it was busy, too—full of men deep in their cups.

Damon stopped the wheelbarrow. "I'm going to have to leave you here."

"No," Hool snarled.

"Hool, there's stairs. Lots of stairs."

"This thing has wheels—*roll me up the stairs!*"

Damon blanched. "But . . . Hool . . ."

"*Do it!*"

Hool saw Damon look up what had to be a long, winding staircase. "Sweet merciful Hann, I'm about to do this, aren't I?"

Hool felt faint. "Hurry up. Before I die."

Damon dusted off his hands, took a deep breath, and began to pull her, step by step, up the winding stair that led to the Dragon's front door. With every bump, Hool found herself yelping. This had two effects: first, the sound of her in pain drove Damon to make it up the stairs without faltering or slipping, though he was cursing in a very unknightly fashion by the top. The second effect was that, by the time they reached the front door, everyone in the place was silent and waiting to see what the hell was about to come in after making that kind of racket.

Hool put an eye to a hole in the blanket so she could see what transpired next.

The place was packed with men—all men— leaning over dented pewter tankards of watered-down beer along a horseshoe-shaped bar that covered one side of the circular room. On the other side was a big iron stove that was burning even though it wasn't especially cold out. The tables on this side of the room were the kind with the benches attached to the tables themselves, and were also packed with the same kind of men—big, bearded, and smelling of sawdust and sweat and weak beer. Some of them were gambling, but most just stared at the door and muttered to one another. Hool felt it was too quiet in here for this many people. Her hackles rose and she hoped Damon knew how to use a sword as well as he claimed.

"No room!" The bartender was a fat, sweaty bald man with only three fingers on his right hand. He pointed this mutilated hand at them and waved them out. "Go somewhere else!"

Hool looked over the tables of dour faces, wondering which two Damon could throw out on their ear to make room for themselves. Damon bowed at the bartender. "Not looking for lodging, sir—I'm looking for a veterinarian."

The bartender grunted. "No room for that, either. Go away."

Hool growled. She didn't like that man.

Damon was pulling out his lute for some reason. "Surely, sir, you have space for someone who can cheer up your guests?" He strummed a chord and looked across the tables. "Well, gents? Anyone for 'The Rose of Amberlee'? 'Skoggin Bridge'? 'The Ballad of Saint Ezeliar'?"

The bearded men stared at them long enough to confirm that Damon had said nothing of interest and then went back to their drinks. The bartender flipped a rag over one shoulder. "Do you know 'The Girls of Ihyn'?"

At the mention of that particular song, a number of men's heads popped up, their eyes suddenly alight. "Yes! Yes—'The Girls of Ihyn'! Play it!"

Damon's expression curdled. "Ummm . . . well . . ."

Hool nudged him with a paw from underneath the blanket. "Play the stupid song!"

Damon whispered under his breath so that only she could hear. "I'm not very good at it."

"You said you learned all the songs to impress ladies."

"'The Girls of Ihyn' does *not* impress the ladies." The knight's cheeks reddened.

The calls for the song had spread throughout the room, now. Men were banging on tables. "Girls! Of! Ihyn! Girls! Of! Ihyn! Girls! Of! Ihyn!"

"Fine," Hool said, "then I will die in this wheel-barrow."

Damon winced. "No! Very well . . . you win. But forgive me—this song isn't suited for noble company."

"I'm *not* noble company."

Plastering a winning smile on his face, Damon hopped up on a table and began to strum his lute very fast. As he began to sing, the men at the bar and at the tables joined in:

> *"Her name was Mazie, she's cute as a daisy,*
> *With tits that could feed a whole army.*
> *I bedded her twice, got me some lice,*
> *But she drove my lancer so barmy!*
>
> *The Girls of Ihyn, best that you've seen,*
> *And all of them willing and purty,*
> *And if you would dare, you'll have any pair,*
> *So long's you don't mind that they're dirty!"*

The song went on like that, and for a *long* time. For a man who claimed not to know it well, Damon knew an awful lot of the verses.

The men were all clapping and slamming their tankards on the tables and stomping their feet—frank discussions of human female anatomy seemed to have an extreme effect on them. Had she not been so gravely injured, she might have found it amusing. As it stood, she felt as though she were being deliberately tortured by a room full of loud drunks.

At some point during the song, however, the bartender came close. Hool held very still, uncertain what she should do. The plan to find a veterinarian, she realized, didn't include what to do when they actually *came upon* a veterinarian. What if he was a spy for Sahand? Surely, even if he wasn't, Sahand would grant an obscene reward to someone who turned her in. Her immediate instinct was to bite off the rest of the man's fingers if he reached for the blanket, but of course that would only make things worse.

So she held still and played dead and hoped she had enough left in her to escape if things got ugly.

The bartender reached for the blanket cautiously, making soothing *shh-shhh* noises as he did so. With a gentle flip, he pulled back a corner of the blanket and got a good look at her.

His eyebrows shot up so suddenly they seemed to be on the top of his head. He immediately replaced the blanket, his face pale. He walked off quickly, looking left and right. He smelled quite suddenly of fear.

He's going to get a guard!

Hool tried to signal Damon, but he was still singing—something about some woman named Cassie and the various dimensions of her buttocks. She wanted to shout to him—she tried gathering the air to do it, but coughed instead. Blood ran down her chin; despite Damon's best efforts to bandage her, her fur was still caked red. The effort to yell made her dizzy. Hool closed her eyes and tried to stop the world from spinning. She needed to stay conscious.

The bartender returned with two big men who had his exact same jawline but much more hair—they had to be his sons. He told them to take her "in back." One of them took the handles of the wheelbarrow. The other cleared a way through the crowd. They began to move.

Hool's heart rate doubled. Why didn't Damon see this happening? How long was this stupid song, anyway? *"Help!"* she whimpered. She felt dizzy again, and among the thousand clashing smells of the men and the beer and the sawdust and the tree and the river, she felt as though she were falling. She had never felt so weak in her life. *Damon*, she thought, *Damon, save me.*

Damon kept on singing. He had the whole inn on its feet now. The Dragon boomed with the raised voices of two hundred lumberjacks.

A door closed, blotting out much of the noise. She heard the bartender say, "Quick, bar that door."

Hool bared her teeth, preparing herself.

The bartender came to stand over her. "I know you aren't unconscious. I'm going to pull back the blanket now and get a look at you. Please don't attack me—I'm unarmed."

Hool growled.

One of the sons took a step back. "Da, are you sure about this?"

The fat man took a deep breath. "Never been so sure about anything in my whole life." He pulled off the blanket.

The two sons gasped.

Hool had her teeth bared. "If you touch me, I will kill you."

"Boys," the bartender said. "Meet Lady Hool, the Beast of Freegate. And she's not joking—she could kill all three of us, even as hurt as that."

The sons—Hool could now see that they were barely men, the eldest just slightly older than Artus— looked terrified, as though they might jump out a window and fall to their deaths rather than remain in this room with her. "Please don't kill us!" the younger one said. "Our da's a good man! We don't mean you no harm—honest!"

The bartender crouched down next to the wheel-barrow. "He's right. I don't mean you any harm at all. Quite the opposite." He spread his hands. "Okay?"

"How do I know you're not lying?" Hool said, letting her teeth drop back below her lips. "How do I know you won't just give me to Sahand?"

The bartender smiled. "Because you'd have to go a pretty long way in this country to find somebody who hates the Mad Prince more than I do. And that's saying something."

There was a banging on the door. Outside, Hool heard Damon yelling. *"Let me in at once! If you've harmed her, so help me!"*

One of the bartender's sons opened the door. Damon burst in, sword drawn. The bartender and his sons put up their hands.

"Put your sword away," Hool snarled. "These men are our friends."

Damon blinked. "They . . . they are? So . . . so our plan worked?"

"I'm as surprised as you are," Hool said. She coughed then, and more blood leaked from her nose.

The bartender looked grave. "My name is Harleck. I'll care for her—if she hasn't died yet, that means she won't die from blood loss. We have infection to worry about, though. Her wounds need to be cleaned, and thoroughly."

Damon paled. "How can I help?"

Harleck put a hand on his shoulder. "You, sir, need to go out there and entertain everyone so damned much that nobody realizes I'm back here with her for the next two hours or so. My sons will tend the bar. With any luck, Sahand will have no idea she is here."

Damon gave Hool a wink. "And you thought this lute would be useless, eh?"

Hool couldn't help but let her tongue pop out in a grin. "You're an idiot. Stop wasting time."

Damon bowed. "As the lady wishes."

He left, along with Harleck's boys. Harleck barred the door behind them and wiped his hands off with a damp cloth. "This is going to hurt."

Hool grunted. "What doesn't?"

CHAPTER 23

ANOTHER DAMSEL,
ANOTHER TOWER

Sahand stumbled backward through the anygate into a fortified courtyard of the Citadel of Dellor. He had the Lady Michelle clutched under one arm like a piece of luggage, and his fur cape smoldered and rotted on his shoulders. "Close the door! Close it!"

His men obeyed instantly, slamming the door shut and dropping a heavy warded bar over it. Their eyes were wide at the sight of their ruler. The captain of the guard stepped forward and bowed. "Your Highness, we were not expecting you so soon. Your table is not yet—"

"Hang that!" Sahand yelled, trying to keep the

panic out of his voice. He threw the girl to the ground at the captain's feet. "Clean this up and bring her to my chambers. Then send for the necromancer."

He took a deep breath and looked around at the soldiers still crowding the courtyard. Many of them had made it through just moments before he did. They were sitting or lying on their backs, panting and trembling. That wouldn't do—not for Dellorans in his colors. "Get up!" he roared at them. "Stand, you dogs, or you'll never stand again!"

Their terror at what they had just seen was eclipsed by their terror at him. They stumbled to their feet, some of them nursing withered limbs and missing fingers or ears or eyes. *Gods,* he thought, walking past them in review. *What in all hells* was *that?*

Again, he swallowed his fear and let it bubble there, seeking that old alchemy that transmuted terror into rage. He got to the end of the line of soldiers and turned on his heel. They were still standing at attention, though barely. Sahand understood how they felt—his own knees felt like jelly and he wanted to vomit. He wanted to check his body all over for any mark that . . . that *thing* had left. "You are men of Dellor," he said, throwing out his barrel chest. "You are not some weak, mewling Eretherian peasants. Remember that—always remember what you are!"

He threw off his half-disintegrated cape and strode out of the courtyard, taking care to keep his steps even and brisk—the stride of a man with purpose, not one who had just fled for his life from some brand of Etheric sorcery he'd never heard of. The broad halls of the Citadel echoed with his steps as he passed rows of triangular alcoves like the teeth of a saw. They were designed to give cover to defenders while denying it to attackers—you could travel in one direction down this hall, but not the other. Not if the defenders wanted to keep you out. His fortress was full of defenses like this. And every one of them would have been useless against that . . . that *thing*, whatever it was.

He had often wondered why the Warlock Kings needed so massive a fortress as this built in so remote a place. Perhaps, after Ayventry, he had part of an answer.

The black . . . smoke? Shadow? Whatever the hell it was, it had eaten through Almor Castle's wards like a mouse through a slice of cheese. He had scarcely realized what was happening before his men started disintegrating on the walls, in the courtyard, up the stairs and through the corridors. Nothing seemed to stop it—not doors, not walls, not sorcery. Sahand had only made it out alive by throwing a pile of his own men against the last door keeping it from the outlet for the anygate. Even then, it had eaten through their bodies so fast it had nearly gotten him. Another second—another *instant* of hesitation and he'd be just so many bleached bones. It was a sobering thought, to consider his own mortality. It would have given a lesser man pause, he supposed.

Sahand was determined to press onward.

By the time he reached his private chambers, two plates of rare meat, hearty bread, and hard cheese had been set out and a flagon of oggra poured for him, a cup of wine for the Lady Michelle. Since he had lost half of his face, he rarely ate with company anymore—the drool was unavoidable, and it made him look like a doddering invalid. This evening's meal, though, was necessary. He threw himself in his chair and broke off a piece of bread, dipping it in the red juice of the meat and letting it soak. He let out a long, slow breath.

And then he noticed Arkald the Strange, lurking in the corner. "Y-Your Highness?"

Sahand barely avoided throwing a deathbolt at the man. "Dammit, Arkald! What are you doing in the dark like that? Come out here, into the light!"

Arkald shuffled forward. Sahand couldn't put his finger on it, but the man looked a little less wretched today for some reason. Maybe it was just a reflection of what he had just witnessed—after watching a man's flesh dissolve off his bones; even a skinny old necromancer like Arkald looked hale. Yes, that was probably it.

Arkald bowed. "You called for me, Your Highness?"

Sahand muttered an augury to detect poison over his food, as was his habit. When he felt the delicate tingle of a pure meal, he took a big bite of the grease-soaked bread. As always, some of the red juice squirted through his cheek and dribbled down his jaw. "What do you know of sorcerous weaponry?"

Arkald rose from his bow and steepled his bony fingers. "Well, my lord, there are death-orbs and warfiends and colossi. Firepikes, of course. Thunder-orbs. All variety of mageglass weapons and armor. It is my understanding that the Kalsaaris are fond of half-real phantasmal soldiers—"

"No, no," Sahand waved off his suggestions. "Something bigger than that—battlefield-scale invocations or possibly conjurations. City killers, understand?"

"You mean, *besides* your attempt to weaponize the Daer Trondor power sink?"

Sahand sipped some oggra and reveled in the heat in his throat. He found he was feeling a bit better. "Yes, besides that."

Arkald twiddled his fingers and shifted his weight from foot to foot. "Ummm . . . well . . . nothing like that has been permitted in literal ages, Your Highness. Saldor would never condone such a thing, and no member of the League, to my knowledge, has ever—"

"That's all I needed to know." Sahand waved him away. "You may go."

Arkald bowed. "I . . . if I m-may, my lord, it *is* possible the Lady Lyrelle might know—"

"I said get the hell out!" Sahand picked up his knife

as though about to throw. Arkald put up his hands and fled, not uttering another word.

When the door was closed, Sahand sealed it with a word and put his knife back on the table. He dabbed at his chin with a napkin, wiping up the bloody grease that had escaped his ruined cheek. Someone had deployed ancient and forbidden sorcery against him today. Who? Lyrelle? Impossible—she could cast nothing from her prison and he had made doubly sure she had no contact with others since his last visit. Surely it couldn't have been Saldor itself—the Defenders would never dare use such a thing. They were probably hunting for the culprit this very moment, filled with righteous indignation. The League, then? No, not them—this kind of sorcery was beyond them. They lacked the vision and the ambition.

In point of fact, he had no idea who it could have been. He didn't even know if they had meant to destroy him specifically. From what he could tell, that sorcery had killed indiscriminately—both armies alike had been consumed by the slithering darkness.

It was possible, however unlikely, that the sorcerer in question was trying to *help* him somehow. The White Army had been entirely within the city limits when the ritual creating the darkness had been enacted, which meant that army was as good as destroyed. His own losses had been substantial—perhaps only half of his men had made it out in time, and gods knew how many Delloran mercenary companies were

THE FAR FAR BETTER THING 347

still hanging around when that thing hit—but he still
had men to draw on and a treasury to pay them with.
He'd have to recall a lot of his border guards and patrols, but he could muster an army of similar size to
the one in Eretheria inside of two weeks at the most.
At least *that* part of his plan was still intact.

But without a White Army to be enraged at his
kidnapping of their Young Prince, who would come
marching to his doorstep? How could he draw out
the armies of the West if there were no armies of the
West anymore? It was difficult to enrage corpses.

There was a knock at the door in a prearranged
rhythm that let Sahand knew it was his guards for
this shift. He put a hand beneath the table, readying a
lode bolt, and called out, "Enter!"

The doors opened and the Lady Michelle Orly
was thrust through. They had cleaned her up a bit—
scraped off the ash and cleaned off the blood and put
her into a linen dress that fit poorly on her skinny
frame—but she did not look well, nevertheless. Great
bags of worry hung beneath her eyes, and her cheeks
looked sunken and sallow. She was shivering.

Sahand gestured to the seat across from him.
"Come closer to the fire. Sit down. Have something
to eat."

Her voice was barely a whisper. "No thank you."

Sahand rolled his eyes. "Are we going to do it this
way, then? You and your pride force me to do terrible things to you to make you comply? Are you,

Michelle Orly, of the opinion that such tactics will give me pause?"

Shuddering, Michelle padded across the vast manticore rug and slid into the heavy oaken chair. She was so slight she looked like a child perching on the edge of her father's throne. Sahand examined her. What he saw was disappointing. He usually liked more curves on a woman—a bit more meat. At *least* in the chest. *One can't have everything*, he thought, snorting. "Eat something. You need it."

Her hands trembling, Michelle picked up the hunk of bread and began to nibble. She never even looked at him. *It's my face*, he thought. *I'm hideous now. That damned gnoll.*

Sahand finished up his own meal in the time it took Michelle to meekly gnaw away perhaps a quarter of her bread. Given her frame, Sahand wasn't convinced that she didn't eat like this all the time, so he resolved to wait no further. "The plan had initially been to kidnap your prince and hold him hostage. Plans like this, however, often go awry."

Michelle froze. "He isn't dead. He got away."

"You can go on believing he's alive if you like—it's of very little importance to me. I, however, am reasonably convinced he's dead. Even if he isn't, his army *is*, which more or less amounts to the same thing in this business. In any event, the thing I am getting at is that plans change."

"Why are you telling me this?" Michelle asked, glancing briefly at his face.

"As far as I can tell, you are the closest relative to the old seat of Davram who is both still alive and not a traitor to the peerage—you never renounced your titles, in other words."

"What titles?" Michelle asked. "A small house in Eretheria city is all I can claim."

"That's good enough in my book. It will also be good enough for Hadda, Camis, and Vora."

This time, Michelle's head snapped up. *There she is—she's getting it now.* "No!" she said. "Never."

"The wedding will occur in a fortnight. You will sign various legal documents and correspondence as they are provided to you, or I will see to it that you very much regret your resistance. I will handle the remainder of the duties. That is all."

Michelle rose, trembling, to her feet. "I will *never* marry you! Never! Never never!"

Sahand rang a bell on his table. The doors opened instantly and two guards came in. "You are dismissed, Lady Orly."

She kept screaming as they dragged her away. By the time the door closed, Sahand was already on to the next problem—how to capitalize upon the usage of such horrifying sorcery in Ayventry.

Of course—it's so obvious. Taking a bite of cheese, he rose and went to his writing desk. After plucking a quill out of the ink, he set it to parchment and began to write:

> *To Polimeux II, Keeper of the Balance,*
>   *As you can clearly see in Ayventry, I am in possession of a deadly sorcerous weapon and prepared to use it against any who oppose me. If you do not comply with my demands by the beginning of autumn, I will destroy one of your cities each week until your wretched domain is naught but ashes. My demands are as follows:*

Sahand couldn't help but smile as he wrote, picturing the expressions on the faces of his enemies when they read his letter. He took care to make certain his demands were outrageous—the more offensive, the better. As the letter took shape, all sense of terror and mortality inflicted by the mysterious black fog faded away. It turned out almost being killed by that stuff was the best thing to happen to him all day.

Lyrelle healed imperfectly from Sahand's beating, but the pain in her ribs and hips and jaw was worth it. Evidently the sight of Banric Sahand brutalizing her in person had jarred something loose in poor Arkald. First had been that cot and the warm cloth, wiping the blood from her face. Then a warmer blanket as she shivered. Then her daily gruel had featured a piece of boiled potato inside, two the next day.

And he spoke with her.

He was, of course, exceedingly cautious. He watched her eat the potato, counting each bite. The blanket had been thoroughly scrubbed of any extraneous material that might upset the establishment of the Astral wards. When he spoke, it was barely more than a mumble, and always very guarded.

Lyrelle decided to match his caution with her own, figuring this would allay his concerns about an ulterior motive more than if she were gracious or complimentary. Mostly, he asked her questions—benign things, designed to indicate human contact but without crossing the line into actual intimacy: "How are you feeling?" or "Was it cold last night?" and that sort of thing.

This morning, however, Arkald was different. He was always nervous, but today he looked positively terrified. His whole body trembled and he kept glancing over his shoulder, as though expecting to be followed. He said nothing at first, emptying her chamber pot and giving her the bowl of gruel—it was still warm. Lyrelle chanced asking him a question. "Are you all right?"

Arkald laughed once—Lyrelle felt the laugh was at his own expense. He wrung his hands. "Why do you think he keeps you alive?"

Lyrelle pursed her lips. How much of the truth to

use here? *Cautiously, cautiously* . . . "He needs me for something. Isn't that obvious?"

Arkald shook his head. "No, that isn't the reason. This I know now. It *can't* be the reason."

And why is that, I wonder? Could it be that Sahand needs sorcerous help of some kind, but has not come to me? Interesting. She hid her thoughts by arranging her blankets.

"Tell me," Arkald said. "Please."

Lyrelle sighed. "He is afraid of me, Arkald. Just as you are."

"Why? Why now?" Arkald gestured to her wretched state. "You are at his mercy. Why not be rid of you forever?"

"Because, Arkald, a long time ago I taught Banric a lesson he has never been able to forget."

Arkald shrugged. "And what was that?"

"That I know him better than he knows himself, and that anything he wishes to do might be something that I anticipated." Lyrelle looked out the tiny window. "I expect it drives him mad. I can see him in bed, tossing and turning, torn between the desire to throw me off the battlements and the deep fear that being thrown off the battlements is *exactly* what I want. *That* is why he doesn't kill me, Arkald." Some steel had infiltrated Lyrelle's voice—she was so tired she had gotten sloppy—so she made sure to let her gaze drop to her ruined hands and leave it there.

"I'm . . ." Arkald began, but then trailed off. He walked to the door, about to leave, but tarried there, one foot partially raised, as though frozen mid-stride. He was deciding something. Lyrelle waited, silent.

He turned back around. "I think Sahand is developing some kind of . . . weapon. A sorcerous weapon."

Lyrelle nodded. "That does sound like something he would do."

"I . . . I don't know for sure. But it seems likely, yes."

"You must be very proud," Lyrelle said.

Arkald blinked. "What? Why?"

Lyrelle cocked her head and feigned confusion— *time to needle his pride again . . . just a little prick.* "Don't necromancers revel in death?"

"No! Those are *lies*! I'm not a . . . not a monster! Necromancy is an art, you hear? An art form!"

And there's that nerve. Lyrelle suppressed a smile. "Please, of all the ridiculous—"

"The skeleton is beautiful!" Arkald snapped, shaking a finger at her. "Decay is a crucial part of the cycle of nature. A necromancer cannot animate or raise the dead without infusing the bones with the Lumen— the very stuff of life and love and joy! My work is art, woman! Art!"

Lyrelle let herself look properly scolded for a moment, allowing Arkald time to settle down. Then she said, "Then you don't think Sahand should have possession of some kind of sorcerous superweapon?"

Arkald leaned against the wall and slid down, his head in his hands. "No . . . no, blast me. Of course I don't."

Lyrelle stared at him. "Then, my friend, what do you propose to do about it?"

"That's just it, don't you understand? There's nothing I can do. There's nothing *anyone* can do."

Lyrelle slowly sat up, her ribs screaming at her as she leaned on the crutch Arkald had brought her and hobbled across the room to stand over Arkald. She reached out her hand and laid it gently on his shoulder. "Why don't you and I talk about *that*, hmmm?"

Arkald looked up, his eyes red. "Well . . . there's this girl being held here. Some kind of princess, I think."

"Good—let's start there, Arkald. *What* girl?"

And Arkald began to talk in earnest.

CHAPTER 24

RETREAT

Tyvian and his companions were not the only people going north. The Freegate Road was clogged with wagons and oxcarts loaded with children and furniture and all the various detritus of a farm quickly abandoned or a city evacuated. These wagons were driven by stern men and hardy women with their eyes on the horizon. Between them and among them were those less fortunate—vagabonds and shoeless wanderers, wearing rags, their eyes seemingly fixed on nothing at all. Tyvian, also shoeless, could guess at what they were seeing, though—the places they left behind, and what had happened to them.

He found himself seeing the same thing. He saw

everything he had once been—dashing, free, respected, *feared*—and wondered where it had all gone. What was he now but just another wretch, shuffling along a vagabond trail to nowhere?

"Where are they all going?" Artus asked one evening. They were camped by the edge of a stream along with a few dozen other refugees. "Camped," perhaps, was a grandiose word—no one had a tent, few had blanket rolls. They had simply flopped on the ground after a day of walking, too tired to go any further.

Tyvian found it hurt to look at these people—at *his* people, he supposed. He looked at the stream instead, or at the shoes he'd scavenged off a dead man just that morning. "Galaspin, most likely. From there some might work their way down the Trell River into Saldor or perhaps keep going to Freegate. Aren't you from Benethor? I would think you would be used to seeing things like this by now."

Artus considered this, looking up at the stars. "Nobody leaves their land in Benethor. There's nowhere else to go, anyway."

Eddereon was smoking a pipe, watching some children trying to spear a fish in the water. "They will be all right. Hann will guide them to a new path, is all."

The sentiment—that the God of Mankind was doing anything to help these people—turned Tyvian's stomach, but he held his tongue.

Artus, though, wasn't thinking about religion. "I did this. We did—Myreon and I. We ruined this place."

Eddereon shook his head. "What part of the match starts the fire?"

Artus frowned at him. "What?"

"He's trying to make a moral analogy," Tyvian said. "He's trying to say that the whole match is to blame and, in this scenario, all of Eretheria was the match, even if you were at the head. But he's wrong." Tyvian glared at Eddereon. "That riddle has an answer, you know. What part of the match starts the fire? Easy—the hand that strikes it."

Eddereon shrugged as he puffed out a smoke ring. "A match will always be struck eventually. It wouldn't catch fire if it weren't a match."

Tyvian threw up his hands. "It's impossible talking to you. You know that, right?"

He looked over at Voth, who was clutching her knees and furiously scratching at her ring. "That won't help," he said to her. "Have a look at Eddereon's finger if you don't believe me. Besides, by all accounts if you take the thing off, you'll go insane."

"Is *this* what happened to you?" Voth held up her ring hand. "Is *this* why you were playing house in that gaming den? Is this what made you soft?"

"I'm sorry, Voth—I didn't want to kill you and this is the only plan that seemed plausible."

"You *should* have killed me," the assassin spat.

"Because I'll make you pay for this, Reldamar. I'll make you pay dearly."

Tyvian leaned back, bunching up his cloak beneath his head. "Promises, promises."

Voth twitched. "Gods! It's inside my damned head!"

Eddereon moved to sit next to her. "Just do the right thing, Voth. You'll feel better."

"Get the hell away from me, you lumbering oaf!" Voth stood up and walked away, sitting down alone further upstream.

Eddereon grimaced at her back. "She's torturing herself. She's fighting it too hard."

"I did the same thing," Tyvian said. "So did you."

"I don't think we made the right choice. The ring isn't for everyone."

Artus threw a pebble into the stream. "Who's it for, then?"

"A noble spirit who has lost their way," Eddereon said.

Tyvian muttered a curse under his breath. "Let's not be grandiose. It's for anyone with a conscience that they'd rather not listen to. I imagine it would work on more people than it wouldn't." He pointed at Eddereon. "*You're* the one nurturing ideas of derring-do and chapbook heroics."

"The ring's capabilities *clearly* intend for the wearer to test the limits of their abilities," Eddereon countered. "It is not a gift for a common cutpurse."

Artus grinned. "Watch it—I used to *be* a common cutpurse, you know."

Tyvian rolled over to one side, putting his back to them. The ring shuddered slightly—it wanted him to go and console Voth, but there was only so much consoling he was willing to do for a woman who kept insisting she would kill him one day. He didn't know exactly what the ring was torturing her with, but he could make a number of educated guesses. A professional assassin walking among numerous valuable targets must present her with a number of adverse moral dilemmas. The only reason she hadn't run off yet, he guessed, was that the ring decided she had to stay.

And that meant it was because of *him*.

His plan to "ring" Voth was a cynical one—he knew she had some kind of emotional connection to him, one he barely understood but that he knew was there. Perhaps it had something to do with the weeping in the middle of the night, or maybe that was related to something from her past. It hardly mattered, in any case—whatever the connection, he had guessed that the ring would act upon it and forbid Voth to betray him. He had been right. It had also been wrong—deeply wrong—for him to do it to her.

And yet the ring—his ring—had no objection to the plan. For the first time since acquiring the wretched thing, he felt as though the ring was the one in the wrong. It *should* have been torturing him over his plot to compromise Voth's autonomy. Instead it seemed to approve.

The world, it seemed, was full of new depths for Tyvian Reldamar to plumb. First he'd gotten Myreon cast out of the Defenders, then he'd unintentionally helped his brother crash the world economy, then he'd managed to sink an entire nation into a bloody civil war. Next to that, enslaving a woman who cared about him seemed, if anything, the least terrible consequence of wearing the ring thus far. For some reason, though, it made him feel just as miserable.

Now, if Artus and Eddereon had their way, they were going to wind up marching into Dellor and probably widowing every woman within a hundred miles. Because that was how this hero nonsense always seemed to work out—pools of blood and burning homes and the world in more of a shambles than it was before. Every. Stinking. Time.

In the distance, Tyvian heard the baying of a hound. His thoughts drifted to Hool. Artus had told him about Brana's death, and he'd been dwelling on it for much of the last few days. Poor little Brana was such a . . . such a *good* person. Positive and happy and kind and enthusiastic. Tyvian had trouble picturing him dead—how could something that young and that full of life wind up dead?

Easy, Tyvian thought, *he hung around with me*.

Another hound bayed and then another. Tyvian

frowned and sat up. Was some idiot conducting a fox hunt in the dark?

Eddereon, though, was already in motion. He slapped a broadsword into Tyvian's hand. "It's Rodall. He's coming for us."

Tyvian's introspective mood vanished with a shot of adrenaline. He was on his feet. "How the hell could he have found us in all *this*?"

Voth's sending stone! He snatched up his satchel and dumped it on the ground.

The sending stone wasn't there. Voth had turned them in. *That* was what was torturing her. "Kroth's Teeth!"

He looked to find Voth. She was on her feet and running along the bank of the stream—making her break for it, he guessed—but then she stiffened and stumbled, clutching her hand to her chest. He heard her swear in the dark.

Tyvian ran to her and pulled her to her feet. "C'mon—this way."

She elbowed him off. "Let me go!"

Tyvian did his best to smile and waved his ring hand under her nose. "Sorry, darling—I can't."

The stream was easily forded and they were all across in less than a minute and running full speed across the broad plains of northern Ayventry. Behind them, the rough voices of Rodall's wolfhounds grew louder and more urgent. Tyvian risked a look over his shoulder—he could see five men on horseback, their armor glinting in the moonlight. They were less than a half mile away. Outrunning them was impossible.

Tyvian pointed north. "That way! The spirit engine tracks!"

"There's no engine coming!" Voth shouted. "Sahand spiked the tracks!"

Tyvian didn't have the time to explain, he simply turned himself northward. The others followed, even if Voth only seemed to do so because her ring forced her. Sahand had spiked the tracks, yes, but that didn't mean they were going to *stay* spiked forever. In fact, if he were a member of the guilds who relied on the spirit engines for trade, he would have a team out here trying to repair them as soon as word got out that Sahand was gone.

"There!" Artus pointed. Sure enough, stopped on the tracks was a small engine—not much larger than a wagon—towing a single cargo car piled with wooden ties and adamant rails. It was only perhaps a three-hundred-yard run.

Which would be fine if you weren't being chased by vicious dogs.

The hounds *were* chasing them, however, and they were closing in. An arrow whistled past Tyvian's ear. A good shot—especially from horseback in the dark. He tried to increase his pace, but he was already in a full sprint.

A big hound darted past Tyvian and snapped at Voth's heel, just missing. Tyvian kicked it hard in the ribs as he went past, launching it a few feet and making it yelp. Another dog leapt on Eddereon's back, but the big mercenary just kept running, dog on his back and all, as though he'd done this a thousand times before.

The spirit engine was manned by a trio of warlocks who were awakened by the commotion. They lit the lamps on the front and back of the engine and waved their hands at the four fugitives coming their way—they wanted no part of this, whatever it was.

Tyvian was wondering how he would explain to them whose side they should be on when one of the warlocks suddenly sprouted an arrow, poking out of his chest. *Gods bless those brutal Delloran bastards*, Tyvian thought, skipping just beyond the snapping jaws of another hound.

An arrow hit Artus in the backside, making him skip-hop, and then he would have fallen but for Voth grabbing him under one arm and helping him along. Tyvian had an arrow graze his forearm, digging a long bloody groove from elbow to wrist. He clenched his teeth—almost there.

The warlocks were getting their engine started, working runes of conjuration into the main spirit vessel. The moans and screams of the engine fiends split the night.

Eddereon was the first to the cab, leaping aboard and finally taking the time to tear the dog off his shoulder and throw it at its fellows snapping at his heels. Artus and Voth were next, hopping onto the guard rail running along the spirit vessel.

Tyvian heard the hoofbeats behind him, too loud to be much more than a few paces back. If they wanted to put an arrow in his back, they could, but the archer—whoever he was—was shooting instead at the cab of the spirit engine. They wanted to stop the thing from moving, and moving it was.

Tyvian found himself running on the tracks behind the moving train, dogs on either side of him, snapping at him; the horses behind with their riders no doubt leaned forward in the saddle, waiting for the moment to strike with lance or saber. His breath burned in his lungs as he reached out to grab the end of the cargo car—missed!

Voth was on top of the car; Tyvian caught a glimpse of blades in one hand—her throwing knives. She cocked her arm back and he half expected it to come flying at him, but instead a dog yelped to his right and then another to his left. Then she cried out—an arrow in her stomach. She crumpled into a ball, about to roll off the top of the cart.

It was the boost the ring needed. Tyvian felt a surge of power fill him and he leapt from the tracks to the top of the cargo car in time to grab Voth by the arm and pull her up to safety. His breaths came in ragged gasps, "Adatha . . . Adatha . . . are . . . are you . . . all right . . ."

She trembled, blood pouring between her fingers. "You better be right about this thing . . . *ughh* . . . making me . . . harder . . . to kill."

Tyvian picked her up as another arrow embedded itself into the roof of the car. He looked back to see the hunting party being called to a halt as the spirit engine picked up speed. He kissed Voth's hair. "I'm sorry . . . I'm so sorry, darling. Stay with me now. Just stay here with me."

Voth curled up in his arms, bent around the arrow buried in her abdomen, as the train screamed into the night.

CHAPTER 25

WALLED IN

The spirit engine didn't stop until it was in Galaspin. The warlocks were kind enough to drop them off before pulling into the berth—the last thing any of them needed was a brush with the mirror men. They slipped through the gates just before dawn and found a place to lie low.

Eddereon knew a fellow in the city—an old mercenary friend of some sort—who let them stay in the cramped attic of his stuffy old house near the walls. Unlike Ayventry, the walls of Galaspin were no mere affectation—standing almost sixty feet high, they kept the house in shadow for the better part of the day. Tyvian always found them claustrophobic and, because of them, he never liked staying in Galaspin for long.

The *last* time Tyvian had been in Galaspin for any period of time, he, Artus, Hool, and Brana had robbed the crypts beneath the Stonewatch—the Duke of Galaspin's castle—and barely escaped with their lives. That had been three years ago, but it still felt recent enough for Tyvian to take care to hide his face when he went out into the street. Since their arrival the day before, he had seen kiosks still affixed with ancient handbills—sun-faded and forgotten—sporting a rough smudge that might have once been a picture of his face. The reward was set for five thousand gold marks.

The thought of turning himself in for the reward was tempting. Just for the laughs—show up, insist on collecting the reward, and then contrive a way to escape with it all. With someone like Voth on his side, it was almost a lock that it would have worked.

Voth, though, was deeply injured. Ring or no ring, it was going to take a few days for the healing poultices to do their work, and until then they were stuck here with nothing to do and nowhere to go. Voth was given use of the only bed in the attic, and so Tyvian had to sleep on the bare wooden floor, thick with dust and the dander of the big orange cat that had at some point claimed the attic as its own. The place stank of cat piss and dead mice.

"You're certain Rodall can't follow us in here?"

Tyvian asked, sitting by the attic's only window and trying to wave fresh air into the narrow, stale room.

Eddereon looked up from polishing his sword with a bladecrystal, making it supernaturally sharp. "No Delloran mercenary will be given admittance to Galaspin, I can promise you that. They'd shoot him on sight."

"Men have been known to wear disguises," Tyvian countered.

"Rodall's metal teeth would stick out anywhere," Eddereon said. "Calm yourself, Tyvian. We are as safe here as anywhere."

"That's what I'm afraid of."

"You're only looking for an excuse to worry." Eddereon pointed where Voth was sleeping. "You're actually worried about *her.*"

"The woman wants to kill me and with good reason. Of *course* I'm worried about her."

Eddereon smiled and shook his head. "Not like that. You know what I mean."

Tyvian scowled. He was about to say something pithy when the trap door to the attic sprang up. It was Artus. "There's an army camped outside the walls!"

Tyvian sprang to his feet. "Sahand? Is he mad?"

Artus shook his head. He was letting a full beard grow in and, for once in his young life, it actually was. His sandy brown mane was starting to be the youthful mirror of Eddereon's midnight-and-silver one. "Not Sahand—some other army. Heard some people talking, saying it might be Saldor."

Eddereon frowned. "Saldor doesn't *have* an army."

"I wanna go check it out," Artus said. "You guys want to come?"

"No," Tyvian said, looking out the window.

Artus looked at Eddereon. "How about you?"

Eddereon got up, being careful to keep his head down so as not to whack it on the ceiling. "I could use a walk."

"What about the medicine?" Tyvian asked.

"Oh, right—almost forgot. Here's the medicine for the woman who wants to kill us all." Artus tossed a paper package on the floor. "I sure hope she gets better soon, that's for sure. I'd hate to stop sleeping with *both* eyes closed."

Tyvian might have said something nasty—*Go look at your army, boy—closest you'll ever get to leading one again*—but he stopped himself. "I owe her my life, Artus. That counts for something, doesn't it?"

"That was just the ring and you know it."

Tyvian blinked at the venom in Artus's voice. "What's eating you?"

"You mean besides the arrow wound in my arse that still hurts like hell? I dunno, let's see—maybe it's the fact that you kidnapped me from my own tent. Or maybe it's the fact that you faked your own death and abandoned me. Or maybe it's the fact that all the time Myreon, Michelle, and I were just barely holding that whole stupid army together, you could have helped us and you didn't!"

"Oh, it's that simple, is it? I just had to show up and scheme you and Myreon out of a goddamned war?" Tyvian couldn't help but laugh. "How the hell can you, of all people, not understand that I make everything worse?"

"Kroth take your self-pity, Reldamar," Artus said. "You're brilliant. You could have fixed things. You still could. You just *won't*."

"I'm not a hero, Artus. I never should have been."

"You are what you chose to be. *You* taught me that." Artus turned to Eddereon. "Come on—light's fading."

They left. Tyvian was alone with Voth. He scooped the package of medicine off the floor and walked over to the bed, head tucked low to avoid the beams.

The assassin had lost a lot of blood on the spirit engine. Were it not for the ring, she probably *would* have died, but she had held on faintly, clinging to Tyvian's arms as he put pressure around the shaft of the arrow to stem the bleeding. Her eyes hadn't opened since Eddereon had taken the arrow out here, in this attic. Her face was now ghostly white, striking a marked contrast with the scar across her face, which was a livid purple. She looked frail and delicate, like a porcelain doll. Tyvian hated seeing her this way. Hated it, he realized, in the exact same way he had hated seeing Myreon as a statue in that penitentiary garden.

He sat on the three-legged stool next to the low bed and ripped open the paper package. It had an array of herbs for boiling into broth and a small vial of some alchemical mixture related to a bloodpatch elixir—it would help thicken the blood, add vigor to a failing constitution. So the alchemist said, anyway. Seeing how he was both dead *and* a wanted criminal, Tyvian was forced to rely on Eddereon's contacts here, and the caliber of alchemist Eddereon put faith in was somewhat suspect.

He pulled out the stopper and leaned over Voth.

Her good eye was open a crack. "If you pour one drop of that vile stuff down my throat . . ." she whispered.

Tyvian found himself grinning broadly. "Or what? You'll kill me?"

"Wh . . . where am I?" Voth tried to sit up, but quickly fell back to the thin pillow with a groan.

Tyvian took her hand in his and rubbed it, trying to warm it up. "Galaspin. Stay still—you've lost a lot of blood."

"No thanks to you." Voth tried to pull her hand back, but was too weak. Tyvian let it go anyway.

"Thank you for saving my life back there. Those throwing knives." He chuckled. "I thought you were going to throw them at me."

Voth looked at him through a half-open eye. "I was. Bloody ring wouldn't let me."

Tyvian was still smiling. "Well, thank you anyway."

"You go straight to hell."

Tyvian didn't respond, but just sat there, looking at her. It was like seeing a cat dipped in water—the grace and dignity of the woman he knew as Adatha Voth was drained away here. He could see so much more in her face, now that she was too weak to hide it. She looked . . . afraid. But of what? Not Rodall, surely.

Wait . . . of me?

Tyvian picked up her hand again and held it. "You don't need to be afraid of me, Adatha."

"That's a stupid thing to say," she said. "You're dangerous. Everyone knows how dangerous you are."

"But not to you. I promise."

She sniffed. "Promises, promises."

Tyvian grinned. "You know why I like you, Adatha Voth? You remind me of myself."

"How narcissistic of you."

"No, I mean it. I was just like you, once," he said. "I was a loner, living life on the edge of disaster, a consummate professional. I did what I wanted and I went where I liked."

Voth rolled her good eye. "Sounds glorious."

Tyvian nodded. "It was, in its way. It truly was."

"Then Eddereon slipped the ring on you?"

"And everything changed." Tyvian's smile vanished. "Everything became more complicated. More difficult. For a while there, I thought it might have been for the better, though. I *felt* better about things. Well, most things."

Voth slowly pulled his hand onto her chest and looked at the ring fused there, black and plain. "How long have you been this way?"

Tyvian thought back. "Going on four years now. Gods, that doesn't seem like such a long time, does it? But it seems a lifetime ago."

Voth looked at the ring on her own trembling hand, turning it back and forth. "I could have escaped a dozen different ways. I could have killed you and your idiot friends a hundred times over." Her voice was bitter. "It wouldn't let me. It was all I could muster to call in Rodall, and then it *made* me jump on top of that cargo car to help you. It got me shot in the stomach and now I'm stuck in some reeking attic with *you*, a has-been underworld kingpin and former monarch, moaning about his bloody feelings. I *hate* this thing, and I hate *you* for putting it on me."

Tyvian knew this kind of venom—he remembered spitting it at Eddereon in much the same way. Unlike Eddereon, though, he wasn't sure she was wrong. He tried to put on a brave face. "It . . . it has its advantages."

Voth pulled the blankets up under her chin. "*Not* the tune you were singing over the ashes of Ayventry, Reldamar."

Tyvian felt a bolt of rage at that one. He threw up his hands. "What, you would have rather died, is that it? Because that was the choice you had, Adatha—the ring or death. You didn't give me any other choice, and I'm *sorry* I didn't want to kill you. I couldn't. I admire you too much!"

"You admired me so much you made me a slave!" Voth snarled, waving her ring hand in the air. "You took away my *choices*, Reldamar! My *freedom!* It isn't right! I don't care how many stupid simple platitudes that hairy oaf throws about—you and I are in *chains*. I won't live that way again, you understand me? Never again!"

Tyvian blinked. "Again? What do you mean *again*?"

Tears welled in Voth's good eye. "Nothing. Never mind. I shouldn't have said that."

"What happened to you, Adatha? Tell me."

Voth began to cry, just like she cried those nights she shared his bed. There was something . . . helpless about it. She rolled in the bed, putting her back to him. "Get out."

"Voth, I—"

"Get out!" She pulled the blanket up over her head.

Tyvian retreated and went downstairs. He borrowed some pipe tobacco from the old mercenary and lit a clay pipe by the back door, which looked out onto a narrow cobbled street with filth caked in the gutters. A couple of boys were wrestling with each other in an alley, laughing and yelling curses. He smoked as the sun set, the shadow of the wall quickly overtaking the neighborhood and plunging it into darkness. The feylamps slowly flickered to life.

Voth was right. It was wrong to put the ring on her—perhaps even more wrong than killing her. He had no right to do it to her, no more than Eddereon had had the right to do it to him. He was sick to death of this heroism nonsense and the wretched trinket that drove him to it, over and over again. Standing there in the doorway, looking at the seedy alleys he once stalked as a smuggler, he remembered that old freedom . . . and he craved it.

The freedom to *not* care. The freedom to let the world take care of itself. The freedom to turn a blind eye to injustice and terror and misery and just look out for the only person he had ever been any good at looking out for—himself.

Where was the great crime in that? Why was *he* required to carry all this weight on his shoulders? *Fix it*, Artus said, but why him? Those boys in the alley didn't give a damn. Neither did their parents or *their* parents. The world was full of people only looking out for their own interests. Why couldn't he be one of them again? Who made it his responsibility?

Right—his mother had done that. His mother, whose misguided attempts to save the world from the same mess she'd made in the first place resulted in her being tortured to death at this exact moment, somewhere in an impregnable fortress in a frozen wasteland. Of all the stupid nonsense, that was perhaps the most egregious.

He tapped the spent ashes of his pipe into the gutter and retreated into the house. If it was an army from Saldor, then he knew where it was going. That meant war was coming to Dellor, and they'd be fools to walk into the middle of it. He'd be damned if he let anybody—Artus, Eddereon, Voth, *whoever*— walk into that mess. He'd meant that before and he for damned sure meant it now. No, they were going somewhere *besides* Dellor, no matter what they thought of the matter.

He pulled Voth's sending stone out of his pocket. It was time to give Carlo diCarlo a call and let them know he was coming.

And tell the old pirate *exactly* how Tyvian wanted to play this.

CHAPTER 26

RETURN TO FREEGATE

In the almost four years or so since Tyvian had last been in Freegate, it had gone downhill. This was saying something, since the city hadn't exactly been on top of the hill to begin with. As the spirit engine rumbled into its berth at the edge of town, the conductor recommended all passengers cover their faces with a damp cloth before disembarking. It turned out to be good advice.

A pillar of angry red fire dominated the sky, shooting up a thousand feet from a blazing crater that had once been Daer Trondor, based high in the mountains above the city. This, Tyvian knew, was the end state of Sahand's *last* play for hegemony and, in a way, directly Tyvian's fault. That didn't make it any less shocking to see. When he'd left Freegate, it had been incognito and he had been recovering from some rather substantial wounds—his eyes hadn't been on the sky. Even then, he couldn't believe he'd missed *that*. It painted the entire city in an angry orange glow. Ash rained down steadily, coating everything in a gray film.

"Gods," Tyvian muttered, staring as he stood in the doorway of the spirit engine.

Voth looked with him. "More of your handiwork, Reldamar? You must be so proud."

Artus shouldered past Tyvian. "C'mon—the sooner we get those supplies, the sooner we can be on our way out of this dump."

"Dump" was apt. Even if not for "the Pyre," the city was in bad shape. The Saldorian Crash had hurt markets here. As they threaded their way through the winding streets, Tyvian saw more than a few shops shuttered up, and a few others showed signs of looting. There had been riots here, and recently. Many of the city's iconic marketplaces were deserted or in severe disrepair—even now, in the early summer, when they should have been bustling. It gave the place a toothless, haggard look. Granted, Freegate had always been a city with rough edges beneath the glitz of naked commerce, but right now the commerce was less "naked" and more "invisible." All that was left was the rough edges.

"Keep an eye out," Tyvian said, leading them through the alleys. This proved to be unnecessary—a lot had changed in the past few years, including the company he kept. Artus was more dangerous than anybody they were likely to bump into in a dark Freegate alley. If the Phantom Guild came calling, they'd be the losers of that exchange.

Or at least Tyvian richly hoped so.

Carlo maintained his same offices with the same private fountain out front. This time, though, he hadn't even made it to the little blue door before it popped open. Beyond squatted the old Verisi pirate, looking not a day older, waving them in with hasty gestures. "Quick. Quickly, if you value your stinking hides, you rogues!"

Tyvian smiled and went in. Eddereon, Artus, and Voth entered with proportionally diminishing levels of enthusiasm.

Carlo waved them through a beaded curtain and into his parlor. He squatted on a cushion and re-moved his crystal eye to dust it off. "Please, sit."

There were cushions for each of them. Artus and Voth remained standing.

Carlo frowned at them and then looked at Tyvian. "Tough crowd, eh?"

"Were you surprised to learn I was alive?" Tyvian asked, making a show of searching Carlo's face for any clue to the old rumormonger's comportment. He needn't have bothered—he could tell nothing. Carlo's face was as inscrutable as the ocean depths. *He hasn't lost a step—good.*

Carlo popped his crystal eye back in its socket. "Each time I receive word that you are dead, you appear on my doorstep within the year. This is a strange coincidence, is it not? Am I some kind of ferryman to the underworld or something?"

Tyvian grinned. "Don't flatter yourself, Carlo. I only visit you when I'm dead because, when alive, I have so many more interesting friends to call upon."

"Ho, ho!" Carlo laughed, his big belly shaking. "It's to be that kind of visit, eh?"

"Tyvian," Artus said, arms folded, "we're in a rush. Can we move it along?"

Carlo looked up at him. "Well, *you've* certainly grown. I think I liked you better as a grasshopper. Easier to squash underfoot, eh?"

Artus rolled his eyes.

Carlo scanned Voth next. His eyes widened. "Hann's Boots, Tyvian—have you brought Adatha bloody *Voth* into my home?"

"Of course I did. You knew it—you saw her from a mile away, and don't deny it." Tyvian laughed. "Gods, old man, I've missed you. I really truly have."

Carlo looked momentarily taken aback. "So . . . you *have* gone soft."

"Tyvian . . ." Artus grumbled.

Tyvian waved him away. "We can't stay—"

"I should say not! Else I'd have to stuff you in sacks and turn you over to Sahand at first light."

"The price on my head is that high?"

"*Your* head?" Carlo laughed. "Your head is priceless at the moment, since everybody thinks it's at the bottom of a big damned lake. But *his* head," he pointed at Artus, "is worth a hundred times its weight in gold in the court of Banric Sahand." Then he waved his hand at Eddereon and Voth. "And these two I could probably sell to that platinum-toothed brute Rodall Gern for a tidy sum."

Voth made for the door. "I can't believe I agreed to this. I'm leaving—"

"Far be it from me to hinder the departure of an assassin from my presence," Carlo said, "but I should note that you are walking about freely in my city because you are Master Reldamar's guests. I wouldn't suggest walking about alone."

Voth froze at the beaded curtain. "I don't take well to threats."

"And you have no goddamned idea who you're dealing with." Carlo pointed at the tufted cushion to his left. "Sit and mind your manners, girly, or I'm likely to get offended."

"*Girly?* Why you ugly, fat—"

Tyvian turned to her. "Adatha—please. This will only take a moment. Artus, you too."

Voth and Artus reluctantly sank into their cushions.

Voth looked ready to bite Carlo. Artus looked like he wanted to punch him. Tyvian decided to take that as a victory and moved on. "We need supplies for a trip through the mountains."

"Trying to avoid bumping into the armies of Saldor and Dellor, eh? Wise," Carlo said.

"How much?"

Carlo shrugged. "That depends on what else you need. Don't give me that look—you didn't walk in here because you needed salt pork and crampons. You're looking for information, too. What kind?"

Eddereon leaned forward. "Is Lyrelle Reldamar still alive?"

"And Michelle Orly—is she? Where is Sahand keeping her?" Artus blurted out.

Carlo gave Tyvian an unreadable look and then, when no one asked anything else, he held up three fingers. "Three secrets and supplies for a mountain journey in exchange for . . . what?"

"Word that I'm still alive and coming for Michelle!" Artus blurted.

Carlo snorted. "Everybody knows that. Worthless."

"The story of how Xahlven Reldamar crashed the Saldorian Exchange!" Eddereon offered.

Carlo shuddered. "I'll pretend I never heard that."

Artus blinked. "Why? It's true! I was there!"

Carlo held up two fingers. "First: nobody would believe me. Second: I'd be found dead the next day, apparently by my own hand. No thank you."

Tyvian smiled. "Can we stop with this ridiculous haggling? I know what you want, Carlo. *You* know what you want. Just ask."

Carlo smiled back. "Fine—cut through all the fun. Here's what I want: I want to know how you faked your own death, I want to know why, and I want to know what you plan to do next."

Tyvian nodded. "Would you like the true version or the fun version?"

"Both. But let's start with the fun one. It is too early in the evening to muddle about with truths."

Tyvian nodded. "Done. First, your end."

Carlo nodded. "Lyrelle Reldamar is alive, or last I heard. She is being kept in a tower of the Citadel of Dellor inside a series of Astral wards of prodigious complexity. The Lady Michelle is likewise alive. She is not being kept in the dungeon, though—she also got herself a cold and drafty tower for a prison. Sahand is a poetic fellow, I'll give him that."

"That's it?" Artus said, shaking his head.

"Not satisfied? What a surprise—you remind me of another sixteen-year-old bravo too big for his britches. Wonder what ever happened to that boy." Carlo gave Tyvian a wink. "Fine, here's a bonus: in a fortnight, give or take, Banric Sahand intends to *marry* the Lady Michelle, thus giving him a legitimate claim to Eretherian nobility."

Artus bolted up out of his cushion. "What! *What!* That's impossible! Michelle would never agree!"

Carlo favored Artus with a wicked grin. "My dear boy, do you honestly think her *consent* is something Sahand cares about? No, I daresay he'll get her to sign whatever paper he passed under her nose if she is in any way interested in keeping all her extremities."

"Why you vicious little—" Artus moved as though to charge Carlo, but came up short as a squat little silver-studded rod emerged from one sleeve. A deathcaster.

A very *familiar* looking deathcaster.

Carlo motioned for Artus to sit. "Manners, *Prince* Artus. Manners. I don't mind if you don't like the news, but you won't be throttling the messenger."

Tyvian glared at Carlo. "That's *my* deathcaster, Carlo."

"It most certainly is not. The owner, I have on good authority, is dead." The deathcaster vanished up one sleeve. "Now, please explain to me how I'm wrong."

Artus was examining his knuckles. They were battered and bruised and scraped. "What about the army heading north? The army of Saldor—I never saw so many Defenders in one place. They'll *destroy* Sahand, won't they? He must have lost practically his whole army at Ayventry. Right?"

"Those are secrets you haven't paid for," Carlo said. Then, to Tyvian: "Now, story. Out with it."

Tyvian nodded. "Call for some tea first, Carlo. This will take a while."

Late that evening, Tyvian shared a bottle of wine with Carlo on his rooftop garden, just as he had so many times before in his life before the ring. It had once been a riot of colorful blossoms and green vines winding around the wrought-iron railings. Now, few plants remained beneath the incessant rain of dust and the perpetual twilight of the city. Carlo was apologetic. "I have to have a servant come up here and dust everything off twice a day, or it will build up. Gods, Tyvian, you should see some of the alleys in the Blocks—impassable. The city watch digs dead vagabonds out from under hills of silt at least once a week."

Tyvian sipped the wine and closed his eyes. It was good—sweet Hann, it was a fine vintage. Carlo had broken out the good stuff, indeed. It was the first glass he'd had in months, and the last one he'd have in months more. In the courtyard below, he could hear Eddereon and Artus discussing how to stow and carry the equipment Carlo had produced in only a matter of hours. Noting Tyvian's raised eyebrow, the old pirate had sighed. "Things are cheaper now in Freegate. All that costs less than you can imagine."

Carlo was looking him over with his crystal eye, paying particular attention to Tyvian's right hand. "That trinket really can bring back the dead, eh?"

Tyvian nodded. "Three times now—twice myself, once somebody else."

"Do you think it's changed you?"

Tyvian looked at him. "Do I seem changed?"

"You seem older. You seem like you've learned a few things the hard way." Carlo swirled the wine in his glass. "Magic rings aren't required for that, though— believe me."

Tyvian watched the Pyre burn, swirling and angry. He remembered the heat of the ritual chamber, the rage-blind madness of Sahand's eyes. "If not for the ring, that wouldn't be there."

"As I understand the story, if not for that ring, none of *this* would be here, either." Carlo motioned to the city spread out around them. "You saved countless lives. In some circles that is admired."

Tyvian felt a grin tug at the corner of his mouth. "And in your circles?"

"I try very hard not to admire anyone. It simply sets you up for disappointment."

In the orange light, Tyvian could see the wrinkles spreading from the corners of Carlo's eyes and lips, could see the many furrows of his forehead. He'd known the man twenty years, first as mentor, then as partner, then as friend. If he admired anyone, it was Carlo—a fixture, the immortal criminal overlord, untouched by time. Tyvian had, in a way, sought to be just like the man—free to live as he chose, do as he wished. But in the angry glow of the Freegate sky, he could now see Carlo was an old man and alone. A man who had to give up an eye so he could constantly be looking behind him.

Tyvian realized he *had* changed. He didn't admire Carlo as he once did. He no longer wanted to be him. But he couldn't remain what he was, either—it cost too much.

"Carlo, do you think I was ever a good person?" he asked, sipping the wine.

The old pirate smiled. "I think about that a great deal, you know. When I found you, I thought I'd found a vicious little rich boy smart enough to be of some use. I was right, too. I set about teaching you to be a coldhearted killer, like me."

"I remember the lessons."

"That's funny, because they never really took. You were always finding ways *not* to kill people. Embarrass them, yes, injure them perhaps, but you were never bloodthirsty, never needlessly cruel. You were always a better con man than a killer."

"Killing is messy and expensive. Lies are cheap and clean."

Carlo waved away the words with a chuckle. "Tyvian, I don't claim to know much about good or evil—I've seldom encountered either in my line of work. Everyone is somewhere in-between what they ought to be and what they know they shouldn't be. My father wanted me to be a soldier, I really *ought* to have been a jeweler, and I wound up a fat old thief with one eye. So it goes."

"This isn't precisely answering my question, you know," Tyvian said.

"My point is, boy, that a man can drive himself crazy wondering whether he's good or bad. Is it his actions that do it? His intent? The *results* of his actions, intended or otherwise? Is it something in his soul that only Hann can see? Pick a method for weighing a man's worth and I'll find you a dozen exceptions in an afternoon and cart them in to shake your hand."

Tyvian grimaced. This wasn't what he wanted to hear, but he really didn't know what would have pleased him more. He sat there, stewing, letting the dust collect in his beard.

"I know what you're getting at, you know," Carlo said, leaning forward. "You want to know what will happen when you rip that ring off your finger."

Tyvian tried to keep his face calm, but he couldn't help staring at Carlo. "That's taking a few leaps, isn't it?"

Carlo held up his hands. "Fine—have it your way—perhaps you called me on a stolen sending stone to ask for directions to the Oracle of the Vale for nothing. Idle curiosity—sure." Carlo laughed and sighed. "I'll tell you this, though: with or without that ring, you are a better person than I've ever been. I sometimes curse myself for ruining you and wonder if everything wouldn't have been better if I just left you where I found you in that run-down brothel in Crosstown. But then I figure there would have been another unscrupulous sort who would have snapped you up, and then *he* would be richer than the Baron of Veris and not myself. You hate what that ring has made you do? Fine—I can't blame you. Go up into the mountains and chat with the Oracle about it until you both have a good cry. But don't think that ring makes you who you are. Life isn't that simple."

"*Tyvian!*" Artus called up from the courtyard. "*We're ready!*"

Tyvian turned back to Carlo and extended his hand.

Carlo took it and shook. "The map is in your shirt pocket. I should warn you: when Captain Rodall Gern comes snooping around Freegate, I'm going to sell him a copy of the same map."

"I expected no less." Tyvian nodded and tapped his shirt to find an old bundle of parchment.

Carlo pointed at the map. "If you can beat that steel-toothed dog to a suspension bridge I've marked for you, you can cut it and he'll never catch up."

Tyvian smiled. "What do I owe you for that?"

"Nothing." Carlo spread his hands. "This is a debt that Rodall Gern owes *me*, and if he winds up freezing to death in the mountains, our accounts will be squared."

Tyvian's smile faded as he thought about where he

was going—a place out of legend. Something from a story. "Carlo . . . the Oracle . . . have you ever been? Can you tell me what to expect?"

"My dear Reldamar, those are secrets you have not paid for." Carlo pulled him into a fleshy hug. "When this is all over, come back. We can start over, you and I. We can rebuild a life for you—Tyvian Reldamar does not need to live like a vagabond."

Tyvian found himself hugging him back. "I'll do that, Carlo. I promise. Take care of yourself."

Carlo released him and dabbed at the corner of his real eye with a voluminous sleeve. "Nobody does it better, my friend. Good-bye."

CHAPTER 27

INTO THE MOUNTAINS

The Dragonspine—the mountainous continental divide that separated the West from the vast plains of the North—was widely considered impassable. Its jagged peaks were so high that travelers couldn't breathe their rarified air, its cliffs and valleys were so sheer as to give even a sorcerously assisted climber pause, and its weather was cold enough to freeze hearthcider. When you combined all this with an indigenous population of trolls, griffons, and mountain lions, just about no one had any interest in exploring the range's secrets.

Except smugglers and thieves, of course. This was where Carlo diCarlo had come in, and why Artus had spent the past week walking along mountain trails so narrow, he could scarcely put two feet on them at the same time. A trip through the Dragonspine on the right trails through the right passes would, according to Tyvian, cut a week off their journey north to Dellor.

Or so he claimed, anyway.

Artus stumbled, his heart pounding in his chest. This far up in the mountains, he couldn't seem to catch his breath. He felt like he was drowning in the air.

Eddereon grabbed his hand and helped him up. "Watch your step, Artus—it's a long way down."

They were hiking along a ridge, perhaps seven or eight feet wide. On either side dropped a cliff of gray stone at a near-vertical angle that disappeared into a bank of fog beneath them. The thought of tumbling down it made him dizzy. "Tyvian better be sure about this."

Eddereon looked at Tyvian, who was at the head of their little company, head down, his walking stick tapping against the rocks as he went. "Carlo gave him a map and we're following it. I think he's right—we're making good time, and we're avoiding the armies marching through the valley below."

Artus picked up his walking stick. "I don't like it. He's up to something. He's not telling us enough."

"It's not that he isn't telling us," Eddereon said, gesturing for Artus to go first. "It's that he isn't telling *her*."

He pointed at Voth, who was stumbling along behind Tyvian, her face pale and her expression pinched beneath a heavy woolen hood. It seemed as though her ring hadn't stopped torturing her since the moment she'd put it on. It was as though the assassin had dark thoughts and urges every hour of every day. The very idea chilled Artus more than the icy mountain breeze.

Of the four people winding their way through the lower peaks of the Dragonspine, Artus was keenly aware that he was the only one with complete freedom of action. Their rings compelled the other three, and Artus was beginning to realize what kinds of problems that created. Chief among these was Adatha Voth—Tyvian refused to abandon her, Eddereon refused to kill her, and yet, even with the ring twisting her right hand into a palsied claw, *she* refused to submit to their company. Artus could see the murder in her eyes as clear as daylight—she was a caged tiger, just waiting for the moment the latch was sprung. No amount of pointing this out to Eddereon or Tyvian in private had made any difference, though. They kept her along—they had no choice.

Artus, though, *had* a choice. One little push and the problem would be solved by gravity. Voth was tiny—it would be so easy.

But then Artus would find himself behind her as they struggled up a steep slope, her ankle easily in reach, and . . . he'd hesitate. He'd do nothing. Even worse, once he even helped her up when she slipped down a rock face. He told himself that he didn't do anything because, after he attacked her like that, the ring would allow her to defend herself, and he knew for a fact that the woman was positively dripping with nasty little blades.

But that wasn't it. Artus didn't kill Voth because he didn't have it in him to try. It wasn't even cowardice—it was sympathy. The woman was in pain, surrounded by her enemies, being forced through the terrible ordeal. Would he act any different than her, were their situations reversed? He guessed not.

But that didn't mean he had to like it.

He tried to pass the time thinking of Michelle. He imagined her waiting for him, praying for her rescue. He imagined what he might say when he at last kicked down that door in that tower and took her into his arms. He could never manage to come up with something pithy enough. He almost wanted to ask Tyvian about it, but decided that would be dishonest. A hero couldn't get his noble phrases from somebody else! That was cheating.

The idea was that thinking of Michelle would keep him going—give him a goal to shoot for. Knowing she was about to be forced into marriage with that monster Sahand was supposed to keep a spring in his step and his sword sharp. But it didn't work, exactly. He felt a bottomless unease at the fact that he was tired all the time, not driven by heroic passions.

He was afraid he would fail, but he was also afraid he would succeed. If he saved Michelle, well, that was it, wasn't it? They were destined to be together. He was destined to be prince of Eretheria.

And that was for life.

His brooding was interrupted when they paused for a rest and Tyvian referred to Carlo's map. "According to this, we just need to crest that pass." He pointed up the ridge they were hiking, which led to a narrow path that wound its way up the face of a mountain with its top frosted with snow. "After that, it should be downhill for a few days."

"How long before we're in Dellor?" Artus asked. "We've been at this for over a week. Rations are getting low. The wedding could have happened already."

Eddereon sat on a boulder. "The boy's right—we can't keep this pace forever. We're going to have to come down into a valley at some point to forage, at the least."

Tyvian looked at Voth. "Anything to add?"

"Other than I hate the mountains and I think all of you are fools? No, I can't think of anything."

"Feel free to stay behind—it's not like you're good company, anyway," Artus said.

Voth waved her ring hand at him. "I've got *this* on my finger—what's *your* excuse, your highness? Maybe *you* should leave—trot down a mountainside and find some country wench to screw that bony noble girl right out of your head."

Artus clenched his fists. "You shut up about her!"

Voth came close enough to look up into his face. "Or you'll *what*? Lay hands on me? Beat up a one-eyed woman? You haven't got the balls, you jumped-up farmboy."

"Will you two stop it?" Tyvian said. "It's bad enough I'm outdoors—do I have to listen to this nonsense, too?"

Eddereon raised his hands in a placating gesture. "Tempers are high, Tyvian. We need a rest. Does that map have anywhere we can go to find decent food or fresh water?"

"Unsurprisingly, the map of the bloody Dragonspine reveals a notable lack of good restaurants," Tyvian sneered.

Eddereon's lips vanished beneath his beard as he scowled. "You know what I meant."

Tyvian patted the map, which he had slipped back up his sleeve. "As I said—through that pass and then downhill for a few days. There's your rest. Forgive me—I thought we were in a rush."

"How long until we get to Dellor?" Artus asked again.

Tyvian paused, exasperated. "It will take a while, all right?"

Artus frowned at the dodge. "How long?"

"The map doesn't say."

"It tells you how long we'll be going downhill, but it doesn't tell you how long until we get where we're going?" Artus yelled. "What's going on, Tyvian? Where are we *really* going?"

Eddereon frowned. "Really going? What do you mean?"

Artus pointed at Tyvian. "I've been with this guy long enough to know when he's conning me, and that's what I'm getting off him right now—I've been saying this for days."

Tyvian winced. "Don't be ridiculous."

"There!" Artus said. "*A-ha!* The ring is giving him a hard time, which means he's *lying,* see?"

Voth straightened. "Gods, the boy's right! Been at this a week and I never noticed. Clever, Reldamar—very clever. Lying by omission, not really lying—it all keeps the pain down, doesn't it?"

"Tyvian," Eddereon said, folding his big arms. "Is this true?"

Artus could see Tyvian struggling with the ring for a moment. He lost. "Dammit all—fine! We aren't going to Dellor. Not directly, anyway."

Artus advanced on him. He wanted to hit him, but instead he simply yelled. *"Where?"*

Tyvian rubbed his temples. "The Oracle of the Vale. That's where."

Voth laughed. "That place isn't even real."

"I've got a map that says otherwise."

"That fat goblin was just taking you for a ride," Voth said.

Tyvian shook his head. "No—he has no motive.

He'll sell the same map to Rodall—he told me as much—but he has no reason to give me a fake one in the first place. Bad for business, for one thing."

"Why in the name of *all the gods* are we going to the bloody *oracle*?" Artus yelled. "We need to rescue Michelle and . . . and your own damned *mother*, Tyvian! What the hell?"

"Artus, do you honestly think the *four* of us can infiltrate the Citadel of Dellor, release Sahand's prize hostages, and then make it out again alive while I'm wearing *this*?" Tyvian pointed to his ring.

Voth raised her hand. "What was that about *four* of you? Count me out of your suicide pact, you idiots."

Artus ignored her. "So are you saying the Oracle of the Vale can, what, remove your ring?"

"It knows someone who can," Tyvian said, shrugging. "Or so I was told."

"By *whom*?"

Tyvian kicked a rock. "Well . . . by Xahlven."

Artus's mouth popped open. "Your *brother*? The same guy who tried to kill you? The same guy who almost killed your mother? *That* Xahlven?"

"Of course *that* Xahlven." Tyvian shrugged, looking at his feet. "It's not a terribly common name, you know."

Voth began to laugh—hopeless, wild laughter that echoed across the mountainside. Artus wanted to join her—it was just so . . . so *ridiculous*—but he couldn't shake the sheer *madness* of the plan. He gaped at Tyvian. "You . . . you *idiot!*"

"Artus, don't you *see?*" Tyvian grabbed him by the arm. "You want me to fix things? This is how I can! I would be unrestricted, understand? Unbound by this stupid moral code which has done *nothing* but ruin lives!"

"It didn't ruin *my* life!" Artus countered. "You'd've ditched me if not for that ring!"

"But I still would have saved you," Tyvian said. "Remember that, Artus—the man who saved you from that burning spirit engine was *me* before the ring."

"I keep telling you," Eddereon broke in. "The ring is not a burden. It's an asset."

"Spare me, Eddereon," Tyvian said. "I don't expect you to understand—it's domesticated you." He turned to Voth. "Don't you see, Adatha? You can get it off, too—I'll free you, understand? You were correct—I shouldn't have put the ring on you—but I can make up for it. It can be like it used to be."

Voth was still laughing. "You poor, naive man. Reldamar, that's not how power works! Nobody's going to just pop the bridle out of your mouth and let you run free! Even if there *is* an oracle and it *does* tell you where to go, do you really think somebody will just *take this thing off?* Why, when they could just alter it to have you dance to *their* tune next?"

Tyvian scowled. "We're going. I've decided."

"Oh yeah?" Artus yelled. "You ain't king anymore, Reldamar. What makes you think you're in charge, huh?"

Tyvian looked at all of them. Artus glared back, Voth still laughed at him, Eddereon looked like he was in shock. "*I'm* the one with the map. *I'm* the one with the plan to get back Michelle and Lyrelle. *I'm* the only one who can get that ring off your finger, Voth. You don't want to come with me? Fine—head west and you'll run into the Wild Territory eventually, and from there you'll find Dellor easily enough. Assuming you survive the journey. As for me—I'm going north, I'm finding the Oracle of the Vale, and then I'm finding the Yldd, and when this stinking ring is gone from my person *once and for all*, then—and *only* then—will I take on Sahand again!"

Artus pushed Tyvian, hard. The smuggler pitched backward and almost fell, managing instead to fall onto his side instead of into the abyss. Artus, at that precise moment, didn't give a damn if he fell. "You're leaving Michelle to marry *Sahand*! You son of a bitch! I should kill you! I should kick you right off this god-damned mountain!"

Tyvian snarled as he scrambled to his feet. "Spare me all this 'Michelle' horse shit, Artus! You don't love the girl—it's just a bloody infatuation. She's the first and only girl who's shared your bed, and now you're feeling all guilty that you got her kidnapped—that's *it*!"

"Go to hell!" Artus took a swing at Tyvian—a

sloppy, wild haymaker that the smuggler saw coming. He ducked the blow and pushed Artus back, tipping him onto his backside, which blazed with pain from the old arrow wound. Artus gasped.

Tyvian stood over him, fists clenched. "How did you think it would all end, Artus? Did you think *you'd* marry that girl? Do you want to be a prince for the rest of your life? Huh?"

Tears welled in Artus's eyes, hot against his cheeks in the frigid air. "Shut up! Just shut up!"

Tyvian nodded. "That's right—you don't. You didn't want that life any more than I did. And you know how I know? Because if you did—if you *really* wanted to be Prince of Eretheria—you would have run back to your people the moment we were out of Ayventry. You'd have raised a new army to go kick down Sahand's doors—and you could have, too. But you didn't."

Artus put his hands to his face. The words hurt more than any wound he'd ever suffered. His shoulders shook as the tears came more heavily.

Tyvian sighed. His voice softened. "It was never going to work out. You're no prince, I'm no king, and there's no such thing as heroes."

Eddereon helped Artus to his feet, his face grim. Behind him, Voth was still laughing.

Tyvian looked haggard—old, somehow. "This is the plan. It's the only one I've got. Follow me or not, but I'm leaving."

He turned and headed up the path, not looking

to see if they came. Eddereon was the first to do so. Voth still chuckled to herself. "We're all going to die. Kroth take me." She started up the path, too, leaving Artus behind.

Artus stayed.

Was Tyvian right? Didn't he love Michelle? He thought about her all the time—didn't that count? Part of him—the part that spoke with Tyvian's voice—told him it had all been an act. That he had "loved" Michelle because he was supposed to and because he had said he would. He wondered if, maybe, it was the same with Michelle—maybe she had stayed with him because she was supposed to stay. Maybe those few months he'd spent as the Young Prince were just a big joke. Myreon needed a figurehead, and he'd been it. That was all. That was all it ever was.

In any case, he knew now that he never wanted to go back. The life of a prince was not for him. Never had been. That was why Tyvian's words hurt.

They were true.

Artus's three companions were almost out of sight when an eagle cried overhead and he looked up. No, not an eagle—a wild griffon, soaring high above, looking for a meal. A little jolt of terror broke him into a run.

He rushed to catch up, cursing Tyvian the whole way.

CHAPTER 28

AMONG THE ASHES

The silence in Ayventry was complete. No birds, no wind through the leaves, no cries of the hurt or fearful. Once the fires died out on their own, there wasn't even the distant crackle of burning wood or the occasional crash of a collapsing roof.

Myreon sat among piles of bleached skeletons, staring into nothing. She did not know how long she had been there. She did not think it mattered.

The Creeping Dark was gone . . . somehow. Not by her doing, at any rate—try as she might, she could no more control it than she could divert the course of rivers with her hands. Perhaps if she were a more powerful sorcerer, perhaps if she had known what to prepare for—perhaps then. Too late now.

The ley of the city had skewed so sharply into the Ether, Myreon could scarcely summon a positive thought, let along the energy to move. Every drip of optimism, every stain of hope had been bleached from her soul. She sat in tattered, rotting robes and felt brittle, as though any movement might make her break. Perhaps it would. Perhaps the Ether had drained the vitality from her body as well as her spirit. Perhaps she was ancient now, and withered.

It would serve her right.

It must have been days before the fires stopped, then the long silence, and then, one day, a crow landed atop a crumbled chimney and looked her up and down with one speck of an eye. It hopped down and made its way across the street, pecking at this thighbone and that skull, before stopping at her feet. It cocked its head this way and that, looking for a sign of life. Myreon realized she was likely the only hunk of flesh left in the city—the only meal.

She shifted her foot slightly and it hopped back, but did not leave. Having no better feeding options in sight, the creature seemed determined to try its luck and see if she died. For some reason, though, she did not.

That night, there was another crow, come to peck at her as she dozed, trance-like, amid the ruin she had caused. The first crow fought with the second and, at last, drove it away. Though not far away.

It occurred to Myreon that the presence of the crows was the ley slowly righting itself. The flow of the great ley line that passed through the city was gradually rebalancing the energies of creation. A part of Myreon's mind that was not despondent—not yet, anyway—woke up and realized that she was witnessing something the magi of the Arcanostrum spoke of only in theory. The Gray Tower worked so hard to keep the Energies in harmony that it had been literal ages since they had been so greatly disrupted. Even in Daer Trondor, the Fey energy had been concentrated inside the power sink, keeping it from completely obliterating the Dweomer and crowding out the other energies. If it had done that, she wouldn't have had a snowball to throw.

She discovered that she was desperately thirsty, yet she still lacked the energy to rise and find water. It might not even be good to drink, anyway, given the ley. Better to wait. Best, perhaps, to simply die. At the very least she would feed the crows, who now waited for her demise with great patience in a flock surrounding her. Their caws and squawks at last supplanted the eerie silence of death.

On what might have been the fifth day, or possibly the fourth or sixth, the crows took to the skies as one. Myreon turned her head, the act itself painful enough to draw tears, and saw a tall man in the gray robes of the Defenders, his magestaff gleaming in the morning light, striding toward her.

It was Argus Androlli. Of course.

He stood over her and she looked up at him and, for some time, neither of them spoke. The bones, she felt, did the speaking for her. At last, when he did speak, his voice was softer than she had expected. "Are you hurt?"

She shook her head.

"Did you see what happened?"

The laugh ripped out of her before she knew it was coming. She laughed and laughed, even though each shudder of her ribcage hurt and her throat was rough and raw as freshly shaved beef.

Androlli's handsome face drew into a frown. He thought she was mad. Perhaps he was right—perhaps she was mad. She had a right to be.

"You are under arrest, Myreon. Please don't resist."

There was no resistance in her—if he could not see that, then she wasn't going to tell him. She sat there, listless; a Sergeant Defender presented himself to Androlli and saluted. "Sir, no signs of life of any kind. Just bones, sir."

"Any sign of any latent disruption of the ley?" Androlli asked.

"The magecompasses are still trending to the Ether, sir, but motion is positive. Whatever did this is gone."

Androlli motioned toward Myreon. "We have at least one survivor, so do a thorough search to see if we can find any other witnesses."

The sergeant looked down at her, his expression grim. "How'd she manage it?"

"She was once a Mage Defender," Androlli said, crouching down and producing a pair of casterlocks. "She went rogue."

Light dawned behind the sergeant's eyes. "The Gray Lady?"

Androlli shook his head slowly as the casterlocks clicked over Myreon's hands. "Not anymore. She's just Myreon now."

Gently, Androlli helped Myreon to her feet. Her joints creaked and her muscles ached with stiffness, but she was able to stand. "Thank . . . you . . ." she croaked.

"If you want to help me, Myreon, you'll tell me everything you know about how Sahand did this."

Sahand!

Myreon almost collapsed to the ground again, but Androlli held her up. "We won't let him get away with it, Myreon. I promise you that." The Mage Defender looked around at the ruined street and the human skeletons scattered as far as the eye could see. "This is the final straw. The Archmagi are in agreement and the Keeper has spoken—Saldor marches to war."

She opened her mouth to say something, though what, she couldn't tell—a confession? A cry of anguish? It never came. The sky seemed to spin and then she was on her back and then darkness.

Myreon woke up. It must have been dawn, judging from the soft light piercing the white canvas panels of the white-and-purple pavilion. She was in casterlocks and had iron shackles clamped around her ankles. She was lying on a flat straw mattress. She tried to get a sense of place and time, but there were no points of reference. All she remembered was the desolate streets of Ayventry and then Androlli being there and then . . . this.

White and purple were Saldor's heraldic colors. Outside she could hear the gentle stirrings of a large camp in the early morning—men talking in low voices, the sound of horses shifting against their tethers. Somewhere a teapot was rattling.

She got up gingerly. She felt wrung out, weak. Her body trembled with the effort of sitting up unaided. Her stomach was so empty it felt plastered to her spine. With shuffling steps, she went to the tent flap and put one eye to the crack. Outside stood two Defenders in their mirrored mageglass armor, firepikes at their shoulders.

She stepped back, trying to put her scattered thoughts in order. What had happened to the Creeping Dark? Had she put it back in the box? No—that was impossible. The box had been destroyed. She had lost total control and everyone died. Everyone.

Then why was she in a tent instead of in Keeper's Court, awaiting trial? Why was she even still alive?

Sahand.

Her last conversation with Androlli came back to her. She shuddered—they thought *he* had released the Creeping Dark on Ayventry. They thought *he* had committed that atrocity. And why not? It was the kind of thing Banric Sahand might do rather than lose a battle.

It was the kind of thing Banric Sahand might do . . .

Myreon fell to her knees, retching. There was nothing in her stomach to come out, though—only a thick string of yellow bile which she spat into the grass.

The flap swung open—it was Androlli. "Good—you're awake."

"Wh . . . where . . ." Myreon stammered as Androlli grabbed her under one arm and hoisted her to her feet.

"Outside Bridgeburg. You've been unconscious for three days." Androlli pushed back the tent flap and guided her through it.

The full light of morning blinded her as she shuffled beside him. When her eyes adjusted, she could see the orderly rows of purple-and-white tents, the firepikes steepled in tripods here and there, the men dusting off mirrored helms after a day's march—an army, then. She was too addled and too confused to possibly estimate the size, but even in their short walk across the camp, Myreon knew there were more Defenders of the Balance here, in one place, than she had ever seen before.

Androlli seemed to follow her train of thought. "The collected resources of Galaspin and Eretheria tower plus the garrisons of every town and city in the north of Saldor's Domain. Impressive, eh? An army not seen since Conrad Varner's days, they're saying."

Ahead of them was a black tent with a banner in front Myreon had seen before but could not place: a portcullis framed by tangled vines. There were two Defenders here on guard, too. They came to attention as Androlli approached. He held up the flap for her and motioned for her to enter. "After you."

Inside were four ebony chairs arranged around a glowing circle of runes scratched into the bare earth. Sitting in one of these chairs was Trevard, Lord Defender of the Balance—a thin man, but full of sharp corners and spiky looks, like a kind of animated splinter of wood. Next to him, resplendent in black and violet, his golden hair perfectly coiffed, was Xahlven Reldamar, the Archmage of the Ether.

Myreon now knew where she had seen the heraldic device before—at Glamourvine. It was the Reldamar family crest. How strange she should have spent so much time with the Reldamars and had hardly ever seen their coat of arms.

Xahlven smiled at her and motioned to one of the empty chairs. "Please, Myreon—sit."

Trevard gave her a look that could curdle milk. "I can't see why we should let the prisoner recline in our presence, Xahlven."

"The woman is clearly exhausted to the point of death, Trevard," Xahlven said, his face open with apparently genuine concern. "We hardly want her collapsing during her interview, do we?"

Trevard's sharp chin shook with anger. "I want a good deal more than *that* for this one. A good deal more indeed."

Myreon collapsed in the chair. Xahlven held out a goblet. "Drink. You need it."

She leaned forward to sip and, as she did, he gently held back her hair. As if he really cared about her. As if any of this were true. She wanted to laugh, but she lacked the energy. The goblet was full of some kind of enchanted wine of the type Tyvian had hated—he had claimed it did the exact opposite of what wine should do and tasted terrible to boot. Despite the sour flavor, she felt almost immediately refreshed.

Androlli saluted Trevard and provided him with a ring of record, which the Lord Defender slipped onto his pinky finger. Trevard then closed his eyes for a moment. She knew he was reviewing Androlli's arrest of her in Ayventry through Androlli's own eyes, though at a more brisk pace. Androlli remained at attention, awaiting his superior's word.

They had a moment before the "interview" was to begin. She knew asking Xahlven questions was like dipping one's toe in a bear pit, but she needed to know and this was her only chance. "What happens in Eretheria? Please, I need to know."

Xahlven assumed a look of suitable regret. "War, I'm afraid. Ousienne of Hadda has declared her support of the missing Prince and called all loyal followers to her banner. She promises an end to the spring campaigns and a reordering of the noble families, among many other promises. Camis and Vora have aligned themselves against her, citing Ousienne's naked ambition."

Myreon couldn't help but laugh. "She didn't declare until after we were through. Now she acts the patriot. What fool would believe her?"

"Most of them, as it turns out. They sing her praises in the capital, where food is scarce and riots are growing more common. The rumor is that the King of Akral is backing the Counts of Camis and Vora. Sahand, it seems, supports Hadda and pursues a marriage with the captive Michelle Orly. And ugly business brews."

"I'm sure *you* had nothing to do with that," Myreon said.

Xahlven cocked his head, evidently concerned. "And why would I?"

Before she could answer, Trevard opened his eyes. "Very well. I've seen enough." He slapped the ring back in Androlli's palm and turned to Myreon. "Explain what happened, girl, so we can get this over with and see you petrified."

Myreon met Trevard's gaze, but couldn't hold it. For so long she wanted to glare at him—this old man who had let her be framed right under his nose, who may have even been *complicit* in her framing—but she couldn't do it. She kept seeing the sack of Ayventry and the piles of bones. She heard the screams of those she'd killed. Her, not Sahand.

But here was the question: should she tell the truth? Reveal Xahlven as the Chairman? Say, *Yes, Magus, I stole a forbidden artifact from Xahlven's mother's house and used it to kill tens of thousands of innocent people.*

"Well?" Trevard barked, slamming his fist on the armrest of his chair. "Don't make me Compel you, girl."

Xahlven put up a hand. "Give her a moment to collect herself, Trevard—the woman is clearly traumatized."

But what purpose would the truth serve, here? Myreon closed her eyes, trying to gather herself. What evidence did she have of Xahlven's collusion? None. Nothing. If she told Trevard the truth, it would be her word against Xahlven's, and there was little doubt which way that contest would turn. No, she would never have Tyvian's infernal brother at her mercy—he was too well prepared, too cautious. She knew it was no accident that he was here now, sitting in this tent, observing her interview.

Androlli was whispering in her ear. "Myreon, just tell them. There's nothing left to hide here. You have nothing else."

But Androlli was wrong. There *was* one thing

she could do—one thing she had. It was clear that Xahlven had anticipated this—that he knew either by scrying or by that same infuriating Reldamar ability to manipulate others that she would be sitting here, in this chair, faced with this choice. Either way, her life was over—that was certain—and since she had dedicated her life to doing good, here at the end there was only one good deed left to her. One thing that could serve the cause of justice.

She opened her eyes and cleared her throat. "I believe Banric Sahand has access to the Seeking Dark, and that he acquired it through his connections with the Sorcerous League, and that he'll use it again if he isn't stopped, once and for all."

Trevard's face was grim, his hawk-like nose pale as parchment. "You will need to tell us everything."

Myreon looked at Xahlven. "Of course, I would hope my cooperation would serve to lessen the severity of my sentence."

Xahlven smiled. "I think that can be arranged."

CHAPTER 29

A STUDY IN MISDIRECTION

By ancient tradition, armies fielded by the Arcanostrum on behalf of the Domain of Saldor were led by the Lord Defender of the Balance and advised by a sitting archmage. This was a historically rare occurrence—even now, over fifteen hundred years after the death of the last Warlock King, armies led by mighty sorcerers were something of a taboo—and therefore there was not a great deal of infrastructure in place to service an archmage in the field. Sorcerers of great power needed access to a great many materials to power their rituals, they required precisely balanced leys to achieve the correct effects, and they also tended to dislike getting muddy. Therefore, the first great ritual enacted by Xahlven and Trevard was to make for themselves an enormous floating palanquin.

It was constructed of mageglass and large enough to accommodate both archmagi and a squadron of Defenders tasked with their defense. It coasted a few feet above the ground on a cushion of faintly glowing Dweomeric force, and its surface held three pavilions—Xahlven's, Trevard's, and a larger one in the center for receiving reports and holding audiences. The front of the large platform had two thrones built into it—a black one for the Archmage of the Ether, and a silver-gray one for the Lord Defender. From its many flagpoles and the spires of its tents the purple and white of Saldor flapped merrily in the breeze. It was an audacious thing—a brazen affront to centuries of Arcanostrum tradition.

But Xahlven had insisted, and Xahlven was very persuasive.

Myreon knew Trevard disliked the palanquin. Over eighty years old and set in his ways, he could not quite accept that in his lifetime the world had changed so much as to permit this thing to exist. Accordingly, he spent as often as he could anywhere else—inspecting the troops or taking meetings with his officers in their tents—only returning to the sorcerous construct in the evening, where he would glower at the serving specters pouring him wine and stomp off to his tent as soon as dinner was finished. Myreon half wondered if he would dispel it all in a fit of rage and they'd all go tumbling into the mud. He never did, though.

Myreon was still in casterlocks, though the Defenders had the decency to let her out of them for meals. She never tried to escape—it would be idiotic to try, there in the company of two of the most powerful sorcerers in the world. Besides, there was nowhere else she had to go, nothing else she had to do. It wasn't even clear to her why she was kept around.

She spent her days shackled to a post near the front of the palanquin—a kind of cautionary tale for rogue sorcerers, she supposed, or maybe a mascot of some sort. Besides the Defenders, who refused to talk to her on principle, her only company was Xahlven.

"A regrettable thing to see, isn't it?" he remarked one day from his throne, looking across the columns of soldiers winding their way across the open grasslands that dominated the northern reaches of Galaspin and the southern reaches of Dellor—a trackless place known only as the "Wild Territories."

Myreon didn't answer. She wasn't sure whether he was referring to the monotonous landscape or the fact that six thousand Defenders of the Balance were marching to war, their purple-and-white banners and mirrored armor clearly visible against the gray landscape.

"To think," Xahlven went on. "If my mother had only listened to Conrad Varner and permitted him to harry Sahand all the way back to Dellor, we might have ended this thirty years ago instead of doing it now. Ayventry was such a lovely city. Such a shame."

Shame? Hadn't he been the one to place the Creeping Dark in her hands? Hadn't he been the one daring her to use it? His hypocrisy made Myreon want to claw off her own ears. She shifted restlessly against her bonds, trying to scoot farther away from him.

What the hell was his game here? If he had spoken the truth in the Black Hall—if he really wanted to see an end to the Arcanostrum—she didn't understand how this would accomplish it. The sorcerous might on display here was astounding. Six thousand firepikes? No conventional army could stand against that. She had spotted at least a score of men wearing colossus amulets, and there had to be thirty or forty Mage Defenders here, each of them trained in practical battle sorcery—lode bolts and fireballs, sunblasts and death bolts, blade and bow wards, sorcerous guards, and a hundred other enchantments and invocations that would spell certain doom to any Delloran force that faced them. How could one destroy the Arcanostrum by obliterating their most stalwart enemy?

It would have been one thing if this army had been mustered without provocation—the other nations of the West were extremely suspicious of Saldor fielding armies of men equipped with invincible magecraft—but, as far as anyone knew, Sahand has just destroyed an entire city of people with forbidden sorcery. They were simply fulfilling their mandate, now—protecting the balance of power that had kept the West functional for centuries.

Myreon *knew* Xahlven was running some kind of plot, here—he was a Reldamar, so of *course* he was—but what the hell could it be? She needed to find out, but needed to do so without letting on that she knew Xahlven was also the Chairman of the Sorcerous League.

At last, she decided on a line of questioning. "Why am I still here?"

"You were a military commander who fought against Sahand—successfully—for several months. We have decided your input could be worthwhile," Xahlven said.

"I'm also a rogue sorcerer wanted for a host of crimes. I should stand trial."

Xahlven nodded, conceding the point. "Your trial will proceed in good time. I am given to understand that Mage Defender Androlli is compiling the evidence against you as we speak. In the meantime, you remain at my disposal should I have any questions that need answering."

Myreon turned to look at him. Xahlven was grinning his dimpled grin, one leg crossed over the other. He looked relaxed as a frog in a pond. "Do you?"

"I am interested to hear what you can tell me about the Sorcerous League."

Myreon's eyes narrowed. Did he know? Was this some kind of test? "Almost nothing. Mostly just rumors."

"Don't be ridiculous," Xahlven said. "I know you didn't learn necromancy in the Gray Tower. Come now—Trevard isn't here and I've made certain he won't hear this conversation. You can tell me without offending the old man's sense of propriety."

Well, I know that you're in charge of the whole thing. But Myreon didn't say that. Instead, she shrugged. "They're just a bunch of pathetic hedge wizards and frustrated apprentices dabbling in arts they can scarcely handle. Other than their connections with Sahand, I wouldn't concern yourself with them."

"You're seeking to deflect suspicion by complimenting my inherent belief in my superiority. Nice attempt—my congratulations. But that ritual in the sewers of Eretheria was not the work of a frustrated amateur or studious dabbler. That was an inspired bit of magecraft. Your work?"

Myreon blinked. "You knew about . . . *you're* the one who dispelled it?"

"Just tying up loose ends for the Arcanostrum in Eretheria. As pretty a job as it was, I couldn't allow it to continue, Myreon. You understand, I'm sure."

Myreon kept her face as passive as possible, but inside her a riot of wild theories was building. He knew about the ritual and where to find it? Impossible, unless the necromancer had told him about it.

This *was* possible—Xahlven was the Chairman, after all. So Xahlven discovers the ritual and then waits to dispel it right at the moment she needed the White Guard most, drawing her army into a bitter street-by-street fight, which of course drives them to sack the city, which drove her to . . .

"Are you all right?" Xahlven asked. "Do you need a drink of water?"

Myreon, her stomach boiling, came back to herself. She felt like she had just run a race. "Fine. I'm fine. It's just . . . it's hard to lose like I did. Like *we* did."

"If their sacrifice leads to the destruction of Banric Sahand, it will not have been in vain. The world will be a safer place without him." Xahlven's voice was soft—he sounded so damned sincere. He *always* sounded sincere.

And yet here was a man who arranged for Myreon to be pushed to use a terrible super-weapon, killing thousands of innocent people, all to get an army to march on *Sahand*, and thereby kill even more people. If the world was to be made safer, Sahand wasn't the only one who needed to be destroyed.

Myreon tugged on her casterlocks, suddenly frustrated at how powerless she felt. If she didn't have anything to look forward to before, she did now. It wasn't enough to be there to see Banric Sahand brought to justice.

Myreon needed to find a way to kill Xahlven Reldamar.

Arkald the Strange was many things—a coward, a shut-in, a freak—but he was not a fool. He knew every piece of information he exchanged with Lyrelle Reldamar constituted a lethal risk from two potential avenues. On the one hand, he had no doubt the woman was a viper who would kill him at the first opportunity, thumbs or no thumbs. On the other, if Sahand found out he had exchanged more than pleasantries with the arch-sorceress, he would find himself in a gibbet hanging from the battlements of the Citadel with ravens tearing out his eyes.

Arkald should have stopped answering Lyrelle's questions. But he didn't. He found he didn't want to. As much as his rational mind understood what was going on, he could not help but look forward to his daily meeting with her. As she was beaten, bloody, battered, and gaunt, Arkald had trouble rationalizing the threat she posed with the benefits she might conceivably offer. Chief among these, it seemed, was the defeat and embarrassment of his own captor—Banric Sahand.

Arkald knew—*knew*—that Sahand had some terrible trick up his sleeve for the encroaching Saldorian army. It was the only possible explanation for the Mad Prince's buoyant mood. He strutted around the Citadel like any man newly engaged, a grin permanently affixed to his half-ruined face, even while rumors of his impending destruction mounted. Arkald had been in Sahand's service long enough to know that the only time he smiled like *that* was when he was about to do something truly terrible to his foes. Arkald recalled that once had included him.

It took Lyrelle to remind him that it *still* included him.

If Lyrelle was representative of the Arcanostrum—the authority that had hounded him ever since he found his calling among the dead—Sahand was representative of the kind of petty, cruel bullies that had driven him to that calling in the first place. In the Mad Prince's vicious smiles, Arkald could see reflections of the mean little brutes who had kicked and beaten him for daring to learn to read and for loving books over wrestling and stone-throwing and also, sometimes, for no reason other than Arkald, with his lazy eye and pale complexion, was just an easy target. Arkald the Strange, the easy target—the story of his life.

Arkald handed Lyrelle a cup of hot broth and noodles. The old woman, her arms trembling, sipped from the bowl eagerly and hugged it close with her mangled hands. "Thank you so much, Arkald."

Arkald knew the gratitude wasn't genuine, but it warmed him much like the broth warmed her. "More soldiers are mustering beyond the city walls. These bore the banners of the most distant garrisons—from the Ogre Hills and even as far as Junor Keep."

"He is recalling all his bannermen, as I predicted," Lyrelle said. "He is making a gamble on one final battle."

"Where he will use the weapon again." Arkald shivered. "If only I could get word to . . ." He caught himself.

Lyrelle's eyes twinkled. "To the Sorcerous League?"

Arkald gasped. "You . . . you *know*? How—"

"Arkald, my dear, it is the purview of the Archmage of the Ether to know secrets and to keep them." Lyrelle reached out and patted his hand gently. "The Black College of the Arcanostrum has known about the League for ages. We permit it to exist since, from time-to-time, the world needs heretics and madmen to make things orderly and sane again." As Arkald's mind reeled at this revelation, Lyrelle went on. "Besides—I am fairly certain the League would be on Sahand's side in this one, even if it isn't already."

"But . . . the *weapon* . . . the League would never—"

"The weapon will be used on several armies in the field, one of which will be exclusively comprised of the League's most hated enemies. The League's desire for their members' anonymity and modest distaste for indiscriminate violence is eclipsed by the fact that the persons they are seeking anonymity *from* will be obliterated. Don't look so shocked, Arkald—you can't have thought the Sorcerous League was an institution with a firm moral grounding, can you?"

Arkald considered this, and in so doing found his heart racing in his chest. "What . . . what kind of man would devise such a weapon? What kind of man would use it?"

Lyrelle adjusted herself atop her stool with a pained grunt. "You want to know why Sahand is like this?"

"I know that you know," Arkald said. "Tell me."

Lyrelle smiled, her sharp blue eyes growing distant, focused on events long past. "Banric Sahand was a mercenary captain and I, then a young mage, employed him on several . . . well, let's just call them *adventures*. You should have seen him then—the very picture of manhood, dashing and bold and *confident*. I liked him very much. He was a trifle cruel and not overly given to mercy, but, being young, I took these qualities to be hallmarks of his profession more than his character."

Arkald tried to picture a *young* Banric Sahand, but failed. He tried to picture a young Lyrelle and, while that was more plausible, it still fell short. The idea of these two young people working together was beyond him. "You . . . you were friends?"

"Yes, we were." Lyrelle sighed. "We were equally ambitious—I wanted to sit atop the Arcanostrum as Keeper, and he wanted to rule as a king. I taught him battle sorcery and helped him attend the War College of Ramisett. He, in turn, taught me much of what I know of military strategy. Unlike me, he always had trouble connecting the two disciplines."

"Is that why he hates you?"

Lyrelle laughed. "Great gods, Arkald—you really don't understand people very well, do you? No, no—

Sahand learned to hate me for a very, very old, very very simple reason."

"You . . . you killed his brother? You stole from him?"

"No, my dear," Lyrelle shook her head. "I married someone else. For his money."

Arkald gaped at her. "He . . . Sahand . . . he . . ."

"Yes. He loved me—or he felt what he *believed* was love. Time and distance have shown me that it was nothing of the kind. And anyway, we both got what we wanted, after a fashion—he with his crown and I with my staff. He hates me now for entirely other reasons. I wonder sometimes if he even remembers those days." Lyrelle's gaze drifted out the window. "And none of that changes what we have to do, does it?"

Arkald rubbed his face. "Of course. She is almost ready. I think I can make the switch tonight."

Lyrelle looked back at him, the wistfulness gone and replaced with that same precise glare. "Have you practiced the glamours I showed you? Can you make the shrouds stick?"

Arkald nodded. "Yes. Of course. But there's a lot left to do."

"And you've let me natter on like an old washer-woman all this time?" Lyrelle shooed him toward the door. "Get moving, boy! Don't let me keep you!"

Arkald staged a hurried retreat. "Don't worry!" he said. "You can count on me!"

Lyrelle grinned widely, revealing the teeth Sahand

had knocked out like black gaps among perfectly white tilework. "I believe in you, Arkald. Hurry!"

He retreated, his heart still racing, his whole body tingling with the terrifying thrill of speaking with her. *Don't be a fool*, one corner of his mind snarled, *she's manipulating you!*

It was true, but it didn't matter. Lyrelle had already given him things he hadn't known he needed. In the first place, he had purpose—stopping Sahand would be an adequate reward for her escape, or so he told himself. In addition, speaking with her had rubbed away some of the terror he bore of Sahand. He was no longer this monster—this insurmountable danger—he was an ambitious man who made mistakes. Lots of them, apparently. It made trying to stop Sahand seem more achievable and less suicidal. It gave him strength he never knew he had.

Last, and most important, Lyrelle Reldamar had brought him back to his work. When he arrived in his chambers, he quickly pulled the sheet off the dead body he had lying on a slab in the center of his bedroom. It was the culmination of almost two weeks worth of labor—carefully selected from recently interred bodies in city cemeteries, she was the perfect height, the perfect build. He had stitched up her fatal wounds, stuffed her collapsed stomach with sawdust to give her some heft, crafted new eyes from polished stones, and expended his supplies of authentic brown hair to make a wig that would match. All that remained were the finishing touches—a few replaced teeth, a few fingertips re-fleshed—and then he could work on raising her. Arkald quickly glanced at the formulas that Lyrelle had helped him sketch out—yes, they could be managed before nightfall, and the ingredients were all on hand. With those glamours and shrouds in place, no one would be able to tell Arkald's animated beauty from the real thing.

At least, this was his hope as he threw himself into his work for the next seven hours. As he was slipping her into a dress, he knew that this was his master-piece—a true work of necromantic art, one rarely achieved. Each of the rituals was completed and the delicate mixture of the Lumen (for imbuing life) and the Ether (for deceiving the eyes of the living) locked into place, an Astral ritual of binding working as a medium keeping the two opposing energies from intersecting and obliterating one another. At last it was time.

Arkald extended his hands and spoke, his voice hoarse from hours of chanting. "Arise, *Michelle.*"

The dead thing—the *physical* simulacrum of flesh and bone—sat up at once, smoothly and gracefully. She was the perfect, spitting image of the Lady Michelle, prisoner of the Mad Prince Sahand and consort to the Young Prince Artus, the future king of Eretheria. Arkald couldn't help but giggle. It worked—*it worked*!

He swallowed his mirth and gestured for the animated corpse to stand up, which it did. Snatching up a candle and lighting it with a wave of his hand, Arkald went to the door to his rooms and poked his head out into the corridor beyond. No one. Perfect.

He turned around and gestured for the simulated Michelle to follow him. "Come along, milady—let's get you to your cell, eh?"

The creature said nothing, but followed him without hesitation. Arkald led the way.

Though it was the middle of the night and hardly anyone was about, Arkald's heart hammered against his ribs as he led the corpse-double of Lady Michelle down out of his tower and across the keep to the tower where the real Lady Michelle was held. If anyone were to see him, the double would be enough to condemn him to an immediate death, and that would be if he was lucky. Worse, they might simply capture him and bring him before Sahand. Just the thought made Arkald want to faint with terror, so he resolved not to think of it.

His candle was the tiniest flicker of light in the cavernous darkness of the Citadel, but Arkald knew the way. He had been going over it in his head for days, paranoid that now, when it mattered most, he would get lost in the dark.

At last he was at the door. The one guard on duty was leaning against the wall, dozing off. Arkald cast a simple sleeping spell to aid him along, and then slipped past with his undead charge.

Up the spiral stairs, up up—the stones cold beneath his slippers and the double silently following. He was going to do it—he, Arkald, was actually going to defy the will of Banric Sahand. He unlocked the door to the cell and pushed it open.

His candle illuminated a cramped room with a big bed, an armoire, and scarcely space for anything else. The Lady Michelle, clad still in that same simple linen dress, sat bolt upright in bed, her eyes wide. "What is it? What do you want with me?"

Arkald laid a finger to his lips to indicate quiet. "You must come with me. Bring nothing. Come now."

Michelle saw the shadow lurking behind Arkald—her double. "Wh . . . what is *that*?"

Arkald executed a half bow. "Your freedom, milady. Come. Come."

Michelle wrapped herself in a shawl and took a few trembling steps past Arkald, her eyes fixed on her doppelganger. "A . . . a simulacrum?"

"No." Arkald permitted himself a smile. "Better." He took her by the hand—she was as cold to the touch as any undead construct—for a moment, he worried that he had perhaps overdone it on the glamours—but this Arkald, what he was coming to know as the *new* Arkald, did not hesitate. Did not doubt. He acted.

Down the stairs they went, quickly and quietly as they could. Past the sleeping guard, his key returned.

"Wait!" Arkald stopped dead. A light was coming.

No candle or torch, either—a feylamp. That meant it was no mere guard.

Arkald's heart froze. *Sahand is coming!*

He pushed Michelle back into a defensive alcove and doused his candle, praying to Almighty Hann himself that the Mad Prince had not seen their light before they saw his. He put a hand over Michelle's mouth and whispered, *"Be silent as death, or dead we will be!"*

Sahand's heavy boots echoed through the vast corridor. He passed close by—close enough for them to see his face. He was grinning, his teeth flashing from the hole in his cheek. He walked with an almost jaunty step.

He turned toward Michelle's tower. They heard him shout at the sleeping guard and then heard the door bang open. He was going up. Arkald's work was about to be put to the test.

"Oh gods," Michelle moaned. "Oh gods, he told me he would do this. Oh *gods!*"

"Do what?" Arkald asked.

But she only shuddered. The two of them remained in the alcove for some time, Arkald listening for the shout of alarm that would come when Sahand realized the truth, and Michelle imagining whatever horror Sahand had intended for her on this night.

But nothing came.

The trick had worked. It actually worked—it fooled

Sahand *himself*! It was all Arkald could do to keep from laughing, both from glee and from intense, physical relief.

He took Michelle again by the hand. "Come, milady. There is someone who wants to meet you."

And off they plunged into the midnight dark of the Citadel, Arkald's feet feeling lighter than the wind for the first time in years.

CHAPTER 30

THE SCORPION'S NATURE

Tyvian noticed they were being followed the day the rations ran out. They were camped on a broad ledge along a sheer cliff of dizzying height, going through their packs again, making sure a ration bar hadn't gone missing. It hadn't—they were out. "Kroth's bloody teeth," Tyvian shouted, kicking an empty sack. "Carlo cheated us! There should have been enough for us to get there! I counted the bars myself!"

"You mean the thief king of Freegate *lied* to you? What a shocker." Artus scowled at him. The boy hadn't stopped scowling since that mountain pass, four days back.

"No. No, that *can't* be it. I saw them—I *counted* them!"

"Phantasms," Voth offered, picking her fingernails with a stiletto. Her face had grown gaunt during the journey. Her eye sockets seemed sunken. Tyvian hadn't gotten her to speak to him in days.

"Carlo is no wizard, and even if he *was*, conjuring phantasmal food is even more expensive than actual food," Tyvian said, rubbing his beard.

"Maybe—" Eddereon began, but then stopped and cocked his head.

A horn echoed through the thin mountain air. All conversation died; they listened as one, the breath caught in their throats.

Threading faintly among the peaks, barely discernible from the wind—the baying of hounds.

Tyvian stood up. "Rodall!"

Eddereon shaded his eyes and stared down the path they had come. "Can't see him yet—he must be miles off. Maybe caught our scent from last night's campsite. Told you we should be carrying out scat."

Tyvian began to stuff things back into his pack. "And I told *you* it would be a cold day in hell before I walked about with shit in my pockets! Get packed and let's go!"

Eddereon knocked a pot out of Tyvian's hand. "No—leave it. Bring only the hearthcider and the blanket rolls. We need to travel light."

They were up and moving in moments, most of

their packs abandoned behind them. The air was too thin to run, but the small party moved at a brisk pace, carefully threading their way along the narrow ledge. Behind them, the horn blew again. It sounded closer.

"You expected this, didn't you?" Voth growled from behind him. "You said you knew Carlo would sell the map to Rodall. What's the plan, Reldamar?"

Tyvian pulled the map out of his sleeve. "According to Carlo, there's a suspension bridge at the end of this ledge—we cross to the other side and we cut it and Rodall will be out of luck. We just need to keep moving."

Voth nodded. "Sounds simple enough."

Eddereon called from ahead. "Less talk. Rodall's probably used potions so he and his men can run up here without getting winded—they're gaining!"

Tyvian put his head down and pressed on. Eddereon was in the lead, then Voth, then Artus. He glanced back to see Artus falling behind. "Focus, Artus! Come on!"

Artus was pale—the altitude was hard on him. Tyvian realized it was because he didn't have the ring to drive him onward. "Coming . . . coming . . ."

"Eddereon!" Tyvian shouted. "Help Artus!"

The big mercenary nodded and edged past both him and Voth along the narrow and uneven path, forcing both of them to press against the rock wall behind them. Once Eddereon had Artus's arm over his shoulders, they carried on.

Again, in the distance, the sound of the horn. Again, it was closer. The horn was a psychological game Rodall was playing, Tyvian knew. He wanted them to panic, wanted them to exhaust themselves and make mistakes so that when he inevitably caught up, the kill would be all the easier.

But Rodall hadn't counted on Carlo's double (triple?) cross.

Tyvian increased his pace to nearly a run. His heart pounded at a rate fit to break out of his chest and he felt dizzy, but he made it to the bridge. It was as the map described—three thick ropes that crossed a broad canyon at the base of which roared a white-capped river. Tyvian wasted no time—he took a rope in each hand, stood atop the third, and began to cross.

Voth made it to the bridge next, but collapsed beside it, panting.

"Voth!" Tyvian yelled back. "Come on—we're almost clear! You can rest on the other side!"

Voth waved him on. "I . . . I just . . . need . . . a moment . . ."

The ring twinged, but Tyvian ignored it and pressed on. She would be all right. Eddereon would help her, if it came to it. One of them had to get across first—everything depended on that. He gulped down more thin air and tried to keep the world from spinning, placing one foot in front of the other on the thick rope. *Concentrate . . . concentrate . . . one wrong step . . .*

Eddereon and Artus arrived next. Tyvian was too far away to hear clearly what was discussed, but it wound up with Artus being left to rest while Eddereon began to make the crossing with Voth just behind him, one hand on the rope, the other presumably on his back or gripping his belt to steady herself.

Tyvian made it to the other side. The sense of vertigo inflicted by the bridge did not immediately pass, and he leaned against a boulder for a moment to get his balance. When at last the world stopped spinning, he looked back. Voth and Eddereon were almost across. Artus was about halfway, moving hesitantly. On the other side, a trio of big wolfhounds paced back and forth, baying at their quarry. They had outrun their masters, but by how far? Tyvian waved to Eddereon and Voth. "Hurry!"

Eddereon made the end. Voth followed immediately after, standing between the two anchor posts. "Reldamar—give me a sword!"

Tyvian hesitated only a moment before he tossed her his broadsword. "Wait until Artus is across." He knew he didn't need to say it—the ring would keep her from trying anything.

Then Voth laid her ring finger atop the anchor post and, holding the broadsword in her left hand, brought it down hard. There was a streak of blood. Voth screamed.

Tyvian caught a glimpse of her finger, iron ring still affixed, tumbling into the void.

"No!" Tyvian yelled.

Eddereon turned to face her. "Voth!"

Voth's face was suddenly alight, a broad grin spilling out from between thin lips. She drove the sword into Eddereon's stomach, angled upward. Tyvian saw the tip tent the back of the big Northron's hauberk. Then she yanked it out again with a savage twist, and Eddereon fell to his knees.

Tyvian tried to charge her, but Eddereon was in the way, cupping his stomach as blood and organs spilled out.

Voth turned, sword held high. Halfway across the ravine, Artus had frozen in place. Tyvian saw him open his mouth to say something, but Voth didn't give him the chance. She brought the blade down on one of the thick ropes, cutting through it cleanly.

Artus stumbled on the bridge, almost falling, but grabbed the foot rope in time and hooked his arms over it, his legs kicking in space.

Tyvian got past Eddereon and tried to grab Voth around the waist, but she was too quick, delivering a back-kick to his groin, perfectly aimed. Tyvian fell on his side, gasping for air.

Laughing, Voth slashed one of his hamstrings.

"Stay with me, Tyvian," she said. "I want you to watch this."

Artus struggled to get on top of the rope, he tried to reach the second one—too far. "Help!" he shouted.

Voth pressed the edge against the foot rope and began to saw, slowly, deliberately. "Bye-bye, your *highness!*"

"Adatha," Tyvian groaned, rolling to his knees and crawling toward her. "Don't!"

"Or what?"

"I'll kill you."

Voth mimed a kiss. "Promises, promises."

The rope snapped. With a scream, Artus vanished into the abyss.

Tyvian surged to his feet and lunged at Voth, a dagger in his hand. She knocked it away with the sword, but they wound up in a violent embrace and rolled along the ledge, Voth's head hanging over the edge. She lost the sword and had only one good hand, but Tyvian was still dizzy, still reeling from the groin hit, and had only one good leg. Voth wound up on top, the blood from her amputated finger raining down on Tyvian's face as they struggled.

She was laughing. "It feels so *good* to have that thing off, Tyvian. Oh, gods, I can't believe you never did that! It's like I'm free—I'm finally *free!*"

Tyvian could see her good eye, and could see madness there. Everything that had been good in her had just been sheared off in one stroke, and what was left was something less than a whole. This wasn't Adatha Voth—this was a lunatic, a splintered husk where the woman had once been. "I would have had it off, Adatha! You idiot! Why *do* this?"

Voth worked on Tyvian's hand, trying to twist his dagger around to stab him. His hand trembled with the effort of resisting her. "Poor Tyvian Reldamar," she snickered. "Always looking for some damsel to rescue. Is that what you thought was going to happen? You'd swoop in, remove the ring, and I'd fall in love with you?"

Tyvian worked his good leg up so the knee was pressed against Voth's hips. She abandoned the hold before he pushed her off and rolled to her feet. Tyvian staggered up, knife out.

Voth swayed in the breeze, blood still pouring from her hand. She drew out a stiletto. Tyvian knew it was poisoned just by looking at the groove down the center.

He limped toward her anyway, trying to shake off the dizziness. "You don't know what you've done, Adatha. You have no idea the . . . the damage you've done to yourself."

"Damage? You don't know what you're talking about!" Voth laughed, almost hysterical. "I'm *better* now. I'm *fixed!* What's a finger compared to a clean soul?"

"You just murdered two men!" Tyvian screamed. He wanted to lunge at her again, but his injured leg wouldn't allow it. Voth danced close to him and offered two quick slashes. Tyvian retreated, but tripped over a rock and tumbled down a steep slope. The world spun.

Voth scrambled after him, cackling with glee. "My tears, Tyvian—remember my tears? Remember me blubbering at night like a fool? You know what caused that?" She stabbed down at Tyvian, but he rolled aside. She pinned his cloak to the ground instead.

Tyvian yanked at it—it wouldn't come loose. He tried to get out of it. "How the hell should I know? Your father taking your eye? Some past trauma?"

Voth drew a leaf-bladed throwing knife and threw, hitting Tyvian in the palm of his off-hand. "It was *you*, Reldamar! *You!* Each and every night you were close, I felt this terrible falling sensation—as though I had lost control of myself. As though I was going mad. And I couldn't fight it! I *wanted* you, come what may. I wanted to be with you! I lived in desperate fear that you might learn that and *use* it!"

Tyvian left the knife in his palm—if it was poisoned, it was too late anyway. He slashed with his own knife, forcing Voth to retreat up the slope. Around him, the wind howled. Flakes of snow drifted through Voth's hair. "What you're describing is *love*, Voth. You're falling in love with me!"

Voth grinned, holding up her mangled hand. "Not anymore."

Tyvian held his knife high, pointed at Voth's face. "I don't want to kill you."

"You won't have to." She pulled a pair of needle-thin daggers from her sleeve. Holding them both in her off hand, she jumped. One she threw, forcing Tyvian to duck. The other she plunged into him, just above his collarbone.

Tyvian countered with a horizontal slash across her stomach, the well-honed blade parting leather and flesh easily.

They fell backward together, Voth screaming as she twisted herself to straddle his neck, one leg pinning his knife arm down. She held the poisoned stiletto up, ready to plunge it into his eye. "Good-bye, you miserable fool of a man!"

But Tyvian was already working his off hand—his *unpinned* off-hand. The one with the throwing knife embedded in it. He plucked it out with the tips of his fingers and spun it around with a little flick.

And then he thrust it into Voth's kidney.

And twisted.

Voth's mouth fused into an open O as what little color was in her face drained away. The stiletto tumbled from her hand as she struggled to pull the blade from her back.

Tyvian rolled, throwing her off. She smacked her head against a rock, tried to rise, blood pouring from her temple. She lost her balance.

She fell.

Crawling, Tyvian peered over the edge. Voth's

body lay crumpled in a heap, seventy feet below. Blood was everywhere, staining the snow crimson.

Slowly, Tyvian worked his way up the slope he'd tumbled down until he was on the narrow ledge where Eddereon lay. It was snowing in earnest now, a storm rolling in. Snowflakes already flecked his thick beard. Tyvian lifted the man's head into his lap. "Eddereon! Wake up! Gods, don't make me kiss you. Wake up!"

Eddereon's eyes flickered open, but he didn't move. "Fat lot of good . . . this . . . this mail did me . . ."

Tyvian found himself laughing even as tears began to blind him. "That's what you get if you spend all your time sharpening swords, you fat oaf. Now get up!"

Eddereon grasped his hand. "Do you think I . . . I did you . . . a wrong by giving you . . . you the ring?"

"Dammit, Eddereon—I am not interested in deathbed confessions. Get your sorry arse up!"

"I think . . . I think that maybe I did." Eddereon looked off into the sky, where the snowflakes swirled and fell. "But it was worth it. It was worth it."

Eddereon's eyes closed. Tyvian grabbed him by the sideburns. "No it wasn't! You hear me? *No it bloody wasn't!* You still owe me big-time, you great hairy fool! Wake up! I'll not lose two friends in the same day, understand?" Tyvian shook him, slapped his face.

He may as well have been slapping a boulder.

Eddereon was dead. Artus was dead. The grief was like a physical pain—another knife, twisting inside him. A knife he couldn't pluck out.

And Voth . . . Voth, too. The pain she must have felt, the fear. He had never spared himself the luxury of imagining a future with her, but now that she was gone, it was all he could think about—what else might they have been? What could they have become? If only he had done more. If only he had had more time. To have driven her to this pass . . .

No, not him.

The ring was still, heavy on his hand. And cold as the wind that blew.

Tyvian slammed his ring-hand against a rock twice, three times. "You miserable piece of garbage! You Kroth-spawned shit! Is this what you think I wanted? *Is this what the world needs?*"

The horn—Rodall's horn—blasted out from across the canyon. Tyvian couldn't see the other side anymore—the growing storm obscured it. But he knew he couldn't stay. It was time to go. By Carlo's map, the Vale was only about ten miles away. So close.

He tried to stand, but couldn't walk. He resorted to crawling on hands and knees, as the snow poured down around him, favoring his injured hand until the cold made it numb. The ring did nothing to help. Tyvian was convinced it never had.

CHAPTER 31

THE KEEPER OF THE VALE

As the storm grew and the snow fell faster and faster, Tyvian found himself not so much crawling as swimming in icy white powder. He was able to take a drink of hearthcider from his canteen, which prevented him from freezing to death in the near term, but it did nothing to stem the pain of his injuries, the numbness of his fingers and toes, or his complete loss of direction.

He could see barely a few inches in front of his face. As night fell, he could see less than even that—he blindly flopped through snow banks and over ledges, he rolled down steep ravines and had to claw his way out of icy crevasses. He had no idea whatsoever where he was or where he was going. He just kept going.

Tyvian expected to die at any moment—to put his numb hand forward and lean, only to find a bottomless gorge yawning in front of him. It struck him as fitting an end as any. It was how Artus had died—how was he deserving of any better? He clawed his way forward, waiting for that sense of free fall.

It never happened.

The snow was over his head now. He could scarcely move. The ring, of course, was cold and inert—he had no "good" intentions to trick it with, no heroic farce to encourage its intervention. If he continued to live, it was only out of spite—to see the ring excised and melted down. The notion of what to do afterward was no longer clear to him. He couldn't even remember. This—this mountainside, this storm, and this slow freezing death was what he had been marching toward all that time. It was what he deserved.

The hallucinations began as sounds—someone calling his name? Myreon? Voth? His mother? He couldn't tell. He shook snow from his beard and called out, his voice raw and hoarse. He imagined the gardens of Glamourvine, the sound of the songbirds in the hedges, the softness of the wet, black earth. He imagined hugging that ground, so warm and humid it seemed to sweat beneath the sun. *Why did I leave?* he wondered. *Could have stayed, entered the Arcanostrum, earned my staff, coasted on my family money. Married some pretty rich girl. Done nothing.*

It didn't sound so bad now. Boring, but painless. Xahlven probably would still have plunged the world into darkness for his own crazy reasons. Tyvian reasoned, though, that when he died in that other life—that fictional, illusory past he was now constructing—he would have died fat and satisfied. Perhaps he would have married Myreon, popped out a few children. Tyvian wasn't fond of children, but he was considering that a failing at the moment. As he died here, alone on a mountaintop, having somebody out there in the world who might miss him seemed an advantage, however slight.

He tried to move. He found he couldn't. The snow was up around his shoulders, covering his back. He tossed his head blearily from side to side. Snow fell over his face and into his mouth.

Fine, then, he thought. *This will do.*

He slept. Or perhaps he died. In any event, he found himself dreaming of Myreon's laugh—that rarest of things—and of Artus. And Hool. And little Brana.

And of his mother hugging him that last time they had spoken.

Tyvian knew he was dying, now, because it didn't even bother him to realize that she had been right.

And then a strong, rough hand had him by the back of his cloak, hauling him upward. "Right—*there* you are!" The voice was deep, like the rumbling of distant thunder.

"Eddereon?" Tyvian muttered, but whoever it was—not Eddereon—was throwing him over his shoulders and trudging through the snowstorm.

Tyvian drifted in and out of consciousness as this happened, and could see really nothing but white and felt nothing but cold and the vaguely dizzying sensation of dangling over someone's shoulder. Then, suddenly, it all stopped. There was light and warmth and quiet—just the crackling of a fire. He was being laid down on a bed. "There," his rescuer said. "Just sleep, Tyvian. Sleep."

Tyvian slept. He didn't even have it in him to wonder how this person knew his name.

Tyvian woke up under some thick fur pelt in some rustic cabin. For the third time in his life.

He threw the fur off of him. "Kroth's bloody teeth, can't a man succumb to death without some imbecile interfering?"

But he was alone. The cabin was small—only one room, with a stone fireplace dominating one wall and a thick wooden door opposite. A cheery blaze flickered in the hearth, and the low beams of the steepled roof were hung with dried herbs and cured meats. From what he could see, there were no weapons apart from a wood axe, and that had a rusted head that was likely so blunt, the axe had to be downgraded to "cudgel" in terms of its purpose. No doubt the sharp one had been relocated, since *something* had to be cutting the firewood around here.

Tyvian's wounds were expertly bound and, though not entirely healed, were certainly much better. They didn't even especially hurt. The ring throbbed at the thought of bashing the person who saved him over the head and diving once more into the storm, so Tyvian seriously doubted this was a dream.

He got up and found that he was naked. The cabin was so warm that it scarcely mattered, and if his savior could handle stuffing a nude Tyvian under a pile of furs, he could bloody well handle a nude Tyvian poking through his belongings.

He found a wedge of cheese and ate it. It was hard and old, but good enough. He found a barrel of ale, too, and poured out a bit into a pewter mug. It was warm and weak, but it would do. He had only to wait until his savior returned.

Tyvian had been awake for about an hour or so when there was a stomping on some kind of porch outside the door—knocking the snow off boots—and then the door swung open. The man beyond was a compact sort of fellow—wide as he was tall, like a wrestler. His hair was pure white, spilling over his broad shoulders, as was his beard, which was so long it was tucked into his rope belt. He wore a patchwork cloak of fur, all caked in snow. Once the door was closed, he threw it off of him and onto one of the roof beams. Beneath, he had a thin shirt, so ancient it was practically transparent, and a pair of patched canvas pants. Of everything he wore, only his boots looked worth anything—black, polished, and heavy, they were the kind of thing that would cost twenty-five marks in a Galaspin outfitter's shop.

"How are you feeling, Tyvian?" the man asked, grinning. His teeth were white and perfectly even.

"I'm going to skip the part where I wonder how you know my name and get right to the 'Who the hell are you and where am I?' questions."

The man nodded as though this were expected. "My name is Abrahann. I found you in the snow and brought you here. I would tell you where you are, but the mountain and the pass where my cabin rests have no name. I will say instead that you are above the Hidden Vale of the Oracle, and so your journey is very nearly complete."

Tyvian shook his head. "All right, I'll bite—how the hell do you know so much about me?"

"I am an augur." The man pointed toward a basin of water on a table—something Tyvian had taken to be a washbasin and used as such. "I've been scrying your future for some time now. Ever since Eddereon saw fit to gift you with the ring."

Tyvian's eyes darted to Abrahann's hands. Sure enough, there on his right hand was nestled an iron ring just like his. The man saw his expression of surprise and held it up. "Yes. I have one, too."

"Then you *must* have asked the Oracle how to take it off!" Tyvian said, standing up. "Can you? Is it possible?"

Abrahann motioned for him to sit. "First, let us get you some clothes and eat a real meal—not that rind of cheese. Then I will answer your questions."

"No. You will answer this question *now*, damn you! Can you take it off?"

Abrahann sighed. Slowly, deliberately, he brought his left hand to his right, gripped the ring between two fingers . . .

. . . and gently slipped it off.

Tyvian was speechless. Watching an iron ring slide off a hand was somehow . . . perverse. Alien. He fiddled with the one on his hand, but it did not budge.

Abrahann slipped the ring back on. "Dress, eat, rest—then we will talk."

Tyvian planted his naked arse in front of the fire. "I'm not hungry and I'm not tired. We talk now."

Abrahann chuckled and sat across from him. He pulled a skillet from the wall and pulled down a pair of sausages from the beams. In a few moments, he had them sizzling over the fire. Tyvian's mouth watered.

"Let me answer the questions you want to ask: The Oracle is not lightly consulted and, were I you, I would leave it in peace. Yes, I do know of the Yldd. No, I will not tell you of them. As for myself: I am the one you seek. The one you have sought all these years but have not thought to give a name. I have been on this mountain for a long, long time. I have met many pilgrims who have toiled into the mountains, seeking the Vale. I have told them all to turn back. They seldom do."

"And those who go down into the Vale? What becomes of them?" Tyvian asked. He was not sure now whether his mouth watered from the scent of roasting meat or the idea that the Oracle was so near at hand.

Abrahann shook the pan to flip the sausages. "It is a funny thing, knowledge. Men see it as a resource—a font of power and wisdom—but I wonder sometimes. I think perhaps the *knowing* of a thing can weaken more important concerns."

"Like what?"

"Faith. Courage. Loyalty. Piety." Abrahann watched the fire. "Only ask questions that need answers. For everything else, is not ignorance, bliss?"

"But that assumes things like loyalty are undermined by the truth. Can't they be strengthened by it, too?"

Abrahann looked at him. His eyes were dark—a color Tyvian could not make out in the dim light of the cabin. They seemed deep as oceans; Tyvian found he could not meet his gaze. "For your almost forty years, have you ever known a perfect person? Has there ever been anyone who, once their secrets were laid bare, had not lessened in your eyes or the eyes of your fellows?"

Tyvian found himself wanting to argue, but hadn't he made the same arguments himself for years? *Lies,* his mother had always said, *are every bit as useful as the truth, but have the advantage of being more flexible.* Faith, loyalty, courage, piety—all traits Tyvian had exploited to varying degrees through his life. They were illusions that people clung to in order to make their world something they could understand and face.

But still . . .

Tyvian held up his ring hand. "Explain this to me, then. If the world is just miserable—if it's just a lie— why does this device exist? Who would design such a thing? What good does it do?"

Abrahann smiled. He flipped the sausages into a wooden bowl and offered it to Tyvian. "Why do you think the ring is concerned with the world?"

Tyvian snatched up one of the sausages, not caring that it burned his fingers, and took a savage bite. He was so hungry, he found himself unable to stop chewing as he spoke. "Isn't it obvious? It's trying to make heroes of us, right? What else is a hero but someone who tries to save the world? What else can a hero be but some selfless naive fool with a sword and a white charger, rescuing maidens from towers and so on?"

"You have it backward, Tyvian. The ring is not

trying to make you a hero—the ring is trying to make you a *better person*. The hero part is all *your* idea." Abrahann pointed at him. "*Your soul* made the ring do what it did; and your will made the decisions that led you here. The ring merely prevented you from doing evil things along the way."

"But what is the point of good deeds if they lead to bad ends?"

Abrahann shrugged. "What good ends did you envision? World peace? An end to injustice? A sack of gold for every pauper and loving parents for every orphan?"

Tyvian took a sip of warm beer. "You sound like my mother now—'there is no justice' and all that. Well, if the world is that terrible, then why bother being the only good man in it, eh? Why not throw the damned thing off my finger and have done? The good man comes to ruin among evil men, yes?"

Abrahann smiled. "You make that sound as if it's a bad thing."

Tyvian shook his head. "It seems as though everywhere I go there is some mystical crank dragging me out of a perfectly good demise only to lecture me about morality." He got up and cast about for some clothing. "I'm going to the Vale now."

"Best wait for the storm to clear. Perhaps in the morning."

"Hang that—I'm going now." Tyvian found a pair of leather breeches and snatched them up. They were a poor fit, but they would have to do.

"The Oracle will not give you what you want, Tyvian."

Tyvian found a fur hat and stuffed it on his head. It smelled terrible. "Oh really? And what the hell do you know about what *I* want, mountain man?"

"I think the bigger question is, what the hell do *you* know about it?" Abrahann countered.

"You know what I want?" Tyvian said, dragging on a loose-fitting shirt and fur vest. "I want Artus to be alive. I want Sahand defeated and forgotten. I want to stop *caring* so much about what happens in the world and go back to merely exploiting it for profit. I want to be left the hell alone. Finally, the *next* time I'm about to freeze to death or drown or bleed out, I would like it very much if I was left to die in peace instead of waking up in another Kroth-spawned barn!"

Abrahann shook his head. "No. You're wrong."

"Kiss my arse." Tyvian dragged Abrahann's heavy fur cloak from the rafters and threw it over his shoulders.

"Do not trust the Oracle, Tyvian. It is not what it seems."

"Neither are you, old man." Tyvian pulled open the door and the snow swirled in. He paused. "Incidentally, which *way* is the Vale?"

Abrahann pointed at the floor. "Down. Just go down."

CHAPTER 32

THE ORACLE

Whether by sorcery or the efforts of Abrahann, the path down from the cabin remained clear of the deepest snow—it was easy to find among the shifting drifts. The path itself was well-worn, the footsteps of a thousand pilgrims having cut it from the rock over the eons. It was an easy trip, such a contrast to the pain and blood and toil it had taken to get this far. Tyvian got a flash of Eddereon's bushy smile, Artus's earnest grin . . .

. . . Voth's deep, throaty laugh.

He shuddered, almost lost his balance. He leaned on an outcropping of rock for a moment before going on. The snow had thinned away by now, the clouds had cleared, and the sun was rising over the mountains. A bright orange line cut across the valley beneath him, illuminating the green treetops and a flat, still lake that glowed like fire.

The Vale.

The stories of the Oracle were a cliché—something to give a children's story that special gravitas, or to make one's moral fable seem more profound. When Tyvian had first learned it was a real place, he had been incredulous—the idea of actual figures from history traipsing up into the northern reaches of the Dragonspine just to chat with some lady in a lake when they had perfectly good magi back at home seemed ludicrous. And yet here he was, doing the same. Hell, he was even a king. *Life's full of its little jokes, isn't it?*

In time, the worn path turned from stone to dirt and moss. Tyvian was among the trees—the fabled glade where sprites traditionally stood guard and knights set camp, where lovers were cursed with confusion and brothers fought to the death, all before the Oracle set it all to rights. Now that he was here, seeing it with his own eyes, he again took stock of the old stories and wondered at the truth of them. He thought, too, of the old man's warnings—that the Oracle would not give him what he wanted. That it wasn't to be trusted.

In truth, he *didn't* know what he wanted, but he didn't trust anybody, not even the Oracle. He figured the two facts cancelled each other out.

The Vale was silent. No birds singing in the branches of the trees, no small animals scurrying in the underbrush. Not even a breeze. Tyvian felt completely, totally alone, as though he'd stepped out of the world entirely.

At the edge of the water, he peered into its depths. A haggard face looked back at him, an uneven beard stained with blood and two eyes sunken in their sockets. He opened his mouth to speak, but the haggard man did, too. It was his reflection. He reached up and ran a hand along his beard, noting the flecks of gray among the rust-red curls. "Gods," he muttered. "I look like hell."

No image in the lake came to speak with him about it, however. Perhaps she was put off by his poor hygiene, though Tyvian couldn't imagine too many people making it here while looking their best. He stood back from the water and swung his arms idly at his sides. "What now?"

He decided to follow the edge of the lake, peering in occasionally to see if the Oracle was handy. Maybe she was restricted to certain parts of the lake. Maybe she liked to sleep in. He considered calling for her or lobbing rocks into the pond, but decided to err on the side of good manners and do what all the knights and heroes in the stories did: just stumble upon her. He even found himself considering how he might feign his surprise at encountering her. For all he knew, the pageantry was part of the whole deal.

The lake cut into the side of the mountains, forming a small grotto with roots and stalactites overhead. Here, the calm surface of the water was disrupted by a little waterfall at one end—the source of the lake, Tyvian supposed. It made the seeing of reflections impossible, so he was about to turn around when he caught sight of something else: right beside the waterfall was a narrow flight of stairs leading to a fissure in the wall. *Intriguing.*

He climbed the steps, taking care not to slip on the slick rock, wishing he had a torch or some kind of illumination. His eyes, though, quickly adjusted—he was not walking into pitch darkness, it seemed. There was a hole somewhere in the ceiling that admitted a single shaft of sunlight, angled steeply across a wide, flat chamber.

At the center of this chamber stood another pool, this one dark as midnight and still as ice. Around its edge was laid a series of rectangular stones, each inscribed with a crude rune. Tyvian's magecraft was not good enough to decode what they meant, but he'd seen similar before in ruins from the age of the Warlock Kings. The hair on the back of his neck stood on end. Given the sheer *quantity* of hair he had back there at the moment, this was saying something indeed.

"Hello?" he called. There was no echo, but there should have been.

Tyvian found his mouth had gone dry. With

careful, shuffling steps, he approached the edge of the pool. He looked in.

Instead of his reflection, he was looking at a tall woman clad in white, her face smooth and perfect, her hair the color of freshly fallen snow. Her eyes were black pools. When she spoke, her lips moved just slightly before her words could be heard, as though she were calling from a far, far distance. "Welcome, Tyvian Reldamar. I am the Oracle of the Vale."

Tyvian doffed his fur cap and delivered a graceful bow. "I am pleased to learn you are not, in fact, fictional."

The joke didn't land. The woman's expression changed not at all. "Ask what you wish to see, what you wish to know, and I will tell you."

Tyvian nodded. "I understand, yes. I have a few procedural matters to attend to first, if that's all right."

The Oracle's face did not move. "I do not understand."

Tyvian licked his lips. "First off, are you able to lie?"

"Have I ever lied? In all the legends, in all the stories, is not the Oracle always found correct?" Tyvian couldn't tell by her tone that she was offended or not, but she was *definitely* dodging the question. He put her down for a big "yes" in the "can you lie" category.

"Second point of order: is there some kind of fee I need to pay, either up front or afterward, in exchange for this consultation?"

"The knowledge comes freely to me. Why should

it not flow freely to you, who have toiled so long to stand here? What would I wish of you if it was not? You have nothing I want, Tyvian Reldamar."

Tyvian looked down at his borrowed rags. She had a point. Either that or she was dodging the question again. "I'm sorry, but I can't help but notice that you have a remarkable tendency to answer questions with additional questions. Is this going to be a theme?" He jerked his thumb over his shoulder. "If so, I can always find augurs who are rather more direct back home."

"Ask your questions, Tyvian Reldamar."

"Any questions at all? As many questions as I want?"

"Ask."

"All right." Tyvian took a deep breath. "Tell me of the Yldd."

The Oracle's expression darkened. Indeed, the whole chamber seemed to dim, as though the word itself sucked the light from the room. "Ask something else."

"No. You are the Oracle, I am the pilgrim—you have to answer my questions. So, out with it."

A long silence followed in which the Oracle hung there, a reflection in the water, but did not move or speak. Tyvian imagined she was wrestling with herself—her duty versus her desire not to speak of the Yldd.

Finally, the Oracle closed her eyes and opened them again—a decision reached, perhaps. Then, she vanished. In her place in the pool was an image—a palace of some kind, or perhaps a city forum. In it sat thirteen robed and bearded men, people gathered at their feet, raising up their hands in supplication. "In the age of mighty Syrin, in the ancient city of Burza, there were thirteen learned men. They were the wisest and the mightiest of sorcerers, descendants of the chieftains of men who had learned at the foot of Hann, their god."

The scene changed, showing these same men linking hands around an elaborate sorcerous ritual, the veta shining with light. "Not satisfied with the knowledge they possessed, they searched for more— and more still. In time, all the secrets of the universe were revealed to them, so great was their power."

Tyvian grunted. "And now comes the fall, yes?"

The scene changed to show those wise men again, but this time all of them haggard and ancient and skeletal, their eyes gleaming with cold green light. "They learned too much. They lost themselves in the knowledge. The world held no more wonder for them, no more joy. They became nothing but guardians of their hoard of secrets, forever cursed."

The scene changed a final time—thirteen men, fleeing a city aflame, climbing high into the mountains, their bodies unnaturally thin.

The Oracle returned. "Now you know."

Tyvian cocked his head. "Ah, but I don't. The story ended early—the thirteen men who, I presume, became the Yldd . . . what became of them? Where are they to be found?"

The Oracle stood silent, as before.

Tyvian grinned. "But I think I know. It's obvious, really—thirteen men who learned everything there was to know, they would have learned the secret of Rahdnost's Elixir, yes? Eternal life. An eternity of sitting in the mountains *knowing* everything."

"You know not of what you speak."

"And now I've caught you in a lie. Because I *know* I'm right. As a know-it-all myself, there is one thing I know for certain about know-it-alls." Tyvian pointed at the Oracle and winked. "They're just *dying* to tell people everything they know."

The Oracle said nothing, her white hair and white gown flowing in some invisible current beneath the surface of the pool. Tyvian pulled his eyes away from her. Instead, he squinted into the darkness of the chamber. "There you are!"

Standing in the shadows, forming a ring around the pool and around Tyvian himself, stood thirteen gaunt figures in black robes, every part of their bodies wrapped and hidden from view with the exception of a deep, dark shadow beneath a thick black hood. They stood perfectly still—still in a way only the dead could manage—but they were not dead. Tyvian was sure of it. "I assume I am speaking now with the Yldd, yes?"

One of the thirteen stepped forward—or, rather, glided forward, as Tyvian saw no indication of legs moving or anything. It did not come into the light, but rather floated just beyond it. "Very clever, Tyvian Reldamar. You do the line of Perwyn justice."

Tyvian scanned the figures surrounding him. He could feel their collective gaze upon him—it was an alien thing, cold and distant. He felt a profound discomfort to realize they had been there the whole time as he spoke with the Oracle.

As though they were reading his mind, the leader of the Yldd spoke. "A simple trick of misdirection. Even the stoutest of hearts quail at the sight of us now. The Oracle has served as an excellent medium for many millennia."

Tyvian licked his lips. "You can hear my—"

"Your thoughts are known to us. Your desires. We know why you have come."

"Well, then." Tyvian held up his ring hand. "I'm waiting."

"First you will ask us questions. Then we will discuss the iron ring."

"Says who?" Tyvian looked around at them. "Who's in charge here, anyway?"

A whispering rustled around the circle—a laugh? "No one," it said.

Tyvian kept holding up his ring hand. The Yldd simply floated there, waiting. It occurred to him that if they'd been hanging out in this dank little cave for thousands of years, the odds of him waiting them out were effectively nil. "Fine. How goes the war? The world? Catch me up."

The lead Yldd moved its black-wrapped arm to point into the pool. "Look. We will tell you."

Tyvian looked.

And he learned the entire world had gone to hell in his absence—or further in that direction, anyway.

He saw the armies of Saldor in tatters, limping across the Wild Territory or lying in heaps on the battlefield. He saw civil war in Eretheria, the remnants of Myreon's rebellion crushed among the juggernauts of the Great Houses of Hadda, Camis, and Vora as they fought over the spoils of headless Ayventry and Davram—cities burning, farmland ravaged, famine not far behind.

He saw the black-armored legions of Dellor mustering in the great courtyard of the Citadel, their swords raised up to salute their prince. Then he saw Banric Sahand, arms raised in victory. At his feet? A broken Artus, chained and battered, awaiting his doom as the mob cheered.

"He's alive!" Tyvian gasped, but it was a foolish exclamation—he wouldn't be soon enough. Perhaps the Yldd intended for him to watch.

The scene changed again. Hool in a burning village, limping from great wounds, Sir Damon at her side, his sword drawn. And again—Myreon in the darkness, Xahlven's black throne looming over her, a cruel smile on his lips. Tyvian watched as his brother raised his hand, some terrible force building in his palm.

Tyvian looked away. "Enough! Gods, enough . . . I . . . I get the idea." He wiped sweat from his brow. "Tell me—are these visions happening now, or are they *about* to happen? Can they be prevented?"

"Perhaps."

"How?"

The leader of the Yldd floated closer to Tyvian—close enough now that he could make out more details of what lay beneath the hood. He caught a glimpse of the bleached jawbone of a human skull. "Now . . . now we shall bargain."

Tyvian nodded. He grinned, despite himself. Of course—what he had just been shown, the horrors he had witnessed, the fate of his friends—this was not prophesy.

It was a sales pitch.

"I wish to have the iron ring removed with no ill effects. Can you do it?"

"It can be removed. There will be consequences—they are unavoidable."

Tyvian thought back to Voth and how she had changed once she cut off the ring. The malice in her eyes, not tempered by any sense of who she had been—the whole woman he had partly come to know. "What are the consequences?"

"The ring is part of you. When it is removed, part of you will be gone."

Tyvian felt his heart sink into his stomach. He had come this far, sacrificed this much, only to be told the same thing his mother had told him in her solarium. "What is the cost?"

"We would keep the ring. You will give it to us."

"That's it? That's all you want?" Tyvian asked, looking around at them all.

"Yes. Yes—a good bargain, is it not? Will you agree?"

Tyvian frowned—something didn't add up here. "Who else has visited you in, say, the last fifty years?"

Silence fell for a moment. An invisible breeze rustled the tattered edges of the Yldd's cloaks. Tyvian guessed they were conferring somehow.

"Why do you wish to know?"

"I'm the one asking the questions here, remember?"

The leader of the Yldd waved its claw-like hand and the pool showed him three scenes, each displaying the ordeal of one supplicant. The first was a woman about his age wrapped in furs, leaning on a mages-taff. When she pulled away her scarf, it took him a moment to recognize her, but when she grinned into the pool, he knew exactly who it was—his mother.

"She came and, like you, saw through our ruse."

"What did she want?"

"For us to lie to the next man who came," the creature pointed.

Tyvian looked at the next scene. Another man, also about his age, with broad shoulders and a soldier's posture, his black eyes wide. It took Tyvian longer to recognize him, as this was a man not yet twisted by bitterness and anger, but one of swaggering confidence and a winning smile. *Banric Sahand*.

"Did you lie to him?"

"We do not lie."

Tyvian snorted. "Did you *selectively omit truths* to produce my mother's desired outcome?"

"Your mother paid well." The image in the pool showed Lyrelle placing a featureless box of black iron at the feet of the Yldd. Tyvian didn't know what it was, but decided he didn't want to know.

The third image was of Xahlven. "Of course it was him. What did *he* want?"

"What your mother paid us." The image changed to show Xahlven receiving the black box from the waters of the pool, a look of stern concentration on his face.

"Did he see through your little ruse, too?"

"No," the Yldd responded. "He only sees what he wishes to. Like most fanatics."

Tyvian looked up from the pool as the images faded. "Well . . . that certainly answers my question."

The Yldd extended its hand. "Will you strike the bargain?"

Tyvian knew his answer now—he knew it in his bones. Still, that didn't mean he was done haggling. "Show me the courtyard of the Citadel of Dellor again."

They did as he asked. Artus was being hoisted up

by his broken arms, his ruined legs flopping about at unnatural angles. The scene made Tyvian wince.

The leader of the Yldd drew closer, almost leaning over him. Its voice was a hoarse whisper. "Without the ring to stop you, you could exact mighty revenge on your enemies. You could avenge your friends! You would be restored to your former self, dangerous and unpredictable."

Tyvian nodded. "Show me the gates of the Citadel."

Again, they did as asked. Tyvian saw them—huge things, studded in iron, twenty feet tall. A team of horses was needed to close them, and the portcullis looked to weigh as much as a treasure galleon. In the image, though, they stood open.

"Without the ring, all this pain you see, all this suffering—it will be as nothing to you. You will be free of it, to act or not act as intelligence dictates. There is no greater reward, no better thing than that."

Tyvian nodded. "I've seen enough."

"Then we are agreed?"

Tyvian laughed. "The hell we are. Kiss my arse, you cut-rate con artists!"

The leader of the Yldd floated back a full pace. "*WHAT*?"

"What kind of fool do you take me for, anyway? All you want is the *ring*? And why would that be, eh? Could it be because you've never gotten your hands on one before?"

The Yldd, ancient cursed seers from time immemorial, sputtered in their raspy dead voices.

Tyvian kept rolling. "You know everything? Nonsense! If you did, you would have made me a better deal than the one you were offering. You think getting rid of this ring and exacting *revenge* is all I want? I've done that already, and you know what it cost me? A premium flat in Freegate and a significant quantity of my blood, and you know what the kicker was? I wasn't even the man to *kill* old Zazlar. *Sahand* did that. He might have done that for bloody *free* if I'd just stayed out of the way!"

"Begone!" the Yldd snarled at him, their voices echoing all around him. "Begone and never return!"

Tyvian turned away from them. "I'm going, believe me. You aren't the ones I need to talk to, anyway. Turns out the old man was right—he's the one I'm looking for."

The dark grotto seethed with the Yldd's frustration, but they did nothing to Tyvian but curse his name as he left. Tyvian ignored them—what had once seemed so terrifying, so powerful, now seemed vaguely pathetic. The way of the world, he supposed.

He pointed himself up the mountain and began to climb. He had one more ancient being to speak with.

And this time he intended to get some straight answers.

CHAPTER 33

THE LORD OF THE RINGS

Tyvian kicked in the door to the cabin. Abrahann was sitting before the fire, his back to him. He did not turn around.

"I can't believe I was that dense," Tyvian said, panting from his ascent. "Abra-*hann*? That's the best you could come up with as an alias? Kroth take me, and you're even wearing *boots*."

The old man looked down at his feet. "I've always liked boots—very comfortable, very functional."

Tyvian stomped across the cabin to come stand between Abrahann and the fire, snow shaking from his feet as he did. "You mean to tell me that you are Hann Longstrider? The God of Men? *You?*"

The old man looked up at Tyvian, and once again Tyvian felt swallowed by his fathomless gaze. "I am Hann Longstrider, the God of Men, who led your ancestors across the trackless Taqar to this Promised Land, when this new world was still young."

"You . . . you son of a *bitch*."

Abrahann—no, *Hann* Himself—laughed. "That's not the reaction I was expecting."

Tyvian pointed at Hann's ring. "You made it, didn't you? The iron ring was your creation. This . . . this *thing* on my hand and everything it's put me through—*your fault!*"

"Yes. It is."

"I should *kill* you."

"And how would you propose to do *that*?" Hann asked. "Don't bother with the threats, Tyvian. I'm a god and you're a man—you are out of your depth."

Tyvian snorted. "You're no god. You're just another sorcerer—a powerful one, maybe, and perhaps an immortal—but you're just another wizard trying to rule the world."

The God of Men gestured to his cabin. "Does it look as though I am trying to rule the world to you?"

Tyvian thrust his ring hand beneath Hann's beard. "Take it off. Now."

Hann enveloped Tyvian's hands in his own—they were thick and muscular, powerful beyond reckoning. Tyvian felt that Hann could rip off his arm as easily as plucking a daisy. A moment of fear welled up inside him—a sense of mortality, or *insignificance*. He glared at the so-called "god" and waited for the sensation to pass.

It did.

"Why didn't you have the Yldd take it off? They could have."

"No," Tyvian said. "Not like that. I saw what that did to Adath . . . to *Voth*. It drove her mad."

"It freed her of her moral obligations, you mean. It excised her conscience." Hann kept hold of Tyvian's hand, his grip warm and firm. "Isn't that what you're really asking me? You want me to remove your conscience so that you can do as you like, is that it?"

Tyvian tried to tug his hand back—it didn't budge. He might as well have stuck his hand in some kind of fleshy vise. "It's not like that and you know it. The ring *prevents* me from doing what must be done. You made it—you know what it does."

"Why don't you tell me about what 'must' be done, then. Let's begin there." Hann smiled at him—a paternalistic kind of grin, saved for toddlers and idiots. Tyvian wanted to slap him.

"Are you kidding me? Are you trying to tell me you don't know what is happening down there, back in the world? People—*your* people—are dying. Sahand is marshaling his armies, war is raging through Eretheria. Starvation, disease, despair . . ." Tyvian trailed off. "Don't you *care*? What kind of god are you, anyway?"

"And you think it is your duty to stop all that?"

"No," Tyvian said. "I think it is *your* bloody duty to stop it, but in your absence, *someone* has to save the world!"

Hann shook his head. "The world isn't about to end, Tyvian. I can see how you might feel that way—you have always hated bullies, even when you became one yourself. Right now, Banric Sahand, the greatest bully of them all, is about to march his army of cowards and brutes over the broken backs of the three northern crowns of the West. It stings to think about. But the world has not ended, Tyvian. Nor will it. The world is merely *changing*."

"Give me back my goddamned hand," Tyvian snarled. Hann released him. The ring was still there.

"I could take off that ring, and then what? You charge down the mountainside to save Artus? You enact some elaborate plan to destroy Banric Sahand? You swoop in to Hool's defense or rescue Myreon from your brother's clutches? Even assuming that were possible—and it *isn't*—people will still die. The wars will rage on. Dellor's new prince will be much the same as the last one—violent, brooding, ruthlessly practical. History will march onward, ignorant of your efforts."

"So what am I supposed to do, then? Stay here with you? Become a hermit somewhere else? Just *shrug* and say 'oh well, guess everything is terrible' and give up?" Tyvian paced in front of the fire. "Aren't you supposed to give *actual* guidance? Isn't that why millions of idiots flock to those ridiculous churches with those ridiculously massive thrones at the front—so that you will listen to them and guide them and *help* them? Kroth, if only they knew their so-called 'god' just sits on top of a mountain, eats sausage, and moans about the inevitability of history."

Hann smiled at him. "Is that you talking, or is that the ring?"

Tyvian stopped up short, scowling. He didn't say anything.

"I only ask because this fellow lecturing me does not sound like the young man who swore off helping people because they were too stupid to help themselves. It doesn't sound like the fellow who wants to cast off his conscience so he can enact wicked plots upon his enemies. It definitely doesn't sound like the man who was willing to risk his own life and the lives of his friends to spare the life of an unrepentant killer."

"I spared Voth for the sex. She was good in bed."

"You used to be a better liar than that, too," Hann said.

Tyvian said nothing, but he felt queasy. Exhausted past all reason. He sank into the other chair before the fire, head in his hands.

"It isn't your fate to save the world, Tyvian—Myreon is born to do that. It isn't your fate to smite the wicked—that is Hool. It isn't your fate to lead men to a better future—that is Artus."

"What good am I, then?"

The God of Men's voice seemed to envelop Tyvian as he spoke. "You, Tyvian Reldamar, are born to be *generous*. To be noble and wise. To be a good person and good friend."

"I have never been any of those things in my life."

"The world has a way of turning us away from our inner selves. Life is hard and it forces us to make hard choices to defend ourselves. We may be unhappy, but we survive. Unhappiness can be borne, sometimes so well we forget we are unhappy and instead find pleasure in other, darker places. You are the bastard child of an imperfect woman who hoped against hope that you would be the means by which her sins might be forgiven. You grew up in a cold world and saw much pain and it hardened you. The thing you are struggling with is not me and it is not the ring. You are simply struggling with yourself."

Tyvian looked up from his hands. "You could have made the world different. You could have guided us better. This is your fault."

"I did not make the world, Tyvian—that was my father. I guided you as best I could, but my brother was right to drive me away from you."

"Ulor the Deceiver? The devil himself? He was *right*?"

"Ulor is not the devil. He's just an arse." Hann's eyes grew distant. "'You cannot rule them,' he said to me. 'If you do, they will never learn.' He was right."

"We *still* haven't learned. We *never will!*"

Hann reached over and laid a heavy hand on Tyvian's shoulder. "You, my friend, are a living example of why you are wrong."

Tyvian tried to meet his gaze. He failed again. "If you won't take off the ring and if you won't stop what is about to happen, can you at least get me out of these damned mountains and show me the way to the Citadel of Dellor?"

Hann waved his hand and the door to the cabin. It swung open. "The way down is shorter than you think from my mountain. You will find that I am never very far away from anywhere. You may take from here whatever you wish, but you will never find your way back."

"Good, because I sure as hell am never coming back." Tyvian got up, looking out the door at the snowy slopes beyond.

Hann laughed. "Farewell, then, Tyvian Reldamar. I bless your journey."

Tyvian adjusted his borrowed fur cloak—the cloak of Hann Longstrider Himself—and strode to the door. "Blow it out your arse, Hann. Just stay out of my way."

He went down from the mountain, leaving the cabin behind and never looking back. It occurred to him that he felt stronger now than he ever had before. He pulled the hood of the cloak up around his haggard, bearded face.

He went down into Dellor.

CHAPTER 34

THE BEAST OF DUNNMAYRE

Harleck, to Hool's surprise, was a competent doctor. He knew how to remove a crossbow bolt without making the damage worse, he knew how to clean a wound, and he knew what herbs to rub into the torn flesh to keep infection at bay. He even was a fair hand at a needle, not that this had ever been a concern of hers—scarring wasn't all that worrying when you were covered in fur. Besides, a few more scars might have made Hool look scarier, and she considered that an advantage.

For all this, though, Hool suffered for days following Harleck's attentions. The herbs spared her from the worst of it, but she took ill with fever anyway, her tongue hanging out the side of her mouth as the walls sang with delirium. She was so weak she could scarcely move, and the stuffy storeroom in the back of the Dragon seemed hot as a furnace. She could taste death.

Hool lost track of time. She lost track of space, too. At times, she felt as though she were back in the House of Eddon, at others she was on the Taqar with her old pack, at others she was on the road with Tyvian and Artus. She tried talking to them, but her words echoed into an empty void. They spoke, too, but she could not understand.

She saw her pups. Api picking wildflowers. Brana jumping at butterflies. Their blood pooling at Hool's feet. Their skulls calling out to her.

The scent of Api's pelt, thick and heavy like tar. It would not leave her nostrils. She howled.

Revenge! Revenge! Revenge for my pups! For all the children Sahand has murdered! Revenge! Revenge!

She raved into a dark room.

The door opened once, and there was Damon. Damon wiping a cool cloth across her snout. Damon gently stroking her arm, her head, her ears as she whimpered into the dark. "It's all right, milady. You're safe. It's all right."

But it wasn't all right. Why couldn't he understand that? Why couldn't he see that nothing was all right?

That nothing would *ever* be all right again? Who was this stupid man, to follow her here? Who was he to interfere with her . . .

With her what?

Her death. Yes. Her death and Sahand's.

"No," Damon said softly. "You don't have to die, Hool. Death is no solution."

She whimpered. She howled.

Damon played his songs. Songs of springtime and rebirth. Songs about eagles and starlight and queens in their castles. He must have come once a day to play, though the days ran together. She marked time by the sound of his voice—a brief glimmer of beauty in the midst of the nightmares. She felt torn between the sound of his lute and the screams of her children. She could not choose.

In time, Harleck's ministrations chose for her. She awoke in midmorning, the little window in the storeroom thrown open and a cool breeze whipping through the room. *Sloppy*, she thought. *What if Sahand's men were to hear me moaning? We could all be dead. The fools.*

She tried to rise; she found that she could, though her legs and arms felt weak. She sat on the side of the benches that had been formed into her bed and tried to shake the smell of sickness from her mane. Her head hurt; she found a pitcher of water on a table and downed it all. The water was cool and clean and the best thing she'd tasted in a long, long time.

Her wounds had healed, or nearly so—the stitches had been removed (when had that happened?) and it seemed they wouldn't leave any scars that would be visible past her fur, more was the pity. She wanted to go outside and look around, but knew better. So she waited, testing her range of movement, her strength.

The door opened, revealing Damon, his lute over one shoulder. His face lit up when he saw her. "You're awake! How do you feel?"

"How long have I been sick?"

Damon blinked. "Uh, well, a little over a week, perhaps? Ten days? I'd need to look at a calendar and nobody seems to have a calendar up here, so . . ."

"How are we still alive? How has Sahand not found us? I was howling! Are his soldiers deaf?"

"That *was* a concern for a while." Damon nodded. "As it turns out, his soldiers aren't *here* anymore. They've been recalled to the capital. Every Delloran bannerman in the principality, it seems, has orders to muster in the Citadel. There isn't a soldier in town anymore."

"So what?" Hool put her ears back. "There's still a reward on my head. Any of these people could turn me in."

Damon put out his hand. "Why don't you come with me? It might be easier just to show you."

Hool frowned. "Show me . . . *what?*"

In the big common room of the Dragon, one of the long tables with benches had been cleared away. In its place was a chair—more of a throne; really, draped with animal pelts and fashioned out of antlers. At its foot were piled little talismans and Hannite crosses and smooth stones painted with symbols Hool recognized as religious but could not say much more about. As the men at the other tables saw Hool enter, they stopped talking and gambling and even stopped drinking. They stared at her.

Hool's hackled raised. "Damon . . ."

Damon gestured to the chair. "Your seat, Lady Hool."

"My *what?*"

Harleck was at the bar. He raised a mug in her direction. "To the Beast of Freegate!"

The men in the Dragon raised their drinks as one. *"The Beast! The Beast of Freegate!"*

Hool's ears shot straight up and she closed her mouth. She held very still. What was going on?

Damon strummed a chord on his lute. *"Ohhhhhh . . ."*

The men, drinks still raised, joined in song immediately:

> *The Tale of Our Lady is Gory*
> *Her enemies many and great,*
> *And this is a tale full of glory,*
> *And of Banric Sahand's worthy fate.*
>
> *Our Lady was once free and wild*
> *A gnoll of a distant cold land*

Until some trappers took her child,
And gave him to Banric Sahand.
Revenge, Revenge for the Beast of Freegate!
Our Lady known only as Hool
She's coming for him, the Mad Prince himself,
And those who would stop her are fools . . .

Dumbfounded, Hool found herself sitting in the big chair after all. The song was . . . different than the ones Damon had sung before. It was *angry* somehow. Angry in a way Hool didn't realize music could be. The great room of the Dragon throbbed with that anger. She saw it in the men's faces—saw it in the vicious grins they gave when the song reached the part where Hool was dismembering the men who had tortured Api. She heard it in how their voices cracked as they sang her praises. Some of the men even had tears in their eyes. She could scarcely understand it.

To the Citadel of Dellor she marches,
No walls and no towers will stand,
'Tween her and her justified vengeance,
On the head of old Banric Sahand!

The song ended. Damon raised his lute in one hand and, as one, the men of the hall shouted, *"REVENGE! REVENGE! REVENGE!"*

Roars of approval. Men stomping their feet and banging their mugs. Damon stood at Hool's side, a smile on his face, as then rows and rows of filthy lumbermen and rivermen and laborers lined up to pay their respects. Hool sat perfectly still, like a fox in a trap, waiting for it to make sense. Men asked to kiss her hand (she refused). They knelt in front of her. They spoke to her, tears in their eyes.

A man almost as big as Hool, weeping like a child, said, "Sahand took my son, too. His brutes murdered him before my eyes. Over a bloody beaver pelt. A beaver pelt, Hann help me . . ."

And then an old man with a hook for a hand. "The Mad Prince's men raped my wife regular for three years, till I stabbed one. Then they took this hand. Had the hook ever since."

And another: "Kill him, you understand me? Kill that murdering bastard twice. My boy's weight in silver don't make no difference to me. I want to hear him scream."

And another: "I'm a good hand with an axe and served in the Mad Prince's army and I'm with you, Lady. If Sahand's blood is at the end of it, I'll travel any road you please."

And another and another and another. Men who spat when Sahand's name was spoken, men who wept over their pain, men who showed her their scars and offered her their blood. It went on for an hour, with Harleck's sons keeping watch at the door, just in case someone they didn't know came up.

But no one did. Damon was right: they had all gone to the Citadel.

Eventually, Hool had to retreat. She left with the chant *"REVENGE! REVENGE! REVENGE!"* ringing in her ears.

When she was alone back in her storeroom, Damon came to join her. "Well?"

"How did you know? If Sahand heard that song . . . if any of them were spies. That was very stupid."

Damon smiled. "I've never been very smart. But I just figured . . . Sahand is a monster, right? No matter how much he keeps his people in line, they *must* hate him. I mean, if Harleck did, then surely . . ."

"It was still stupid. Those people are all talk. They just want me to kill Sahand—they won't help."

"That's true," said Harleck, standing in the door. "But it still means more than you think it does."

"Explain," Hool said, rubbing her shoulders, testing their strength.

"Dellor has always been ruled by tyrants. Before Sahand there was a man named Ferrod Bosh—a foreigner from some distant place in the south. Sahand came with a mercenary company, defeated Bosh's soldiers, took his head, and so became prince. That's been the way of it for three hundred years or more."

"So?"

"So, the people stood aside when it was Bosh's time. They'll stand aside when it's Sahand's time, too.

He might rule us, but we are not his people. He keeps order and he defends us against bandits and such, but his wars are for his own gain and only fools think otherwise. His men are bandits themselves, taking what they please and doing what they like. You heard the stories—we are waiting for a new ruler." Harleck nodded to Hool. "That could be you."

Hool snorted. "When I kill Sahand, it will be for myself, not for any of you."

Harleck smiled. "Spoken like a true Princess of Dellor, Lady Hool." And with that, he bowed and left.

She was left alone with Damon. Damon was still grinning like an idiot. "What do you think?"

"About what?"

"Princess of Dellor? Has a nice ring to it, eh?"

Hool punched him in the nose.

She was pleased to find that her strength, though depleted, was still enough to drop a grown man on his backside. Damon grabbed his face as blood poured down his chin. "Owwww . . ."

Hool grabbed him by the collar and hoisted him up. "Why don't you *listen* to me? There is only one thing I want in the world—there is only one thing that matters anymore. And that is Sahand dying. That is *it*! I am not going to be princess. I am not going to rule Dellor or be your friend or even be *alive*. Do you understand me?" She shook him. "I am going to die in Sahand's castle! I am going to kill him and all his soldiers and all his friends and allies and then I will die. Then, finally, I will be able to rest."

Damon hung limp in her grip, his face sad. "You don't have to, Hool. There is more . . . there is so much more to life."

"You have never lost a child. You do not understand." She threw him to the floor. "You can't ever understand." She turned her back to him, curling up on the benches, hiding her face in her own fur.

Damon got up slowly and straightened his clothes. "You're right. I can't understand—not exactly. But I do know this: the only reason you want to die is because you don't think there's anything else left for you. And on that score, you're wrong, Hool. You're dead wrong. I only hope you realize that before it's too late."

Hool said nothing. Eventually, Damon went away. Then, when she was finally alone, Hool thought of Brana and Api and quietly moaned herself to sleep.

That night, Tyvian visited her in a dream. Or, at least, she assumed it was a dream at first. He was there, sitting at the foot of her bed, dressed in a way Tyvian would never dress. He had a great mane of red hair streaked with white and he wore a huge fur cloak. He smelled of blood and filth and sweat and a kind of acrid magic that made Hool's eyes water. Were it not for his eyes—sparkling and blue—she would have never thought it was him.

"I've come to apologize to you." He cleared his throat. The sound was sharp and clear—not the fuzzy sounds of a dream. Not a dream, then. Perhaps he was simply a ghost.

"Go away," Hool said. "I have had enough of dead people."

Tyvian seemed not to hear her. "I've come to realize my priorities have been messed up for a long, long time. I've spent so long trying to get this damned ring off . . . I just . . . I guess I didn't even know what it was trying to teach me. I didn't care to know."

"I don't care either. I want to go to sleep." Hool laid her ears back. Even as a ghost, Tyvian talked too much.

"You were right, Hool. You've always been right. And I never listened."

"Obviously. That's why you're dead."

Tyvian smiled, those bright white teeth shining through the beard like the sun through the clouds. "You're right. Again. I had reputation, but it didn't matter. I had wealth, and it didn't matter, either. I even had power, and I had to fake my own death to escape it."

"I told you all of those things were stupid. You did them anyway."

"Because I thought I was smarter than you."

"You weren't."

"No," Tyvian said. "I never was. My mother told me once that the most important things in the world were peace, food, home, and children. I thought she meant them as a kind of political goal—the purpose of a good ruler is to provide those things for their subjects. But that's not what it means. It means that those are the only things that matter in our *own lives*."

Hool folded her arms. "How long do you plan on staying?"

Tyvian looked at her. "I'm confessing something here. Do you mind?"

"Can you confess faster?"

The smuggler's hairy face fell as some dark thought crossed his mind. "You had all those things, Hool. And for years I had the power to give them to you again. Instead . . . instead I stripped them away from you."

Api and Brana's faces—ghosts she was far more familiar with—rose up again in Hool's mind. Her ears drooped and her mouth clapped shut. "No . . . don't say it. Don't."

Tyvian hung his head. "It's my fault, Hool. Their deaths—my fault. I'm sorry, I—"

Hool pushed him. Instead of him flying away or bursting into clouds or some other ghostly thing, he fell over and landed on his back on the floor. He grunted with pain. Hool leapt out of bed. "You . . . you're *alive*?"

Tyvian rolled slowly to his feet. "What? Of . . . of *course* I'm alive. What the hell did you think was going on just now?"

All the things she was going to say to him, all the howling angry oaths she was about to hurl at his spirit . . . they all fell away. Hool picked him up off the ground and enveloped him in a big, warm hug. She found herself whining, on the edge of howling, even. It was pain, but a different kind of pain. Not the pain of emptiness, but the pain of something lost being replaced.

Tyvian pushed himself out of the hug. "I'm going to make it up to you, Hool."

"You can't."

"I've died and spoken with oracles and gods and I know your moment is coming. I'm convinced of it. But I can't stay. There are other things I have to do first."

"This is another one of your crazy stupid schemes, isn't it?" Hool's ears went back. "I hate those."

Tyvian placed a hand on his heart. "This is the last one ever. I swear it. Look for me." He squeezed her hand one more time and then left, silently as he had arrived. Hool watched him go. As soon as he entered the common room of the Dragon, he vanished among a hundred other fur-clad, bearded men and was gone. Only his scent lingered—the same old Tyvian scent, but . . . different somehow. Blessed.

"Who was that?" Damon asked, strolling up the hall. "Another admirer?"

"Yes," she said.

CHAPTER 35

WORKING A HUNCH

Myreon couldn't tell if Xahlven knew that she knew he was the Chairman of the Sorcerous League, so she chose to operate under that assumption. If he knew, then he was taking a big risk keeping her chained up here, an easy cry for help away from dozens of mage-hunting Defenders. But of course, that risk itself was camouflage—any accusation could be easily deflected as nonsensical. No doubt a search of his sleeping quarters would turn up nothing of note. Myreon would expect a mage of his resources to be using an anygate to go to and from his offices back in the Arcanostrum, at any rate. No—any direct confrontation with Xahlven was doomed to failure.

It occurred to her that the same could be said of Lyrelle or even Tyvian (in his day). This struck her like the dawn itself—the whole world seemed suddenly illuminated. If you wanted to trick a manipulator, you needed them *to think you were being manipulated*. She needed to act as she might normally act, but needed to select the "normal" behaviors that would get her closest to her goal. She needed to make it seem as though she were stumbling toward victory *by chance*, not heading there on purpose. If Xahlven got wind of any breath of her intention, and she was done for.

As the armies marched north in generally fair weather, Myreon considered her options carefully. She had time—it would be another week before they crossed the border into Dellor, which was marked by an ancient and mostly ruined series of watchtowers that Sahand kept intermittently manned. Trevard had a team of augurs working constantly to predict when and where they would make contact with the enemy or whether Sahand would deploy his weapon and, while the future was very much in flux, one thing seemed certain—there were no Delloran attacks in the near term. As this was Myreon's third military campaign, it was becoming clear to her that most of war was simply walking for long periods of time and eating rustic food.

Myreon took care to eavesdrop as much as she could on Trevard and Xahlven's exchanges. She doubted this would arouse much suspicion—what captive *wouldn't* take a keen interest in the conversation of her captors? As two people went, it would be hard to find anybody more ill-suited to one another's company. Xahlven was gracious and intellectual and cultured; Trevard was brusque, practical, and dreadfully dull. The Lord Defender had no idea how thoroughly Xahlven was directing his actions—Myreon would have missed it herself had she not been looking for it specifically. Trevard disliked Xahlven, and Xahlven used that dislike as a fulcrum upon which to lever Trevard into the actions he preferred. If Xahlven wanted the army to move faster, he would suggest that such travel was wearing and that they ought to camp earlier to give Trevard's men a rest. Trevard, predictably offended at the implication his men couldn't march, would insist they carry on, even if what Xahlven said was technically true. The Archmage of the Ether seemed to be a savant at saying the right thing at the right time to nudge his colleague this way and that. This ought not to have surprised Myreon—he'd done it to her several times—but it was shocking to witness, especially to one considered as learned as Trevard.

She might have pointed out this manipulation to Trevard, but he didn't trust her. This was, of course, partially Xahlven's doing—he often spoke of her in positive terms and would even debate her merits with the Lord Defender. This served to calcify Trevard's opinion of her as a traitor and a turncoat and a rogue element. If she remained on the palanquin, it was only because sending her anywhere else was too risky.

In that suspicion, though, Myreon thought there might be a weakness. If she could convince Trevard to send her back to Saldor, she might be beyond Xahlven's surveillance, if only temporarily. Of course, if she were transferred back to Saldor, it was Keeper's Court and a quick sentencing for her—that solved nothing. There was no Tyvian to break her out anymore. No Artus. No Hool. Nobody at all.

Except maybe Argus Androlli.

"Good morning, Argus," she said one day as he came to the palanquin to deliver a report. He had come before, of course, and he had always said hello to her—he was gracious that way—but her decision to initiate the contact instantly put a wary expression on the Mage Defender's face.

He gave her a half bow. "Myreon. I trust you are well."

She held up the casterlocks. "I'd like to get these off, to be honest."

"We all bear our burdens, eh?"

"I'd like to speak with you before you leave. Will you?" she asked.

Androlli gazed around at the guards, the palanquin, and the vastness of the barren plains around them before answering. "Why?"

"There's something I think you should know."

Androlli pursed his lips thoughtfully. "Anything

you tell me will be conveyed to the Lord Defender immediately. You know this, correct?"

Myreon gave him her sweetest smile. "The Lord Defender won't listen to me, Argus. Maybe you will."

Androlli didn't answer her. He went into the tent where Trevard was poring over a map of mostly blank space that ran between Galaspin and Dellor. After he'd delivered his report, he left without so much as looking at her. This was expected—Myreon had planted the seed. Androlli was a climber—ambitious, confident, ever eager. The fact that he might get a piece of intelligence Trevard had overlooked was a delicious prospect that he would be unable to deny, but it wouldn't happen overnight. It would take time. Chained to her post on the big floating palanquin, Myreon knew that time was one of her only assets at the moment.

To keep up appearances for Xahlven, Myreon kept trying to draw Trevard into conversation or catch his eye as he was surveying the troops. Her efforts only repelled the Lord Defender. If what she had to say had nothing to do with the sorcerous weapon that had destroyed Ayventry, he didn't want to hear it. "I am not your judge, woman," he had snapped once, slapping a table. "Save your bargaining for them."

Xahlven was almost impossible to read, but Myreon hoped it was enough to throw him off the scent. She was under his power; he didn't have anything to fear. That was how he liked it, so why should he worry? Besides, even if he did suspect something, what could he say? Who could he warn? She was a criminal—*of course* she was up to no good.

Still, she could not sleep. In her tiny tent at the back of the palanquin, the casterlocks digging into her fingers and the shackles biting her ankles, she lay on a thin pallet of straw and stared into the utter darkness, dreaming of all the terrible fates that might befall her—and everyone else—if she failed.

It was going to be another long night.

"Myreon!" someone whispered from outside the foot of her tent. It was Androlli.

Myreon rolled onto her front and pushed herself up on her elbows. She returned his whisper. "What are you doing here? It's the middle of the night!"

"I'm working a hunch," Androlli said, waving his hand. The shackles around her ankles fell off.

Myreon hadn't expected this—she hoped Xahlven hadn't either. She shuffled out of the tent and Androlli—disguised as a Defender-at-arms—took her by the elbow and led her down off the palanquin and a short distance to an empty tent. It had a smooth floor and all the equipment needed for a wide variety of sorcerous rituals. One of them was already in action—an anti-scrying circle, glowing faintly around the edge. Myreon took care to step over it.

Once inside, Androlli took a peek through the flap and then sealed it behind them. "We can talk freely now."

Myreon looked at the circle and recalled Lyrelle's comment about scrying not being the only means to collect intelligence. "Ward against eavesdropping, too. Just in case."

Androlli nodded and then altered a few of the runes in the veta. The world beyond the tent—the quiet bustle of an army camp, even in the middle of the night—vanished. The silence seemed to envelop them.

Androlli produced a smooth white crystal ball—it would record everything said. "Now, what is it you need to tell me?"

Myreon assumed that Xahlven would find out what was on that ball—it seemed safest. She was, on some level, performing. Putting on an act. "First I need some assurances."

"Don't toy with me, Myreon. I'm taking enough risks even doing this. What is it you can't say to Trevard? Out with it!"

Myreon shuffled her weight around on her feet to make her look nervous. Hell, she *was* nervous. "Trevard won't listen to me, and I don't trust Xahlven."

Androlli rolled his eyes. "Gods, Myreon—Xahlven Reldamar is the only decent Reldamar in the damned family. I trust him more than I trust *you*, that's for certain. Is that what all this caution is about?"

"No!" Myreon said, holding her casterlocks against his arm as though tugging on his sleeve. "No, it isn't—it isn't at all!"

Androlli frowned at her display of fear. He looked concerned. *Good.*

She pressed on, shaking her immobilized hands above her head. "Argus, I can't go back into stone. I . . . I just *can't*, all right? Before we start, I want assurances that what I tell you won't count against me in court."

The Mage Defender looked her in the eye and spoke softly. "Myreon, you toppled a *government*. You escaped imprisonment. You used bloody *necromancy* in war. How much worse can this get?"

Myreon licked her lips. "I'm a member of the Sorcerous League."

Androlli stared at her. She knew that look—he was deciding whether to believe her or not.

"I can prove it. The necromancer beneath Eretheria—he inducted me."

A moment of silence was all it took before Androlli made his decision. He spoke carefully, as though she might misunderstand something. "Names, Myreon. Get me the names and whereabouts of members. This could go a long way to alleviating your sentence."

Myreon tried to summon up some tears, just to make it stick, but couldn't quite manage it. Instead, she made her voice tremble. "I . . . I can't. Everyone uses aliases, shrouds—it's a cell-structured organization. Nobody knows more than one or two other members."

"Do you even hear yourself? Myreon, you sound like any dozen other crazed hedge witches we drag in every year. They *all* say things like that, and there isn't damned scrap of evidence they can produce."

"They aren't trained sorcerers—*I* am. I can prove it."

"How?"

Myreon took a deep breath. *Here it goes.* "I know where they meet. You need to perform a ritual to get there. It isn't complicated, but it's time-consuming. Ether-and Astral-based, you know?"

Androlli scratched his chin, no doubt considering the implications for his career. "All right—teach it to me."

"And then let you cast me aside while you steal all the credit?" Myreon snorted. "Fat chance. I'm going to *show* it to you, and then you and I are going to go tell Trevard *together*."

Androlli chewed it over for a moment. Myreon knew what the answer would be, though—maybe just enough to erase the stains Tyvian Reldamar had put on his record and secure a good posting after this little war was over. Maybe. "Fine," he said. "Deal."

She held up her casterlocks. "Take these off, then, and we'll get started."

Androlli shook a finger at her. "Nothing funny, Myreon. You'll never make it out of this camp alive if you try something."

Myreon gave him an innocent grin. "Me? Try something? You must have me confused with a Reldamar, Argus." She shook her casterlocks at him. "Let's go—this thing takes hours."

They came off. Her fingers trembled and ached, but Myreon was able to go through marking out the veta that would take them into the Black Hall, even if it took an hour or so longer than usual.

Androlli watched her carefully, seeking to follow the complex forms and straining to eavesdrop on her recitations. Myreon was pleased at the looks of frustration that crossed his face—though a competent investigator and interrogator, Androlli had never been an especially talented theorist. His sorcerous style was functional and direct—the kind of thing Trevard encouraged in his magi. Lyrelle Reldamar's influence had made Myreon something different—had given her the edge she needed to get ahead . . .

Only so men like Androlli could abandon her when it was politically convenient.

The thought filled her belly with bile—it was an Etheric thought, probably encouraged by the ritual. No matter. It was true, anyway. It was important to keep things in perspective—Androlli was no friend, even if he had been, once. She was using him. Just like he hoped to use her. That was what life was like—user and used, the exploiter and the exploited.

Another Etheric thought. Myreon pressed on.

When the ritual was complete, it was nearing dawn. Myreon knew her absence from her "cell" would be noticed within the hour. She desperately hoped that, within the hour, she would be beyond anyone's reach. "There," she said, standing up and wringing her hands.

The runes of the veta darkened, seeming to drag all the light from the pavilion. Androlli gripped his staff tightly, ready to bind Myreon if she made a move. She simply stood there and let the ritual overcome her. Soon, the darkness was all around, obliterating any sense of place or sign of their location.

Androlli pulled a shard of illumite from one of his uniform's pockets, but it was dark. "Dammit—what is this place?"

"A pocket world—on the edge between the material plane and the Ethereal." Myreon stepped forward and offered her hand to Androlli. "Come on."

Androlli followed her, squinting into the dark. As they walked, details began to solidify—walls of pure shadow, a floor of dusky flagstones, an arch of midnight black. She whispered to him, "This passage goes to the main hall and will lead us back to where we came from. I don't know if anyone else is here, so be quiet."

Androlli nodded, sliding down the visor to his mirrored helm. "If there is, I'll take care of them. Just stay behind me."

Myreon rolled her eyes. Typical Rhondian chivalry.

She led him into the Black Hall. It was empty, as she had hoped. Thirteen terraces leading down to the ink-black Well of Secrets, and not a rogue mage present for

Androlli to duel. The Mage Defender pointed at the Well. "What is that?"

"An artifact of fairly incredible design—it's called the Well of Secrets. It detects lies. I'm fairly certain it is the primary reason this place exists."

Androlli gaped up at the semi-real architecture as they walked down the stairs toward the center. "The League . . . *built* this?"

"I don't know—maybe they did, maybe they didn't. I have no idea how old the League is, but I get the sense they've been around for a long, long time. For all I know, this was a courtroom used by Rahdnost the Undying that they somehow inherited."

He looked at her as if she was crazy, but she just shrugged.

When they arrived at the center of the hall, Androlli examined the Well in detail with a few auguries. All the Lumenal ones he attempted failed. "I can't tell how this is supposed to work."

Myreon walked to the opposite side of the Well. "If you lie, a light shines from the depths. That's all I know. Here—tell me a lie."

Androlli looked at her. "I trust you completely."

The dark, still liquid in the well glimmered for a brief moment, as though a white flare had been cast into its depths. Androlli slid back his visor. "Impressive."

Myreon fixed him with a hard stare. "Are you in Xahlven Reldamar's employ or otherwise under his direct influence?"

Androlli blinked. "What? No. Why would I be?"

The waters of the well remained still and dark. Myreon exhaled. "Do you accept that this thing works?"

Androlli looked at the Well and then back at Myreon. "I . . . suppose it does. It seems to. What's this all about?"

"Argus, I need you to listen closely to what I say: Xahlven Reldamar is the Chairman of the Sorcerous League."

Androlli snorted. "What?"

Myreon pointed at the Well. "Did it glimmer? Did it shine?"

"Well . . . no, but—"

"Xahlven Reldamar is planning to topple the Arcanostrum and the current world order. I very much suspect that the army of Saldor is walking into a trap and that the Arcanostrum is in grave danger."

"Myreon, that's ridiculous. Even if *you* believe it, you can't expect me to—"

"That's not the issue, Argus—the issue is whether or not I lied." Myreon looked him in the eye. "Did I? Did I *lie*?"

"I suppose not." Androlli sighed. "But you could be insane."

"I *could* be. But there also could be evidence I'm right that we—you and I—could go and collect right now."

"Where?"

Myreon licked her lips. "Xahlven's private offices in the Black College."

"You can't be serious!"

Myreon nodded. "I most certainly am. It's the most secure place I can think of. No one but a former archmage has access to that place, and what just happened to that former archmage, eh?"

"You're asking me to commit treason."

"Magi can't commit treason, Argus—we recognize no king, remember? Xahlven is not our ruler—not once we attain our staff. That is the *most basic* principle of the Arcanostrum—it's the first damned thing they teach you."

"That still doesn't mean we can go breaking into an archmage's office without consequences!"

Myreon took a deep breath. "Argus, I can't do this without you. If you only knew the . . . the *terrible* things Xahlven is responsible for. If you only knew what he's done, you'd understand."

"Then *tell* me!" Androlli spread his arms. "I'm here—I'm listening!"

Myreon pursed her lips—she couldn't tell him about the Creeping Dark. How could she tell him what she'd done? He'd never believe her when she said Xahlven *made* her do it. She scarcely could believe it herself. "I'll make you a deal, Argus—if I'm right, and we find the evidence we're looking for, you get to be a hero, but *I* get a pardon. But if I'm wrong, you get to be the one who apprehends me and I get turned into a statue for a long, long time. It's win-win—you can't get a better deal than that."

Androlli frowned. "This will be very dangerous."

"You found me among a pile of skeletons in a dead city—you think I care about *danger*?" Myreon could tell Androlli was debating with himself. She could tell by the way he kept tightening and relaxing his grip on his staff. On the one hand, he could just turn her in now and get plenty of credit. On the other, though— saving the whole Arcanostrum would make him famous. He'd be a shoo-in for Master, maybe even manage to sit in the Lord Defender's seat someday. "Argus—this is a once-in-a-lifetime opportunity. Don't play it safe for once."

Androlli smiled, his white teeth gleaming in the permanent gloom of the Black Hall. "You always were the crazy one." He extended his hand. "I'm in. Let's go."

CHAPTER 36

THE CROSSING AT DUNNMAYRE

Trevard, Lord Defender of the Balance, was explaining strategic concerns as if he, a glorified constable, understood them. Xahlven was nodding along, pretending that what Trevard said was revelatory and not plainly obvious to any fool with a map.

"Here," Trevard tapped the worn old map of Dellor—the most recent one they had. Not a lot of cartographers jaunting about the area, it seemed. "The main problem with laying siege to the Citadel of Dellor is crossing the Whiteflood, which is several miles wide. There is a ferry at Dunnmayre—a small trading outpost at the edge of the forest. If we can sneak a small raiding party across the river incognito, we can ambush the mercenary garrison and take control. The army can then be ferried over."

It was fiendishly difficult not to look bored. Xahlven nodded and stroked his goatee. "Clever. What do your augurs say?"

Trevard stood at attention before his map, arms folded behind his back. He was briefing Xahlven, and the man was determined to look the part. "There is some interference scrying the ferries themselves—they're on the water, after all—but our raiding party should reach the river without incident. Anything beyond the crossing is too unpredictable at this moment, since we cannot yet establish what happens on the water to get a reliable reading."

Xahlven hummed with interest, as though how scrying worked was foreign to him. "And Sahand's armies?"

"Our aerial scouts haven't seen a Delloran banner since we began the march north. Sahand must have taken more casualties in the Ayventry incident than we thought—he is probably stocking the Citadel with whatever rearguard he can muster, preparing for a siege. Scryes of the city have shown a lot of troops marching in, but Sahand has a lot of wards on his gates, so getting a precise read of how many are coming and going is difficult. My best estimates put his garrison at two thousand men at the most. Still a significant force, granted, but we are more than equipped to take him on." Trevard chuckled at that last point.

Probably imagining the kind of sorcerous ruin the Defenders can rain on Dellor. Xahlven elected to chuckle along, though for different reasons entirely. The chuckle was an important release for him—he'd needed to laugh in Trevard's face for weeks now. The idiot. The bombastic moron.

After they had shared their chuckle, Trevard relaxed a bit. "We should have done this years ago. If only Varner were here—you never saw a man who hated Sahand more. Gods, what I wouldn't give to have him with us."

Xahlven expressed his sympathy with a smile. "Yes, a shame. But Varner has his own king now, and his own wars." *And if Conrad Varner were here, he'd know that Sahand is going to punish your river crossing in ways you cannot imagine, you trumped-up court bailiff.*

Trevard put his hands on his hips, surveying the campaign map as though it showed territory already conquered. "Well, the raid should be underway in a matter of hours. Best get some rest. Tomorrow is a busy day."

Xahlven stretched and said good night. It was late—practically dawn. He went to his tent, which was really an anygate back to the Archmage's Labyrinth in the Arcanostrum, and threw himself into his high-backed chair at its center.

He ought to sleep as Trevard proposed, but there was too much to do. For starters, he had to write some League-related correspondence. At that moment, a few dozen of the League's most talented invokers were in Dellor, awaiting his word that the Grand Army of Saldor was about to reach Dunnmayre. Xahlven wasn't sure how much of a difference they would make in the coming battle, but Sahand had requested them there, and far be it from Xahlven to get in Sahand's way at the moment.

A little serpentine puddle of shadow leaked beneath a door into the room and pooled at Xahlven's feet. "Master . . . master . . . Jyanix returns to you!"

Xahlven drew his foot away by reflex. The little demon was largely harmless, despite its ability to eat through wards. He sighed—the last thing he needed right now was a prolonged negotiation with a demon. "What is it?"

"Hungry . . . so hungry, master! Good Jyanix, loyal Jyanix—does Jyanix not deserve a treat? Yes? Yes yes?"

Xahlven slipped off one of his rings—one with a moderate enchantment warding him against intoxication. The little serpent of shadow pounced upon it at once and wrapped it up in its coils, sapping the sorcery away.

Xahlven watched the thing eat for a moment and then tapped his staff on the ground. "I told you never to return here unless you had something to report. Out with it."

Jyanix was positively delighted to be of service. It bounced around the floor like a spring. "The girl! The girl has escaped! Gone away! All gone!"

Xahlven straightened. "What? How? Where?"

Jyanix giggled—a high-pitched, screeching sound. "She lied! Lied! Got a mirror man to help her! So naughty—so, so naughty. Went in tent with wards. Jyanix eats the yummy wards, finds them gone. Wicked girl, tricking friendly Master!"

The creature was, of course, delighted by the subterfuge. Xahlven sat back in his throne, hand beneath his chin. Myreon escaped, eh? Not altogether unexpected, given Trevard's refusal to listen to her, though it did create certain loose ends. Where would she go to be heard about the Sorcerous League? In whom would she confide? She had no one of consequence left in Saldor, now that Lyrelle was out of the picture.

It seemed probable that she was headed here, to the Arcanostrum. Xahlven imagined she probably goaded that idiot Androlli to help her by explaining how helpful to his career it would be to show up an elderly Lord Defender and expose an ancient conspiracy. Not that anyone was likely to listen. Worst-case scenario meant the Black Hall would be compromised. A major loss, but one Xahlven would be willing to accept, as it would be only temporary. The Arcanostrum only had a matter of days left to interfere with his plans and then . . . well . . .

"More food? More food for greedy little Jyanix?" The demon was still cavorting at his feet.

Xahlven moved his hand once and banished the

creature from the plane of existence. He didn't need it anymore. He needed something slightly different. At a twitch of his head, a cloaked figure stepped out of the shadows of the labyrinth—it was nothing *but* cloak, a semi-real phantasm of his own design, pure darkness folded in on itself and made semi-solid. A specter of sorts, and so not terribly intelligent. Significantly more trustworthy than any Master of the Ether living in the Black College, though. "Go," he said. "Bring me the woman named Myreon Alafarr and her companion, Argus Androlli. I would speak with them."

It departed, passing through the door that the demon had wriggled under. Xahlven watched it go and sighed. Sleep was not his to have tonight, it seemed. No matter. He always did enjoy the dark, and sleep would wait.

Tomorrow, he needed to oversee a slaughter.

Banric Sahand sat in a small room—too small, really, for his purposes—a half-dozen sending stones arrayed in a half moon on the table in front of him, each showing the face of a different lieutenant. Sahand absorbed their reports, relayed to them by his field commanders. He steepled his gauntleted hands beneath his chin, brushing the edges of his close-shorn beard.

Trevard had raided the village of Dunnmayre in the middle of the night with a few dozen Defenders who seemed to come out of nowhere—sorcerous tricks, no doubt, but of little strategic importance, as he had left no garrison to speak of. Sahand expected Trevard to seize control of the ferries next.

He *wanted* him to.

His own scouts now reported that the whole Grand Army of Saldor was in the process of ferrying themselves across the river. There was, of course, only one ferry, so Trevard had ordered makeshift ones fashioned from commandeered riverboats—the crossing, Trevard knew, had to be quick, and six thousand or so soldiers and their supply train would take a long time to ferry. Sahand was getting reports of boats of every kind, filled to the brim with the martial strength of the Arcanostrum, tottering slowly from one bank of the Whiteflood to the other.

Which was why Sahand was sailing an armada of armored barges down on them at that exact moment.

The reports done and his orders dispatched, Sahand ducked his head to escape his tiny cabin and walk onto the deck of a floating castle. It was square, sixty feet long to a side, with three decks. The bottom deck, closest to the water, had a gunwale of shields and sharpened steel stakes backed up by a company of men with pikes and bows. The second deck, the one on which Sahand stood, had three ballistae to a side, their bolts coated with all the nastiest things Sahand's private collection of alchemists and thaumaturges could devise. The top deck, last, featured the small sails and navigational equipment that fulfilled the barges' modest maneuverability requirements—namely that they not run aground or get hung up on a sandbar.

Ten such barges were cruising quietly downstream. One thousand hard-nosed Delloran killers, trained by life on the frontier and the tender attentions of Sahand's best captains, all waiting for the enemy to come into sight. It was a beautiful thing.

Well, for now.

The captain of this particular barge—Orten was his name, or something like that—saluted him. "Sire, Dunnmayre will be in sight shortly. Would you care for a viewing glass?"

Sahand took the offered glass without comment. When it became clear that he had nothing more to say to Orten, the captain trotted off to inspect the war machines one last time. Sahand squinted into the glass as he pointed it downstream. They had to be close . . .

There!

In the midsummer sun, the calm waters of the Whiteflood glittered, almost obscuring the boats staggering across the river. There were dozens of them, each packed beyond what would be considered safe weight—they rode low in the water. Sahand grinned as the lookouts atop the masts of his armada took up the call, blowing horns. Men scrambled around him, winding their ballistae and stringing their bows. Orders were barked and the deck thundered beneath hurrying feet.

"Captain," Sahand said, "I want four war barges athwart their crossing point. The other six are to anchor wherever the targets seem the most plentiful. Anything flying purple and white dies before it lights us aflame. Understood?"

Orten saluted. "As you command, sire!"

The commands were relayed via a series of flags waved from the top deck. Those barges closest to the center of the river gradually aimed themselves to stand as impassable bulwarks against crossing ships. The others split their attentions between each bank— one half to attack that part of Trevard's army trying to organize itself outside Dunnmayre, and the other half to face the remainder of the army camped on the southern banks and awaiting its turn across.

Sahand watched the banks closely. He could see griffons taking flight and saw banners waving. There was commotion in the ranks—the Saldorians weren't ready for this, their augurs hadn't foreseen it. Sahand couldn't help but laugh—all the sorcerous might in the world, and they'd forgotten all about *boats*.

The first war barge came into range of a ferry that was frantically trying to row itself back to the southern bank. A few men aboard discharged firepikes, but the range and accuracy weren't sufficient to do more than scorch a few of the shields of the barge's bottom deck.

The volleys of arrows, however, found easy purchase among the pressed ranks of Defenders, glancing off mageglass helms just to get stuck in arms, legs, feet, and hands. Sahand could not hear their screams, but he imagined them, he savored the *idea* of them.

The first ballista bolt raked the deck of the ferry, exploding in green fire and throwing men into the river. The second struck at the waterline in the bow, blowing off a chunk of the barge. The whole thing listed to one side, and the men went into the water. The arrows kept falling.

The other war barges were soon engaged. They fired from three sides at the soldiers crossing the river, sinking boats and killing those who tried to swim away. One boat rowed *into* a barge and tried to board it—he was almost impressed. Sahand watched the desperate melee from a bad angle, but the outcome was never really in doubt. The barges afforded their pikemen a solid footing with which to repel boarders and they had numbers on their side, anyway. The river was as good as his.

A screeching cry split the air—griffons. A flight of three swooped overhead, the riders tossing thunder orbs down on the decks of the barges. One hit near Sahand, and he was barely able to take cover before it exploded, destroying a ballista and killing five men. His ears rang with the power of the concussive force, but he was yelling anyway. *"Bows! BOWS! Shoot them down! Shoot!"*

He was not alone—other barges were also hit, but volleys of clothyard shafts arced up from the decks, forcing the griffons to keep their distance. His initial worry was quickly allayed. They were doing some minor damage, but they were a distraction—griffons tired quickly and would have to land before long. No, nothing was going to stop him. Not today.

Then one of his barges burst into flame—the whole thing, top to bottom, immolated in an angry red fireball. Even Sahand's breath caught at that. *Sorcery.* But his barges were warded!

At least, they were supposed to be . . .

Scanning the banks, he spotted two cadres of magi pointing their staves and carrying on in a way that could only be some kind of incantation. Sahand couldn't hope to decode their exact purpose, but he made an educated guess—one group was dispelling the wards and a second group was calling down the fire. He ordered a man to bring him his sending stones just as a second barge was pummeled by an unnatural barrage of heat-lightning that lit it on fire.

The soldier came back, cradling the six stones in his arms like goose eggs. Sahand picked up one and yelled into it. "Tell them to shoot the magi! Shoot the magi!"

It was an unnecessary command. Two other barges began sending ballista bolts their way, only to see them deflected by guards and potent bow wards. *Dammit!* Sahand felt acid biting in the pit of his stomach. He hadn't realized the wards would be so easy to dispel at that range. Perhaps it had something to do with the ley. He cursed the death of his wyvern—that would have come in damn handy right now.

A third barge burst into flame, but the men on board were doing a good job of fighting it this time. Well, until the river itself rose up and threw it onto shore. The massive barge tipped over sideways, an upended top, and men and materials spilled out. The soldiers on the shore pounced on them and Sahand looked away—those men were as good as lost.

Three barges down! What could be done about those magi?

Surveying the river, the rest of the battle was going well—his own cavalry was charging the half of the army that had already crossed, catching them off guard, while they were being shot by the barges in the river—those were as good as surrendered. No more crossing was possible, either, but Sahand could scarcely rain destruction down on the *other* half of the enemy army if it was guarded by those thirty or so magi. A crushing victory would turn into a merely decisive one, and that wasn't what he wanted. He didn't want the armies of Saldor to merely *retreat*—he wanted them routed, scattered to the winds, and left for the ravens and the wolves to peck at. He wanted *this* to be their Calassa—an embarrassment from which they would never recover.

Another barge was crippled with lightning. "NO!"

Sahand screamed, kicking a helmet across the deck. "No, no, no!"

"Sire." Orten was there, saluting again. "We cannot get close to the southern bank. Not so long as . . . AHHHHH!" Sahand grabbed him by his hauberk midreport and hurled him off the barge like a bale of hay.

The men on deck looked at him, wide-eyed. Sahand met their stares with his own. "Order all barges to make for the southern bank."

A man wearing lieutenant's epaulets blanched. "But sire, we can't—"

Sahand put a spike of pure fire through the man's throat and, with a twist, popped his head off. "No man tells Banric Sahand what he can and cannot do! Fly the flags, dogs, or drown here!"

The orders were relayed. The barges pivoted from their moorings and slowly made their way toward the enemy army.

From behind the magi, great colossi arose, their mageglass armor glittering in the afternoon light. They threw boulders at the barges, doing heavy damage. Some waded into the shallows of the river, trying to come to grips with the enemy. However, most could not sustain too many direct hits with enchanted ballista bolts and faltered, either coming apart or flickering out of existence. A few had to be fought in close, with a legion of Sahand's best men wedging pikes between armored plates until the wearer of the colossus could be exposed. A bloody business, but the men of Dellor were equal to the task.

Arrows rained down on the magi and still their guards and wards held. The other five barges were suffering severe damage. Most were at least partially aflame. Sahand's own flagship had sustained heavy losses from a volley of mageglass darts that materialized out of nowhere and fell to the deck.

But he was close enough now. And the Fey was strong enough here, in the madness of battle, that he barely needed to reach out to seize it.

And seize it he did. Enveloping himself in a ball of crimson fire, Sahand launched himself from his barge onto the shore just in front of the magi. This they hadn't been expecting. Guarding parties of Defenders pivoted to confront him. Sahand laughed at them.

"Too late!"

The Mad Prince of Dellor lashed out with a wave of fire that incinerated the mirror men closest to him and forced the party of magi to alter their wards to deflect his attack. This was long enough for a volley of arrows to get through, injuring several magi and killing two or three more.

Sahand strode toward his enemies, a shield of flame swirling around him. He threw a lance of fire at the closest mage. She wasn't quick enough to defend, and she was reduced to ash in a blink of an eye. The second threw a lode-bolt at him, but it was eaten by his fire-shield with little trouble. Sahand responded with a fireball that blew the mage off his feet.

Sahand's assault and the steady volley of arrows from the war barges forced the magi back, falling behind ranks of Defenders-at-arms, these armed with halberds. Sahand raised his arms, ready to smite them all into cinders. He roared at them, *"I am Banric Sahand, Prince of Dellor—kneel or die!"*

And then his shield of flame vanished. His arms locked up, as though turned to stone. He couldn't move.

From the chaos stepped a tall, thin man with a pointy bald head, leaning heavily on an elaborate gray magestaff.

He spoke to Sahand in calm, even tones. "I am Trevard, Lord Defender of the Balance, Archmage of the Astral. I do not kneel before any man."

Sahand struggled against his binding, but he could not move. He could scarcely even breathe. As archer fire fell toward him, Trevard raised one hand and stopped the arrows midflight. Indeed, the entire battle seemed to freeze. A deathly quiet fell.

Trevard stepped between the frozen missiles and came before Sahand, a faint smile on his thin lips. "Banric Sahand, you stand accused of forbidden sorcery, biomancy, and the atrocity of Ayventry. How do you plead?"

Sahand could only growl through his paralyzed jaw. "Kiss . . . my . . . arse . . . old . . . man . . ."

Trevard frowned. "I will call that an admission of guilt. No need to stand on ceremony." He raised his staff, light warping around its end. "Now, let us proceed to your sentence."

Sahand hissed and cursed through his teeth, struggling like mad. It could not end here—*it couldn't*!

But the blow never fell. The battle resumed suddenly, and Trevard blinked, surprised. He turned to look behind him. "What the . . ."

Sahand was free! He had his sword out in the blink of an eye and, before Trevard could turn back around, Sahand cut his leg off at the knee. The Lord Defender shrieked and fell over. Three arrows embedded themselves in his side and the old man groaned again.

Sahand stood over him, sword raised. "Here in Dellor, it is the Prince who passes the sentence. And yes, there is no need to stand on ceremony."

Trevard held up one hand to ward off the blow, so Sahand cut off his hand first. Then, as the old man's eyes rolled back in his head, he plunged his blade into the fool's heart.

The Lord Defender of the Balance was dead.

He looked up to see three Defenders flicker and vanish to reveal robed figures in their place—shrouds. The lead one saluted Sahand, placing her fist to her chest. "The Sorcerous League sends its regards, Your Highness."

"Took you long enough."

The sorcerers bowed and then vanished again. That was all the help they were going to provide, it seemed. Sahand looked around—it didn't matter. His own forces were storming the shore by now. The Saldorian army was in disarray. He grunted—even that little bit of assistance was all the help he needed.

He hefted his blade and charged back into the fray.

CHAPTER 37

THE BLACK COLLEGE

When Androlli and Myreon at last emerged from the pervading gloom of the Black Hall, they found themselves beneath an enormous elm tree in the center of a small lawn bordered by cobblestone streets and flickering feylamps. There were two teenagers in drab brown robes nearby whose heads perked up when they saw them, but when they saw Androlli's mirrored armor, their eyes were once again buried in the scroll they were sharing between them.

They were Initiates. Students. For the briefest moment, Myreon felt like she'd stepped back in time. That could have been her, studying augury or enchantment.

"Don't make any sudden moves, understand?" Androlli said, grabbing her by her upper arm.

That single, perfect memory of her past crumbled away as quickly as it had arrived. She forced herself to be calm, to hold her head high. "I know my part, Argus. Don't forget yours."

The lawn and the elm tree stood just beyond the grounds of the Arcanostrum itself, deep within Saldor's Old City. It was under this elm tree that Myreon had stood awaiting her entrance examination, and under this elm tree that she had spent so many summer afternoons going over her notes from various lectures. She knew it was the same for Androlli—probably the same for every mage in the West—and so it had made the perfect focal point when leaving the Black Hall.

Beyond the lawn and across Polimeux Street stood a wrought iron fence, nine feet high, that marked the perimeter of the Acanostrum's grounds. Beyond the arched gate were paved walkways and tall trees whose branches concealed the towering spires of the colleges themselves. In the daylight, one could catch glimpses of the silver domes of the Blue College or the seashell-ivory towers of the White through the branches. Here, in the dead of night, only the flicker of fireflies and the bob of illumite lanterns lit the darkness.

They crossed the street and passed through the gate. No one raised an alarm, no sorcerous guardian came to challenge them. No guards were set because nobody actually *broke into* the Arcanostrum of Saldor—ordinary people wouldn't dare cross the border if they could avoid it, and those who knew anything about the place understood the consequences of mischief all too well. Even Myreon, knowing they were not yet in any danger, felt a flutter in her stomach as the gravel pathways crunched beneath her feet.

Androlli said nothing as he marched her along the winding paths beneath the ancient trees and past archaic sculptures of this or that famous mage. They both knew they were being watched by *someone*, and any conversation they had at this point could be easily overheard. It was Myreon's hope that a Mage Defender marching a traitor to the doors of the Black College would not be sufficiently noteworthy to activate the suspicion of the Master Defender keeping an eye on them.

Very soon, the colleges themselves became visible. Each had a different challenge needed to be overcome in order to gain entry—it was a rite of passage for Initiates who achieved the First Mark. Once they could enter the College of their choice, they could be officially declared Apprentices. Many—most, in fact—left without managing it, going on to a life of relative wealth as a private sorcerer of some kind.

The Blue College had a mighty djinn who demanded a riddle answered before the doors would open. The riddles were reputedy of the most fiend-ish difficulty and you only got one guess (though you were free to think about it as long as you liked). As they passed the gates of the Blue College, there were three would-be apprentices sitting on the stairs, heads in their hands. One was talking to herself.

The White College required the admission of painful truths and acts of atonement, the Red College demanded you best a mage in a wrestling match, and the Gray Tower—the place Myreon and Androlli had both entered—gave you an exhaustive examination on Arcanostrum law and history that lasted two days.

The Black College, though, was simply a laby-rinth. If you couldn't find your way through it, you never got in. Some went in and never returned. No black-robed mage Myreon had ever interviewed had given her the same answer when she had asked them why. The challenge with mages of the Ether, as always, was figuring out when they were lying and when they were telling the truth.

The Black College itself was a trapezoidal build-ing overgrown with the thorny vines of innumerable rose bushes. Nestled deep within the grounds, it was difficult to determine how far back the college went or how large it was compared to the others. The gate was open, as it always was—a yawning rectangular portal thirteen feet tall. Beyond was a kind of dark-ness somehow thicker than the night itself.

Myreon's instinct was to pause and consider their

options carefully before proceeding—there could be some kind of trap. Androlli, though, did not break stride and dragged her along behind him.

Next thing they knew, they couldn't see a damned thing. Myreon looked behind them—the gates were gone, as was the faint light of grounds. If they had slammed behind them, they made no sound.

Androlli grunted. "Well, *this* is familiar."

"Illumite won't work," Myreon said, and summoned up a little ball of Fey fire in one hand. The harsh orange light illuminated the floor beneath them and gave the impression of walls to either side, but not much more.

"What do we do, then? Just wander around until we stumble upon Archmage Xahlven's quarters?"

Myreon pursed her lips. "Let's try following the left wall. If we keep doing that, we should find our way through."

"Says who?"

"It's a logic puzzle, Argus—that's all it is. Stay positive."

They shuffled along in the darkness, coming upon a few intersections, but stuck to the wall to their left at all times. The darkness and the silence of the place was disorienting. Myreon felt at alternating moments like she was headed down an incline and also up. She felt dizzy and hallucinated flashes of light in her peripheral vision. Or, perhaps, it was all real, intended to disorient her.

It was working.

After almost an hour of them bumping into walls, casting spells, and making no progress, Androlli stopped and leaned against a wall. "This is officially the stupidest thing I have ever done."

"Oh, stop it," Myreon said. "If apprentices can figure this out, two staff-bearing magi should be able to."

"It's got to be some kind of illusion—where would a huge maze like this even fit, anyway?"

"They could just be expanding space Astrally to accommodate it. Besides, none of our dispels worked. We should keep going."

"Going *where*?" Androlli kicked the wall. "I can't even say for certain we're not going around in circles."

"We should have brought a spool of thread or something," Myreon said.

"What are we, seamstresses? Who in hell wanders about with spools of thread?"

"Stop complaining! Gods, you're always *complaining*."

Androlli folded his arms. "And you're hopelessly naive. We're trapped, understand? We can't get out."

"We *can* get out. Plenty of people have."

Androlli snorted. "You know what I think? I think this is some kind of trap."

"Of course it is—we knew that going in!"

"Not this maze—*you*, Myreon. You led me down here, convinced me to abandon my unit, and now are going to get me caught with a fugitive trying to infiltrate the Black College. It will be the end of my career. If they don't take my staff, they'll have me posted in some godforsaken dump in the middle of the Eddonish frontier. I'll be eating beef jerky and freezing my arse off for the rest of my days."

"Will you stop thinking about your career for one damned minute? None of that nonsense is going to be of any help right now."

"I think of my career, Myreon, because thinking that way has gotten me everything I have. Maybe if you had spent more time thinking about *your* career and less time thinking about justice or social equality or whatever other nonsense we learned about in Gulter's civics lectures, you wouldn't be where you are now."

"Riding other people's coattails isn't a career, Argus," she sneered.

"Very pithy," Androlli sneered right back. "You pick up that kind of wordplay from your dead boyfriend?"

Myreon's stomach went cold. "You leave Tyvian out of this. You have no idea what you're talking about."

"Of course not," Androlli said. "That's the whole point, right? Argus Androlli, the human joke, has no idea what he's talking about. How many times did that conceited, grinning scum make me look like a fool, eh? Every time I thought I had him pinned down, he'd weasel out of it. I take it back—you aren't the reason I'm stuck here, Myreon. It's all because of Tyvian bloody Reldamar!"

Myreon wanted to hit him, but as she was thinking about it, something else occurred to her. Tyvian had always said that the best tricks were the simplest ones—the ones that merely confirmed the mark's assumptions. Lyrelle had said much the same thing to her over the years; Xahlven was a living embodiment of the theory. Xahlven, it was well known, had solved the Black College Labyrinth when he was younger than *Artus*. What if . . .

Androlli was looked at her. "What?"

"There *is* no labyrinth!" she said. "Of course!"

Androlli rolled his eyes. "We've been through this, Myreon—the dispels didn't do anything."

Myreon shook her head. "That's because we were dispelling the *wrong thing*!" Pointing a hand at herself, she performed a simple Astral dispel that would knock any enchantments off her person. There was a breath of icy cold across her shoulders and a soft pop.

She was standing in a corridor lined with black marble pillars, lit by sconces flickering with green demonfire.

Androlli had been leaning against one such pillar. He stood up, his eyes searching for her. "Myreon? Myreon, where did you go! *Myreon!*"

They hadn't been wandering in an illusory labyrinth at all—they had simply been enchanted to *think* they had. Laughing, Myreon dispelled Androlli's enchantment as well. The Mage Defender's eyes bugged out as he realized the ruse. Then, eventually, he chuckled. "Damn. Damn—I really *am* a fool, aren't I?"

Myreon only smiled at him.

"Myreon Alafarr and Argus Androlli?" The voice, flat and cold, came from an . . . entity that emerged from the shadows of the hall. It was little more than darkness, somehow folded and given solid shape. The look of it made Myreon's skin crawl.

Androlli put an arm out to ward Myreon and leveled his staff at the thing. "Who are you and what do you want?"

If it was bothered by Androlli's show of bravado, it didn't show it. "Archmage Xahlven would see you now. Please follow me."

It did not turn around, but it floated away a few paces, barely visible among the actual shadows cast by the thick pillars of the hall. It was waiting for them to follow. "So much for the element of surprise," Myreon said.

"At least we're going to find his office." Androlli winked at her. "Stay positive, right?"

The shade led them through a number of secret passages and blind turns. Myreon tried to keep her bearings, but it was difficult—the place was a painstakingly built optical illusion, subtle and elegant. Where the hanim's palace in Freegate had been a maze of brazen phantasms, the Black College confounded with the truth as often as it did with lies. Stairways that looked painted turned out to be real, and doors that looked as though they could not possibly go anywhere revealed whole rooms behind them.

In time, they entered a winding corridor with many branchings—a kind of confused nautilus chamber, with doors in seemingly every corner. They wound their way, somehow, to what Myreon would consider the center. And there, seated on a throne of onyx, a scrying pool at his left hand, was Xahlven Reldamar.

He rose, giving Myreon a suspicious look and then favoring Androlli with a stern nod. "Mage Defender Androlli, I assume there is an explanation for this."

Myreon watched Androlli out of the corner of her eye. She prayed he would have enough guile to know what to say and what not to say. She found herself holding her breath.

Androlli pointed at Myreon. "It has been revealed to me that this woman is a member of the Sorcerous League. She is trying to get a more lenient sentence by providing us with evidence of the association's existence, but she claims Trevard won't listen to her. I did."

Xahlven steepled his fingers beneath his chin. "And so you've come to me, then? Hoping I'll put in a good word for you with the judges, Myreon?"

Myreon said nothing. She was too busy trying to tame the raging beast inside her—the one that so desperately wanted to accuse him to his face of what he had done. But that wouldn't work—it was becoming obvious to her that things like that never worked.

"Am I the first person you've come to?" Xahlven asked Androlli.

Androlli nodded. "I, of course, will file my report with Trevard as soon as I'm back with the army."

"I'm glad to hear it." Xahlven rose from his throne and reached out to shake Androlli's hand.

Androlli grinned and took it.

Xahlven pulled the Mage Defender close and pressed something small and black beneath Androlli's chin. There was a hissing sound and Myreon was hit in the face with some kind of dust.

Androlli's headless corpse sank to the floor, the stump of his neck smoking. The mageglass helm fell backward and bounced into a corner.

Xahlven slipped the deathcaster back up his sleeve. It was then that Myreon realized what had hit her in the face—the dust that had once been Argus Androlli's head.

The Archmage of the Ether sat back down in his throne. "Now, Ms. Alafarr—let's you and I have a more . . . *candid* conversation, shall we?"

CHAPTER 38

BLOOD IN THE WATER

Hool watched the Battle of Dunnmayre from the roof of the Dragon, where Harleck had built a small but comfortable porch concealed on three sides by the thick boughs of the tree. Harleck had a Kalsaari spyglass—some contraption that allowed somebody to see something far away without the use of sorcery. They passed it back and forth as they watched the fleet of war barges intercept the crossing Saldorians. In the distance, she could see the signal flags on Sahand's command barge. He was there—Banric Sahand, the Mad Prince, the monster of her dreams. No more than a mile or two away, almost taunting her across the water. She thought about making Damon row her out there, just close enough to get her alongside . . .

Damon nudged her. "Don't be ridiculous, Hool. You'd never make it."

Hool put her ears back. "How do you know what I was thinking?"

"Your thoughts are always all over your face," he said, shrugging. "Shroud or no shroud."

Hool balled her fists. Over the last few days, she'd eaten well—nearly eaten Harleck out of business— and she felt that her strength was back, if not all her flexibility. The wounds still hurt, but that was to be expected—they were wounds. She was more than a match for any dozen Dellorans. More than a match for any Banric Sahand. "We should do *something*."

No one answered, since the answer was clear. There was nothing to do but watch the Whiteflood stain itself red with blood.

"Why do they do this?" she asked Harleck. "Why do they fight for him? Why do they kill? If you hate him, why do your brothers and sons wear his mark?"

Harleck considered. "Because we fear the alternative. Because we are afraid of what might come after, or that there might not *be* an after. The Mad Prince is the tyrant we know. We have learned to live beneath his heel."

"And they *kill* for him? They do *this*?"

Harleck nodded. "Sometimes it is better to be the heel than the throat beneath it."

Hool felt a new fire inside of her. A new kind of hatred for Sahand was growing—one born of something different than her lost pups. She saw that Sahand was like a blight that killed everything it touched. It rotted the world from the inside out. He needed to die not just for his deeds, but also for what he had made others into. She thought back upon all those brutes she had murdered in Sahand's service. They were men who had taken an oath, like Damon. But unlike Damon, they had done it because they were afraid, and that fear transformed them into monsters. It made her sick to think about it.

One of the barges buckled, some invisible force breaking its hull. There was an explosion of water from its center, throwing men through the air. It began to list to one side, sinking in the river. Hool waited to see if the two other barges would move to assist their ally. They did not. A series of flags flashed from the top deck of the command barge, and they turned away, heading toward the opposite bank.

Beneath them, the Saldorians cheered—a minor victory. A short-lived one.

"I've seen enough of this," Hool growled. "Get me some rope. Big, thick rope."

"Wait, what are you going to do?" Damon asked, but she was already heading down the stairs.

As she passed through the common room, she saw the men all crammed around the doors and windows, watching the battle. "You! You fools of Dellor! Come with me!" She pushed them away from the door. "Bring rope and things that float."

"Like what?" someone asked.

Hool rolled her eyes. "I have no idea what floats! You live next to a big river—you figure it out!"

She went down the stairs and out of the tree. On the ground, mirror men were running back and forth, their firepikes on their shoulders. It was not immediately clear to Hool what they thought they were doing. She grabbed one. "You!" she bellowed. "Where is your leader?"

The man's eyes bugged out. "Wh . . . what are you?"

Hool shook him. "Leader! Now!"

He pointed, and so Hool found herself standing in front of a short little man in a big mirrored helmet waving around a sabre. She didn't waste time introducing herself, she just started telling him what to do. "We are going to save men out of the river now. If you shoot at me, I will kill you. If you help me, I will save your people, too."

The little man froze, staring up at Hool through his visor. He took a deep breath and straightened his breastplate. "Sir, if you have a plan, I've got men to make it happen. For me, I'm fresh out of ideas."

At that point, somehow, it was collectively decided by everyone in Dunnmayre that Lady Hool, the Beast of Freegate, was in charge.

Hool's entire knowledge of the water was limited

to fishing, which she was not very good at but the basic principles of which she understood. The only difference between fishing people out of the water as opposed to fish, was that the people were on the *top* of the water and the fish were under it. So, she reckoned that she needed fishing lines that went *on top* of the water.

One of the things Dunnmayre manufactured was long, strong ropes—a Roper's Guild existed, somehow taking the fibers of various trees deep in the forest and braiding them. Rope, therefore, was available in great abundance. Men also appeared with a variety of barrels, jugs, washbasins, bottles, and other things that could be said to float. Collecting all this took almost no time—the Defenders and the natives of Dunnmayre worked with frantic haste, as their friends and countrymen were drowning with every passing minute.

Hool tied a rope around a barrel and then assigned a man to a barrel. "Can you swim?"

The riverman nodded.

Hool pointed at the river. "Swim out there, tell people to grab the rope. When they grab it, we pull it in. There—fishing for people."

The man smiled. "Right. Fishing. I get it."

His smile spread across the tired faces of Saldorians and Dellorans laboring in the muddy shallows of the river. They got it—they all did.

They got to work. Saldorians clinging to capsized boats, Dellorans floundering in their armor, injured men nearly drowning—all of them were put on the rope and hauled in. They had twenty such ropes operating, the swimmers trading off with others when they were too tired or too cold to continue. Any man who could make it within two hundred yards of shore had a decent chance of being plucked from the water. Hool and teams of broad-shouldered lumberjacks heaved on the ropes, bringing coughing, sputtering, pale soldiers onto the banks.

"Hurry up!" Hool yelled, looking out across the river. "There are still more!"

Somehow, the men found the strength to hurry up, as their Lady commanded.

The rescue efforts continued for over an hour. In that time, the battle on the far shore seemed to have ended. Trumpets were sounding.

They were not the trumpets of Saldor.

Hool stood amid piles of exhausted, filthy men—men covered in blood and ash and mud. She could barely tell who was a Saldorian and who was a Delloran; she didn't think they could, either. While the ropes went out and the soldiers were dragged in, it scarcely seemed to matter. Now, it became clear that it was going to matter again.

Hool turned at the sound of hoofbeats. Sahand's cavalry was retaking the town. They formed a ring around the huddled survivors, their lances red with blood, arrows nocked in their bows. An officer was shouting orders. "Lay down your arms or die!"

His face pale, the Sergeant Defender gave the order. Firepikes fell to the muddy ground.

Hool stepped forward. The officer pointed a sword at her. "Stop! One more step and you're dead!"

Silence fell. A cold wind, bearing the smell of fire and death from the far side of the river, swept over the town. Hool drew the Fist of Veroth; its head blazed to life. The horses beneath the soldiers shifted uneasily. "I just saved hundreds of your friends," Hool said. "And you think you can just *kill* me for it?"

The Delloran officer gave her a mean grin. "They ain't my friends."

"Sergeant!" a man gasped from the crowd of survivors. He staggered to his feet. "Stand—" he coughed roughly, then recovered himself. "Stand down!"

The cavalry sergeant squinted at the man. "Captain Orten?"

"You know me," Orten said, his throat hoarse, "and so you know I have the ear of the Prince. And I say let this creature pass."

"But Captain, the Prince has orders—"

"Let her pass, damn you! She saved a hundred of our own men today. Let her go!"

The other Dellorans present nodded, muttering agreement.

"Captain, if the Prince finds out, it'll be my balls!"

Orten was shivering. "Then he doesn't find out, does he?" He looked around at the other survivors. "Does he? This was our idea, wasn't it, men? We did it. There was no beast, was there?"

Hool remained on the balls of her feet. She had five bows trained on her right now, but the men were tired. Perhaps they'd miss.

The sergeant put up his sword. "It's on your head, Orten." With a jerk of his chin, his horsemen parted. He looked at Hool. "You get a day's head start, beast."

Hool swung the Fist of Veroth over one shoulder and sauntered past the sergeant. "Then enjoy your last day alive, *man*."

Damon scurried to her side, his pack already on his back. "Bye, everyone," he called. "Congratulations on your victory and what-not!"

Hool scowled at him. "Shut up, Damon!"

No one followed as they left—there was too much to do, she guessed. She heard Dellorans barking orders and pushing Saldorians around even before they were beyond the stockade.

"That was a wonderful thing you did back there, Hool," Damon was saying.

She shushed him. She stopped—there was a scent in the air. A scent she'd not smelled since . . .

"Hello, Hool." It was Tyvian, still in his big furry cloak, sitting on a rock just outside the town among the tattered remnants of Sahand's battle to retake Dunnmayre—discarded weapons, dead men and horses, and muddy banners. He was picking his fingernails with a knife.

When Tyvian threw back his hood, Damon's mouth fell open. "You . . . Your Highness?" He fell to his knees.

"I've been thinking about what you said." Hool yanked Damon back to his feet. "And you're right. You *do* owe me."

Tyvian grinned. "Then it's time I made it up to you."

"Explain. Quickly this time."

He pointed at the river, where Sahand's war barges were mopping up any stragglers from the battle as they tried to escape downstream. "Where do you suppose Sahand built those things so the magi couldn't see?"

Hool put her ears back as she thought. "Inside his giant castle?"

Tyvian grinned and clapped her on the shoulder. "Let's walk. And then let's you and I have a discussion about architecture."

Hool's stomach grumbled at the thought. "That sounds terrible."

Tyvian winked at her. "Trust me, Hool—you're going to *like* this conversation."

CHAPTER 39

PRINCE TO PRINCE

It was becoming increasingly clear that Artus was never going to regain sensation in his legs. He was a cripple—now and forever.

This was not one of his top five problems.

Once the storm had cleared, Rodall's dogs pulled him out of the mountains on a makeshift sledge fashioned from a shield and a fur cloak. It did very little to protect his head, and so he had regained consciousness as a direct result of his head whacking against a rock. For the remainder of the journey, he did his best to keep his chin tucked to his chest until his neck was screaming with the effort.

It was a company of three that had caught him—

Captain Rodall and the two Delloran spies, Hambone and Mort.

Of course it was those two.

Of the pack of hounds that had pursued them in Ayventry, only four remained. Those four were the ones that had found Artus in the river and dragged him out before he drowned. He supposed he ought to be thankful, but waking up to see Rodall's platinum-capped smile leering over him had put a damper on that.

"Half a prince is better than no prince at all, eh boys?" he chirped in his shrill voice.

Hambone and Mort chuckled dutifully.

"Where are you taking me?" Artus asked.

"Prince Sahand wants a piece of you, boy," Rodall said. "So, to Dellor we go."

The other two had nothing to add. Artus was left to imagine what "wanting a piece of him" meant when Banric Sahand said it. He assumed it was literal. He looked at the flat gray mountain sky and imagined blood and pain and public spectacle.

Beyond moving his head, any further movement was largely impossible. His legs lay lifeless and, judging by their angle, shattered. His arms he could feel, unfortunately—they, too, were lumps of flesh pierced by jagged shards of bone. It hurt when he breathed, and he frequently lost consciousness.

As a result, the journey out of the Dragon-spine came to Artus in pieces, some dreamlike. He felt himself floating in space once, only to realize he was being lowered down a sheer face by rope. He dreamed of Michelle kissing his hand, only to awaken to realize it was one of Rodall's hounds licking the blood from his fingers. At night, when the cold descended, he shivered beneath a thin blanket laid over him, ironically unable to sleep. Around him, the dogs snored, twitching and grumbling in their dreams.

There was always one of the three Dellorans on watch at any point in the night. According to Rodall, he wanted them keeping an eye out for nurlings or trolls or, worst of all, bandits holed up in the foothills.

One night, when Hambone was on watch, Artus caught him looking at him. "You were one of my knights," Artus said. "You swore yourself to my service."

Hambone, his beard shining in the moonlight, did not move. After a moment, he spoke, his voice hoarse. "I said and I done a lotta things I didn't mean. This ain't no different."

"I saved your life, and this is how you repay me?"

Hambone looked away. He was noticeably thinner than he had been in the White Army—the punishing pace of Rodall's pursuit, Artus guessed. At this angle, the moon showed his cheeks. Once full, they now seemed sunken. "World ain't like that. We all do what we got to."

Artus considered that statement—he'd heard it a

lot back home. He cleared his throat. "That ain't true, Hambone."

Hambone threw a rock. "What ain't?"

"We all do what we got to—that ain't true. Some of us don't."

"Yeah," he grunted. "Look at you, eh?"

"That's not the point." Artus strained his neck to get a better look at the broad Delloran. "Point is you gotta make that choice. World doesn't make you do nothing—you choose. It's the choices that make us."

"What're you—a priest?" Hambone turned his back on Artus.

Artus let his head drop. Sleep still did not come.

The Dragonspine gave way to the Ustavar Hills, and after a few days of that rough, rocky terrain, Rodall's hunting party found themselves in Dellor. They found a small trading post by the edge of a narrow river, and Rodall commandeered a riverboat to bring them the rest of the way to the capital city.

Artus's overtures to Hambone had earned him a gag, but it didn't stopper his ears. He lay and he listened as his captors exchanged gossip they'd heard on the river from other boats.

The Grand Army of Saldor was destroyed. A total rout, with Sahand as victor. A few thousand prisoners, Trevard dead, and magi being ransomed. The question now was whether Sahand could attract enough recruits and draw enough mercenaries to invade Galaspin again.

Rodall had laughed at this and kicked Artus in the ribs. "That's where you come in, boy!"

Those people they happened to meet never asked about Artus, but they looked at him carefully. Once, a girl of about twelve on a passing boat had called her little brother to stare at him for a while before finally passing out of view. Artus found himself wondering what it was like to grow up here, under Sahand's thumb. It was a thought that stayed with him for the days that followed.

From what he saw, life in Dellor was rustic but . . . normal somehow. He saw lots of armed men and hard faces, but it wasn't that different from where he grew up. Trade happened on the river, money and pelts and goods were exchanged, and soldiers in black livery took their cuts and bossed people around. The few villages they came across were tiny and the people weren't exactly welcoming, but he saw no heads on pikes or roads of skulls or any of the evil things he somehow expected. These were Sahand's people, these were Dellorans—the people who had invaded Galaspin and Eretheria and put towns to the torch and slain children—but they didn't seem inherently different than any other people Artus had ever seen.

They just seemed poorer.

The houses were stone and thatch with no glass in the windows. The people dressed in rough furs with cheap shoes. Most people were filthy and hungry and looked tired. Much about life here on the frontier was similar to life on the broad fields of Oscillain in Benethor, where Artus grew up.

But that was the North, and this was still technically the West. That was the difference. These people knew that about two hundred miles south across the Wild Territory lay warm lands of unimaginable wealth. Wealth someone had told them they couldn't ever have. Rage couldn't be that far behind such thoughts.

For all the good that revelation did him now, crippled and helpless, being carried to Banric Sahand on a platter.

The city of Dellor was smaller than Ayventry, but had walls of rough-hewn stone twice as tall, with iron spikes set along the top at each crenel. From the river and his forced angle, Artus could see nothing of the city inside the walls. The dominant feature, though—even more so than the wall—was the Citadel itself.

Artus had heard accounts of it before, but seeing it in person was something else entirely. A fortress just about as large as the city that surrounded it, it had a monstrously tall curtain wall—seventy feet, perhaps—in a star pattern. Within, a host of broad flat turrets and soaring towers all competed with one another to attain the highest altitude, like weeds growing through a crack in a boulder. It was dark and gray and cold, with loopholes like gaping mouths dotting its blank face. At a glance, it seemed to mirror the reputation of its ruler perfectly—overbearing, heartless, and threatening.

And Artus was headed right into it.

There was a river entrance to the Citadel—the tip of one point of the star jutted into the water and, at its base, a thick, spiked portcullis was being hoisted up. Beyond was a dark tunnel, poorly lit by guttering torches. It looked to Artus like he was being poled into hell.

Once his eyes adjusted to the gloom, he saw a massive artificial harbor—a perfect half circle, a few hundred yards across, above which yawned an incredibly high dome. It was construction the likes of which he hadn't seen since the Peregrine Palace or the Arcanostrum, which, of course, meant one thing: this place had been built by wizards.

The riverboat pulled up to a dock and Artus was dragged out by his armpits. His broken arms shrieked with pain and he couldn't help but cry out. The black-mailed soldiers lining the quay laughed at him. Rodall led the way, a tattered red cape thrown over his shoulders. Behind him, Mort and Hambone brought up the rear.

Artus screamed the whole way from the harbor to the feet of Banric Sahand himself.

The throne room was huge and forbidding, like everything else in the Citadel. Artus's eyes were so blinded by tears by the time he arrived that he could not make out the details—banners hung on the walls, or perhaps tapestries. There were several dozen people here and the floor was bare stone. Artus was thrown down on his face, which split open his chin and clacked his teeth together as he hit.

The hall roared with laughter.

Despite his broken arms, Artus tried to push himself up, but it hurt too much and he fell to the floor again. His useless legs were only dead weight behind him. He gasped into a slowly growing puddle of blood around his mouth.

The laugher died. Heavy boots thumped down a few steps and Artus heard the jingle of mail. Someone was standing over him. He twisted his head to look up.

It was, of course, Banric Sahand. "Well, well, well—look what my dogs finally ran down."

"Kroth take you, you—"

Sahand interrupted him by pressing the heel of one of his boots on Artus's shattered forearm. He screamed until, at last, Sahand relieved the pressure. "Manners, manners, Your Highness. Rodall tells me that his men saved your life and, therefore, *I* saved your life. Where is the gratitude, I ask you?"

Artus was panting. "I . . . I don't . . . owe you . . . anything . . ."

"You have courage—no man here doubts that." Sahand adjusted his fur cape. "The question, my boy, is whether you possess *wisdom*."

"What are you talking about?"

Sahand nodded to his retainers. "Flip him over. I want him to see me while I talk."

Rough hands rolled him like a log and spun him around. Flat on his back looking up, Artus could see that Sahand had returned to his throne—a giant construction of the bones of many large animals. Human skulls capped the armrests.

"I feel as though my general ambitions have been clear for some time," Sahand said. "I wish to rule—I wish to usurp the corrupt magi and guild bureaucrats who have dominated this region of the West for centuries too long. I wish to be king of Saldor, of Galaspin, and of Eretheria. In short—I wish to be the most powerful king since the warlock king Spidrahk. Even you, a boy, understand this, yes?"

Artus didn't nod. It was fairly clear his participation in this conversation was to be discouraged anyway.

"The armies of Saldor and Eretheria are in shambles—two down, one to go. My own forces, however, are weaker than I'd like. I need allies. This is where *you* come in."

"You can't be serious." Artus coughed.

Sahand grinned at him—a very wolfish look indeed. "You have a choice now, boy. If you were to swear fealty to me, many of the soldiers who followed you to Ayventry—who fight for you even now in the Eastern Basin and along the Eretherian Gap—would change their allegiance. Especially if I were to take up the causes of your late general—no levies, lower taxes, the elimination of the noble houses."

"You'd lie, in other words?"

"What lie?" Sahand spread his hands, as though giving the world himself. "I would *do* these things, if it meant victory! I have no need for levies, as my soldiers *volunteer* themselves as a means to a better life. As for taxes, they would pay the same as any of my vassals—and you will find that is less than you imagine. The noble houses I have little use for and would be putting to the sword in any event. You see? Join me and achieve your aims."

Artus gaped at him. He felt like he might be going mad. "But you don't believe it. You don't care about any of it—you'd just be doing it to win!"

"So what?" Sahand leaned back in his throne. "Who cares why it is done, if it is done? Come down off your pulpit, boy. Good intentions got the Gray Lady nothing but despair. Show a little more intelligence—accept my offer."

"And if I refuse?"

Sahand's grin vanished. "Then . . . well, then I execute you. Publicly. In exchange for your head, I have House Hadda, House Camis, and House Vora of Eretheria ready to assist the conquest of Davram and Ayventry, seats in the Congress of Peers, and a promise not to interfere with my Galaspin and Saldorian campaigns. As you can see, I win either way."

Artus bit back the curses that flew to his lips.

"What about Michelle . . . let her go! Release her, at least!"

Sahand laughed. "You mean my lady wife? Why-ever would she wish to go?"

"What are you talking about?"

"Ask her yourself." Sahand stepped back and ges-tured to a chair just to the side of his throne, but off the dais. In it sat Michelle in a black gown and white fur stole. Her eyes were fixed on a distant point, her face blank.

"Michelle!" Artus gasped, trying to crawl toward her, but succeeding only in clawing the flagstones. "Michelle, it's me, Artus! Snap out of it! Oh gods, say something!"

The room erupted in laughter. Sahand raised a hand to quiet them. "I'm afraid your young lady has had a bit of a mental breakdown. Hasn't spoken a word in days. Very convenient, I must say—I've always enjoyed *agreeable* women."

More laughter, but this time with a more vicious edge. Artus closed his eyes, trying not to picture what Sahand had done to her. He felt ill. "You . . . you bastard."

Sahand laughed. "I've been called much worse. Come now, boy—make your choice. Choose your fate. I've wasted enough time on you as it is."

Artus looked around the room. A line of armored, bearded warriors glared down at him, each of them more unfriendly than the last. His words to Hambone came back to haunt him—here it was, his choice. Did he do what the world was forcing him to, or did he say no?

And by saying no, he condemned Michelle to her fate. No one would come to rescue her. She would remain like this, forever.

But if he said yes, would he be the man Michelle thought he was in the first place? Wouldn't that be just another kind of death—becoming Sahand's creature, just like all these men had become at some point? Men whose desire to survive had overridden any grander desires they might have once harbored. Shells. Husks. Stooges.

I'm sorry, Michelle. I just can't.

Artus let his head fall back to the floor. "Go to hell, Banric. I'd choose death over you any day."

Sahand's men muttered among themselves. Sahand, though, laughed loud and hard. "Good! You don't disappoint, eh? A hero to the end. My congratulations."

Sahand stood and clapped his hands. "Take the hero to the dungeon. You needn't be gentle."

Rough hands seized Artus by the broken arms again and began to haul him away. Even though he braced himself for the pain, he couldn't help but scream as he was dragged down, down into the darkness of the Citadel.

CHAPTER 40

AN EXTRA SET OF HANDS

Michelle Orly was a shivering wreck of a girl, but she did not whimper and she did not say foolish things, so there was a bit of steel in her somewhere—being held prisoner by Banric Sahand was no mild ordeal, and for her to remain silent even now was a feat of will. Still, Lyrelle wasn't going to have much use for a trembling leaf.

Michelle was seated on the floor of the tower, her back pressed to the wall, her eyes fixed on the door. She was deathly pale and her collar bones were poking through her thin linen shift with alarming clarity. Her thin lips were blue.

Limping to her, Lyrelle laid her blanket over the

girl's legs and chest. "With luck, Arkald will bring an extra helping of stew today. A little food and you should feel better."

Michelle said nothing, not taking her eyes from the door.

Lyrelle kept the smile on her face as she limped back to her stool, but inwardly she was frowning. She didn't know very much about Michelle—she had not featured in any of her scrying and so there had been no real reason to investigate her in depth. She was a physical representation of the limits of watching the future—there was always that which you could not anticipate. It was fortunate that she was now here, for sure, but getting her to do what Lyrelle wanted was going to be a challenge. She was forced to manipulate her blindfolded, as it were.

She kept smiling down at the shivering girl. "Everything is going to be all right. You can trust me."

"I *know* everything is going to be all right!" Michelle's eyes flashed with anger. "Artus—the Young Prince is coming for me. I know it."

Lyrelle felt her stomach turn. *Oh. One of* those. *Wonderful.* "You are worried, then, that your prince will fight his way to your tower only to discover your decoy?"

Michelle hugged the blanket closer to her chin. "What if . . . what if *Sahand* finds out what you've done?"

Lyrelle saw no reason to sugarcoat the situation.

"I will die. Painfully. I expect you will have the opportunity to watch."

"Then *why*? Why do this?"

"Because I am an old woman, Lady Orly." Lyrelle let her smile slip. "And so I know what to expect out of princes."

"He *is* coming for me! You will see!"

"I agree that maintaining hope is important," Lyrelle said.

The lock in the door clunked and then in came Arkald. He looked worse than usual—he and Michelle made quite the cadaverous pair, though in Arkald's case there was something of a professional requirement he was meeting. In his hands he had a single bowl of stew. "I could not get more. They would notice."

Lyrelle sighed. "Will the decoy you prepared eat?"

"No. I ordered it to throw its food out the window, though. That will have to do."

"So long as no one is walking underneath." Lyrelle frowned. She had expected complications like this. It only remained to best them.

Arkald offered the stew to Lyrelle, but she waved the bowl toward Michelle.

When the young noblewoman sat forward to take it from him, she winced. Lyrelle had noticed it before—her back was injured. "How did Sahand's men hurt you?"

Michelle took a dainty sip from the bowl as Arkald watched her. "They did not lay a finger on me, besides a few blows. Sahand . . ." She shuddered. "He only made threats. Promises."

"How did you hurt your back, then?"

The girl shuddered and took a bigger sip of the stew. "I . . . I would rather not say."

Lyrelle looked at Arkald. "Would you step outside for a moment?"

Arkald's eyes narrowed. "I need the bowl back first."

Lyrelle frowned at him. If he left, he might not come back, and that food was important. She barely had the strength to stand as it was. "Very well—stay. Lady Orly, I need to see your back."

The girl still had the sense of self to blush.

Lyrelle twirled her finger at Arkald. "Face the wall." Then, to Michelle, she said, "Hurry up, girl. Give us a look."

Staggering to her feet, Michelle turned around and lifted her shift so it was bunched beneath her armpits. Her sickly porcelain skin was marked with an array of yellowing bruises—that much was expected—but her back had a number of odd strips of dead skin, much of which was in the process of sloughing off, revealing tender pink flesh beneath. Lyrelle could understand at once her discomfort—the new flesh was tender and the harsh cloth of the shift and the wall against it was chafing easily.

Lyrelle ran a finger along one, making Michelle shudder. "How did you get these?"

"I'd . . . I'd rather not—"

"Speak!"

Michelle shivered. When she spoke, tears strained to escape between her words. "Some . . . some kind of sorcery. It was chasing us. I . . . I don't know what it was. Please . . ."

That clinched it. Lyrelle knew wounds like these—she knew them well. They were the essential principle behind weaponized Etheric energy—deathbolts, deathcasters, orbs of oblivion, rot-curses, the lot of them. Those injuries on her back were distinct from most known applications in a number of ways, but most importantly was this one:

It was *chasing* her.

Michelle slid back down her shift and returned to the blanket and the stew, covering herself up again.

Arkald turned around. "Well—what was it?"

Lyrelle pursed her lips. "I now know what kind of weapon Sahand has—or claims he has. And I know how to counter it." At that, though, Arkald deflated—something had happened. Lyrelle watched him closely. "Arkald, tell us."

The necromancer looked at the floor. "I just received word. Sahand has destroyed the Grand Army. He is victorious—he didn't even have to use his weapon. It's over."

"What about Artus? What about the Young Prince?" Michelle asked.

Arkald said nothing for a moment, shuffling his

feet on the floor. He sighed heavily. "Captain Rodall of the Ghouls just brought him in yesterday evening. He's in the dungeon, awaiting execution."

Michelle began to cry. "No. No—you're lying. No."

"There's nothing anybody could have done," Arkald said. "You're doomed."

Lyrelle rolled her eyes. "Enough. Stop it, both of you! Do you know when a man is most vulnerable?" They blinked at her. As one was a man and one was a girl, they obviously did not. "You must forgive my language: a man is most vulnerable when he thinks the fucking is over, but his pants are still around his ankles."

Michelle blushed, but she also chuckled. Lyrelle staggered to her feet and pointed to the stool. "You, girl—pick up this stool."

Michelle rose, uncertain, but did as she was asked. "Where do you want me to put it?"

Lyrelle ignored her, moving so that Arkald was between her and Michelle. "As for you, Arkald, I believe your pessimism to be misplaced. No situation is hopeless."

"How is this not hopeless? Sahand has won, understand? He's *won*. The Young Prince can't save you, the Lord Defender of the Balance is dead, the armies of the West are scattered . . . and you . . . you're trapped here. There is no way out."

"Correction, Arkald—there *used* to be no way out. Now there is."

Arkald blinked at her. "How?"

"Michelle, please hit Arkald in the head with the stool."

Arkald's eyes grew wide. He spun around, tried to raise his hands . . .

Michelle brought the stool down on his bald head with a deeply satisfying crack. The look on the girl's face indicated she was as surprised as Arkald was.

Lyrelle smiled at her. "I knew you had some steel in you, girl. Grab his key."

She did. They were out the door of the cell in a moment, and Michelle locked it shut behind them. Then it was down the stairs, step by step, Lyrelle's hips screaming the whole way.

But it didn't matter. With each and every step, she felt some of her power returning to her. Some of her *self* returning to her. It only remained to be seen how much of what she had done with ten fingers could now be done with *eight*.

"Come," she said to the girl beside her. "Let's see about rescuing your prince."

Myreon gaped down at the headless body of Argus Androlli, blood still pumping from the stump of his neck. From the shadows of the room, formless demons crawled forth to feed on the corpse.

"Now, I'm curious exactly what you promised him?" Xahlven asked, looking at Androlli's body with disappointment. But disappointment in *what*? Was Xahlven so insane that he couldn't turn off his act if he wanted to?

"Evidence of your betrayal. Something he could bring to Trevard." Myreon stepped away from the body and backed herself toward the wall, her hands out, ready to cast.

Xahlven laughed at her. "Trevard? Really, this is too much. Evidence? Even assuming I were some kind of traitor—"

"You *are*!" Myreon screamed. She couldn't take this anymore, couldn't *listen* to another word. "You are the Chairman of the Sorcerous League! Don't deny it—I *know*! You spoke before the Well of Secrets a truth—irrefutable truth—that you want to see the Arcanostrum cast down and the order of the world usurped! You said the words!" She pointed at Androlli. "And what about *him*? How will you explain *him*? You've incriminated yourself!"

Xahlven held up two fingers. "Wrong for two reasons. First, I will not have to explain him—he will be listed among the casualties lost at the battle of Dunnmayre, along with hundreds and hundreds of others. Nobody will ever find his body and nobody will miss him. Second—that I incriminated myself— only holds if *you* are able to tell anyone of what transpired here. I can assure you that, by the end of this conversation, such a thing will be impossible."

Myreon erected a ward against deathbolts around her. "I'm harder to kill than you think."

"Oh, Myreon—please, give me a little credit. I don't intend to *kill* you. I intend to *convince* you."

Myreon scanned the room quickly, looking for a way out. None was evident—she wasn't even sure where she had come in. "Of what?"

"That I'm right, of course." Xahlven waved his hands and the little blob-like demons dragged Androlli's body into the shadows. Myreon watched it go. *An exit concealed there, perhaps?*

"You, of all people, ought to sympathize with what I am doing, Myreon." Xahlven leaned forward as he spoke, eager, it seemed, to finally talk about this. "The Arcanostrum is a system of *oppression*. It's a blight upon human endeavor. Do you have any idea how much better off humanity would be without it? Look at the wars they have driven us to. Look at the misery their hoarded secrets have inflicted upon humanity! They have made us covetous and vain and *weak*. No, it all has to come down. It must be destroyed for the good of everyone, before it is too late!"

Myreon shook her head. "No—lies, all lies. Every damned word out of your mouth! You aren't doing this out of some philanthropic impulse. You don't care about the common people. This is about *you*!"

Xahlven rolled his eyes. "Because I'm a Reldamar, right? Because you think I'm like my brother was?

Spare me—I've been cursed with his reputation for long enough. He's dead, Myreon, and I am not now nor ever was like *him*."

Myreon cocked her head. Was that a nerve she had touched? She bore down on it. "I don't believe you. You're just like Tyvian, except . . ."

"Except *what*?" Xahlven sneered.

"He was better-looking."

The Archmage of the Ether stared at her for a moment and then burst out laughing. "Oh . . . oh . . . I see. Trying to taunt me into an error, eh? Gods, watching you manipulate people is like watching a dog ride a horse. Honestly, Myreon—didn't your disaster with the White Army teach you anything?"

"*You* killed them!" Myreon shouted. "You . . . you put that *thing* in my hands and . . . and manipulated me into . . . into . . ."

"You can't blame me for that, Myreon. And you shouldn't blame yourself, either. They did it to themselves. It was a fate they had all earned— vicious, short-sighted brutes, the lot of them. Even the citizens of Ayventry are just as guilty. They stood by as Sahand took control, they ate the spoils that Sahand's armies brought to their tables, they let a monster rule them in exchange for some momentary comfort."

Tears welled in Myreon's eyes, threatening to blind her. She wiped them away. "And so they *all* have to die? Is all humanity too diseased to live, is that it?"

"It isn't humanity that's diseased, Myreon. It's *society*. It's *modernity*. It is this age and these structures we have built that make us less than we once were."

Myreon edged toward where Androlli's body had vanished. "And what were we, once?"

"We were like the gnolls. We were like the nomads of the Taqar or the Salasi of the great southern deserts. Tribes of people, bound by honor, steeped in a tradition of simplicity and survival."

Myreon wanted to laugh, but the whole situation was too perverse. "And barely surviving, scraping a life out of a world of death and pain and ignorance. That's a *solution* to you?"

Xahlven's expression darkened. "And where do you think *this* society ends, eh? A world teeming with people, all devouring each other. Cities of towers with their tops in the clouds, packed full of slaves laboring for invisible masters they barely see, much less understand. The principles of your revolution dashed beneath the march of a million booted feet, charging off to meaningless wars that will enrich people like me while people like you die and are forgotten."

Myreon was taken aback. She searched for the words.

"It's already happening, Myreon—you know I'm right. It will only get worse. Humanity will come to rely more and more on sorcery for more and more things. The very energies of existence will be tapped to their breaking point. In a matter of centuries, the entire world will be on the brink of sorcerous cataclysm, the likes of which have not been seen since Rahdnost the Undying's fall. I have *seen* this, Myreon. I am not destroying the world, I am *saving* it from certain doom."

"Saving it . . . how?"

Xahlven raised one hand. Myreon tensed, ready to deflect whatever spell he hurled at her, but instead his hand came down, and in it rested a rough iron box.

Myreon knew that box. She saw it in her dreams. "What . . . that's *impossible!* It was destroyed! Totally . . . totally destroyed!"

"The Warlock King Spidrahk fashioned *thirteen* coffers such as this, Myreon." Xahlven held it up, gazing on it like a prizewinning rooster perched in his hand. "That one you used was one of two in my family's possession. The first my mother traded away. *I* traded to get it back. The trouble was, of course, *how it worked*. I didn't know and could find no one who would tell me—not even the Oracle of the Vale was willing to part with that knowledge. So—"

"So you arranged for me to steal it so that I would . . . *test* it for you?" Myreon could scarcely control her horror. She felt like vomiting, weeping, and screaming all at once. "I was just . . . all those *people* were . . . just a *test?*"

"Don't sell yourself short. There were a number of other useful side effects to your use of the Seeking Dark." Xahlven shrugged. "But yes, I needed to see how it worked and how, if at all, it could be controlled. So thank you."

Myreon took another step toward the shadowy corner. "And now you're going to use it here, aren't you. Right in Saldor."

"Once the Arcanostrum is gone, there will be no Defenders to keep the peace among the nations of the West. There will be nothing to stop the Kalsaari Empire from invading again. The world will be plunged into an age of war and violence not seen for two thousand years, from which will emerge a new society. A *healthier* society." Xahlven held out the box. "You and I could be there, Myreon—side by side, controlling, guiding. We could remake the world together. This is it—my one-time offer."

Myreon kept her eyes on Xahlven, on the box. A plan—a crazy, desperate plan—was forming. She would only get one shot at it. "Why offer it at all? Why not just kill me?"

Xahlven chuckled. "I've always been partial to blondes."

Myreon threw a deathbolt right at Xahlven's head with her left hand. He easily deflected it, but the distraction was all she needed. At the same time as she threw the deathbolt, she reached out with a telekinetic hook from her right hand and snatched the Seeking Dark right out of Xahlven's grip.

The next few seconds seemed to take place in slow motion. The coffer tumbled through the air in a gentle arc and Myreon was there, scrambling beneath it. As Xahlven shouted, she caught it in both hands and turned to run. Deathbolts sizzled around her, but her wards held—if barely. She dove into the darkness where Androlli had gone. Sure enough, where it looked like there was a wall, there was nothing—a little passage, barely large enough for Myreon's shoulders.

But she did fit.

She wriggled into the darkness of the Archmage's labyrinth, the sound of Xahlven's roars of frustration behind her. She did not look back.

I bet he didn't foresee that.

CHAPTER 41

A SENSE OF THEATRICS

The hours and the days were unclear to Artus now, so deep and constant was his pain. The dark of the dungeon was filled with petty horrors—a kick to the face, a twist of the arm, the hard, uneven rock of the floor. The food they poured down his throat was foul and tainted, probably with his jailor's urine. He lost consciousness frequently and awoke suddenly to find himself the victim of some new indignity.

Then they took him out into the light. Just before, as he was being strapped onto a wagon that would transport him, someone waved a vial of something pungent beneath his nose. "Here now, boy, have a sip of this. His Highness wants you bright and awake now—down the hatch!"

The vial was stuffed in his mouth and poured down. He gagged on it—it was like drinking liquid fire—but his mind cleared and the fog of pain lifted as the white heat of adrenaline surged through him. He found himself able to struggle and he began by smashing his forehead into the nose of the man who had slipped him the potion. The man howled and Artus was slammed backward by a half-dozen other hands. He screamed and he growled but then a leather strap was forced in his mouth—he was bound up like a hog going to the slaughter.

Which, he now realized with his newfound clarity, was exactly what he was.

They wheeled him up a ramp and through a square of sunlight. When his eyes adjusted, he was looking at a massive parade ground enclosed by towering walls and packed with thousands of armed men, their pikes so numerous as to look like a forest of dead trees stretching out for a quarter mile in every direction. The men were in neat ranks, the standards of their companies unfurled for review. When they saw Artus, they cheered and banged their pikes against the dirt—a thunderous sound, like cavalry charging.

His cart was positioned on the top of a broad rampart that overlooked the parade ground. Craning his neck as best he could, he could see this wall was the outer edge of the Citadel's keep. Given the lack of a parapet, Artus imagined its entire purpose was for inspection and review of the troops in the broad bailey that stretched out beneath.

Standing there already, and flanked by Michelle on one side and some of the same bearded captains that had attended him in the throne room on the other, was Banric Sahand. He had his arms raised in triumph, pointing to Artus as though he had captured him single-handedly. When he spoke, his voice was sorcerously amplified so it could be heard by even his farthest legions. "Behold, men of Dellor—the Young Prince of Eretheria!"

The roar of the crowd was once again deafening. Sahand kept speaking, but Artus ceased to pay close attention—he knew the gist, here. Sahand was singing his own praises and mocking Artus—the symbol of his crushed, beaten foe. He was speaking lies—that Artus was at some battle he wasn't, that the White Army was responsible for the slaughter of Delloran prisoners. The precise charges scarcely mattered. What mattered to Artus was Michelle.

She stood there, clad in furs, her eyes still fixed on some distant point. Why didn't she fight? Why didn't she *do* something? She wasn't even looking at him.

And why should she? He was as good as dead. She was broken, beaten. Why feel the pain? Why not go numb?

She was doing what she had to do. It stung, but

he understood. What they had together . . . it wasn't love. It never had been. He understood that now. It still hurt him, though. Hurt him worse than anything Sahand was about to do. He felt hollowed out, empty and aching. His eyes blurred with tears.

No gallows had been constructed on the rampart, no gibbet was waiting for him. Artus didn't see a headsman anywhere, nor the wheel or the rack or even a stake at which to burn him. Were anyone else his captor, he might have been relieved—perhaps mercy was on the table after all. But this was the Mad Prince of Dellor—the lack of an obvious means of execution simply meant something even more terrible awaited him. Artus hoped, whatever it was, it was over quickly.

He seriously doubted that would be the case.

Sahand was wrapping up his speech, bellowing promises of riches and feasting to be had once the rich hills of Galaspin and the green fields of Eretheria and the bountiful vineyards of Saldor were compelled to kneel to them. His armies drank it all in, cheering him on despite everything he had done to them—*had* to have done to them—over the years. The faces of the hungry, starved of everything, stared up at Artus by the thousands. They were not men, this howling mob. They were beasts, whipped into a frenzy, deprived of everything until their minds could no longer separate the true from the desperately wished for.

"And now, it is time to deal with this little one."

Sahand pointed at Artus. "And I have something special planned for him, oh yes."

The Mad Prince reached into his cape and drew out the hilt of a rapier. Artus recognized it instantly—it was *Chance*. Tyvian's sword.

"See his eyes!" Sahand bellowed. "He knows this blade! It is the blade of his father, Tyvian Reldamar—the cursed King of Eretheria who ambushed your brothers as we came to parley, to show respect to a new monarch."

Sahand mumbled the words "bon chance" and the translucent mageglass blade extended from the hilt, gleaming coldly in the pale Delloran sunlight.

"How fitting, then, that this traitor's blade would be the implement of the Young Prince's demise, eh?"

The mob cheered again. They began to chant something, but Artus couldn't make it out over the rhythmic thump of pike butts against the hard earth.

The legions parted. A team of four horses—wild-eyed beasts, their nostrils flaring—was driven down the center of the bailey. Behind them trailed a harness as yet unattached. A squadron of soldiers turned the horses around so their backs were to Artus, and another ran a pair of study ropes up the rampart and attached them to Artus's bindings. One man slapped the horses on the rumps, making them jerk and strain in their harness. Artus could feel the power tugging him, even anchored to the rampart as he was.

Artus was about to be dragged by these horses until dead. A brutal death, and not a brief one, either.

Below him, ranks of Sahand's best troops stood, looking up at him. At their front was none other than Captain Rodall, his metallic smile gleaming amid a howling sea of open mouths.

Artus felt *Chance*'s tip scrape at his back, near where he was bound to the frame that was keeping him in place. "With one stroke, I cut him loose from this anchor and deliver this traitor, this wretch, this cowardly deserter into your midst, men of Dellor. I trust you will show him what we do with our enemies, eh?"

The chant had spread. Artus could hear it clearly now, pounding in his ears. *"WE WANT BLOOD! WE WANT BLOOD! WE WANT BLOOD!"*

Artus wanted to say something, wanted to scream something, even if just a prayer. He had been so resigned to his death until now, when it was at hand. He struggled against his bonds, to no avail. His useless legs merely dangled before the faces of those who were about to beat him to death, to tear him apart as he was dragged past.

"Artus of Eddon," Sahand said. "Crown Prince of Eretheria, for crimes against Dellor and its Prince, I hereby sentence you to death!"

Chance cut through the air, and Artus felt his body come loose from the wagon to which he had been bound. Someone slapped one of the horses again with the flat of a blade and off they went. Artus was ripped from the rampart, wind whistling through his ears. He hit the muddy ground of the bailey with a heavy thump and then was dragged at the speed of four galloping horses. Rocks and clods of earth pummeled Artus on the back, the legs, the arms, the head. He tried to scream as the soldiers whipped past him, many throwing things or striking out with weapons. He took the briefest consolation that he was going too fast for them to hit anything.

He flipped onto his side, then his chest, then his back again. His nose and mouth were clogged with filth; light and dark spun together. In his agony, he only knew he was being driven toward the open gates of the Citadel—that Sahand was going to see his corpse dragged all through the city beyond and then maybe onto the roads and then . . . who knew. He'd be dead by then.

There was a roar from the armies of Dellor. A roar loud enough to drown out the noise of Artus's own death. Then the horses . . . *turned*. He felt himself being dragged upward, draped across the back of a horse. He cried out against his gag as the beast bucked beneath him, but he blinked up into the light anyway.

There, standing atop two horses, a foot on each, their reins in his hands, was Tyvian Reldamar. He was wearing Delloran livery that fit him poorly and a huge fur cape that flapped in the wind. The smuggler looked down and gave him a wink. "Sorry about that. Try not to fall off, eh?"

Tyvian hauled on the reins and steered the horses into the ranks of soldiers. They scattered. Many were packed too tightly to get entirely out of the way, and so they were kicked to the ground or knocked aside. When they had reached the rampart again, Tyvian picked up Artus like a parcel and leapt up next to a totally dumbfounded Banric Sahand.

Tyvian dropped into an en garde position, ran through two guards that came at him. He dumped Artus to the ground and threw off his helm. Then he faced the Mad Prince. "Hello, Banric. I believe you have my sword."

Sahand's eyes nearly popped out of his face. His wicked grin was gone, replaced with a look of complete disgust and shock. "YOU!"

Tyvian saluted him with his blade. "So much for playing this off as the act of some random madman, eh?" He nodded to the mob, which were now watching with a mixture of confusion and morbid fascination. "What say we settle this the old-fashioned way?"

Sahand faced Tyvian, *Chance* outstretched.

And then he shot Tyvian with a lightning bolt, knocking the smuggler clear off his feet.

"Yes," the Mad Prince said. "Let's."

The cavernous halls of the citadel were always empty—Sahand could never hope to support a court large enough to fill them—but on this morning they were *particularly* empty. Lyrelle only wished she were well enough to run. "Hurry," she whispered to Michelle, on whose shoulder she was leaning heavily, "we must hurry—they are all in the courtyard, watching the execution."

Michelle, her lips pressed into a line, her brow furrowed, pulled Lyrelle along a bit faster. "Which way?"

"Follow the doors. Those that take us deeper into the citadel open *toward* you, those that lead you further out open *away*. A . . ." Lyrelle groaned as a spike of nerve pain shot up her back. ". . . a defensive feature."

Michelle did as she was told, and soon the skinny girl and the withered old crone could hear the chants of the crowd and the bellowing taunts of Sahand's voice. They were close.

"Magus, look!" Michelle screamed, pointing through an ancient loophole to the vast bailey beyond. There they could see Artus's broken body displayed before the rabid masses of Sahand's troops. "We're too late!"

Lyrelle nodded as she hugged Michelle close. "I'm afraid so, child. But you needed to see this."

Lyrelle winced as *Chance* cut through the rope. She closed her eyes as the crowd roared.

Michelle yelped in pain as she watched Artus drop into the crowd—as she watched him die. She looked up at Lyrelle. "What do you mean . . . I *needed* to see this?"

Lyrelle cupped Michelle's face in her hands. "We were never going to save him, Michelle."

Michelle's face twisted in horror as she drew away from Lyrelle. "What? *WHAT?*"

"Listen—*listen* child, for this is the last and only lesson I will teach you: the fate of the world does not rest with true love or with noble princes or daring heroes. It never has. It never will."

"What are . . . what are you *talking* about?"

"The fate of the world rests with those who are willing to *sacrifice* to change it." Lyrelle's voice was hard. "Do you, Michelle Orly, wish to save your country from desolation and civil war?"

The soldiers in the bailey were roaring in what sounded like bloodthirsty ecstasy. Michelle shuddered at the sound, closing her eyes. When she opened them again, they were hard and focused. "Yes."

Ahhhh, Lyrelle thought, *there's the steel.* She gestured behind Michelle. The girl turned to see that they had come into the courtyard containing Sahand's anygate. With a wave of her hand, Lyrelle activated the runes to take Michelle back to Peregrine Palace. The portcullis raised, the gate swung open. "Then go. Do it. Do it yourself, Lady Orly. Let no man stop you."

"But . . ." Michelle paused, looking back toward the bailey.

Lyrelle pushed her toward the gate. "Remember

him well, girl. He did come. You were right about that. But he is dead. And he will remain so."

Tears welled in Michelle's eyes. "Thank you, Magus. Thank you."

Lyrelle kissed her hand. "Go."

The girl hiked up what skirts she had and ran through the door. Lyrelle slammed it behind her and scrambled the combination—no one would follow her, and no one could come back.

It was then that Lyrelle noticed silence had fallen over the armies of Dellor. She shuffled to a loophole to look out. When the man on the rampart threw off his helm and revealed his mane of red hair, Lyrelle felt an energy fill her that she hadn't known she lost. It was a power deeper than any connection to the ley, deeper than any desire to destroy Sahand. "Yes!" she said, tears coming to her eyes. "That's *him*! That's my little boy!"

The air cracked as Sahand's lightning bolt struck Tyvian off his feet. The surge of elation was replaced with one of sheer adrenaline. Her work was not yet done. The anygate—and her own escape—would have to wait.

CHAPTER 42

DESPERATION

For the first time in years, uncertainty filled Xahl-ven's guts as Myreon vanished into the shadows of his own labyrinth. It burned at him like acid—here was not something he had predicted! His auguries had been too weak, too unclear to see this. *What if she gets to Dunnmayre? What if she releases the Seeking Dark prematurely?*

His first act was to smite apart his scrying pool with one enchanted blow of his staff and immediately channel the thunderous release of Astral energy into a time-dilation. His body shuddered with the effort, Lyrelle's curse gnawing at his reserves, but this was his inner sanctum—he could work this spell here.

He was not sure how quickly time would be passing outside of his labyrinth, but enough, he was certain, to pull them well past the battle and perhaps a few days following it. The armies of Saldor and the Lord Defender would be dead and gone long before Myreon Alafarr could save them. *There—let her try and stop me now.*

Now, it became simply a matter of finding her and getting back what was his.

He paced silently through the twisting halls of his labyrinth, staff at the ready, his wards and guards at the closest thing to full strength he could manage after channeling that powerful time spell. He spoke into the darkness, his voice calm. "Myreon, Myreon—be reasonable. There is no escape. Come out—face me."

He caught a glimpse of filthy gray robes and blasted it with a bolt of demonfire. Nothing—an illusory decoy. She was using the deeply Etheric ley to assist her efforts to hide, to confuse him. Clever, but a waste of everyone's time. "What is your endgame, here, eh? You can't hide the Seeking Dark from me forever—I *will* find you."

Myreon's voice echoed off the walls around him—another trick to hide her location. "I'll destroy it before I let you have it! I've used it before—I know how!"

Xahlven couldn't help but laugh—the audacity of this girl! "Myreon, if generations of Reldamars couldn't figure out how to destroy it, *you* certainly cannot. You are simply prolonging the inevitable." Xahlven threw another bolt of demonfire at another shadow—still not her. "And you are making me angry."

He heard a faint echo coming from a parallel corridor. Xahlven slipped through a secret door to come out behind the noise. "I have you," he whispered.

But he didn't. Instead, he found himself standing on a blazing rune of crimson energy. A trap! The explosion would have torn Xahlven's legs off, were it not for his guards. As it was, his curse-weakened defenses barely held. He was slammed back against the wall.

Myreon dropped on him as though from nowhere, swinging Androlli's staff in a wide arc. Xahlven moved to block it, but she had twirled it to a different angle. The blow took him in the shoulder, knocking him to one knee. The follow up would have hit him in the temple, either killing him or knocking him unconscious, but he phased himself through her weapon and then displaced himself behind her. His counterattack was a fist of Dweomeric force powerful enough to kill a horse, but Myreon was quick—she had been a Defender, after all—and she deflected it upward, knocking a hole in the vaulted ceiling. The falling stones forced Xahlven back; they were separated by the cave-in.

Myreon had vanished into the darkness again.

Xahlven tried his shoulder—it hurt like hell. "Bitch!" he shouted into the darkness. "I'll boil your bones into soup! I'll eat your heart!"

Myreon's laughter floated through the air. "You'll have to catch me first, Reldamar!"

Xahlven slammed his staff into the floor. "Servants! Attend your Master!"

The walls of the labyrinth writhed as a score of tiny demons of a dozen different phyla emerged. There were disembodied floating eyes, amorphous blobs, black winged things, and pools of darkness with eyes of bloodred. "Find the intruder! Kill her! Bring her things to me and be rewarded! Go!"

The vicious little beings cheered as one and vanished into the darkness. In moments, the halls of the Archmage's labyrinth echoed with wicked laughter. *Let's see her deal with that.*

A pair of pale yellow eyes coalesced in the darkness before him—the demon he had set to watch his mother. "I see you, wizard."

Xahlven scowled. "What now? Speak!"

"First, my reward," the demon responded.

In a fit of rage, Xahlven seized the creature with tendrils of blue fire. "Speak now, and your reward shall be your miserable life!"

The demon howled and struggled to free itself—it was losing power. Xahlven was, in essence, destroying his own servant, but he did not have time to haggle with child-eating monsters at the moment. "Mercy!" it shrieked. "Mercy!"

"Speak!" Xahlven pressed it harder, until its eyes grew even paler.

The demon's voice was frantic. "The . . . the woman! The woman . . . escaped! Escaped!"

Xahlven dropped the bands of flame. "What? *HOW?*"

But the demon was gone, never to return.

Xahlven stood there, hand outstretched toward where the demon had been. His mother had escaped. Escaped! It was impossible. How could Sahand be such a fool?

And the time dilation! Who knows how long ago she escaped, or how much time she has had to plot!

The nagging knot of uncertainty grew into full panic. What if she had planned this? What if this had been her endgame *all along*? No, no—it couldn't be. Nobody allowed their thumbs to be cut off as a ploy.

But this wasn't just *anyone*. This was Lyrelle Reldamar.

Xahlven whirled—his demons would deal with Myreon.

He needed to get to Dellor.

Myreon watched Xahlven carefully from a little alcove full of shadows, a simple camouflage spell making her effectively invisible so long as she didn't move. Thinking he was unobserved, Xahlven's demeanor was less guarded, less calculated. It spoke volumes.

When the demon screamed that Lyrelle had escaped, Myreon almost squeaked with joy—she was *alive*!

Xahlven's face told a different story. He looked worried, possibly even afraid. He stood for a moment, thinking, seeming to debate with himself. Then he turned and walked with purpose toward a sliver of darkness Myreon had been sure was a solid wall. But it wasn't—another secret passage in this thrice-damned labyrinth.

She knew exactly where he was going.

Slipping out of her camouflage, she cast a simple silence spell over her movements and stole across the room, quiet as a whisper. She was through the secret passage a second later and caught a glimpse of Xahlven walking down a corridor. She made her way after him . . .

. . . only to find she couldn't move. She looked down—a solid brick of darkness had formed around her leg, paralyzing it. She couldn't even feel it. "What the . . ."

From the ceiling dropped Xahlven's legion of demonic servants. Horrid things that defied description, reaching for her with cold, damp tentacles and black talons, screeching in delight—they fell upon her as one.

Her guards blazed with light, thrusting them away, but this also expended them and Myreon fell on her back, stunned. The leech-like things—the things that formed the anchor of darkness paralyzing her—began to ooze up her leg. Everything they touched went numb, conjuring horrid memories of the Seeking Dark and the death of Ayventry. Around her, the demons gathered, rimless mouths slavering with hunger. "Wait! I have an offer! An offer!"

The beasts paused, giggling among themselves. "Let it beg!" one said.

"Yes, yes, yessss! Beg! Beg for mercy!" the little things chorused.

Myreon was no summoner, but she knew well enough what demons wanted—they were simple things, driven by vice. "Revenge! I offer revenge upon your Master!"

The demons froze. "How can it do this? How how?"

"He is right now seeking to escape! Take me to where he is going and I will tell you the name of his most dangerous enemy."

The demons drew back without hesitation. Myreon found her leg coming back, tingling with pins and needles all over. She staggered to her feet.

"Follow, follow—do not be slow! The Master is almost there!" the demons chorused and took off down the corridor. Myreon followed at a limping gallop, leaning heavily on Androlli's staff.

Three turns and two more secret passages, and they were in another chamber of the Archmage's labyrinth—this one with an actual door. Not just any door, though—the runes inscribed in the stones around it revealed it to be exactly what Myreon had hoped.

An anygate.

It had evidently taken Xahlven a moment to find the proper runes to connect the enchanted door with a door in the Citadel of Dellor, as Myreon arrived just as the door slammed closed behind him. She lunged across the room and yanked the door open before Xahlven could cancel the link.

The demons behind her howled. "Payment! Payment! Payment or treachery!"

Myreon smiled at them. "Her name is Myreon Alafarr."

She went through . . .

. . . and burst into an airy gallery somewhere high in the Citadel of Dellor's soaring architecture. It was, in fact, a footbridge connecting two of the larger turrets in the main keep, a yawning gulf of open air on either side displaying a dizzying view of the Whiteflood, the sprawling courtyard filled with soldiers, the star pattern of the massive curtain wall.

Xahlven hadn't heard her follow him—he was darting through the door on the other side and leaping up the stairs beyond. *He's going to check on her cell!*

Myreon followed him, Spidrahk's Coffer banging against her back as she ran up the stairs. *This is crazy,* she said to herself. *You're bringing his weapon back to him.*

This thought should have stopped her short. She couldn't hope to defeat Xahlven in a sorcerer's duel—he was a bloody archmage. But she had a plan. A ridiculous plan that relied on a lot of luck. *Tyvian would be proud.*

The stairs wound up and up, at last coming to a small chamber stuffed with sorcerous materials and drawings and the various grisly trappings of a working necromancer. Xahlven didn't pause here and neither did Myreon. She was so close behind him now, but her silence spell was holding and he hadn't looked back. Just as long as he didn't . . .

Xahlven sprinted up the last flight of stairs, taking them two at a time, and stopped outside a locked door. Myreon hid around the bend of the stairs, holding her breath.

Xahlven was examining the runes on the door. "It's . . . the Astral wards are still in place! How is this *possible?*"

He waved his hand over the lock and it sprang open. He looked inside. "What . . . who the hell are you?"

A man's voice whimpered from inside. "Please . . . please don't hurt me! I mean you no harm!"

"*Where is she, you miserable wretch?*" Xahlven screamed.

In the midst of his rage, Myreon snuck up behind him and pushed Xahlven inside. She followed him in and slammed the door behind her. "Got you!"

Xahlven whirled, his steely eyes wide. "You!"

The cell's current occupant—a gaunt, malnourished man with an enormous bruise on his bald head, held up a three-legged stool and backed toward the wall. "Who . . . who *are* you people?"

Xahlven ignored him. "I expected more from you, Myreon. What does this nonsense gain you? You can't hope to face me."

"Not with sorcery I can't," Myreon grinned. "But this room is *Astrally warded*, so . . ."

Myreon struck Xahlven on the wrist with her staff, making him drop his own. She followed up with a blow with the other end into the side of the archmage's knee, knocking him to the ground.

Xahlven thrust his deathcaster at Myreon, but nothing happened.

Myreon jabbed Xahlven in the solar plexus, making the archmage go white with pain. "I've got you, Xahlven. Game over."

The door behind her slammed open. Myreon glanced over her shoulder—it was the skinny man fleeing. The distraction was telling, though.

Xahlven had a knife in his hand. He plunged it into Myreon's calf and then rolled to his feet, his black robes falling over his head.

Myreon staggered back from the injury, gasping, but was able to block as Xahlven picked up his own staff and took a wild swing at her.

Xahlven pressed the attack, pounding on Myreon's guard. His technique was basic, but he had two good legs under him and was better rested. It was all Myreon could do to keep from being bowled over. She got in a few hits herself, but nothing solid—nothing to take him down. Xahlven's face had taken on a wild expression—he was desperate, angry, crazed with frustration.

Xahlven feinted and Myreon fell for it. His real blow struck her in the wounded calf. She screamed and fell down. The archmage knelt on her back and tore the satchel containing Spidrahk's Coffer from her. He giggled. "Mine! You lose!"

Myreon struggled to get up, but he twisted the knife in her calf and she nearly fainted. Then Xahlven was up and at the door. "Enjoy getting down those stairs again."

Then he was gone.

CHAPTER 43

THAT WAS YOUR WHOLE PLAN?

Tyvian's ears rang from the thunderclap that had come with the lightning. His whole body twitched as he struggled to get up. *Damn*, he thought, *should have thought this through.*

Sahand laughed and walked toward him, *Chance* still in his hand. "I thought you were smarter than this, boy. Perhaps I gave you too much credit. Why in all the hells would you go to all that incredible trouble to fake your own death only to reveal yourself here, *now*?"

Tyvian struggled onto all fours. His sword? Where the hell was his sword? He struggled for some banter, his face twitching. "Oh . . . just bored, I guess . . ."

"Usually men have better reasons for suicide." Sahand thrust out his hand.

Another lightning bolt streaked through Tyvian's body, setting his hair on fire and making him bounce five feet in the air. He had expected to be dead, but the ring seemed to think keeping him in a state of perpetual agony was more in line with the heroic idiom. He struggled again to his hands and knees, letting go any thought of strategy and just concentrating on controlling all his muscles at once.

Sahand cocked his head to one side, giving Tyvian a good look at the hole in his face, the teeth inside clenching and unclenching like the beak of some undersea monstrosity. "Still alive? If you're wearing a life ward, I must say that I pity you. I think you'll find death to be preferable by the time I'm done with you."

Tyvian saw that Delloran soldiers were coming up the ramps to the top of the rampart. Artus was struggling weakly against his bonds. Michelle just stood there, blank and meek, as though the mayhem surrounding her held no interest for her. No help was forthcoming from either of them, it seemed. He wondered if there was some kind of backup plan he could use to survive.

Nothing came to mind.

Oh well, he thought, *the plan will still work anyway.*

Sahand raised his hand, ready to throw more lightning at Tyvian. "Third time's the charm, eh?"

But that third lightning bolt never hit him—it was deflected away, into the troops of soldiers in the yard, throwing a half dozen of them into the air. Sahand looked around, enraged. "What in blazes?"

"Hello, Banric!" said a voice, echoing across the courtyard. Tyvian thought he must be dreaming—he'd thought his mother was dead. He had been sure of it.

Sahand's expression was no less shocked. He spun around, searching the parapets and towers and galleries of his fortress for the source of the voice. "You *witch*! That fool of a necromancer! I should have him killed!" He pointed to his men. "Fan out! Search the palace! I want her dead!"

"A little late to the party on that score, my old friend," Lyrelle said. "You had your chance to destroy me. Now it's my turn to destroy you."

Sahand shouted into the air, loud enough for any and all to hear. "You're bluffing! You're barely able to stand, barely able to cast. A cold wind would kill you dead as a canary. What possible threat could you—"

"How about . . . this." The men on the rampart braced for the impact of some kind of destructive sorcery. Instead, the Lady Michelle was suddenly . . . not. Some kind of shroud fell away, some kind of subtle glamour. Instead of the waifish Eretherian lady in a wedding gown, there was the animated corpse of a woman very clearly dead and very clearly *not* Michelle Orly.

"The wedding is off, Banric. No claim of legiti-macy now—no play for the Falcon Throne." Lyrelle chuckled. "And shame on you, anyway—the girl is a quarter your age. Really, now."

Sahand stared at the undead construct standing there, a look of horror on his face. "No! NO! How is it possible?"

"You treat your servants very poorly, that is how. What's the matter? You didn't . . . sample the wares before the wedding night, did you?" Again, Tyvian heard his mother's airy laugh echoing off the walls of the vast courtyard. "Goodness, how *awkward* this must be."

Tyvian had recovered enough to crawl, and crawl he did—right to the edge of the rampart. The soldiers were mostly watching Sahand. A few, Tyvian noted, were chuckling among themselves. The mighty Banric Sahand, embarrassed in front of his entire army. It was a thing of beauty.

Sahand managed to recover himself. "What are all you fools looking at, eh? *Go find that woman!*"

Tyvian sought to roll off the rampart and hope-fully slip away unnoticed, but Sahand stepped on his chest. Drool dripped from his ruined face. "And just where do you think *you're* going? Slinking away in defeat? How like a *smuggler*."

"Sahand, I've got news for you. I'm not a smuggler."

"What?"

"I'm a *diversion*."

From somewhere deep inside the Citadel, a bell began to ring. An alarm bell. Sahand's mangled face went from angry to completely wild—he knew. He knew the mistake he had made.

Tyvian didn't get the chance to witness Sahand's full tantrum firsthand, but he heard enough of it to smile as he and Artus were roughly dragged inside the Citadel where, he figured, he and Artus would either be stashed in a cell for yet *another* elaborate public execution or, alternately, they would have their throats slit and be thrown in a hole. Of the two, Tyvian guessed the second one likely, if only because Sahand would probably prefer to save money on catering.

The good news was that the convulsions that had been paralyzing him were fading. He kept on twitching anyway—no need to let his captors know just yet. He just hung over the shoulder of the big fellow carrying him, limp as a dead snake, and threw in the occasional mimicked muscle spasm.

As they moved through the corridors, Tyvian saw that there was very little order to the search, as it was being conducted in haste by literally thousands of men without the benefit of planning or foresight. Brute force, it was assumed, would win the day. Tyvian didn't know they were necessarily wrong. He just hoped his mother had some kind of escape plan. At least, he hoped it was better than his own escape plan, which currently involved grabbing Artus, jumping in the river, and hoping for the best.

Tyvian was thrown on the floor with a heavy thump that knocked the wind out of him. Artus was dumped next to him. They were in some kind of side room—unfurnished, small, with a single loophole overlooking the river. The two guards removed their helmets.

It was Mort and Hambone.

"Hey, Duchess."

Tyvian sucked in a painful breath. "Hambone. You lost weight."

The two men exchanged glances. Mort nodded. They drew knives.

"The prince told us to make you die slow. But . . . well, you've done us right in the past. Both of you. So we're gonna make it quick and painless." Hambone managed a weak smile. "Wish it coulda been different, but orders are orders."

Tyvian sighed. "You've got to do what you've got to do."

"Yeah, well . . . hold still." Hambone came close.

Tyvian kicked him in the knee—the knee he'd broken all those months ago in Eretheria. The Delloran howled and fell over. Tyvian rolled to his feet more smoothly than he had any right to and drew his own knife.

Mort made a wide slash with his own blade, fumbling for his sword with his off-hand. Tyvian opted not to fool around and simply threw his knife, planting it deep in Mort's throat, just below his jaw. The giant man staggered backward, hit the wall, and slid to the floor, mutely grabbing at the hilt of the knife as his life's blood poured out.

Hambone tried to get up and Tyvian kicked him in the groin hard enough to turn Hambone's face green. Then he went over to Mort and drew out his broadsword. This was slow and turned his back on Hambone—a dangerous choice. But Tyvian did it on purpose. He wanted Hambone's life to be in his own hands, not the hands of the bloody ring.

He turned to see Hambone on his feet, his sword drawn. "You killed Mort! You . . . you . . ." Hambone struggled for the words.

Tyvian held the borrowed blade down to his right side and pointed at the floor. "He made his choice. Now make yours."

Hambone lunged. Tyvian's beat was savage, knocking the broadsword out of Hambone's hand and across the floor. His backswing slashed the man across the throat—a precise, quick, killing strike. Hambone fell back against the opposite wall from his companion, and slid down in the exact same way.

"Painless, as you said." Tyvian looked into Hambone's dying eyes. "The best I could do. You understand, I'm sure."

Turning away, he checked on Artus. Still alive, if broken in a half-dozen different ways. He wrestled the gag out of Artus's mouth. As soon as it was out, the boy started moaning. "Where's . . . Michelle? Where . . . is . . . she . . ."

"Gods, boy, you do *know* other words, don't you?" Tyvian took the straps that had been used to dangle Artus over the mob and threw them over his shoulders, hoisting the young man on his back. He then threw Hann's big cloak over both of them. With any luck, he'd just look like a hunchback in livery. "Now be quiet!"

Back into the mayhem of the Citadel they went. All he needed now was a wall to jump off . . .

Lyrelle leaned over the puddle of water, doing her best to scry the future. The result was too murky to be useful, and her hands were too ruined to force the issue. That sense of overwhelming *blindness* that she'd felt ever since her capture would not leave her. All she could see with any clarity was the present: Tyvian was alive. Michelle Orly was saved. Sahand was shown to be an ass in front of his entire army.

There was nothing more to be done. Slowly, leaning on the wall for support, she made her way back to Sahand's anygate. As she came around the corner, she knew what she would see. She knew *who* she would see.

Xahlven stood blocking the way. "This doesn't

bear the markings of a well-arranged plot, Mother. Playing things by ear, are we?"

"Given the bruises on your face, I could say the same thing to you," Lyrelle said. "Here to finish the job, are you?"

"It's almost done. I needn't concern myself with it." Xahlven produced Spidrahk's Coffer from beneath his robes. Lyrelle recognized it immediately. "I came to show you that you have failed, once and for all."

"That depends, ultimately, on what you think it is I intended to achieve."

"Don't be coy—not now, when it is all over." Xahlven shook his head. "You wanted to save your new world—the one you created, with Sahand as your spoiler. The world you sold *this* to the Oracle to guarantee. But it's failing, Mother—it is crumbling to dust all around you. And now"—he stroked the edge of the iron box gently—"this will be the final stake in its heart."

Lyrelle looked at the ancient artifact long and hard, remembering everything she had risked in stealing it from Xahlven's father. Remembering how she had manipulated Sahand into becoming the terror that would lead the West to what it now was. She looked back on a long, impossibly complicated life—kings crowned and nations crushed, a world on the end of the string—and saw it for what it was:

Over.

Her work was finished. She had done her best. She deserved rest.

She smiled at Xahlven. "My poor son. I wish I could have done better by you. You could have been . . . so . . . so *talented*."

Hatred blazed in Xahlven's eyes, so bright it seemed to glow. He grabbed her by her tattered gown and threw her to the floor. Lyrelle felt her hip break again, the pain bright and intense. She slipped into unconsciousness as Xahlven, his face drawn and pale, backed away.

Rest.

CHAPTER 44

ONE LAST DUEL

Hool bashed the lock off the door with the guard's head. Beyond was a staircase, going deep into the bowels of the Citadel. In the distance, the alarm bells rang.

Damon, wearing Delloran livery, looked down the dark tunnel. "Are you sure about this?"

Hool yanked him by the arm and pulled him down the stairs. "Hurry up, stupid—this entire place is about to go crazy."

Damon squinted in the torchlight. "How do you know?"

"Because Tyvian is involved—stop asking so many questions. Follow me." Hool led him down, through winding passages and moldering tunnels, always following her nose toward the water.

Damon held the torch high, trying to decipher some kind of ancient writing on the wall. "I'm so glad you decided to bring me along. I wasn't sure you would, you know, considering . . ."

"Shhhh!" Hool hissed. "This is not a time for feelings! This is a time for doing things! We will talk later."

"Right. Of course."

Hool pulled them into a defensive alcove as a troop of soldiers ran by. They were all going *up*, not down. Just as Tyvian had predicted.

"Where are they going?" Damon whispered.

"Tyvian," Hool said.

"And where are *we* going?"

"To destroy Sahand, just like I said before."

Damon looked down the passage they were heading through, empty save for stagnant pools of water and mossy walls. "I still don't see how this is going to work without . . . you know, both of us dying."

She ignored him and drew the Fist of Veroth, its head already swirling with Fey energy.

Damon took a full step back. "Now, Hool—I'm aware this is a ridiculous statement, given where we are, but, well . . . let's not be *rash*."

Hool glared at him. "You are right, Damon Pirenne. There is more to life than revenge. You are right, too—being with you is more important than killing Sahand. But revenge is also important. My Brana and my Api deserve it. And if you love me, you will help me."

Damon paused, but not for long. Then he bowed. "At your service, my lady."

Hool displayed all her teeth in a wolfish grin. "Let's go knock down a castle." She kicked open the last door to reveal the artificial harbor in the bowels of the Citadel. There were a few guards here, but only a handful—Damon and Hool dispatched them quickly and sent the survivors running for help.

The Fist of Veroth resting heavy in her hands, Hool strode to one of the big, fat supports that held up the huge domed roof—and, according to Tyvian's boring lecture on architecture, the *entire castle above it*. She drew back, the head of her enchanted mace flaring to life.

And she struck.

Myreon limped slowly into the necromancer's quarters beneath the cell and paused long enough to treat her leg wound with a bloodpatch elixir she had spotted on the way up—at least now she wouldn't bleed to death.

Not that it mattered much—Xahlven had the Seeking Dark. He could be heading back to Saldor at this exact moment, and she could never stop him in time, never make it down the stairs like this.

So, instead, she jumped out the necromancer's narrow window. She timed the slowing spell just right, landing with a rough thump instead of a meaty splat on the top of a turret beneath. She got inside and clambered down the stairs into one of the keep's great halls, its vast table laden with an elaborate feast.

And soldiers everywhere.

She ducked back into the stairwell. Alarm bells were ringing—she could hear them clearly now. Then, the floor beneath her shook, causing dust to be knocked loose from between the stones on the ceiling. What was going on?

A soldier stepped into the stairwell, coming face to face with her. Myreon's knee came up instantly, catching him in the groin. He groaned and sagged back against the wall. She had her fist balled, ready to punch him in the throat, when he managed to gasp, "Gods, Myreon! What the hell?"

She froze. Indeed, the whole world seemed to freeze. Was that . . . it . . . it couldn't be.

But those eyes. There was only one family with those eyes.

"*Tyvian!?*"

Tyvian smiled through his bushy beard. "Guilty as charged."

Myreon grabbed him and pulled him close and hugged him as tightly as she could. Tears welled in her eyes. "What the . . . what the Krothing hell . . . you . . . you son of a *bitch*! *I thought you were dead!*"

Tyvian hugged her back. "Yes, well, sorry about that. It was . . . complicated."

Artus's muffled voice came from underneath Tyvian's huge, furry cloak. *"I told you so!"*

Myreon blinked. "Artus? What the hell are you all doing here?"

Tyvian waved his hands. "Let's all assume, for the moment, that our stories are far, far too long to exchange at this precise moment and just accept that we are all here because terrible things are about to happen and we're trying to prevent them. Fair?"

Myreon couldn't seem to stop smiling. "Fair."

"Then let's go."

They stepped back into the hall.

It was filled with soldiers, surrounding them immediately. At one end of the hall, standing atop the huge table that ran its length, was Banric Sahand. "Well, well, well—if it isn't Myreon Alafarr. What a pleasant bonus. Now, where were we?"

Tyvian loosened the straps on his Artus-pack and lowered him to the ground. Artus, who seemed to have regained consciousness, folded himself up neatly, as though he really were just a large pack. Tyvian left Hann's cloak over him. He leapt up on the table to face Sahand down about a hundred feet of polished hardwood and plates full of roasted meat. "I really *would* like my sword back, please."

Tyvian felt his skin tingle as Myreon worked a series of wards over him. The feeling made him buoyant. Despite being surrounded by scores of hardened enemies, he felt for once like he had things under control.

Sahand drew out *Chance*. He dropped it on the table and kicked it toward Tyvian, knocking over candles and goblets and place settings as he did. "Take it," he said. He looked at his men. "Kill that man."

Tyvian threw his broadsword at the first man who came at him with a pike and began to sprint toward *Chance*. Spears and polearms were thrust at him, but the quarters were too tight to swing them. Tyvian dodged left and right, ducked and weaved. The weapons rebounded off Myreon's wards and guards, even as Myreon herself started throwing fireballs and lodebolts. A chandelier exploded with the Shattering, sending iron shrapnel hurtling out in all directions and deafening everyone in the room.

Tyvian reached forward.

His hand clasped the hilt of his old sword.

It felt like coming home.

Then Sahand kicked him in the face so hard Tyvian practically did a backflip.

Sahand had a sword of his own—a longsword that glittered with bladecrystal and was inscribed with Dweomeric runes Tyvian was familiar with. They let the blade hold a Fey enchantment without melting it—very expensive. But then, he *was* the Mad Prince.

The sword blazed down at him with a speed belying the weight of the weapon. Tyvian rolled off the table, plates flying, and Sahand left a thick divot where Tyvian's ribcage had been.

Soldiers tried to close in and Tyvian swung *Chance* in a wide arc, keeping them at bay. Sahand lunged at him, jumping off the table. Tyvian side-stepped and stuck the Mad Prince in the armpit between his armor—a quick touch, not deep. Enough to draw blood. Enough to enrage.

Sahand swung his sword in graceful arcs, driving Tyvian back as he tried to parry or dodge. The sword had the blessed side effect of keeping the soldiers from interfering—nobody wanted to get their arm chopped off—and besides, the rest of the hall was degenerating into a legion of Sahand's troops against the blazing sorcery of an angry Myreon Alafarr. At the moment, it seemed a stalemate—soldiers were hunkered down in cover, behind heavy furniture or in doorways. They would be trying to work their way around to ambush her from behind.

Tyvian was too busy to tell her that, though. He only hoped she knew.

Sahand bound Tyvian's blade with the crossguard of his sword and threw an elbow at Tyvian's face. Tyvian ducked, abandoning *Chance* to Sahand and, drawing his dagger, slashed Sahand's hamstring. The Mad Prince howled, stumbling forward.

Tyvian kicked *Chance* back into his hand and tried to run Sahand through from behind . . . only to have his attack knocked aside by the broadsword of none other than Captain Rodall. His teeth gleamed. "I know you—I never forget a deserter, *Duchess*."

Tyvian disengaged his blade and backed away from the Captain. He didn't have much idea of how good the man was with a sword, but he couldn't afford too many mistakes just now.

Sahand was drinking something he had taken from his belt and standing up. "Rodall—bind him up!"

The mercenary captain smiled and attacked, making short, tight cuts that Tyvian was able to parry, but not effectively riposte. Rodall's necklace of human ears jiggled as he fought. "You like them, eh? Soon you'll be joining them!"

Tyvian tried for a feint, but Rodall didn't take it. He ducked inside Tyvian's guard and wrapped him in a bear hug. The wiry mercenary captain was much stronger than he looked, and Tyvian gasped at the force of his grip. "I have him, my prince!" Rodall crowed. "I have him!"

Sahand nodded. "Good. Hold still."

Then he thrust his sword through Rodall and Tyvian both.

The blade took Tyvian just below the ribcage, passing through his stomach, but the blade wasn't quite long enough to pierce out Tyvian's other side. His reflex was to push himself away from Rodall—a good instinct, as Sahand ripped the blade sideways, cutting Rodall practically in half.

Tyvian fell backward, blood pouring out of his stomach. He was back about where he started, at the end of the room near where Myreon had made her stand and where he had laid Artus under the fur cloak. But this time Myreon was nowhere to be seen.

No time to worry about that now.

Chance was still in one hand, and Tyvian held it out. Sahand knocked it savagely aside and knelt on Tyvian's wound, letting his knee grind into it. Tyvian practically passed out from the pain.

Sahand planted the tip of his sword on Tyvian's breastbone and grabbed hold of the crossguard, ready to drive it down through his heart and pin him to the floor. "Never have another man do what you ought to do yourself."

"I agree," a voice said, and Artus threw off the cloak and leapt up behind Sahand, driving a dagger to the hilt into the Mad Prince's armpit. Sahand paled and fell sideways.

Tyvian's eyes bulged. "Artus! You . . . you're *walking!*"

Artus spat on Sahand and then smiled at Tyvian. "Yeah—where'd you get that cloak, anyway?"

"Behind you!"

Delloran soldiers came at Artus, but the Young

Prince pulled a sword from a corpse and started fighting, leaving Tyvian a moment to recover.

Tyvian tried rolling onto all fours. He was losing a lot of blood—too much blood. The ring was weakening. What had Artus just said . . .

The cloak.

He reached out to grab it.

But Sahand's hand was there first. Though badly injured, he was still bigger and stronger than Tyvian, and he threw a punch into Tyvian's jaw that made his eyeballs rattle. "Die, smuggler! Why the hell won't you *die*?"

Tyvian tried to keep the ceiling from spinning. "Same . . . to you . . . you Krothing arse . . ."

Sahand pulled the cloak over him. "You . . . you can't win. I've got . . . thousands of soldiers . . . they'll . . . they'll be here soon . . ."

And then the entire castle shook, as though struck by a catapult stone the size of a dray wagon. Even Sahand looked worried. "What in all the hells *is* that?"

"That . . . is what . . . I . . . was diverting . . . you from."

There was another blow. And another.

Then the floor began to collapse.

CHAPTER 45

WHEN THE WALLS
COME TUMBLING DOWN

The battle pushed Myreon out of the great hall and into a separate gallery. Not suicidal—even at Sahand's command—the Dellorans were taking potshots at her with crossbows while taking cover behind seemingly innumerable pillars. These attacks she could ward off with bow wards easily enough, but advancing was slow and she was weakening. She wanted to help Tyvian, she wanted to save Artus, but there was still Xahlven to worry about.

Using as much of her remaining energy as she could manage, she created a simulacrum of herself to use as a decoy and sent it on her own suicidal charge at the Dellorans surrounding her.

It worked. As they swiveled their attention to follow the fake Myreon's progress, she limped out a side entrance, sunblasting the only soldier there.

Then it was a maddening, staggering climb through the endless halls and stairways of the Citadel, trying to make it back to the door to which Xahlven had linked his anygate. She channeled all of her power into a few feyleaps; she hastened her pace with the use of the Astral and the Dweomer. Images of the destruction of Ayventry haunted her, the sound of the city dying screamed in her ears. She had to make it.

She *had* to.

Somehow, she did. Xahlven was waiting for her on the footbridge, the anygate just behind him. Spidrahk's Coffer rested in his hand. "Come to see me off?"

Myreon didn't talk, she just attacked. She threw everything she had into one massive bolt of fire, hoping to burn the mad archmage to bones. Instead, Xahlven simply evaporated as though he had never been there at all. Because he hadn't.

It had been a simulacrum. Left here only to taunt her.

Breath caught in her throat, she ripped open the door. Nothing but more stairs—the anygate connection had been broken. Xahlven had already escaped.

She had failed.

Saldor. All those people. Everyone she had ever known. The Arcanostrum itself . . . doomed.

She sank to her knees, weeping. "No . . . no . . . no no no . . ."

When the castle began to come down, Myreon did not notice at first. She only assumed it was her heart breaking and the sky falling upon her, as it justly should.

The Fist of Veroth, blazing with Hool's righteous anger, struck the next support like a meteor. Masonry flew everywhere and great cracks ran up the huge column. Hool struck again. And again. Into each blow she poured every ounce of her anger, her misery, and her will. This castle would not stand so long as her pups were dead. Each strike was cathartic—as the stone blasted apart, she felt as though some part of her were free again.

Hool wrecked another column. And another. And another. The men down here had long ago stopped trying to kill her—they were running for their lives. They had winched up the great river gate and were paddling off in small boats—canoes and sailboats and small barges. Hool grunted her approval—at least *these* fools would not die for Banric Sahand.

"Hool!" Damon was at the quay, standing in a longboat, waving her over. "You've done enough! It's falling down! Come on!"

She looked up at the domed roof. Cracks had run almost all the way to the capstone at the top. The whole citadel seemed to be trembling with her wrath.

But it hadn't crumbled yet.

Hool reared back with her enchanted mace and struck another blow. Another thunderous boom, another shower of stones, and more cracks.

"Hool!"

She didn't listen. She was back in that old place, that place she had been for so long—he hadn't lost them, hadn't lost everything. He was just a man—a stupid, simple man. She struck another blow. A whole edge of the dome above collapsed, dropping tons of material into the artificial harbor. A huge wave washed up on the quay. Damon clung to the boat, nearly tipping over.

"That's enough, Hool! It's coming down! Do you want to die?"

Hadn't he listened to her? Why shouldn't she die? What else was there? A gnoll without a pack. A mother with no children.

Her body shuddered. She realized that she was howling. That she had been howling this whole time. She dropped the Fist of Veroth and sank to her knees, hands on her face. "My Brana . . . my Api . . . gone . . . gone . . ."

Damon was there, though, putting himself under her shoulder. Lifting her up. "You damnably stubborn woman," he grumbled. "How many times must I explain that *I* love you? Get in the goddamned boat."

Hool was too distraught, too weak from her rage and grief to care that she was being pushed into a boat. A piece of stone the size of a house fell into the water just beside them, showering them with spray.

Damon began to row, his eyes wide, fixed on the crumbling castle above.

And the sky began to fall.

Tyvian couldn't see—dust in his eyes. He couldn't move much, either—the strength had gone out of him. The ring had at last given up. Someone grabbed him by the wrists and started pulling him out of the rubble.

"C'mon, Tyvian—stay with me! Not like this, you hear me?"

Tyvian blinked a few times and made out Artus standing over him, pulling. Behind him, a shaft of light shot through what looked like a door . . . or a window . . . or who knew what. The castle was falling down. Defeat the evil wizard and his castle falls down—just like in the stories. It was almost funny.

Artus slapped him. "Snap out of it! You're acting like you've never been stabbed before!"

The boy had a point. But then the castle shuddered again. Somewhere close, a huge amount of stone was collapsing into the earth. Tyvian tried to wriggle his wrists loose. "Just go, Artus. No sense in all of us dying."

Artus grabbed Tyvian by the beard and yanked. "You listen to me, Tyvian Reldamar—I ain't got no father, as he died when I was little, so you're the closest goddamn thing I got, and if you think I'm going to let you die *again*, you're out of your Kroth-spawned mind. Now *snap out of it!*"

Tyvian blinked up at the boy. The boy he'd picked at random in the alleys of Ayventry all those years ago. The boy who seemed to have driven him all this time. Who had, just by existing, made him a better man.

He snapped out of it. Together, they worked their way clear of the rubble in time for the next blow to shake the castle to its foundations. They stumbled off together.

Whereas the first part of Tyvian's loose plan—get back Artus—had not gone to plan at all, the second part—jump into the river and hope for the best—went pretty much exactly as predicted.

Artus carried him to the curtain wall as the world seemed to be coming apart at the seams. The great towers of the Citadel fell like stacks of children's blocks. The keep seemed to swallow itself—the noise was deafening, louder even than the pounding of Tyvian's heart.

He would have liked to say they jumped together.

Instead, Artus threw him off the side like a dead body and then dove in after him. As he was half-dead, he was a bit unclear on what followed—a little drowning took place, he believed.

But someone pulled him out. Someone bandaged his chest. Someone was holding his head in her lap.

It was Hool.

"I should have known it would be this crazy. Nothing crazy ever happens without you."

Tyvian smiled. "Sweet heavens, Hool—are you in a boat?"

Hool put her ears back. "Don't remind me."

Tyvian lifted his head a little to see that Damon had stowed the oars and was reaching over the side of the boat, helped by Artus. They dragged someone in.

Myreon.

She was injured, but not badly. But she looked worse than Tyvian did. She coughed the water out of her lungs and stared up at the sky.

"Whatever is the matter with you?" Tyvian asked, his voice weak. "Did Sahand run you through, too?"

"Saldor," she said, her voice equally fragile. "It's gone, Tyvian. I couldn't stop him. He got away."

"Who?"

"Xahlven!" Her eyes were red with tears. "He had this weapon—an ancient, terrible weapon—the one that killed Ayventry."

"Gods—that can be used *twice*?"

"No, no—he had another one. An iron box,

enchanted—once he opens it . . ." Myreon trailed off, hugging her knees. "I failed."

Hool grunted. "Sounds like it."

Something tickled at Tyvian's memory. "Was the box about this big?" He made the shape with his hands. "Black metal, looks like iron. Very plain, a bit battered around the edges?"

Myreon nodded, unable to speak.

Tyvian started laughing. It hurt so much, but there he was, doing it anyway.

"What?" Myreon asked, scowling at him. "What could possibly be so funny?"

Artus looked grim. "Yeah, this isn't funny, Tyv."

Tyvian shook his head. "Saldor is fine."

"I *saw* him with it!" Myreon countered. "You don't understand!"

"Trust me, Myreon—Saldor is *fine*."

"How could you possibly know that?"

Tyvian let his head fall back into Hool's lap. "Because a con man can always spot a con a mile away."

Hool sniffed the air. Her ears went back. "Damon, row me to shore. Back to the city."

"What? Why?"

"Yeah, Hool," Artus said, "that sounds crazy."

"Do it," the gnoll said. "I'm not done."

Damon met her gaze. Something passed between them—Tyvian couldn't tell what. Something that needed no words. "As you wish, milady."

Sahand held the magic cloak tightly to his body as he stumbled through the muddy streets of Dellor-town. The dust from his collapsed Citadel dulled the sun and rained down over the city like a light snow. The people were lining the streets—filthy, dressed in rags, their eyes wide with terror.

"Help!" Sahand barked. His hands were slick with blood. The cloak had healed the boy—why wasn't it doing the same for him? Where were his men? Why were there no soldiers here? "Bring me a healer!"

Everyone watched. Nobody moved.

"Bring me a damned healer or I'll eat your eyeballs!" Sahand roared, stumbling and falling in the muck. "I am your prince! Obey!"

The people, though, drew back from him. They retreated inside their houses. They closed their shutters and barred their doors.

Sahand struggled to his feet. "I *made* this country! You would all have *nothing* without me! Nothing, you hear?"

He'd lost a lot of blood—too much. The world was somehow gray; his heart pounded in his ears. *"Traitors! Fools!"* He lunged toward a ragged bunch of peasant children, watching from the top of a fence. They screamed and fled. But not from him.

There was someone behind him.

Sahand knew who it was. Knew it before turning.

He could feel her growl in the soles of his feet, rumbling like distant thunder.

He turned to face her.

The gnoll stood unarmed, clad only in her golden fur. She towered over the Mad Prince, her teeth bared. "It is time, Sahand."

Sahand forced himself to his full height. He threw off the worthless cloak. "Come then, dog. I am in need of another pelt."

She came, her jaws flashing.

It was over quickly.

As Sahand lay in the mud, his life's blood pouring out of his ravaged throat, his last sight was that of the gnoll leaning down and picking up his iron circlet—his mark of dominion over Dellor—and of her setting it upon her golden brow.

"This land is mine now," she said.

They were the last words Banric Sahand ever heard.

EPILOGUE

Xahlven strode into the Chamber of Stars with a spring in his step, Spidrahk's Coffer under one arm. He had been called to report to the Keeper of the Balance himself on the massacre at Dunnmayre, and so he had gladly acquiesced.

All the archmagi were to be there, after all. And their council of masters. And the halls beyond the chamber? Filled with staff-bearing magi. All the most prestigious, most powerful, most *knowledgeable* magi in all the world, all gathered in close proximity.

It was *perfect*.

As he arrived to take his throne, a troop of Defenders came to attention. These would probably be the last true Defenders of the Balance the world would ever know. In a few moments, they would be naught but dust and bones. Xahlven tried to assume a sense of solemnity for the event—a solemnity that warranted the end of the old world and the start of a new—but he couldn't. He was beaming.

Delkatar, the Archmage of the Dweomer, glowered at him over his four-foot-long white beard. "*You* seem cheery for a man who has failed so colossally."

At the center of the room, seated upon a high dais that overlooked all the other thrones, the Keeper of the Balance, Polimeux II, steepled his bejeweled fingers beneath his hook nose, his rheumy eyes distant. "There will be no banter, please. This is a matter of much gravity."

Hugarth, Archmage of the Fey, laughed and put his feet up on the armrest of his throne. His bare feet were muddy. Xahlven hoped he died first.

"Of course, Keeper." Talian, the Archmage of the Lumen—across the room from Xahlven—looked severe as always in her white robes and rose-colored spectacles. Like a schoolteacher. "In the regrettable absence of Trevard, we shall forgo some of the pageantry—let us have the report, Xahlven. You were at the battle, correct?"

"In point of fact, I was not."

A rumble among the Masters present. They hadn't known—which means they didn't know what came next.

"Xahlven," Polimeux said gently. "Explain." The Keeper, mad as a rabbit, did not even look at him, his attention somewhere far away.

Xahlven held up Spidrahk's Coffer. "Gladly."

He raised his other hand over it and, with a dramatic gesture, disintegrated the box. "BEHOLD!"

Nothing happened.

In Xahlven's hands was just . . . dust.

"We're *beholding*," Delkatar sneered. "Well?"

Xahlven spun around—had it slipped away? Where was it? What had happened? "I . . . I don't . . . how is this *possible*?"

Hugarth started laughing. His masters joined in, slapping each other on the back, stomping their feet.

Talian stood up. "Gentlemen, if you *please!*"

Xahlven looked at his hands, his mouth hanging open in shock. There was . . . nothing. It was empty. *The Oracle had lied to him!*

The Keeper of the Balance raised one hand, and the commotion died. He looked down at Xahlven, his eyes suddenly clear and sharp. He had a knowing expression, as though various pieces of various puzzles had only just then fallen into place.

Xahlven's whole body experienced a kind of terror that made it seem as though he were in free fall. *He knew. Polimeux had known all along.*

The Keeper had been feigning his own senility. And Xahlven had fallen for it.

"Now, young Xahlven—I believe we were on the topic of your failure at Dunnmayre and your dereliction of duty." The Keeper smiled, eyes twinkling. "Please—do elaborate."

The foothills of the Dragonspine appeared no more inviting than they had from Freegate, but Tyvian found himself looking forward to them. After a month recovering from his injuries in a small cabin, staring at nothing but fur pelts and smoke-stained rafters, the fresh mountain air and stunning vistas were a nice change of pace.

Artus finished checking the harnesses on the pack mules and dusted off his hands. "We're all set."

"This is it, then," Myreon said, leaning on her staff. "This is good-bye."

Tyvian hadn't fully realized how much he missed Myreon until this past month, when she was there every day, talking to him, rolling her eyes at his jokes, arguing with him about . . . well, everything. "It needn't be," he said, but regretted it immediately.

"No, Tyvian—our paths are different ones. Xahlven is still alive. With your mother gone, someone has to stay to stop him. That someone is me."

"I know. I'm just . . . just glad—"

Myreon hugged him. "I'm glad, too—I'm glad we're friends again. I'm glad you're alive. I'm glad about so many things. But I can't leave."

Tyvian released her. They held hands for a moment, but then parted. "Perhaps we'll be back. The North is unlikely to hold my interest forever."

Artus snorted. "Says you. Wait until you taste my Ma's cooking."

"That's exactly what I mean."

Both Artus and Myreon exchanged glances, and then Myreon hugged Artus as well. "Are you sure about this? Michelle is still alive, Artus. We could use you."

Artus shook his head. "I'm not a figurehead anymore."

"I didn't mean it like—"

"No, I know. But . . . it ain't my fight, you know? Never really was."

Myreon opened her mouth, ready to argue, but she stopped herself. "Try not to get in *too* much trouble."

"Same to you," Artus said. They said their last good-byes, and then Myreon retreated into the cabin. She was already hard at work on a series of sorcerous rituals, the purpose of which Tyvian could only guess at.

He hadn't asked.

Artus shouldered his pack and took the mule's reins. "Ready?"

Tyvian slapped him on the shoulder. "Come on, Artus. Let's get you home."

ACKNOWLEDGMENTS

Here, at the end of Tyvian's journey, there are so many people to thank. I shall begin with my wife, Deirdre, whose patience is without limit and whose indulgence I scarcely deserve. Also my agent, Joshua, without whom this book would have likely never existed. And also David, my editor, without whose advice this book might have been a much shabbier affair.

I again would like to thank Jason, Brandon, and Katie for all their help and good advice over several books and for assuring me that I am not, in fact, insane.

Here, at the end, I'd like to thank Christine, DJ, Josh, Perich, Serpico, and Will for helping build a foundation for Tyvian's world and for bringing that world to life with me for a time.

Finally, a big thanks to my parents, whose encouragement and trust in me as a young man allowed me to take this precarious path leading to publication. May all children have parents who believe in them as much as mine did.

ABOUT THE AUTHOR

On the day **AUSTON HABERSHAW** was born, Skylab fell from the heavens. This foretold two possible fates: supervillain or sci-fi/fantasy author. Fortunately, he chose the latter, and spends his time imagining the could-be and the never-was rather than disintegrating the moon with his volcano laser. Auston is a winner of the Writers of the Future Contest and has had work published in *Analog*, *The Magazine of Fantasy and Science Fiction*, and *Galaxy's Edge*, among other places. He lives and works in Boston, MA.

Find him online at aahabershaw.com and on Facebook at www.facebook.com/aahabershaw, or follow him on Twitter @AustonHab.

Discover great authors, exclusive offers, and more at hc.com.